SUMMONED

THE SUNDANCE SERIES

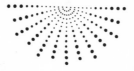

C. P. RIDER

Diane,
Be good. Try.
Love you tons.
C.P. Rider

VC GROUP, LLC

For Jeff Martin. The best gift Mom and Dad ever gave me. Thanks for the support, little brother.

C.P. RIDER
URBAN FANTASY ROMANCE

LIKE YOUR URBAN FANTASY WITH A LITTLE ROMANCE?

To find out how to sign up for new release notifications and bonus content not available anywhere else, follow the links at the back of this book.

CHAPTER ONE

EVER SINCE THE PARANORMALS IN TOWN FOUND OUT I COULD KILL THEM with the power of my mind, business at La Buena Suerte Panaderia had been slow.

If the residents of Sundance, California had been less reactionary, I could have told them I had rules. I didn't use either my telepathic or spiker abilities unless necessary, didn't read friends without permission, spiked no one unless there was no other option.

Then again, people would only have my word that I followed my rules and, with my wolf shapeshifter uncle gone, there weren't many paranormals in the vicinity who trusted me.

Two of the exceptions were standing at the counter ordering an obscene amount of pastries for a gathering later that evening. The Blacke shifters loved sweets—also fresh meat, but I didn't sell that.

"Another two dozen *conchas*, I think." Chandra Smith, Blacke group alpha second, hyena shifter, and all-around badass, drummed her boot heel on the tile floor.

"Four." Amir Gamal, Blacke group alpha fourth, eagle shifter, and male model—I didn't know that for sure, but I suspected—crossed his arms, tucking his hands beneath biceps the size of mangoes.

"Maybe we should get six just to be sure," Chandra growled. "Damn Dan and his ridiculousness. He should be doing this."

I said nothing, only scratched out the numbers two and four on my notepad and scribbled in 6.

"Sorry, Neely." Chandra scrubbed at her black hair. The spiked cut coupled with her pale brown complexion reminded me of the singer Joan Jett, but I'd never tell Chandra that unless I was sure that was the look she was after. "I'm sure he'll get over it."

"Yeah." My pencil lead broke, and I reached beneath the counter for an ink pen. "He seems to be a real open-minded sort of guy."

"Normally he is." Amir shuffled his feet. "I believe you frightened him the day your uncle—uh, the day we found José."

In fairness, I'd scared myself with the amount of power I'd manifested the day my uncle died. I guess I could understand why Dan Winters—a coyote shifter, and Lucas Blacke's third—would be nervous around me. Sadly, he wouldn't talk to me about it. Just took off in the other direction every time we crossed paths.

"How are Lucas and his new shifters?"

"Alpha hasn't called you?" Amir asked.

I shook my head. The Blacke alpha and I had left things unsettled between us, and he didn't seem in any particular hurry to settle up.

Chandra replied, "He says it's going well. This group is the last of the Vegas shifters to be pledged. They're aquatic animals, so he took them snorkeling in Baja. Should be back in a couple days."

"Roso had aquatic shifters in his pack? In the *desert*?" Seemed unnecessarily cruel, but I shouldn't have been surprised. Saul Roso had been an unnecessarily cruel man.

"Only three. Roso slaughtered their alpha and most of their school, and then forced them into his pack." The way Amir's jaw clenched told me everything I needed to know about how he felt about that. "The real question is why they'd want to stay here in *our* desert. Alpha suggested they meet with a friend of his, an aquatic alpha in San Diego, but they insist they want to be part of our group."

"They trust him." It didn't surprise me. Lucas, the alpha leader of the only shifter group in our little desert truck stop town, was slowly becoming known for being a fair alpha leader—a rarity in the paranormal world.

"And they don't trust anyone else," Chandra said.

2

A few weeks ago, Lucas had helped me kill Saul Roso, a Las Vegas wolf alpha hellbent on turning me into his own personal paranormal weapon. While hunting me, he had gone on a murder spree in Sundance, and we weren't able to stop him until after he'd killed several people, including my beloved uncle.

So, I carried that on my soul.

Lately it seemed as if all the bad luck in town emanated from me, as if I were some kind of anti-four-leaf clover.

I didn't realize I'd murmured the words out loud until Amir said, "What you did was brave. You didn't have to sacrifice yourself for us."

Never mind Roso would never have come to our little corner of the southwestern desert if I hadn't lured him here. Being a spiker meant being feared by the weak and coveted by the despotic. In Roso's corrupt eyes, I had been a weapon, nothing more. I couldn't be happier that he was dead, but I regretted my inability to contain the fallout.

The shifters left after that, and I took their order to the back of the bakery and handed it to my temporary baker, Diego Vargas. He scanned the receipt.

"Pity order, do you think?" I asked.

Diego nodded, the hair net keeping his longish dark brown hair from moving. "Yes. But we'll take it. Pity money spends the same."

"True. So, when do you start the new job?"

After months of looking, Diego had finally found work at a sugar beet processing plant in the town an hour away. Dan Winters, the coyote shifter who hated me, had gotten him the job. It wasn't personal. Diego needed retirement benefits and better pay, and his job at the bakery could offer him neither.

"Two weeks. I'm sorry, Neely. I said I'd help you and—"

I held up a hand. "Stop apologizing. I'm happy for you. I really am." I was. If I wasn't, I wouldn't have told him so. Diego was an empath and can sometimes sense when a person is lying.

"I'll come in and help after work until you find another baker to take over."

Diego really was a sweet man. "Thank you, but I haven't decided if

I'm going to keep the bakery going. This was Tío José's dream, not mine."

"What is your dream?" He shook flour over the freshly scrubbed worktable and dumped out the *concha* dough I'd made early this morning. A cloud of white danced on the surface of the table.

"No idea. I always assumed I'd know it when I saw it."

He smiled. "Maybe you will."

The bell on the front door hit the glass with a sharp crack.

"Did you hear that? Someone wants an iced coffee badly enough to brave the presence of the evil spiker." I widened my eyes and made a woo-woo noise.

"Don't be so *dramática*."

My stomach clenched, because it sounded exactly like something my uncle would have said and it had only been two months since I lost him. I missed him so much my entire body ached whenever I thought about him not being here.

Diego stopped what he was doing. "I'm sorry it hurts you so much."

The challenge of working with an empath.

"Thanks. I just ... miss him. I'll be okay."

I plastered a fake smile on my face and went back into the café.

CHAPTER TWO

IT WAS PAST NINE AND I'D SHOWERED, THROWN ON MY PAJAMAS, AND was lying in bed with a book. A romantic suspense with a serial killer I wanted the couple to hurry up and kill so I could concentrate on the juicy romance. Not that I could concentrate on much. I kept thinking about what Diego had asked me in the bakery this morning.

What is your dream?

If he had asked me the same question a year and a half ago, I'd have said my dream was to co-own a bakery with my uncle, and marry and make cute babies with Julio Roso, my fiancé.

Of course, that was all before Julio told his maniacal brother Saul that I was a spiker, and before Saul told Julio that it would be in the best interests of all involved if I let him make me into a crossbreed.

The crossbreed ceremony would have turned me from a telepathic spiker into a shapeshifting telepathic spiker. It would have sent my abilities into the stratosphere, at the same time making me emotionally unstable and a danger to everyone around me. It would also have tied me to Saul Roso for the rest of my life.

There was the chance Julio didn't know I'd be practically married to his brother. I was almost willing to give him the benefit of the doubt because there was a stupid part of me that held out hope that he'd really loved me and hadn't been using me all along.

"Why can't I get you out of my head, Julio Roso?"

"Who are you talking to?"

I leapt out of bed with my pillow held in front of me as a shield, my chest pumping like an accordion playing Cajun-zydeco music. *What the hell?*

A tall, dark blond, and very handsome man leaned against the wall beside the stairs. "Good evening to you, too."

Lucas Blacke had sauntered into my apartment the way he always did, quiet as a whisper and with blatant disregard for my privacy. It was late, but he was dressed as if on his way to a business meeting. Charcoal suit tailored to fit his slim, muscular body, hair smoothed back, tie precisely knotted. It was a look he'd shown me only once before, and it was completely un-Lucas-like.

He glanced at the stainless steel Tag Heuer watch on his tanned wrist. "Not too late, is it?"

"Yes, it's too freaking late. I have to be up at four."

"Please. It's not as if you have a long commute. You live where you work."

True, my apartment was on the second floor of the bakery, which was convenient. But there were both pros and cons to living where you worked. Con: some people assumed I was always open and had no problem knocking on my door after-hours for a pastry. Pro: I never needed air freshener because my apartment always smelled like fresh baked cookies.

And the commute, of course. Lucas was right about that.

"I'm going to figure out what hole you're using to sneak in here and I'm going to board it up." I set my jaw, glared at him.

"Lie. If you were really worried about me sneaking in, you'd have found it by now." He pulled away from the wall, hips first, and strolled past my bathroom and into my small kitchen. Opened the fridge and frowned into it.

My place was compact, but it had everything I needed. Bathroom with a tub, kitchen with a full-sized oven, living area with a modular sofa, and a full-sized bed on a pine platform, sectioned off by strategically placed glass walls and bookcases. Tonight was one of the times I wished I'd paid the extra to put in a bedroom wall instead of leaving my bed visible to anyone who walked in.

"What are you doing here and why are you dressed like that?" I climbed back onto my bed, crossed my legs tailor-style, and arranged the pillow on my lap.

"Like what?"

"Fancy pants."

I'd expected him to smile at that. He didn't. He closed the fridge without taking out anything and crossed the room to me. "I had a last-minute meeting in San Diego today."

"With whom?"

Lucas perched on the edge of my bed, leaned over me to read the title of the book on my nightstand. "Romance?"

I crossed my arms. "With *whom*, Lucas?"

"You're nosy." He picked up my book, flipped through it.

"*I'm* nosy?" I crossed my arms over my chest. "You know what? I don't even care. Why are you *here*?"

"Why is the binding on this book broken?"

Talking to Lucas was an exercise in patience. "I'll tell you if you tell me why you're here."

He snapped the book closed and fixed his amber eyes on me. Probably silently judging my white flannel nightgown. When it was boiling out, I liked to run the air conditioner at just under "hang meat" temperature and pretend I was somewhere wintery. I would not apologize to anyone for sleeping in comfort.

"I was summoned to San Diego by my old alpha."

My heart stuttered. "Xavier Malcolm."

"The one and only."

Lucas didn't talk about his old pack alpha much, but when he did it wasn't complimentary. "Can he do that if you aren't a member of his pack anymore?"

"No, but he can ask really nicely with the power of a thousand-strong wolf pack behind him."

"Oh."

"Yeah. Oh." He looked down at the romance book in his hand.

"So, what did he want?"

"He wants to meet you." Lucas tossed the book on the bed. "I told him you aren't part of my group, so I couldn't force you. He asked me to extend an invitation."

Fear drenched me. My breath started coming in shallow pants. "No." I'd never met an alpha besides Lucas who didn't want to use me for my ability and, if I was being completely honest, I still wasn't a hundred percent on Lucas. "*No.*"

"You can say no. But he'll keep asking. It may get … messy." His shoulders slumped and he raked his fingers through his hair, leaving it mussed and much more Lucas-like. "I'm sorry. I didn't tell him what you were, but someone here did. He has his spies."

Shit, shit, shit. "Do you think I should see him?" I wrapped my arms around my knees, rested my forehead on my kneecaps.

"You probably should."

"I'm afraid."

I raised my head, caught him twirling a lock of my spiral-curled hair around his finger. He did that often, touched my hair. Anyone else tried it and I would have backhanded them, but Lucas was … well, Lucas.

"Afraid? You?" He let my dark chestnut curl spin out, stroked his fingers over my jaw. "You're the warrior who took down Saul Roso. What do you have to be afraid of?" He said the words as if he meant them, but his lashes lowered over his eyes and I knew he was worried.

Sure, I took down Saul Roso. But without Lucas's help, I would have died doing it, and that was the absolute truth whether he wanted to admit it or not.

"I'm not a warrior. I'm just a baker's niece." And now I wasn't even that.

"I'll go with you."

He played with another strand of my hair. This time I did slap his hand away.

"Will he think we're together if you go with me? Like a couple?"

Lucas lifted one shoulder. "He might."

"Would that be best? For him to believe that we're lovers?"

"Yes. He should also believe that you're considering joining my group." Lucas reached for my hair again but stopped short of touching it. "And this will all be easier if we stick close to the truth."

"The truth? Are you saying I *really* have to be your lover and potential group member?" If this was his way of sneaking into my bed, I was going to junk-kick him.

"No sex necessary, but I'm game if you are."

I was losing patience with his flippant answers. "Lucas, *talk* to me."

"I am talking. Listen, it's all semantics with alpha leaders like Malcolm. If I said we're sleeping together, he wouldn't think we were having pillow fights and painting each other's nails. This is me we're talking about." He shrugged out of his jacket, dress shirt, and under-shirt, kicked off his shoes, and climbed into bed with me, wearing only a pair of trousers that sat low on his hips.

I tried hard not to stare at the two shallow grooves on either side of his abdominal muscles leading into his waistband. What was the term for it? Apollo belt? Penis cleavage? Whatever it was called, it was really nice to look at. I bet it would be nice to touch, too.

"Is this my side of the bed?"

I came to my senses. "You don't have a side of my bed—Lucas, that's my pillow, you can have this—wait, what am I doing?" I scooted to the other side of the bed as he made himself comfortable. "What are *you* doing?"

"Read my mind and find out." His tone was teasing, but those aged-whiskey eyes were serious.

"No." I'd stopped reading the people who came into my bakery once I had taken down my uncle's murderer. I was back to my rules, which included respecting my fellow humans and paranormals and keeping myself out of their heads. After all, I owed these people at least that. If it weren't for me, Roso never would have come to Sundance.

"Guilt is a shitty emotion," Lucas whispered. "You should let it go."

My voice trembled a little. "Tell me what you're doing in my bed."

"Semantics, I already told you. Pay attention. Also, reading. It's not John D. MacDonald, but it'll have to do." He picked up my book, opened it. A smile curled the corners of his sexy, deceptive mouth. "Also, never mind."

"Never mind what?" I dropped onto my pillow and pulled the blanket over my shoulders.

He flipped the pages in my book. "Never mind explaining why the binding is broken here. I get it. This is sexy stuff."

"Go to sleep, Lucas." I flipped over, facing away from him.

I had to admit, there was a small part of me that was glad he was here. I hadn't slept well since the town had turned on me. Kept picturing Dan Winters showing up with a vampire stake while I was sleeping. I knew Lucas would protect me—he'd already proved it—but if he wasn't around, no telling what his shifters might do.

"You first. I'm going to finish this chapter." I heard the page turn. "You *sure* you don't want to have sex with me after reading this? I'm sweating over here."

No, I wasn't sure, and it didn't have a thing to do with the book, either. It had to do with the way he made me smile when I didn't mean to, the fathomless loneliness inside me that called out to him, and it was that damn penis cleavage.

I rolled over, snatched the romance out of his hands, tossed it on my nightstand.

"Be that way." He hunkered down beside me and ran his fingers over my flannel sleeve. A shiver went through me at his touch.

Why was I so weird? I couldn't find a nice, normal man to be attracted to. It had to be this one. I was a *tonta*, my uncle would say, a fool, and I had terrible taste in men.

"Neely?"

"Oh my God, *what now?*"

"You look like someone's virgin great-aunt in that nightgown."

"Shut up and *go to sleep.*"

WHEN I WOKE up the next morning, Lucas was snoring beside me. He'd slept on top of the covers with his arm around my waist. If he'd made the gesture sexual, I'd have shoved him away, but it had been about comfort more than anything.

Only I wasn't sure which of us was more comforted by it.

As was my custom, I went downstairs to take the chairs off the tables, wipe them down, and start up the ancient coffeemaker. Sometimes I whipped up pastry dough at this time, but the orders were low right now and I'd made up enough yesterday to last through today.

Surprisingly, I still had regulars who came in for iced coffees and *pan dulce* who did not treat me any differently than they had before they knew I was a spiker. There were also regulars who came in and treated me like I had a communicable disease. I didn't mind. At least they came in.

That done, I dashed upstairs to condition-wash my hair. It took some time to dry, so I rarely washed it on a weekday morning. However, I'd slept like wild beasts were chasing me in my dreams and my hair was a fuzzy mess on one side. It needed conditioner, styling cream, and gel. Stat.

Lucas was sitting at my kitchen table when I walked out of the bathroom in a blue cotton sundress with a microfiber towel on my head.

"Where's the flannel nightie, Grandma Esther?" he asked.

"I will wear what I like in my own home."

"It's a hundred degrees out."

"Not in here, I—*wait a sec*. Grandma Esther? How do you know about *The Waltons*? That's a bit before your time." I squeezed the towel on top of my head, trying to absorb water without creating frizz, always a trick with my curls. "I grew up with Tío José, who practically welded our living room television to the classic TV station. How do you know about it?"

"Chandra."

Did not see that coming. "*Our* Chandra?"

He nodded. "She binges on seventies shows when she's sad. After she and Cynthia broke up, she power-watched the entire series over the course of a month. Anyone who dropped by got an eyeful of John Boy, Jim Bob, and the rest of the gang. I'm just relieved that we didn't have to watch *Welcome Back Kotter* again."

"Better than binging on ice cream, I guess."

"She did that, too. And corn nuts. I smell coffee. I need it inside me right now." He was still shirtless and shoeless, and now he was scruff-jawed and sleep-rumpled. The jewel-eyed watercolor tiger tattoo climbing up his left arm appeared to be watching me every bit as closely as its owner.

"Get dressed and come downstairs. I'll pour you a cup."

He shook his head. "I'd rather have it here. With you."

"Yeah, well, I have to open up in five minutes." I scrunched my hair with the towel and let the curls hang damply down my back. "As you know, there's nothing in my fridge except leftover frozen pizza. Come down with me and I'll get you a pastry."

"Okay." He stood and started toward the stairs.

"Hang on." I put my palm against his muscled chest. His skin was hot. Most shifters ran a few degrees hotter than regular humans, but Lucas ran hotter than most. Or was that just me? "Get dressed first. Try to look like you arrived this morning instead of last night."

One perfectly shaped brow went up. "Maybe I want people to know we're sleeping together."

"We're not sleeping together."

"We just did."

"Yes, but we're not *sleeping* together," I said.

Lucas tugged on one of my damp curls. "Why aren't we?"

Because I'm terrified of you. Because it would never work. Because you're you and I'm me and that's that. "We're barely figuring out how to be friends."

"Friends?" He let go of my curl, watched it mix back in with the others.

"What? You don't want to be friends?" I dropped my hand from his chest, took a step back. It was getting a little too intimate between us.

And I was a little too comfortable with that.

"I do. It's just I normally separate people into two camps: friends and lovers. You don't fit neatly in either category."

"Yeah." I backed away, heading toward the stairs. "If it makes you feel any better, I'm just as confused as you are about what this is."

CHAPTER THREE

My REGULARS CAME AND WENT IN A STEADY STREAM FOR THE FIRST twenty minutes after I unlocked the doors. I served cookies and *pan dulce*, hot and cold coffee. The glass display cases were starting to look bare, which was a good thing, but also a bad thing, because Diego wasn't due to come in until tomorrow and it would be difficult for me to break away with him gone.

A half-hour after opening, Lisa Cesar sauntered in with Margaret Lentz, the busybody of the Blacke Shifter group. I heaved a heavy inward sigh and resolved myself to the inevitability that one or both women would be pissing me off soon. They were two of the few shifters who overtly and aggressively hated me. Most people hid it better.

Margaret was an alpha wolf shifter with the Blacke group. She had steel gray hair curled to within an inch of its life and her right eye blinked more than her left when she was in full sermonize mode. She'd been born middle-aged—I was absolutely convinced of it. I could not imagine her under forty.

"I'll have a small iced coffee." Lisa brushed her straight brown hair over her shoulder. She was as tall as Margaret, around six foot, and in her mid-thirties. She was also a rattlesnake shifter with Lucas's group and the town's elementary school teacher, which made a strange sort of sense when you thought about it.

"I'll have the same." Margaret fanned herself. The ceiling fans were running full blast and the air conditioner was set to sixty-five, but she was sweating like a televangelist in a confessional. "Oh, and a muffin. One of those." She pointed to a *mantecada*.

I filled two cups with ice and added coffee, cream, and my home-made sugar syrup. I set them on the counter along with two paper straws, and grabbed a small sack for the *mantecada*. I didn't ask if Margaret was taking it to go—that damn woman was taking it to go.

"I'm surprised you stayed in town after your uncle was *murder*—" I glared at the busybody and she caught herself. "—since your uncle's passing."

"It was her fault he was killed." Lisa tossed her money on the counter. "Maybe staying here is her penance."

That one stung. Mostly because she wasn't wrong. Not entirely.

"Now, Lisa. That's unkind." Margaret's eyes gleamed with a sort of wicked delight at the scene unfolding in front of her. She took her money out of her wallet and laid the bills in a precise pile on the counter as sweat trickled down the sides of her face, dribbling on my clean countertop. The woman was up to something.

I swept up the cash and shoved the pastry bag at Margaret. "Will that be all?"

"You don't belong here." Lisa's gaze was hooded and dark. "You brought that murderer to our doorstep. How do we know there aren't more? You're a danger to us."

"I would like to add that if you're staying because of our alpha, you should know that he's fickle when it comes to affairs of the heart. He's what the young people call a 'player' or a 'manwhore.'" Margaret's eye twitched at the speed of a hummingbird wing flap, and the curly gray hair that edged around her face was soaked. "I'm not saying this to be unkind, dear. I'm trying to help you."

God save me from Margaret and her help.

"Yeah, well, *I* have no problem being unkind. No one wants you here, *spiker*. Even the ones who come in every morning and order their pastries just like they always have." Lisa downed her coffee and set her cup on the counter. If she thought she was getting a free refill, she was wrong. "They've been *ordered* to be nice to you. They wouldn't come in otherwise. We all know you brought death to this town with your lies and secrets."

"Everyone in this town has a secret." I grabbed a rag and disinfectant spray from behind the display case to my right and mopped up Margaret's sweat. "You wouldn't live in Sundance if you weren't hiding from something. My something just happened to show up this time. Maybe next time, it's yours." I pointed at Lisa with the spray bottle. "Or yours, Margaret."

"Well now, I don't... That is, I—"

"I stayed and fought mine. Would you do the same, Lisa? Or would you turn rattle and run?"

The snake shifter's eyes faded from dark brown to pale gold and her tongue lengthened, forking at the tip. "I wouldn't have to. I don't have *enemiesss*."

"Oh, so you're here for the amazing weather?" I laughed humorlessly. "It's September and supposed to be a hundred and five degrees this afternoon."

"Maybe I like the heat."

"Or maybe no rattlesnake rhumba would have you." The way she flinched, I knew I'd hit a nerve. Imagine that. I hadn't even read her, and I happened upon a nasty little truth.

Margaret stepped between us. "Please, we're only trying to help..."

I slammed the spray bottle down and tossed the cleaning rag into a bin behind me. "Get out of my bakery and take your help with you."

The older woman drew back as if I'd slapped her. "There's no need to be rude."

"Get *out*."

Lisa's serpent tongue flicked over her lips. "Or what? You'll *sspike uss*?"

"No." Damn her for suggesting that when I hadn't even read them. I was following my rules, the rules my uncle had helped me develop when I was a kid. I was doing everything the way I was supposed to, and still no one trusted me.

"Then what can you do to hurt me? You can't *physsically forcce* me."

15

"She can tell me, and I'll kick your ass out." Chandra strolled through the bakery front door, sending the bell attached to it jingling against the glass. "I'd consider it a bonus. I only came in for coffee and a *concha*."

Lisa pointed at me, keeping her eyes on Chandra. "You know what *ssshe isss*. How can you defend her?"

Chandra moved. Faster than my eye could track, she went from the doorway to directly in front of Lisa. "Because I *know* what she is. I saw her sacrifice herself for this ungrateful town. I know you all, every shifter in the group, and I don't know many who would do the same."

Lisa's eyes glowed white gold and her mouth cinched up on either side. She was shifting to her hybrid form and it was not a good look on her. "She's not one of *usss*."

"Exactly. She's not part of the Blacke group, yet she protected us when she could have run." Chandra took a step into Lisa's personal space. She had to be five inches shorter, but in her own way, she managed to tower over the rattlesnake shifter. "She's also a friend to our alpha. Would you challenge him on that? Would you challenge *me?*"

Lisa backed up, her mouth working but no words coming out. Her tongue thickened and shortened as it retracted into her mouth, and her eyes bled to their normal dark brown.

"Alpha Second, we meant no offense to you or to Alpha Blacke." Margaret's face went sheet white and shiny. She was really working up a sweat now. "We were just—"

"Leaving." Chandra cocked her head to one side, crossed her arms over her chest. "You were just leaving."

"BAKERY BITCHES," Chandra said after Margaret and Lisa hurried out, "they're the worst sort of bitches."

Normally I hated that word—especially when directed toward women—but I had to agree. "Iced coffee? It's on the house for getting rid of those two."

"Sure. I'll take a pastry, too. A pink *concha*. And that I pay for."

Lucas appeared in the kitchen doorway, fully dressed, the ends of his freshly washed hair dampening the collar of his shirt. "I heard Chandra threatening someone. What did I miss?"

"The Margaret Lentz and Lisa Cesar Welcome Wagon," Chandra muttered.

"Did you tell your shifters they had to come here?" I thrust my hands on my hips. "Because that is not okay with me. I don't want people coming in because you threatened them."

"No, I did not. I hardly ever threaten my shifters." Lucas jerked his thumb at Chandra. "That's her job and she does it better than I do. Why? What happened?"

Chandra gave him a rundown as I scooped ice into a cup and poured coffee and syrup over it. Lucas's jaw tightened as she told him what she'd heard.

"Is there anything else?" This he asked me.

"That pretty much covers it." I set Chandra's iced coffee on the counter. "Oh, Margaret Lentz called you a manwhore."

Chandra snickered.

Lucas's mouth fell open. "*What?*"

"She warned me away from you. Called you a 'player' and a 'manwhore.'"

"Margaret actually said 'player?'"

"Yep." I poured him a cup of hot coffee and added a little cream to it.

"She's on Twitter now," Chandra said. "It's obviously having a positive effect on her understanding of slang."

"No." Lucas shivered. "It's not."

"What?" Chandra arched her brows in surprise. "You going to tell me she's wrong?"

"Yes, I am. I'm not a manwhore or a player. That makes it sound like I charge for it. I'm just ... friendly." He picked up his coffee. "So, did you read Margaret and Lisa? See what they're up to?"

I shook my head. "They were up to threatening me. I didn't need to read them."

Lucas and Chandra exchanged a look that I pretended not to see.

"We need to talk." Lucas took a sip of his coffee, swallowed. "Neely, take a break."

"Uh, I'm working here, Captain Highhanded." I picked up a clean rag and sprayed and wiped the counter again.

"Working?" Lucas surveyed the empty cafe. "Seriously?"

"Fine." I went into the kitchen and washed my hands, poured myself a coffee and tossed three *conchas* on a plate. Plopped down across from Chandra at a table beside the window Saul Roso had shot out one of the times he'd tried to kill me.

It had since been repaired, along with the cracks in the terracotta Saltillo tile floor, the bullet holes in the sunny saffron walls, and the broken lacquered pine tables and chairs. This poor bakery had gone through a lot two months ago.

Lucas sat beside me and bit into one of the pastries. Chewed, took a sip of coffee, and said, "I'm taking Neely to see Malcolm."

Chandra's expression told me everything I wanted to know about what *seeing* Xavier Malcolm meant. "No offense, Alpha, but ... *are you out of your goddamned mind?*"

"Chandra." Lucas's voice went low and growly. His alpha tone.

"I said no offense," she grumbled. He stared at her. "Okay, I apologize, but taking Neely to see Malcolm? That's a huge risk. You remember what happened with Suyin."

"Yes, I do." He showed Chandra his teeth. They were human, but no less menacing for being so.

Chandra fell silent. Finally, she said, "This is political. You have no choice."

"There's always a choice. I'm trying not to make a bad one." Lucas growled then, low and long, and I nearly genuflected and crossed myself.

It was at times like this that I remembered Lucas was a top-of-the-food-chain predator. A prehistoric shapeshifter. Most shifters evolved physically and mentally over time. Some did not. In his prehistoric form, Lucas was one of the most powerful beings on the planet—the Smilodon, otherwise known as the saber-toothed tiger. I'd only seen a fraction of what he could do while in that form, and it had been astounding.

18

The hyena shifter's demeanor did a complete one-eighty after that growl, going from incredulous to serious in seconds. "I go in under the radar?"

Lucas nodded. "Your focus is Neely. I want her kept safe."

"Sorry. Can't do that."

"I *order* you to."

I spoke up. "Protecting you is Chandra's job as your second. I don't think you can order her not to do her job. Especially if she thinks you're in danger."

"Danger? I can shift into an eight-hundred-pound saber-toothed tiger. There aren't many things scarier than me out there."

"No," Chandra said. "There aren't. But Xavier Malcolm comes damn close."

CHAPTER FOUR

THE WEEK WENT BY THE WAY THE WEEKEND HAD—UNEVENTFUL, SLOW. I had a few customers roll in for coffee and pastries. Not many. Fewer than the week before. Only our restaurant orders in Nopales, the town nearly an hour east of Sundance, were keeping the bakery afloat.

At this rate, I wouldn't have to worry about whether or not I wanted to keep my *tío*'s bakery open. The choice would be made for me.

The night before Lucas and I were scheduled to leave for San Diego to meet with Xavier Malcolm, I slept fitfully. I dreamed of my mother, and the dream was accompanied by the usual shame and despair and pain.

"Mama, who was that man?"

I watched in the mirror as my mom worked a fat-toothed comb coated with watered-down conditioner through my waist-length curls. They were dry and frizzy again. Everything was dry in Texas—especially in August.

"What man, mija? We need more of that good conditioner. This stuff is garbage. Remind me to pick some up in town."

"Okay, I will. You're not going to town today?"

"No."

"Good. I don't like it when you're gone."

"Sometimes I have to leave. I always come back, don't I?" She snagged the comb on a knot. "Dang these tangles."

I picked up a loose curl, glared at it. "Is my hair bad?"

"Bad?" Mama laughed. "Hair is just hair. It's not good or bad." Her silver and turquoise bracelets jingled as she worked the comb through another section. The long braid she always wore slid over her shoulder. Her hair was silky black, thick, and straight. Unlike me, she hardly ever got tangles.

"What do you think about cutting it?" she asked.

"Daddy will say no."

"Not much he could do if we decided we wanted to cut it, is there?" Waggling her eyebrows at me, she took hold of a handful, pulled it up. "We could trim it to your shoulders. It would be easier to manage. Your curls would be even bouncier."

"Daddy will still say no."

"Yeah. He will." Mama's slender shoulders slumped. She reminded me of a soccer ball with the air let out. "Another knot." She sank nimble fingers into my hair, worked at the snarl until it was gone, and then resumed combing.

"The man you were with has fur like Tío José when he's a wolf. Only he's more brown."

The comb flipped out of her hand and landed in the sink. I handed it back to her.

"Why are your hands so cold, Mama?"

"Where did you see him?" Her voice trembled. Her hand, too, which meant the comb got away from her again.

I retrieved it, gave it to her. "In you."

"In ... me?"

"Yes. You know, in here." I pointed to my head.

She met my eyes in the mirror. "No, I don't know. Mija, are you telling me you can read my ... thoughts?"

"I don't know what that means."

The lines that appeared between her eyes when she was angry or worried made an appearance. Those lines scared me. Made me think I'd done something wrong.

"Mija, do you hear voices that no one else hears?"

"No."

"Do you see pictures?"

21

"Sometimes." *Slowly, I raised my hand, splayed my fingers over my head.* "But in here. Like I saw you with the man and you were hugging him. Then you both shifted to your wolves and ran for a long time together. You're a pretty wolf, Mama." *I added that last bit, my six-year-old mind thinking a compliment might soften those angry lines.*

It didn't. If anything, it made them deeper.

"Dios mío." *Mama sank down on the closed toilet lid and grasped my shoulders. Held me at arm's length.* "Never tell anyone what you saw."

I huffed. "I'm not a little kid. I know it's bad to talk about shifters with anyone who isn't paranormal."

"Not just humans, Nelia," *she growled the words out.* "Anyone."

Frightened, I could only nod. Mama had never spoken to me with her wolf in her eyes before. I didn't understand why she was doing it now. I tried to move closer to her, but she stiffened her arms, held me at arm's length.

"It's not right. Seeing inside other people's heads. Sometimes people have bad things happen to them that they don't want anyone to know about."

Then it happened. My mother's memory, the one that popped into her brain the second she said, "bad things happen to them," *appeared in my head. We were in a bedroom. I didn't recognize it, but the bedspread was pink and there were dolls and stuffed animals strewn about. A child's room.*

A man stood over a huddled little girl with straight black hair and my brown eyes, a thick leather belt doubled over in his hands. His whole body smelled like my daddy's breath after he watched football with my tío.

"Mentirosa. Bruja." *Liar. Witch.*

"Por favor, I won't tell. I promise. Please, Papa," *she cried as the belt cut into her skin.*

Though I couldn't feel the actual pain of the lashes, I saw them as if they were aimed at me and I sensed her fear.

"Stop it, Nelia."

"Mama, what's happening?"

"Y-you." *Her voice was so small I had to bend close to hear it.*

"Mama?"

"Please. It ... hurts."

I was doing this. Somehow, I was hurting her. Making the memory come alive in her head, too.

"I'm sorry, Mama." With more luck than instinct and more instinct than skill, I pulled out of her head. *"I'm sorry, I'm sorry."*

"Not a telepath," she whispered. *"Por favor, dios, no mi hija también."*

"Mama?" I didn't know all the Spanish words, but I knew what she'd said. Please God, not my daughter, too.

"It's all right." She wiped her face, rolled her shoulders back. She didn't touch me, seemed to be carefully avoiding doing so.

"I'm sorry."

"You must control this ... thing. If you aren't careful, you'll hurt someone." Someone besides her, she meant.

My throat stung and I could barely push out the words, *"Am I bad?"*

Mama gave me a too quick hug, a nervous smile. *"Of course not. But you need to keep what you can do a secret. You can't tell anyone."*

I wanted to cry, but I only nodded.

"It's just—people won't understand, Nelia."

The lump in my throat hurt when I swallowed. *"Are you like me, Mama?"*

She shook her head. *"Not anymore. I had the gift when I was a child. It wasn't good..."* She stopped, seemed to reset herself before continuing. *"It went away the first time I shifted."*

"Will I be a wolf, too?"

"No. You're different." Her voice fell into a papery whisper. *"Damn your father."*

"Mama?"

Dabbing at her eyes with her fingers, she said, *"Promise not to tell your daddy what happened today or what you saw in my memories. None of it."*

That frightened me. She'd never asked me to keep secrets from Daddy before. *"I promise."*

"Go to your room now." She ran her hand through her hair, loosening the braid. *"Mama needs a moment."*

"But what about my hair? It's still tangly."

"Yes. Your hair." She handed me the comb. *"You work on it. I'll be back in a little while."*

Later that night, I overheard my dad talking to my uncle. *"I don't know what happened. Alma just said it was too hard."* His strong, sure voice was thready with fatigue.

"What happened after she said that?" Tío José asked.

"She walked out on us."

"Neely?"

My eyes blinked open and I bolted upward, tumbling off the bed and landing on my ass on the floor. I pushed back my hair. The frothy mass of curls had been in a ponytail on top of my head when I went to bed but was now hanging in my face. The ring I was wearing snagged in it, and when I tried to pull free, there was a tearing sound and bites of pain on my scalp.

"Lucas?"

"It's me."

"Oh God." My face was hot and damp, my hand was stuck in my hair, and my nightgown was up around my waist. Thank God the room was dark.

Then I remembered that Lucas could see very well in the dark.

"Nope, not God. Just me." He crouched down beside me as I used my free hand to yank my gown over my thighs. Dressed in chocolate brown board shorts and an ecru Golden Girls T-shirt with the neck stretched out, he looked more like himself than he had in the business suit. His feet were bare, his hair stood up all over his head in wind-blown disarray.

"What are you doing here?" Again, I tried to yank my hand free of my tangled curls. "What time is it?"

"Eleven-something. Careful, you'll rip your hair out." He straddled my legs and leaned close to slowly unwind my hair from around my fingers. He smelled like the desert—sunshine, sand, and clean air. Everything in me responded to those scents.

I plucked at his T-shirt. "This cannot be yours."

"Why not? I'm probably Blanche's biggest fan."

I laughed a little. Sniffed. Laughed again.

"What were you dreaming about?" His warm breath ruffled the ends of my hair. I shivered. I wanted to move closer to him, but Lucas and I were in a weird place and it wouldn't be smart to confuse things too much.

"The day my mom walked out on my dad and me."

I wiped my face with my free hand, and it came away wet. Crying

24

in my sleep? It felt a little pathetic, seeing as how my mom had left us nearly a quarter of a century ago.

"Bad idea. You should dream about me, instead."

"Like I can help what I—*wait*." I hiked up an eyebrow. "Dream about you? Why?"

"I'm good looking and excellent in bed. Those would be tears of ecstasy instead of sorrow."

I rolled my eyes. "It's breathtaking, the depth of your narcissism."

"Now you know why I like Blanche so much." He tsked at me and moved my head to the side. "You've really got yourself knotted up in here."

"It's my ring. I wore it to bed and my hair must have gotten caught on the diamond. It's a solitaire, and the prongs sometimes—"

"Ring? What ring?"

"My old engagement ring." I'd gotten caught up in old memories and took the stupid thing out, fell asleep with it on my finger. I should have gotten rid of it by now, but I never seemed to be able to cut that last tie to Julio.

"Don't wear rings to bed anymore."

"Sound advice, since it got tangled in my hair."

"Especially *his* ring," he snapped.

"Hmm. You seem to be leaving the advice zone and entering the possessive zone."

I yanked on my hand and he flicked it aside, frowned at me. "Stop it. I'm working here."

"My arm is numb. Please hurry."

"I'm moving as fast as I can. Your ex wasn't good to you. Never look back on a past it's best to forget." Lucas's very good-looking face —he hadn't been lying about that—was intent and as serious as it ever got.

"Sometimes the past won't leave you alone. Sometimes you have to look back in order to move forward," I said.

"Digging into your past rarely ends well. Trust me on that."

"I have questions."

"You'll always have questions. Let them go. Why would you want to invite pain back into your life?" He gave my hair a final tug. "You're free."

My hand dropped into my lap. I stared down at the half-carat, round-cut diamond. Julio had blown his entire savings on it and I'd cried when he got down on one knee and asked me to marry him.

Lucas was right. I shouldn't wear it anymore.

I massaged away the pins and needles in my arm with my other hand. "Thank you."

"Welcome." He helped me to my feet. "You're going to do what you want to do, but be careful."

"I will."

"Ask for help if you need it."

"Okay."

He kissed me on the forehead and walked out.

Sighing, I slipped off Julio's ring and dropped it into my nightstand drawer. Put my hair back up in a ponytail on top of my head and climbed into my rumpled bed.

I was halfway asleep when I realized Lucas had never told me why he was in my apartment.

CHAPTER FIVE

"Did you put the pink *conchas* in? I wanted pink."

"Yes, Dolores."

Dottie and Dolores Fairfield, better known as the Tower Witches, shuffled into the bakery early Friday morning. I was surprised to see them. According to their assistant Tim, they didn't normally surface before noon. Entirely understandable, considering the amount of wine they consumed in the evenings.

Dolores narrowed her blue eyes at me. "Are they fresh?"

"You can plainly see they are. Neely wouldn't serve us anything but her best." Dottie shook her head.

Dottie Fairfield was the exact opposite of her sister in build—short and generously proportioned where Dolores was tall and flat and sturdy—but her twin in coloring. The sisters were of Scandinavian descent with ivory skin, eyes like blue topaz, and silver-blonde hair they wore in chunky braids that hung down their spines.

With a smile and a wink for Dottie, I responded to Dolores's question. "Whipped them up this morning. The only way they could be fresher would be if they were still rising in the bowl. What else can I get you? Coffee?"

"Oh, that sounds lovely." Dottie squinted at the chalkboard style menu on the wall. "An iced coffee, please."

"Same here." Dolores thumbed open the bakery box. Sniffed. "Why are you dressed up? Don't think I've ever seen you in anything but a cotton sundress or shorts, kiddo."

She was right. I wore a cheap cotton sundress and Converse sneakers nearly every day. They had become a sort of uniform for me.

Today I was in heels, a pair of wide-leg charcoal pants that hugged my behind like it was never going to see it again, and a sleeveless coral blouse made of some silky material I had to wash by hand. My hair was down, the fluffed coils brushing my shoulders and trailing down my back. Even I had to admit I looked good, and I was usually my own worst critic.

"I'm going to San Diego."

"To see Alpha Xavier Malcolm?" Dottie asked.

I did a double take. "How did you know that?"

"Well, one hears things—"

"Dot's been doing the parallel polka with Earp." Dolores picked up a *concha* and bit into it, dusting the counter, the floor, and her chest with pink topping.

"Dolores, shame on you." Dottie's forehead wrinkled. "Jedidiah is a good friend." She turned her attention to me. "He mentioned that he was going to keep an eye on the bakery while you were away with Alpha Blacke. He's worried about vandals."

"Yeah, the town has turned against me." I said it matter-of-factly, but it stung.

"Jerks and cowards." Dolores muttered as she chewed.

Dottie said, "Well, I can tell you there are several people in this town who don't feel that way about you at all. Mr. Earp is certainly one. I do believe he's your biggest fan."

I'd saved Jed Earp's life when Saul Roso came to town, so I supposed I could see why he'd feel that way—even if I was the reason he had been in danger to begin with.

"Yeah, and if you can change that old grump's mind, you can change anyone's. Besides—" Dolores frowned down at the box of pastries. "—you've got us."

That made me smile. I may not have much, but I had my witches.

"So, how's the tower coming along?"

28

The tower was a three-story brick structure with a dilapidated wood balcony wrapped around the third floor. It was round and broad and stone, vaguely medieval, though it didn't look as much like a castle as it did an above-ground dungeon. The building stood atop crisscrossing ley lines and, according to the witches, had the potential to be very powerful—when it wasn't dormant.

Dolores shook her head. "We thought we'd revved her up when those shifters attacked a couple months ago, but the old girl has gone to sleep again."

"We're preparing ourselves for a three-day chant." Dottie grinned. "That's why we came in for pastries. We need the extra sugar."

"Three *days* of chanting?"

"Don't sound so surprised," Dolores said. "We might be half past our seventies, but Dot and I can still whip out a three-day chant. Once, we performed an anti-possession spell that required around the clock chanting for two weeks."

Dottie wrinkled her nose. "Yeah. Too bad about that man."

"He knew the risks going in, sis." Dolores stared down at the bakery box. "Hey, there's only four pink ones in here."

"You only ordered four *conchas*. You said you wanted to leave room for cookies." I made their iced coffees and took the box back from Dolores, placing a dozen *sandias*, watermelon-shaped sugar cookies, inside. "Thanks for the support, guys."

"No problem, toots. When you get back from seeing that devil alpha in San Diego, you come over and we'll pickle ourselves with strawberry wine by the hot spring. Dot's just about got the recipe right."

"I'm very close." Dottie plonked her straw into the iced coffee lid. "It's a fine balance between strawberries and sugar. My acid blend is perfect."

"I will." I'd visit, but I doubted I'd be drinking Dottie's wine. I'd had a bad experience with that stuff once. Twice. Certainly no more than three times. "If I can have a margarita instead."

"You and those prickly pear margaritas." Dolores grabbed a watermelon-shaped cookie from the box and pointed at me with it. She pulled out a chair and indicated that I should do the same.

With a sigh, I wiped down the counter with a clean cloth—a never-ending task—and joined them. It occurred to me that Dolores and Lucas were a lot alike, but I'd never tell her that, as the two shared a somewhat adversarial relationship.

"You liked my prickly pear cactus syrup?" Dottie grinned. "I'll teach you how to make it if you like."

Oh, I liked. That stuff was delicious. How the witch could get wine so wrong and margaritas so right was beyond me.

"Later, Dot." Dolores shook her cookie at me. "Now that we've got our snacks, you can sit down and tell me why you're going to see the scariest shifter I've ever met in my life." She held up a hand. "No, don't tell me. It's that damn tiger isn't it? It's always that guy."

I sat, rested my chin on my hands. "It's not Lucas's fault."

"Bullshit." She chomped on her cookie, chewed viciously. "You better be careful around that one, bakery girl, or you'll wind up a crossbreed or dead, and I'm not sure which would be worse."

Dolores was blunt and sometimes rude, but she wasn't wrong. I'd had the exact same realization. I liked Lucas, was drawn to him, but I couldn't trust him. He was an alpha leader who knew my secret and I'd spent too many years being burned by people like him.

"My presence in San Diego was requested by Alpha Malcolm through Lucas."

Dolores looked like she just bit into a lime instead of a cookie. "The nerve."

"Yeah, well, if you know how scary Malcolm is, then you know what I have to do."

"Run," Dolores said.

"No, I'm going to—"

"Run," Dottie said.

"Look, Lucas said he'd stay with me. I … trust him."

Dolores swallowed her bite of cookie. "You almost got that out with a straight face. Good for you."

I waved my hand around in dismissal. "Fine. So, trust doesn't come easily to me—particularly with alphas. That's not Lucas's fault." I leaned back in my chair, crossed my arms. "Now, will you please tell me what you know about Alpha Malcolm."

"Wolf shifter, alpha leader, San Diego pack. He's got roughly a thousand or so wolves under him. Handsome—most alphas are, for some strange reason—and mean as a snake. People who stand against Xavier Malcolm don't live long, happy lives."

"Dolores and I ran into him while we were searching for our tower. There was land on the Tijuana side of the Mexican border that we thought might be enchanted enough for us to grow one."

"You can build them from scratch?" The witches' current tower was the oldest structure within a hundred miles.

"Grow, not build," Dolores said. "And yes. Though the process takes a lot of time and a tremendous amount of magic."

Dottie played with a cookie crumb. "Alpha Malcolm doesn't like witches. So, he very firmly asked us to leave."

"What did you do?"

Dolores scowled. "What do you think we did? We skedaddled the hell out of there."

"But you're witches. Why didn't you use your magic and stand up to him?"

"We'd have had to kill him." Dottie delicately sipped her iced coffee. "If we didn't, he'd have killed us. He's not a nice man."

"Yep." Dolores put some money on the table, gathered her bakery box in her arms, and stood. "So, if you end up having to spike him, you'd better not half-ass it or he'll hunt you down."

Didn't that sound familiar?

"This Malcolm guy," Dolores said, "he's nothing like that Roso was. He's completely sane, for one thing. For another, his power … it's like comparing a wildfire to a torch. Saul Roso was nothing compared to Xavier Malcolm."

Dottie patted my hand as she got up to leave. "You're very powerful and growing more so by the day. But at your current level, you won't win against Xavier Malcolm and his wolves. Whatever you do, don't challenge him. Have a nice trip, dear."

"IF YOU TOUCH that thing one more time, I'm going to break every single one of your goddamn fingers."

Chandra yanked her hand away from the knob. "The stations keep going out."

"It's satellite. They don't go out. You just don't like the songs." Lucas hit a button on the console and the radio switched to an easy listening station. "There. It's staying on this station."

"You know, *Alpha Blacke*, the main reason why I agreed to join your group was because you told me you did not torture your shifters."

"Suckered you right in, didn't I?" Lucas smiled aggressively at her.

"This is cruel and unusual—oh God, *is that flute music?*" Chandra gagged.

"Wait for the jazz flute solo. That's the best part."

"You're killing me."

Personally, I liked the flute music. It was calming. As I was headed into the lion's den, I needed to be calm and centered and, unfortunately, these two were ruining it with their bickering.

"Take the offramp after this one, turn right." Chandra unzipped the desert camouflage duffel at her feet, rifled through the contents. Knowing the hyena shifter as I did, I assumed her packing consisted of ninety-five percent things that could kill people and five percent black clothing. "You'll see a gas station with a bathroom in the back. Pull around and have Neely go inside to get the key. While they're watching her, I'll slip out. I've got a ride waiting nearby."

"Sounds good," Lucas said.

It sounded dangerous to me.

I poked my head over the back seat. We were in Lucas's silver BMW M6 that he'd purchased for trips into the city, and I'd been relegated to the back seat by Chandra, who'd called shotgun with an actual shotgun in her hands.

"What if Alpha Malcolm finds out you're doing this?" I asked her.

"If his recon team is any good, he will."

"I don't understand."

"Malcolm knows us," Chandra said. "If we don't take some precautions, he'll get suspicious. I'm giving him a focus for those suspicions. We'll be fine as long as his team is as stupid as they were last visit."

"They aren't stupid," Lucas said. "You're just the best."

"That's true." Chandra reached for the radio knob again. Lucas gave her the side-eye and she lowered her hand.

The closer we got to town, the more anxious I became. Unable to hold back my panic any longer, I rapid-fired questions at them. "What am I supposed to say to him? What am I supposed to do? Are we staying? How long? Diego agreed to run the bakery through the weekend, but I have to be back, and what does Alpha Malcolm expect from me, because—"

"Chill, spiker," Chandra said. "It's not as if you don't have any way to defend yourself. If Malcolm gets out of line, spike the shit out of him."

"No," Lucas said. "No spiking."

She shrugged. "Bummer."

Lucas gave Chandra the side-eye again. "Neely, I'll be with you as much as I can. The important thing with Malcolm is balance. He'll want you fearful, but not too afraid to look him in the eye. He'll want you brave, but not so brave you make him look weak in any way. Follow my lead."

"Okay."

"And make sure you read everyone, including me," he added.

I didn't say anything to that.

As we pulled to the back of the gas station and Chandra rolled out the passenger door, I contemplated rolling out with her, hitching a ride to the airport, and flying the hell away from Lucas Blacke and Xavier Malcolm.

Instead, I went into the mini mart to get the key to the restroom and create a distraction that was purposefully designed not to work. Once Chandra was gone, I climbed into the front seat of Lucas's car, clicked myself in, and stared sleepily out the window as the mountains flattened into city that rolled into gorgeous southern California coastline.

A little under an hour after we had dropped off Chandra, Lucas poked me. "Wake up, Sleeping Beauty. We've arrived in Hell."

"Hell" turned out to be an enormous Victorian-style house that doubled as a bed and breakfast in Carlsbad, an affluent seaside resort city that stretched across seven miles of beach in northern San Diego county.

Lucas parked and escorted me inside. He grabbed the room key from the front desk attendant and immediately went upstairs, carrying our bags himself, grumbling about how he trusted no one here with his things.

Although the exterior and common areas of the bed and breakfast were distinctly historical Victorian, our guest room was fitted with every luxurious amenity one could ask for.

"This is beautiful."

The ornate headboard of the room-dominating king bed was black-washed pine, the bureau and settee were in a matching wash. The marble-topped antique nightstands were just big enough for a cell phone and a white pillar candle. Our bedding was sumptuous, buttery soft to the touch and layered in shades of white and ivory. One entire wall consisted of tall, rectangular windows overlooking the beach across the road, and a salt-scented breeze eased into the room through one of them.

Lucas stepped into my space, pulled me into his embrace. "Read me." His voice was a feather stroke over my ear.

I stiffened and he tightened his hold but kept his voice low. "Don't be a pain in the ass about this. Read me, Neely. I'm inviting you in."

An invitation meant I wasn't breaking any rules. And a read wouldn't be so bad. I didn't get that addictive euphoria from using my telepathy the way I did when spiking someone.

I reached for him with my ability.

...watching us right now. Two cameras. Above the bed and above the bathroom door. Be aware.

I stroked my hand over his back and whispered, "Cameras in a B&B?"

For shit's sake, don't say it out loud—and yes. Cameras. Nothing in the bathroom, though. One in the living area, one on the balcony.

"How can you tell?" I whispered.

I can hear them. Only if I concentrate, though. Whoever put them in is good. Really good. I need to get their name.

He buried his face in my hair. Being this close to him was starting

34

to feel a little too comfortable. I shivered as he trailed his fingers down my spine.

Don't be afraid. I won't let anything happen to you.

Yeah, not why I was shivering, but a good enough excuse—and accurate. I was terrified of Alpha Malcolm. Anyone that had Chandra and Lucas operating at this level of caution was not a person to be trifled with.

"There's only one bed," I whispered. "You couldn't have gotten a room with a sofa?"

What? There's a settee right there.

"That is a bench with a back and even I couldn't stretch out on it. I know you can afford a suite, Lucas Blacke."

I'm not paying for this. He made a jabbing motion in the direction of the bathroom and we headed into the spacious en suite.

"Who is then?" I pushed the door closed behind us and kept my voice low.

"Malcolm."

"*Malcolm?*"

"This is his place. He owns several B&Bs in the county for visiting shifters. This is one of the nicer ones, actually." He surveyed the spacious bathroom with its sunken tub and two-person shower. "Anyway, we've slept together before."

I cracked the door and peered out at the enormous bed in the center of the room. Tossed Lucas a threatening look over my shoulder. "Okay, fine. Just keep to your side."

"Hey, I've got no problem with that." He leaned against the wall beside the towel rack and stared at himself in the mirror over the sink. "Maybe you're the one who should worry about losing control and jumping my bones."

"I'll do my best to contain myself, Blanche."

He grinned. "You say that as if you think it offends me."

"Offend you? Mr. Bulletproof Ego?" I peeked at the bed again. "Is that *chocolate* on the pillows?"

Lucas stepped closer to the mirror, examined a spot on his chin. "Probably."

"Hallelujah." I flung open the door and headed straight for the bed, watching him over my shoulder to make sure he wasn't following me. I didn't feel like sharing.

"I should have brought peanut butter cups." Lucas leaned against the bathroom door frame. "That's how I bribed you last time."

I snatched the wrapped squares off each pillow and sniffed them.

"There's room service here, you know," he said. "We can order in lunch."

"Order lunch here? No way. Might be poisoned." More like it might be not-chocolate. I peeled away the first candy wrapper and shoved the melty little square of pure heaven into my mouth. "Oh, this is good quality."

"You know, if I was going to poison anything, it would be the chocolates housekeeping puts on the pillows." Lucas pulled away from the doorway, crossed to the window. "Plausible deniability and all that."

I stopped chewing. Thought about spitting it out.

"Nah, too obvious," I said.

BEFORE LEAVING SUNDANCE, Lucas had told me that I'd be expected to dress for dinner. Dresses for the beach, I had in spades. Dresses to "dress" for some bourgeois dinner? Not so much.

So, I borrowed one from Chandra, which in hindsight might have been a mistake. For one thing, she was slimmer than I was, and for another, she was far more daring than I'd ever dreamed of being.

"Wow." Lucas walked into the bathroom as I was putting on herringbone-patterned thigh-high hose.

The dress was a band of black microfiber that hit me at mid-thigh. The halter top left my upper back bare, revealing a tattoo on my right shoulder.

"I'll take that as a compliment." I slipped my feet into a pair of four-inch platform pumps. Thankfully, they were excellent quality shoes. I'd bought them three years ago when I was getting out of the house more.

Lucas straightened the lapels of his jacket and moved behind me.

He was resplendent in shades of charcoal and white. I don't think I'd ever seen him look so haute couture—and so utterly un-Lucas-like. Even his business clothing suited him better than this, though he was as sexy as ever.

"You should. You look incredible." He loosened his collar, fanned himself for effect. "Did you get a tattoo? Is that *José*?"

I glanced over my shoulder in the mirror at the pearly silver outline of a wolf's head and the faded moon. The silvery ink glimmered beautifully against my brown skin. I loved it.

"In his younger days. It was from a photo he'd had taken of his wolf. I found it after … after he died." My chest still hurt when I said those words. "I took it to Dottie's tattoo artist in Pacific Beach and he captured my *tío*'s essence perfectly."

I'd cried all the way home after I got it.

"You're lucky to have that photo. Most shifters don't allow themselves to be photographed in animal form." He ran his fingers over my shoulder. "It's a beautiful remembrance of a good man."

I shivered beneath his touch. Lucas's breath quickened.

Neither of us called attention to our reactions.

"You're going to have to read people tonight, Neely. I know you don't want to, but we need the information." He spoke softly, gently, as if he felt it was necessary to coax me into compliance.

"I have rules."

"Yes." He sounded sad. "I wish I didn't have to be the one to ask you to break them."

I half-turned to face him. "Then don't."

Our gazes locked, and my heart beat a little faster. After a moment, he gave me a brusque nod and backed away. He still wanted me to read Malcolm and the others, and I still didn't want to do it. But I would do it and he knew it. He also knew that he was asking me to compromise my moral code and it didn't sit well with him. Nor should it.

I faced the mirror again. "I'm almost finished."

"We have ten minutes."

I'd spent a lot of time on my eyes—nailed the smoky eye look on the third try, thanks to a couple of online makeup tutorials. I bent over to fluff and spray my curls, and then flicked my head so that my hair tumbled down my back. Tiny hairs stuck up all over my head like little antennae, but my hair was also full of body—the double-edged sword of frizz.

"Should I put it up?" I asked. "The salt air is making it puffy."

"No." Lucas's eyes flashed gold in the mirror. "Leave it down. Loose." He cleared his throat, seemed to catch himself. "Unless you want it up."

If leaving my hair down had that effect on Lucas, it must look good. Frizz or not, the hair was staying down.

While I smoothed gloss over my lips, Lucas retreated to the doorway. He studied me the way most people would read a book. Smiling once in a while, frowning, his entire focus on me.

I zipped up my cosmetic bag and then spun in a circle to show him the whole package. "Too much?"

"No." His gaze raked over me. "You're perfect."

CHAPTER SIX

I DON'T KNOW WHAT I'D EXPECTED. THE WEIRD DINNER PARTY FROM *Eyes Wide Shut* maybe? But the vibe here was more "cocktails with the boss" than hedonistic rich people wearing deer antlers and ceremonial robes.

Lucas laughed when I told him what I'd expected. "Antlers?"

"Well, I've never been to anything like this. I assumed the worst."

I gripped his elbow tighter as we milled around the gathering area adjacent to the dining room. The room was so generic it could have been a movie set in an old whodunit movie. Polished oak side tables, uncomfortable red-cushioned Victorian sofas, green patterned wool rugs. An ornate gold mirror hung on one nature-themed papered wall. Built-in oak shelving lined the one across from it, an expensive looking, but otherwise uninteresting, collection of vases on the shelves.

Most of the women wore black, which made me wish I'd worn another color. Three waitstaff in white dress shirts, black ties, and black trousers weaved through the guests, drinks on trays balanced on one hand. The mingled scents of spent firewood, alcohol, and salt-water should have given the room a cozy atmosphere.

It didn't.

"It's no big deal. We'll eat an expensive meal, watch everyone here kiss Malcolm's ass, and have drinks in the solarium with the 'chosen few.'" He half-smiled at a woman in a black and white checked skirt and jacket who tipped her head in his direction. Everyone here seemed to know Lucas, but very few people had stopped to talk to us, and several of them were obviously keeping their distance. I glanced over their brains, a light telepathic read.

They were afraid of him.

"What does that mean?" I continued reading people as I made my way to a quiet corner where another bookcase was stocked with expensive-looking volumes that seemed chosen for aesthetics rather than reading enjoyment. The colors of the bindings perfectly matched the hunting-themed tapestries hanging on the wall on either side of it.

Lucas followed. "Out of the twenty people here right now, he'll choose anywhere from four to six to accompany him to the solarium, or perhaps for a walk on the beach. We'll be chosen. He wants to talk to you."

"You're really not convincing me this isn't like *Eyes Wide Shut.*"

"No masks, robes, or nude women." He swiped a whiskey from the tray of a passing server and took a long swig. "Yet."

I shot him a quelling look. "What's the deal with everyone? Why do they look so frightened? Are they that afraid of Malcolm? That afraid of you?"

"I see you're reading people again." He took another gulp from his glass.

Before I could respond, a green-eyed, red-haired man walked into the room and made a beeline for our corner of it. He was Lucas's height, but built softer.

"Do my eyes fail me, or is that the dastardly Lucas Blacke?" The man held out his hand and Lucas shook it.

"William Scott. Been a while."

"It has, it has. I told my sister you'd be here tonight." He yanked on his navy blue and charcoal striped tie and gestured to the woman approaching at a more sedate pace. She had the same pale white skin, red hair, and green eyes as William.

"I believe *I* told *you.*"

The woman straightened her brother's tie. Her silver sheath dress

40

hung perfectly on her slender frame, her hair was artfully arranged in an elegant chignon, and her makeup was of the barely-there-but-probably-took-an-hour-to-do style. A diamond solitaire the size of a child's marble sparkled on her middle finger. Her ring finger was bare, as was her brother's.

"Willa's right. It probably happened that way." The man was obviously American, but he had a hint of Scottish brogue in his voice, the way a person would if they'd been raised around native Scottish parents or grandparents. "It's good to see you."

I read him. He meant it, which was a nice change from how everyone else in the room regarded Lucas.

The feeling was mutual. For the first time since we'd walked downstairs, there was a genuine smile on Lucas's face and his posture had softened. "How have you been?"

"He's been an absolute terror. Refuses to take his medication. Tell him, Lucas." Willa put her hand on Lucas's sleeve. Despite the fact that she and her brother were barely north of forty and Lucas was in his mid-thirties, there was something maternal in the gesture. She patted Lucas as if he were a beloved child or cherished younger brother. "Tell him he needs to take his blood pressure medication."

"There's never been a wolf with high blood pressure in our family. The doctor was wrong." William crossed his arms over his chest.

"Human doctor?" Lucas asked.

"Dr. Penbright," Willa said, with a raised brow and a frown.

Lucas glared at his friend. "Take the medicine, William."

"Never mind that, introduce me to your beautiful date." His devilish gaze snagged mine and I couldn't help but smile. "Or is it beautiful *mate*? Have you finally found someone willing to put up with you, old friend? About time." Both Willa and her brother appeared excited at the prospect.

"You two are worse than my grandmother," Lucas muttered. "This is Neely Costa MacLeod. She owns a bakery in Sundance."

Grandmother? Color me intrigued.

"Hello, lovely." William smiled at me, and then sighed dramatically. "You know, perhaps I should give Luciana Blacke a call. Ah, but it's been a while since we had a nice chat. I could tell her all about your mate."

Lucas glared at his friend. "And you call *me* dastardly."

William pressed his hand to his heart. "I'm a saint and you know it."

I leaned against the bookcase and watched the two men volley the conversational ball between them. Dipped into their heads just long enough to see that they meant each other no harm, and then relaxed.

Willa stopped a passing server and plucked two glasses of white wine from his tray. Handed me one.

"Thank you." I meant it. My last few bottles had been at the Tower with the witches. I'd almost forgotten what good wine tasted like.

She smiled. "Neely, right? I'm Willa."

"Yes, and pleased to meet you, Willa."

"Likewise. So, you're a baker?"

"Sort of," I replied, smiling at her quizzical frown. It was the truth, after all. I had no idea if I was still a baker. The only thing I knew tonight was that I was a spiker, and that yet another alpha leader had wormed his way into my life.

"Best baker in Sundance." Lucas jerked me in front of him, nearly spilling my wine. "To answer your question, no, we're not mated— yet." He brushed his lips over my ear. "Neely, meet Saint William."

"Oh, is it Saint now? That's not what you called me last time we met." He extended his hand and I shook it. "You don't look like a baker, Ms. Costa MacLeod."

"Is that so? What do bakers look like?"

"Like they sample their product. So, a bit more like me rather than him." He thumbed in Lucas's direction. "MacLeod? Perhaps our families knew each other once upon a time. Wouldn't that be something?" He whisper-kissed my knuckles like a hero from an old movie. I almost curtsied, but managed to keep my knees locked.

"Put your eyeballs back in your head, William."

"Come on, Lucas. Only paying my respects to the most beautiful baker I've ever met." He winked at me, and I had the feeling that he was playing a game with Lucas and was including me in on the fun.

So, I winked back.

Lucas growled.

Really growled. The couple nearest us took several steps back. The male lowered his head submissively. If Lucas noticed the man's reaction, he didn't let on.

William's eyes widened. "Wait a minute, you said you aren't mated."

"She's *mine*." This time the growl was unmistakable, seeing as how it was accompanied by a flash of teeth. I shivered. The submissive couple shot off to the other side of the room.

William and Willa didn't seem put out at all by Lucas's reaction. In fact, they grinned like Cheshire cats at each other. I read them, and again picked up no malice from either one. They seemed to genuinely like Lucas.

Willa lifted her wineglass to her lips. "I give them until the end of the year."

"Didn't you see the way he came at me, sis?" William asked. "Six months, tops."

Behind me, Lucas's entire body tightened in annoyance. I didn't know what had gotten him so worked up, but I knew it wouldn't be wise for him to shift here. Not with Xavier Malcolm in the house.

"Lucas." I pulled his arm around my waist. Squeezed his palm against my hip. He brushed the cup of my ear with his lips.

"Read me," he murmured, so I did.

Old memories swam in the shallow waters of his mind. Heavy, painful remembrances that made me want to take Lucas by the hand and lead him out of this place—for his sake as well as mine.

It's not them, it's me. I hate this place.

"I know you do," I whispered.

Someone rang a bell—a damn *bell*—signifying dinner was beginning, so we all made our way to the enormous oak table in the next room. Wolf paw-embossed place cards at each plate directed us to our seats. Mine was between Malcolm's and William's chairs, but Lucas picked up William's card and flicked it away.

"I give it *three* months." William laughed and flicked Lucas's card away, and then stood behind the seat across from me.

I started to pull out my chair, but Lucas halted me with a hand on mine. He indicated the other dinner guests with a sideways look and a

43

raised brow. Everyone was standing behind their chairs. It was like a scene out of a stuffy period drama.

"Are you freaking kidding me?" I whispered.

Malcolm loves ceremony. Pomp. Eclat. It's a real pain in the ass, putting up with all this feigned elegance bullshit.

"How did you do that?" I asked. "I wasn't..." I pointed to my head.

You weren't reading me?

"No."

A smile curved his handsome mouth. *Guess my thoughts are powerful.*

I gritted my teeth. "Just when I thought you couldn't get any more arrogant."

William and Willa gave me a curious look. I smiled and tried to seem only half as nervous as I was. I downed my glass of wine and reached for Lucas's. He grabbed my hand before I could, and threaded his fingers through mine.

"Gimme," I muttered.

Take it easy, woman. Try not to embarrass me in front of all these lovely people who hate me.

There was an air of expectancy as we waited for the "lord of the manor" to take his place at the head of the table. I was breathing too fast. My pulse was in my ears.

God, I hated alpha leaders—with the exception of the one who stood beside me. Although at the moment, he wasn't high on my list of favorite people, either.

Hey. Lucas leaned into me a little. *Calm down. I promise I won't leave you alone with him.*

My eyes felt as wide as a flashlight lens. Lucas wouldn't leave me, he'd promised, but I was still scared. I'd been conditioned to expect the worst of alpha leaders who knew what I could do.

"Swear it."

I swear it. You're safe with me.

I nodded too fast.

Breathe. It's only dinner.

I couldn't figure out if Lucas was thinking to himself or to me, but I went ahead and took a couple of deep breaths anyway. Circumstances what they were, I figured I'd be using my telepathy a lot this weekend and I was glad I'd been practicing control with the witches. Although I'd been practicing *keeping from* reading people more than actually reading them.

My telepathy used to be uncontrollable. I heard the thoughts of everyone I came across unless I purposefully blocked them, and this had given me massive headaches. For a while I'd worn a spelled charm, but with the help of Dolores and Dottie, and a lot of practice, I no longer needed it. I was now able to turn my ability up and down like the volume on a stereo. Unfortunately, it seemed Lucas was the one person able to break through my mute setting.

It figured. The man took being an annoyance to an entirely new level.

A door creaked open at the far end of the room. The voices of the guests died out, one by one, until the dining room was completely devoid of sound. It was so quiet I could hear pots being stirred, though the kitchen door was closed. Could hear the ocean waves breaking on the beach across the street.

Could hear the sound of my heart hammering in my chest.

"Good evening, everyone."

My heart jumped from my chest to my throat as Xavier Malcolm strolled into the room. His smile was charming, and the corners of his ice blue eyes were carefully creased as if to convey the idea that he did, in fact, smile a lot. He was white-skinned with a Southern California summer-tan, and exceptionally fit. Dressed entirely in loose-fitting white linen, with his silver hair cropped stylishly short, he looked like a Hollywood-style prophet.

I turned up my ability and tried to read him.

Nothing. I couldn't sense a thing.

That happened sometimes.

Not often.

"Welcome, treasured guests." Alpha Malcolm's voice was both charismatic and sharp. An alpha trick. Saul Roso had been a pro at it, and Lucas could do it when he chose to, which was almost never.

"Please, be seated. No need to stand on ceremony here." The

chuckle accompanying this invitation was as manufactured as his smile. As were the self-conscious laughs of the wolves in response.

Bullshit. If any of his pack had sat down before Malcolm gave them permission, there'd be hell to pay. Lucas thought this to me as he pulled out my chair.

Again, I wasn't reading him. It bothered me that he was able to send thoughts to me without my opening up to him. Having Lucas in my ear was trouble enough, but having him inside my head? So much worse.

We sat and waited for the alpha to make his way to his chair. As per the place cards, I was seated between Alpha Malcolm, at the head of the table, and, now, Lucas. My chair was across from Willa, who was seated beside her brother.

"I hope you all enjoy dinner." The wolf alpha infused even more power into his voice. The sound set my teeth on edge. "Our chef has outdone himself."

Himself must have been the secret password, because servers suddenly burst into the room, arms weighed down with platters and bowls. The dinner guests, who had gone conspicuously silent when the alpha entered, grew noisy again. It seemed shifters could ignore nearly anything unpleasant if there was food in front of them.

The alpha shook hands and offered individual greetings on his way to his seat, but his eyes remained laser-focused on Lucas.

"You rearranged the place cards," he said as he lowered himself into his chair.

"I wanted to sit beside my date." Lucas nodded as a young male server offered him soup from a silver tureen. He kicked up an eyebrow at his old alpha. "Look at her. Would you let her sit next to William if you were me?"

"Unkind, Alpha Blacke." William winked. "But astute."

Alpha Malcolm set his attention on me, his cool blue eyes taking in my appearance. I had the unsettling feeling that this wasn't the first time he'd seen me tonight. Had he been watching Lucas and me in our room earlier? Or just now, while we were having drinks in the gathering room? Perhaps through a hidden camera or by peeking through paintings with the eyes cut out? I made a mental note to check the artwork.

"You must be Miss Costa-MacLeod, the town baker." His perfect smile reached his eyes and made his face shine, but there was no warmth. It was as cold and empty as a poor man's freezer.

"Neely, please. And I used to be the town baker. These days I'm exploring my options."

The alpha's eyebrows hiked up, which made me worry I'd just said something stupid.

"I hope the accommodations suit you."

"The room is lovely, thank you." I nodded at the server, and received a ladle of creamy soup in the bowl in front of me. There was broccoli in it. As broccoli and my digestive system were cautious friends at the best of times, I shoved the green bits to the side with the edge of my spoon.

Alpha Malcolm shook his head at the server offering him soup. "If you'd prefer your own bed, *Neely*, I'm happy to move you to another room."

Asshole. Lucas wasn't holding back his thoughts at all. In fact, he was pushing them at me.

"Thank you." I smiled as if I hadn't heard my "date" think a thing. "But I'm happy where I am."

Lucas sat up a little straighter, shoulders back, head up. He lifted his glass of wine, winking at Malcolm as he took a sip.

"Very well." The alpha gave me a curt nod and Lucas a narrow-eyed once over. "Alpha Blacke of the Sundance group, how are you?"

Xavier Malcolm alternated between sounding like a petulant king and a charming icicle. When he spoke to Lucas it was in a downward drift, as if he were regarding him from the peak of a mountain. I tried to read the man again and failed.

Disturbing.

Lucas replied, "I'm doing well, thank you."

"And your people? They aren't being murdered left and right anymore?"

Bastard. "Nope." Lucas popped a kalamata olive into his mouth.

There was a dish of assorted olives and cubed cheese between us I hadn't noticed until now. He'd already eaten half of it.

"You located the culprit? Dealt with him or her?"

As if he doesn't already know the whole damn story. "Yep." Lucas said aloud. He chewed, swallowed. Popped another olive into his mouth. "Neely spiked the guy straight to Hell."

A hush swept over the table, from end to end. Every eye was on me. If they weren't all staring, I'd have smacked Lucas upside the head for bringing that up.

"That's right. I understand you're a spiker?" Alpha Malcolm asked.

Apparently, we were playing some sort of weird game where we pretended he didn't already know everything about me. I went along with it.

"Yes."

"And you're joining Alpha Blacke's group?"

An errant stalk of broccoli floated onto my spoon. I guided it to the edge of the bowl. "I am considering it."

"One of those options to which you referred earlier?"

"Yes." I felt like I was tiptoeing through a minefield.

Lucas tossed another olive into his mouth.

"So, you're a spiker, huh? Don't meet many of those." William pointed across the table at me with his whiskey glass. "If you spiked me right now, how long would it take you to kill me?"

My eyes slid to Lucas, who was now chomping on a cube of gouda. He didn't look at me, neither did he think anything at me. Guess I was on my own.

So, I told the truth, but kept it vague. "Not long."

William's eyes went wide. "Remind me not to cut you off in traffic, then."

A nervous laugh tittered down the table. It was a church giggle, the kind you tried to hide from your parents and the minister, all of whom in this case would be Xavier Malcolm.

"You have nothing to fear from me." I smoothed the napkin on my lap. "I'd never use my ability on anyone who wasn't trying to kill me first."

"No?" Willa picked up her wineglass. "Not to insult you, Neely, but

48

there are those in Alpha Blacke's employ who wouldn't hesitate to abuse an ability like that at the slightest provocation."

Lucas sighed. "Chandra apologized. She thought you were a danger to me."

Willa huffed. "I was *hugging* you goodbye."

"Your fingers grew back. Besides, it was the early days and she was learning the ropes of her new position."

"As your *second*," Alpha Malcolm said with distaste.

"You don't think a woman can be an effective second alpha?" I spoke without thinking, as I was thoroughly annoyed at the suggestion, and defensive on Chandra's behalf.

The wolf alpha's clenched, cold smile made an appearance. "I believe a woman can do anything a man can do—especially a paranormal woman. But I don't believe an assassin can be an effective second."

"*Ex*-assassin." Lucas ate another olive.

Alpha Malcolm picked up his fork and serrated knife, and delicately sliced into the chicken breast on his plate. "Where is your killing machine, Alpha Blacke? Slinking around my city?"

"Chandra doesn't slink, she skulks. And I don't know where she is right now."

At the other end of the table, an older male voice said, "Because you don't have control of your shifters. You're no alpha, Lucas Blacke."

Lucas ignored the man, so I did the same, keeping my eyes on Malcolm instead.

"That's enough, Richard." One of Alpha Malcolm's eyebrows shot up. I was sure he agreed with the old man, but his face registered annoyance at the interruption. "Did you bring the eagle this time instead?" This he directed to Lucas.

"I couldn't say where Amir is, either. He is his own man."

"No control, I tell you," Richard muttered to the wolves at his end of the long table.

This time I looked at him—glared, really. Richard appeared to be in his mid-seventies, fit, with hair more salt than pepper. He sported a short-cropped white beard and dark gray mustache that lent him the look of a cut-rate Sean Connery.

49

Alpha Malcolm stabbed his fork into the chicken breast and took a savage bite. It was so at odds with his civilized exterior that it startled me. "You learned nothing from me during your tenure here, Alpha Blacke."

Lucas picked up my refilled glass of wine, handed it to me. His was already in his other hand.

"On the contrary. I learned everything from you." The implication being that Lucas knew his old alpha well enough to know the man was up to something.

"Not everything." The edge in Xavier Malcolm's tone brought the already-faltering conversation at the table to a screeching halt.

"Not *anything*," the rude older wolf muttered.

A muscle pulsed in Alpha Malcolm's cheek. He picked up his serrated knife and examined the pointed tip. With an almost casual gesture, he flung it at Richard. The blade sank deeply into the older man's upper arm, the wood handle quivering like a feather in a windstorm.

Richard gasped, but didn't cry out, nor did he remove the blade. Blood oozed around the wound, staining his pearl-gray dress shirt. "Ap-pologies for the interruption, Alpha."

The wolf alpha said nothing, merely picked up his fork and began to eat his chicken. The old man left the blade sticking out of his arm as he finished his meal. Muted chatter among the dinner guests resumed, forks and knives scraped plates, dishes were set down and removed, ice clinked in water glasses.

Lucas said and thought nothing. He seemed neither surprised nor horrified by what Malcolm had just done. I was both.

Before Lucas could, I nabbed the last olive and popped it into my mouth. Washed it down with a huge swig of wine.

It was going to be a long night.

CHAPTER SEVEN

Lucas was wrong about the solarium. Malcolm didn't choose six, or four, or even two people to accompany him to the glass-walled room. He chose one.

Me.

"You said you wouldn't leave me, you giant ass." I hissed this at Lucas during digestifs in the gathering room after dinner.

Digestifs. I had to surreptitiously look up the meaning of the word on my cell phone. Booze after dinner. The opposite of *aperitifs.* What the hell was I doing here? I was so not a *digestifs* person. I was a prickly pear margarita and bad homemade wine person.

"I'll be close. But I'm curious about what he intends to say to you, and he won't say it in front of me for some reason. Why do you think that is?"

"How should I know?" My hands shook so badly, brandy sloshed in my glass.

Lucas took the drink away and set it on a polished oak end table. I didn't care. It tasted nasty anyway.

Calm down before someone notices.

He'd pushed the words into my head again. No one else could do that, and both Julio and my uncle had tried several times. Why was it so easy for Lucas?

51

"No one is looking at me."

These are shifters. Most of them can smell fear.

"If Alpha Malcolm gets me alone, I'll probably wet my pants and they won't have to go to the trouble of sniffing."

"You are not without power, Neely."

I scowled at him. "Power you said I can't use."

"There's a reason for that." He threw back the last of his brandy and set his glass on the table by mine. "You can read him."

"No, I can't. Not even a little bit."

Lucas stared at me for a beat, then rolled his eyes. "Sounds about right. Malcolm brings fresh meaning to the word inscrutable. It's no surprise he'd be difficult to read."

"Not difficult. *Impossible.*"

He clasped my hand in his. "No one is impossible for you to read. You'll just have to push a little harder with him is all. He's an alpha."

"The only way to do that is for me to spike him."

"No." His fingers tightened on mine. He let out a slow breath and loosened them. "Do *not* spike him."

"So, my only defense and I can't use it. Thanks a lot."

Lines appeared around his eyes. "You won't need it. He won't hurt you. Not yet."

"That makes me feel worlds better."

"You know what?" He released my hand. "Let's go, then. Sneak out the back to wherever Chandra is skulking—seriously, slinking? Does he even *know* her? —and go home."

That sounded like a fantastic plan, and it brought up a question I'd been wanting to ask. "Why doesn't Alpha Malcolm like Chandra?" There was no way it was the assassin thing. He looked like the type of guy who had the numbers of several assassins on speed dial.

"Because he knows she'd kill or die for me and she can't be bought. It irks him when he can't compromise someone."

"He tried to compromise her?"

"Malcolm has tried to turn every paranormal in my group against me. He's relentless."

"Is he trying to compromise me? Is that why I'm here?"

"Maybe. He's never forgiven me for leaving his pack. That alpha holds a mean grudge, and he's single-minded to a fault."

Realization sank in along with Lucas's words. "Single-minded."

"Yeah."

"So, if the reason he wants me here is to change me into his cross-breed, he won't stop until I'm changed or dead."

"We can't be sure that's what he wants."

"There are better choices." Slowly, I tipped my head up, stared into his amber eyes. "Amir Gamal, Margaret Lentz, Lisa Cesar, King Jones. Powerful shifters who are *in your group*, unlike me. There's no reason to compromise me, Lucas. I'm nothing to you."

"You may not be in my group, but Malcolm believes we're lovers."

I shook my head. "He half-believes it. And he didn't believe that much until *after* he'd decided he wanted me here, did he?"

A muscle pulsed in Lucas's cheek. "*Neely.*"

"It's happening again." My chest tightened. "If I run, he'll come at me through the people I care about. Roso wouldn't stop until I killed him. That's how alpha leaders are."

"Some."

"Damn you." My eyes dampened, but I held back the tears. "I have to meet him alone. You *promised* you wouldn't leave me alone with him."

"I meant it." Lucas's expression hardened. "You're going to have to trust me."

"And if I don't?" I said through clenched teeth.

"Then we're both screwed."

"YOU DIDN'T WANT to meet with me."

The solarium was a window-walled room on the ground floor of the house, filled with ferns and flowers and a bunch of plants I didn't recognize. Instead of overlooking the ocean, it offered a 270-degree view of the expansive garden at the rear of the house. Someone had threaded fairy lights through branches and leaves inside and out, giving the place a magical cast, like something from a child's dream.

"You're the lead alpha of the San Diego wolf pack. I was—" I played with a fern frond. "—nervous."

"Nervous. Is that all?" The alpha sat on a cement bench beside a plump succulent plant. His elegant fingers glanced over the prickly edges.

I shrugged. Made my way over to a clay pot with a froth of pink flowers spilling over the side. I was so scared I could feel my heart beating in my throat and I couldn't get my hands to stop shaking.

"She answers me with her silence." He gave me a snake oil salesman smile. "You don't like me."

"I don't like alpha leaders in general. Don't take it personally."

He laughed. It sounded real, but like so many things about him, might have been a lie. "It must have been tough for you, growing up a telepathic spiker."

So, he knew about the telepathy. I wondered if Lucas had told him, then decided Lucas wouldn't have shared anything he'd consider an advantage.

"It wasn't easy. Who told you I was a telepath?"

"Does it matter?"

"I suppose not." I straightened, turned to face him, my back to the flowers. "What do you want with me? Why have you summoned me here?"

"Summoned?" He chuckled. "You make me sound like a feudal lord."

"Is the comparison so far-fetched?"

He tipped his head, squinted. "I don't demand fealty."

"Yes, you do." I crossed my arms over my chest. Though my tone was on the heated side, the gesture was more protective than combative. "All alpha leaders demand service and allegiance. That's the *definition* of fealty."

I was tired of playing this game. The rules kept changing according to his whims. Feudal lord fit him perfectly, and I wasn't going to pretend otherwise.

"You *really* don't like alpha leaders." He stood, shook the creases out of his pants.

"No." I dropped my arms, took a nervous step to the side and back. "Sorry."

The alpha advanced toward me, sending my pulse into hummingbird territory. "But you like Lucas Blacke."

Choppy waters ahead, navigate with care. "Yes. I like Lucas."

"You trust him?"

Well... "As much as I trust anyone."

"A safe answer." He continued advancing. If I backed up now, it would be obvious I was trying to avoid him. The last thing I wanted to do was insult him or anger him in any way, especially since spiking him was out of the question.

"It's the truth."

"The truth." He was too close. Air lodged in my lungs like a paste, but I didn't want to gasp, so I did my best to hold my breath. I took a moment to hate Lucas a little bit for bringing me here, for breaking his promise to me by leaving me alone with Malcolm, and for forbidding me from using the only weapon I possessed.

"Yes." I drew in a shaky breath as Alpha Malcolm leaned in, sniffing me, his eyes flashing to gold and back so quickly I almost missed it. Despite Lucas's command, I opened up, let power flow into me. Spiking wouldn't be my first choice of defense—it never was—but I wasn't just going to sit back and let the wolf alpha kill me either.

His eyes flashed gold again.

Was he going to shift? Here? And then what?

"You don't really trust him, but you're sleeping with him?"

"I, uh—"

"What can she say? I have bewitched her with my rock-hard abs and boyish charm." Lucas stepped out from behind a plant with silky green fronds as long as my legs. "Hello again, Malcolm."

The air in my lungs thinned enough for me to catch my breath and my heart slowed until it only felt as though I'd run up two flights of stairs instead of ten.

"Hello, Blacke. I was wondering when you'd make your presence known. You've been lurking back there long enough." Alpha Malcolm took one last sniff of me and backed off. He returned to the cement bench and sat down.

Lucas came up behind me and stroked a finger down my spine, making me shiver, and then circled around to stand between his old alpha and me. "You knew I was back there? Thank God. I was worried you were slipping in your advanced years."

The older alpha's grin was all teeth. "Sharper than ever, thank you."

"Good to know." Lucas's smile was aggressive. "I worry."

"Do you?" Alpha Malcolm's eyes flashed gold. "So why are you here? Did Neely accuse you of abandoning her to the big bad wolf?"

Wow. Lucas wasn't telepathic, but I was starting to think Malcolm might be.

"She did mention her preference for not being stabbed with a steak knife in the solarium, Professor Plum."

"That wasn't Richard's first knife to the bicep, and it won't be his last. Besides, it's not as if you haven't done much worse." Malcolm's smile slithered over his mouth. "Need I remind you of the breakfast with the Tijuana shifters eight years ago?"

"You *needn't*." Lucas mimicked Malcolm's tone.

There were no knives in the vicinity I could see, but there were gardening tools, so I decided getting their attention off one another might be a good idea.

"Alpha Malcolm?"

"Yes, Neely?" He spoke to me, but kept his gaze pinned to Lucas, who was feigning nonchalance as he ran his finger over a fuzzy geranium leaf.

"Why did you ask me to come here?"

With a sigh, he turned away from Lucas and let his eyes bleed back to blue. "I requested the honor of your presence because I need your help. As a spiker and a telepath."

"I'm not an assassin. I don't kill people, if that's what you want."

He shook his head. "Now that's not entirely true, is it? You've killed before."

I crisscrossed my arms over my chest, rubbed them like I was cold.

"Wow. He's usually much smoother than this." Lucas backed up until he was by my side. He made the move look casual, but I knew it was protective and Alpha Malcolm probably didn't miss it, either. "So, either he doesn't respect you enough to display good manners or there's something really wrong here."

"Apologies, Neely. Blacke is right. I'm usually not this ham-fisted." He held out his hands, palms up. "I didn't ask you here to kill anyone for me. *Au contraire*, I would like for you to *heal* someone."

"I'm not a healer."

"Exactly. You're a spiker."

Curiouser and curiouser. "Setting aside the fact that I can't do any such thing, who do you want me to heal?"

The alpha swallowed. I watched his throat work, and for a moment, a single second, I sensed real fear in him. "Me."

"I don't understand. You look fine."

"I'm not. Please. Sit." Alpha Malcolm patted the bench beside him. Not knowing what else to do, I crossed over to him and sat down. Lucas moved closer, but didn't join us. No one spoke for a long moment.

"Alpha Malcolm." I cleared my throat. "I'm a spiker. If you're sick, you should see a doctor."

"Allow me to explain. And please call me Xavier. Or just Malcolm. Either works." He flexed and released his hands repeatedly, and his knee bumped against mine.

"Okay. Malcolm. Please explain."

"I was married to a spiker once." He glanced up at Lucas. "Did Blacke tell you about her?"

Suyin Chen. The woman had been a close friend of Lucas's, and she was the only other spiker he'd ever known. Malcolm had turned her into a crossbreed—with her consent—and she'd lost her mind and tried to murder everyone in sight, including him.

"I told her a little," Lucas said.

"It was a business match. We were friendly, but neither of us was in it for love. But it was consensual."

"Lucas said that Suyin liked power the way you do."

"Did he?" Malcolm's forehead creased. "From your tone, I take it you don't appreciate that quality."

"It's not something I admire, no."

"Should I apologize for liking power?"

I tipped my head, squinted at him. "I don't know. Should you?"

"I don't apologize for—" He caught himself, huffed out a laugh. "I see why Alpha Blacke likes you."

"Oh, I annoy him plenty."

"I'll bet not for long." He patted my knee. One quick pat.

A low growl rippled through the room. I gazed up at Lucas. His whiskey eyes glowed softly gold in the dim light of the solarium.

Lucas was furious.

Malcolm let out another low laugh, this one accompanied by a watchful look toward Lucas. The alpha knew what he was doing, knew Lucas was unhappy with the intimate way he was speaking to me. Malcolm didn't address it, though, simply continued as if he hadn't heard the growl or seen Lucas's eyes.

"Neely, when an alpha turns someone, paranormal or human, we take part of them within us. And they take part of us within them. It's why most alphas won't do it under any circumstances. It amounts to a commitment akin to marriage. Deeper, in some ways. A connection that can only be broken through death."

I'd heard something similar from Lucas. "Any alpha or only an alpha leader?"

"Any alpha strong enough to change someone. Those alphas tend to become leaders, but it's not a requirement."

Interesting. "So, what you're saying is part of you went into Suyin."

Malcolm nodded. "And part of her went into me. It's not as simple as it sounds, and yet it is."

"So, what happens when the person you're connected to dies?"

"As I mentioned, the connection breaks. Ends. You mourn the part of that person in you that's gone, and move on. In cases where the couple is connected by affection, it can be quite brutal. Some alphas don't live through it."

"Is that what happened when Suyin ... died?"

When Lucas had to kill her to save your life? I wanted to say. I didn't. Malcolm was being forthright, and I wanted him to keep talking.

"No. I was sad to lose a friend, but I didn't love her. The mourning period was short." He cleared his throat, tugged on the knees of his pants. "The problem isn't that I was connected to her by affection. The problem is that I am still connected to her by whatever bond we formed when I changed her."

"Are you saying you *still* have a connection with Suyin? How is that possible if she's dead?"

"I don't know." He raked his fingers through his short silver hair. "I can only tell you there's something still there, something connecting me to her. And it's driving me insane."

CHAPTER EIGHT

"That's not what I expected. Frankly, I'm surprised Malcolm still has the capacity to shock me," Lucas said.

When we returned to the room, he decided to take a bath in the oversized tub in the bathroom, the only area that he had declared free from Malcolm's listening devices. He'd called me into the room a few minutes earlier, but I told him not until the bubbles had completely covered him, to which he'd replied, "Chicken."

"It's not what I expected, either. *Hey*, is that my vanilla ice cream bubble bath?" I perched on the commode, seat down, and swiped the bottle off the sink counter. "I don't recall packing it."

Lucas held a cluster of bubbles to his face and sniffed. "I took it from your bathroom when I stayed over. It smells like you. I like it."

I wasn't sure how I felt about that on a whole bunch of levels, so I made him promise to replace what he used and changed the subject. Or, rather, U-turned the subject back to Malcolm.

"Nothing about tonight was what I expected. Though, it makes me feel a little better that Malcolm doesn't seem interested in changing me into a crossbreed."

"Tread carefully, Neely." Lucas poked at the suds piled on his chest. He had to have poured half the bottle of bubble bath into the tub. "Don't let this act fool you."

"That's just it. I don't think it's an act."

"But you can't read him, so you can't be sure." He leaned his head back on the lip of the tub.

"True. It's just ... Malcolm felt different in the solarium. I can't explain it."

"The man is a master at manipulation." Lucas picked up a handful of bubbles and blew them at me. "He's not to be trusted."

I reared out of his line of fire. "It's not trust, exactly."

He groaned out a sigh and plunked his hand into the water to wash off the bubbles. "You think Malcolm is really worried about a part of Suyin still living in him, like some sort of spirit?"

"Yes."

"Even if he does think that, you can't do anything about it. Are you going to spike his ghost wife away?" He picked up the soap, began washing his feet. I was not a foot person, but his were nice—lean and perfectly formed. It seemed unfair that every part of him was perfect. The man should have ashy heels or bunions to make him seem more human.

"That's ridiculous. But I'm thinking ... the thing is—" I faced away from him lest I see more than I needed to when he lifted his left foot. "—I can't read him."

"You mentioned that."

"I can read anyone. Not always clearly, but I can pick up on things. I always know their brain is there and working and even if I can't see images or words, I can feel the person being alive. But Malcolm is ... off. It's as if I'm trying to read the brain of a dead person. I can't get in."

"Could it be a spell?"

"Possibly. I'll call the tower witches."

Lucas groaned. "Not those two again."

I heard a splash and figured he'd put his feet back into the water, so it was safe to look. I peeked behind me, saw that not only was I right, I was also very wrong. He'd plunked his feet back into the water, but now his top half was under and he'd sort of jutted up his lower body to make room to dunk his head in the tub. I got an eyeful of his assets and quickly looked away.

Okay, not *quickly*.

When he resurfaced, I twisted away from him, pretended to be interested in my cosmetic bag on the counter. "Be nice. You said you'd try to get along with Dolores after she and Dottie promised to stop siphoning solar power from you."

"I know what I said."

I peeked over my shoulder again to make sure he was decent before swiveling back around. "Lucas, what if what Malcolm's saying is true? What if the reason I can't read him is because Suyin really is still active in his brain?"

"Not possible. She's dead." Lucas picked up the soap and scrubbed his chest a little too vigorously, sending water splashing over the side of the tub. His mouth was a hard line, bracketed by parenthetic creases. "No one knows that better than me."

His words echoed off the tiles, a haunting self-recrimination.

"Hey." I touched his arm. "I'm sorry to bring it up. It hurts you to think about it."

"It was a long time ago," he snapped.

Ouch. I retracted my hand. "Not so long."

"Sorry, I..." He ducked his head for a moment. Water dribbled from his hair over his shoulders, running in tapering rivulets down the sinews of his back. I wanted to comfort him, but I didn't know how.

When he spoke again, he was calmer. "What makes you think there's any truth to what Malcolm is claiming? The man lies like he's getting paid by the hour for it."

"A feeling. Supposedly, telepaths go one of two ways with other telepaths. They either connect with them very easily or they find them impossible to read. Could be the same with spikers, which would explain why I can't read him. If Suyin was somehow still in there, I mean."

"Where'd you hear that?"

"The witches. There's more information on telepaths than there is on spikers, so we've been researching that side of my ability."

"Them again." Lucas stood in the tub. I covered my eyes so I wouldn't catch his reflection in the mirror, but I heard the water dripping down his body, the whisking sound of the towel against his skin, and I had an imagination. A damn good one.

"It would be nice if I could ask another spiker about things like this. Unfortunately, I don't know any, so the witches are helping me."

Lucas didn't respond, but I sensed him coming closer. A blast of water droplets spattered all over me. Pinching my eyes shut, I scowled in his general direction when I heard him snickering.

"Did you just shake off *like a dog?*"

He snickered again, the man-child.

I lowered my hand and opened one eye. He stood over me, arms akimbo, a bath sheet knotted around his waist. I opened the other eye.

"Neely, would you please tell me why you stupidly told Malcolm you'd spike him to see if his dead ex-wife is still in there? Because that's what we're really talking about here."

That rankled, even if he had a point. "The 'stupidly' part is a bit harsh. I was a smidgen impetuous, maybe."

"*Impetuous?*"

A droplet of water dripped from his hair onto my top, dampening a spot on my breast. Lucas stared at the spot until I scowled up at him. "It's just ... I think I can help Malcolm with his spiker-ghost."

"His head is not a haunted house, Neely."

"I know that. But maybe, in a way, it is. We all have bad memories and sometimes they stick in our brain. Maybe that's what's going on here. If so, I might be able to help him."

"Why would you even want to try? You hate alpha leaders."

"I thought if I helped him, maybe he'd leave us alone."

Lucas stared at me. "Us?"

"Yes. You and me and the rest of the Blacke shifters."

Cursing under his breath, he paced the bathroom. His glutes worked beneath the towel, dropping it low on his waist. Once again, I was distracted by the sight of the muscled vee leading down to his groin.

"Pull up your towel, Lucas. I can see your penis cleavage."

"My what?" He peered down at himself and poked at the muscle above his groin with his index finger.

"Anyway, what are you so worried about? I'll just pop in and out of his head." I snapped my fingers. "A quick spike."

"What am I worried about?" He snapped his fingers back at me. "You spiking him dead. If you kill him, his shifters will have to kill you, Neely. It's the way it works."

Tired of looking him straight in the pelvis, I stood so I could look him straight in the chest. "I can spike without killing someone." It wasn't pleasant, but I could do it.

"Have you ever done so?" The water beading on his heated skin was creating a sort of haze between us. If I were wearing glasses, I was sure the lenses would be fogged up.

"That day with my ... *tío*." I tipped my head back to look into his eyes. "A couple of other times."

"I'm overflowing with confidence now." He played with one of my curls. Curls that were rapidly becoming frizz in the steamy bathroom.

"I can do this. I'm thinking of it as occupying the middle ground between a telepathic read and a spike—like when you shift to hybrid form and you aren't human, but you aren't a tiger, either."

"You're saying this is an *experiment* for you?"

He made it sound dumb. "Kind of, yes."

The brackets around his mouth returned. "His wolves *will kill you*. All one thousand of them. It'll only take one to do it, but they'll all want to get their claws into you, so it won't be a quick death."

I yanked my hair out of his hand. "The Vegas shifters didn't kill you or me after we took down Roso."

Lucas jerked up his chin. One brow arched high on his forehead. "I was challenged. I won."

"What?" I'd had no clue that's what he'd been doing while he was in Las Vegas. "*Why didn't you take me with you?*" I yelled. Then I remembered where I was and lowered my voice. "It was my fault Roso came for you. I could have helped—Lucas, damn it, you could have been killed."

"Nah." He leaned against the counter, grinned. The towel drifted lower, into temptation territory. "They weren't really into it. Just had to make a good showing. None of the challenges were to the death. I didn't kill anyone, and no one was trying to kill me. They hated Roso."

"Then why fight?"

"Because there's a way these things are handled in our world." The grin fell away. "Malcolm, believe it or not, is respected, even admired by most of his group. They will challenge you and it will be to the death."

Lucas ran his hand through his hair, knotted the towel tighter around his hips, and paced from one end of the bathroom to the other. It took him exactly four strides, which was more an indication of the length of his legs than the size of the bathroom.

"This is an angle."

"An angle?" I perched on the edge of the tub, watched him fume. "Could you be paranoid?"

"Paranoia is a healthy state of mind in Malcolm's vicinity. He's got something planned—it's what he does. He's ingratiating himself to you, playing vulnerable, which reminds me, what was all that touching-thighs-on-the-bench bullshit about?"

Irritated, I sat up straighter on the tub. "What was all that jealousy bullshit about?"

"It's expected. If I didn't react, he'd know I'm not sleeping with you and then we'd both be screwed."

"Oh." It was weird that his response disappointed me a little. I should have been relieved.

I stretched out my legs, wiggled my toes. After wearing flat sneakers to work for months, walking around in heels tonight had taken a toll on my feet. "Should I act jealous when a woman gets too close to you?"

"Is that something a spiker-telepath would be likely to do? Shifters tend toward the base emotions. We can be jealous assholes." He stopped pacing and snatched a pair of lounge pants off a hook on the wall. With a flick of his hand, the towel around his hips dropped to the floor.

I covered my eyes. "Would you warn me before you do that?"

"I'm a shifter, I don't care." There was the sound of cloth whisking over skin. "Fine. You can look now. I'm dressed."

I lowered my hand. He was dressed, but in a pair of black silky pants that left nothing to the imagination. "I don't know if other spiker-telepaths get jealous like shifters do. I've never met anyone like me."

"Think back to a time when you felt jealous." He watched my face so closely I knew he expected an answer. I thought about my only serious adult relationship and tried not to get depressed.

"When we lived in Las Vegas, Tío José, Julio, and I worked at a counter bakery together. We did wedding and birthday cakes, cupcakes, that sort of thing." I picked up my toothbrush, ran my thumb over the damp bristles. "Once, I caught a spinning instructor from the gym down the street flirting with Julio and I wanted to pick her up and throw her out on her perfectly sculpted butt."

Lucas resumed pacing. "What did you do?"

"Took her order myself so Julio wouldn't have to."

"You're a real badass, MacLeod."

I slammed the toothbrush on the counter and shot to my feet. "You know what? I am a badass. I'm someone who feels strong emotions and is capable of controlling them. Not someone who lets his tiger do his talking for him."

"I told you, *it's expected*. If the situation between us were real, I would retain control of my emotions just fine."

"Is that right?" I planted my hands on my hips.

Damn that shifter speed. He went from the other end of the room to pressed against me in a half-second and I never saw him move.

"There are things I can't control about myself, but I can and do control my emotions."

The moment would have been a lot more ironic if I didn't know what he was referring to.

A couple of months ago, Lucas had asked me something similar to what Xavier Malcolm had asked tonight. He'd wanted me to use my spiking ability to help him control his Smilodon form. It had been difficult for him to admit to the berserker rage that powered through him, shredding his control while in that form. He was a killing machine with no conscience and no loyalty, and he hated it.

"Whoa." I picked up his hand where it dangled by his side. "That's not what I meant. I'm sorry if it sounded that way."

"You're helping Malcolm." He flexed his hand around mine. "Why wouldn't you help me when I asked?"

I swallowed. "Because I was afraid."

"What, that you'd hurt me?"

"Yes, but also..." I wrapped my other hand around his other hand. "That I'd fail you."

His whiskey gaze locked on mine. "What if you fail Malcolm?"

"Then he realizes I'm not that powerful, that I can't help him, and we go home. I don't mind failing Malcolm." I swallowed. "But, for some reason, I really don't like the idea of failing you."

He stared at our clasped hands. Said nothing. The room felt ten degrees hotter than it had the moment before, and I was acutely aware of every point of contact between us. Hands clasping hands, thighs touching knees, breasts brushing chest...

"*Neely.*" He buried his face in my neck and inhaled, his damp hair grazing my jaw. In that moment, I felt everything he was feeling without reading him. Pain and desire and fear and fury all rolled together. The emotion in him was tremendous.

Without another word, he took a step back and, using that annoying shifter speed, blazed out of the room.

"Good goddess. The wolf alpha *wants* you to spike him?" Dottie sounded appalled.

The next morning found me lying in the dry bathtub with several pillows behind my head. I'd layered two fluffy towels on the cold surface, too. If I was going to be doing a lot of talking in here, I figured I should make myself comfortable.

"Sounds like a lunatic." Dolores spoke from wherever she was in the room. Dottie had me on speaker.

"That's debatable." And the pot calling the kettle black, but I didn't say that. "Are either of you aware of a spell that could keep a telepath or spiker out of a person's head?"

"There are a couple." I heard something creak in the background and figured Dottie was checking her spell books. "There's a spell that thickens the brain fluid until nothing can penetrate. Is he slurring his words, has his voice deepened at all?"

"Not that I noticed. But I never spoke to him before yesterday."

"That's the blockhead curse, Dottie," Dolores said.

"Oh, that's right. It's a curse. No one would do that."

"Not unless they were suicidal. The backlash is enough to turn out the lights on a warlock."

I stared up at the ceiling where two black dots of mildew had formed. "There's something else. He feels ... this sounds weird, but he feels dead to me. I mean, he's obviously alive, but I can't sense his life force."

"That is curious," Dottie said. "And the question isn't only what the spell might be, but why would the alpha need to keep you out of his brain in the first place? If he's the one doing this, that is."

"The question had crossed my mind."

Lucas didn't trust that Malcolm was being genuine with us, and despite what I'd said to the contrary, I respected his take on the situation. He'd known the wolf alpha leader a lot longer than I had.

There was a ten-second pause, and then Dolores said, "What about *lapis cerebrum*?"

"The stone brain spell. Brilliant. Let me get my grimoire. I left it on my nightstand." Dottie's voice trailed off.

"Yeah, stop doing that. Damn thing cries all bloody night," Dolores shouted. In a more conversational tone, she said, "So how's it going with you and the tiger? You guys doing the horizontal mambo yet?"

"*No.*" My voice echoed off the tiles, so I lowered it. "No. We're sharing a bed, but it's platonic." I dangled my leg over the side of the cold tub. Should have brought Lucas's pillows, too. The tub was a great place to bathe, but it was darn uncomfortable to lounge in.

"'You sure about that, kiddo?"

"I'm sure."

Thinking of his pillows reminded me of how I'd woken up. On top of the comforter, my left leg slung over his right one, his arms wrapped around me, my cheek pressed against his warm chest. I tried to convince myself that I'd told Dolores the truth, that our affection for each other was based in friendship and nothing more, but the more I thought about it, the less sure I was.

"Bummer. I was hoping you could get him to help me with some zoning issues. I believe I mentioned that I want to turn the tower gift shop into a bar while we're waiting for it to wake up. Thought it would give us something constructive to do. Bring in a little extra cash."

"Dolores, are you saying you wanted me to leverage a sexual relationship with Lucas to get you a *liquor license*?" Why was I surprised? It was precisely something she would do.

"Hey, I was even going to offer you free prickly pear cactus margaritas for life. But since you guys aren't having sex, I'll find another way to get the license. You've probably got him all frustrated and worked up and I don't want him taking it out on me." Before I could form a response, I heard Dottie ask, "Is Alpha Malcolm wearing a necklace with a bright red stone?"

"I don't think so."

"He could have it in his pocket, too," Dolores said. "Remember that fella in Phoenix who tried to pull one over on us?"

Dottie giggled. It sounded tinny through the speaker on Dolores' phone. Before I left, the witches had mentioned that until the tower was fully awake, telecommunication distortions were going to be a regular occurrence.

"He wore white pants, the silly man. I could see the stone in his back pocket."

"Yeah, he wasn't the sharpest pencil in the box." Dolores paused. "You know, *lapis cerebrum* isn't hard to break. All you need is a spelled bag—a hex bag."

"Spelled? Hex?" I sighed. "Look, you know I adore you both, but we've had a little trouble with spells in the last few months, haven't we?"

"I told you that was because our tower wasn't awake. Anyway, this is a different sort of magic," Dolores replied. "You'll want a black one, preferably drawstring, or you can make it into a sachet, but the point is it needs to be closed."

Okay, a bag. That didn't sound so bad. And if it wasn't a spell…

"Inside the bag you'll want to add an amethyst the size of your pinky nail, a splinter from lightning-struck wood, and a chip of toad-stone," Dottie said.

"Toadstone?"

"It's just a fossilized shark tooth, dear, not a true toadstone. The real ones are rare and quite pricey."

Because, of course, stones grown in the head of a toad were an actual thing. Wonderful. "It may as well be real. Where am I going to find a fossilized shark tooth? Doesn't sound like something I can pick up at my local DiscMart."

"Bill Bill, of course," Dolores replied. "You'll need to stop by his tattoo parlor/shrunken head shop. Good thing you're close."

CHAPTER NINE

LUCAS INSISTED ON COMING WITH ME.

"I think I can handle a trip to Pacific Beach alone." I smoothed moisturizer on my face, working it down my neck and into my décolleté.

Lucas's eyes followed my progress. "I'm coming."

"For the love of... Just give me the keys to your car."

"No." He reached into my cosmetic bag and pulled out one of my Korean sheet mask packets. He ripped it open and stared at the dripping, folded tissue wad in his hand. "What the hell is this?"

"Hey, I was going to use—*stop touching it.*"

"I'm trying to open it."

"Ugh. Since you've already messed with it, bend down and tip your head back." I snatched the lavender mask out of his hand and, carefully unfolding it, draped the oozing tissue over his face, making sure to center the holes over his eyes, nose, and mouth. "Leave it on while I take your car to Bill Bill's and your skin will be as fresh as a newborn's by the time I get back."

He raised the packaging to eye level without moving his head. "Says twenty minutes here. It won't take that long to get to Pacific Beach."

"You are *not* wearing that face mask in the car."

I was really getting tired of being wrong about things.

Lucas drove and I sulked all the way to Pacific Beach. When we arrived, I snatched the white mask off his face and wadded it into a ball.

"You do *not* need to come in with me."

"Maybe I want to poke around the shop, pick up a crystal or a spelled charm or some hemp cream..." Lucas patted his cheeks. "I'm feeling very moisturized."

Lavender liquid dripped from my fist onto the BMW's console. "You owe me a face mask and a bottle of bubble bath. Don't think I won't remember."

"Knowing you, you've made a list."

"I have you on a variety of lists, Lucas Blacke."

He smirked at me as he parked the car behind the shop and used a coffee chain napkin to mop up the console.

We circled around to the front of the building on foot and walked up to the beachfront shop, salty breeze in our hair, sandy grit on the asphalt crunching beneath our feet. I pulled open the shop's front door and bells tinkled delicately against the glass. This was odd because there appeared to be no bells hanging anywhere on the door, neither was there any sort of electronic chime.

"Hello, my Sundance desert brethren. Good to see you again."

Bill Bill had black hair and a bushy black beard, and he looked like he belonged in a biker gang or on a pirate ship, but he smiled a lot and it wasn't mean or complicated and, my God, I needed that today.

I raised my hand in greeting. "Hello, Bill. The tattoo healed up nicely."

"Did it?" He blinked a few times, wrinkled his forehead.

His reaction made me think that he'd forgotten about doing my tattoo. Odd. Or not. According to the witches, the man did a *lot* of tattoos.

I patted my shoulder, where the tattoo was hidden beneath my top, to remind him. "Yes. Thank you."

"Good, good. That's good. And how are you, Alpha Blacke?" Bill asked in his low, deep voice.

"Doing great, thanks for asking." Lucas riffled through a stack of handmade rolling papers. "So, Bill, hypothetically speaking, would you happen to have magic-coated, armor-piercing ammunition in stock? Something that could take down, say, a whole bunch of pissed off wolf shifters? Massive quantities a plus."

"Hypothetically, of course," Bill said.

"Of course."

"*Lucas.*" I smiled nervously at Bill.

"What?" He shot me an innocent look. "Chandra's birthday is coming up and I wanted to pick up something on her wish list."

I glared at him.

"How massive a quantity and how soon do you need it?" Bill Bill asked.

I whipped my head around. "*What?*"

"*Massive.*" A cunning smile crawled over Lucas's face. "And as soon as you—"

"*So, the tower witches said they were going to call you?*" I said loudly.

"They called." Bill set a paper bag on the counter and handed me the purchase order. "It's all here. Not trying to gouge you or anything, but there's a shortage of lightning-struck wood right now."

"Can't a witch just summon a bolt of lightning to strike a tree?" Lucas picked up a pink quartz the size of a half-dollar and weighed it in his palm.

"Has to be natural, or it doesn't work so well. The Fairfield witches specified that it be redwood. Those trees are under protection, so we have to wait until one falls down naturally. Can't cut down a protected tree."

I stared at Bill for a long moment. "Something tells me you aren't talking about the protection of the U.S. government."

"Fairies," Bill Bill said with a straight face. "They take their oath to protect their forests very seriously. The only lightning-struck redwood I'll buy is from a fairy-authorized representative. I'd like to survive the afterlife, thank you very much."

I didn't know what he meant by any of that, but I decided then and there that I'd never cross a fairy.

"Here." Lucas handed Bill an ivory business card and a black credit card. "This, too." He set the pink crystal on the counter.

Bill rang up the purchase and handed back the black card. He tucked the business one in his shirt pocket. "I'll be in touch about the ammo."

"As much as you can supply. See ya soon, we gotta go." Lucas scooped up the bag, his card, and the quartz, and ushered me out of the store.

"Jeez, where's the fire?"

Lucas hauled me to his car and urged me into the passenger seat. "Stay down. We're being stalked."

"You said Chandra was undetectable."

"Not by Chandra. By Malcolm's wolves." He slid behind the wheel and started the car. "Why do you think I wouldn't let you come here alone?"

"Because you're nosy and wanted to know what I was doing. Also, you don't want me driving your precious car."

"That's all true. But it was also to protect you. What Malcolm is asking you to do isn't going to be popular with the pack. And whether or not he assured us that the pack won't attack, once he's dead, they'll do what they want."

"And in the meantime?"

We cruised down a Pacific Beach street lined with cozy bungalows —the way beach houses used to be built in San Diego and Los Angeles before ocean-front mansion monstrosities were a thing. I pushed the button to lower the window and inhaled the salt-laced breeze. It was a beautiful day to overreact in San Diego.

"If they can kill you and make it look like an accident, they will. Win-win for them."

I broke a nail jabbing the button to close my window as I sank down in my seat. "Where's Chandra?"

"I sent her on an errand."

"What? Why would you—oh, never mind." I peeked at the side mirror, saw nothing but traffic reflected back to me. "Are they still there? Can you see them?"

"Blue Ford. Two blocks back. From this point on, you go nowhere without my permission, got it?"

Permission? Uh, no. "I don't like the sound of that, Alpha Blacke."

"Then be prepared to kill some shifters, my little pacifist spiker, because that's what it will take."

"*You told me not to spike.*"

"Yeah, well, stop taking everything I say so literally."

I wanted to choke him. "*Fine. I'll stay with you, but it's my choice.*"

He continued as if I hadn't spoken. "Also, I'm going to make Malcolm swear to me that you won't be harmed. If I get his word, he'll destroy anyone who even thinks about hurting you." Lucas made a quick succession of turns that brought us out of the bungalow neighborhood and onto the freeway. "I should have done it in the first place."

"You trust his word?"

"It's a thing with him. He's manipulative, but his word is gold. He gives it out rarely, and when he does, he stands by it. Have to watch the wording, though. He's a slippery bastard."

Takes one to know one. "Then why doesn't he respect Chandra? All she's done is given her word that she'll protect you."

"Never said he doesn't respect her. He just doesn't like her." Lucas glanced in the rearview mirror, sped up.

"I find it odd that those things are separate in his mind."

He shrugged. "They're separate in my mind, too."

"Guess you really did learn something from him."

"I learned how *not* to be an alpha leader." A muscle in his jaw flexed. "And yes, I also learned how to be a damn efficient one. Our methods are not the same, Neely, don't make the mistake of thinking that he's as tolerant as I am. You don't have an inkling of what Malcolm is capable of, and I hope to God you never find out."

That made two of us.

Lucas drove north on Interstate 5, changing lanes, accelerating and slowing according to whatever it was his keen eyes picked up in his mirrors. It had taken us half an hour to get to Pacific Beach from Carlsbad, but something told me it wouldn't take nearly that long for us to get back. Lucas was hunched over the steering wheel weaving through traffic like a man with the devil on his heels.

"Neely." He squeezed the BMW's steering wheel until it creaked. "You're going to hear about me while we're here. Well-meaning people, some not so well meaning, are going to want to regale you with my exploits as Malcolm's personal enforcer. They'll tell you I did some very bad things."

"I won't believe them."

Expressionless, he replied, "You should."

I wasn't sure how to take that, so I kept my reply to myself.

"Damn." He glanced into the rearview mirror again and growled. "If those wolves scratch the paint on my M6, I am going to rip their throats out."

"No throat-ripping over paint, Lucas."

"Those wolves will heal, but my car? I had to special order it because they only stock this model in black." He rolled his eyes. "Does everyone in Southern California drive a black BMW? How boring."

"Some of us don't drive BMWs at all, and would be thrilled to have any color," I muttered.

He ignored my comment. "Glacier silver metallic. Look at it."

"I like your truck better."

This wasn't Lucas's only car. In fact, I was convinced he had an entire fleet in a secret hideout somewhere. Of all his vehicles, though, my favorite was his early 2000s Toyota pickup truck. To quote him, the truck, "...has a hundred fifty thousand miles on it, the seats are worn, it's always dusty for some reason, the air conditioner doesn't work, and the paint is peeling off the hood."

I liked it because it showed me a side of Lucas that he didn't let just anyone see. That there was more to him than arrogance and snark, though that was definitely a part of him, too.

"My truck is in a class of its own. This is a precision automobile and an expensive one at that. If they even think about messing up my paint job, I will come unhinged."

"Sounds like you're already halfway there. Calm down. Nothing has even happened. Maybe nothing will."

Ping.

Lucas let out a string of curses.

I popped my head up, looked around. "What was that? Did we hit something?"

"That was a bullet. Damn it, I'm going to have to take my car to the dealership. Do you mind if I detour into Kearny Mesa before heading back to Malcolm's?"

"What the hell, Lucas? Someone is shooting at us and *you're worried about your stupid paint job?*"

"I told you, I had to special order it. The dealer makes you pay extra for that. They don't say it, but it's not like they're going to make you a deal for a car they know you love everything about. I mean, they aren't stup—"

Ping.

He fired off another set of curses. "Well, now I can't take it to the dealership."

"You should be grateful neither of us has been hit." I said this from the floorboard where I was now huddled. Unlike Lucas, I did not heal quickly.

"Get up here and put on your seatbelt. If I take a bullet to the skull, you'll be glad you had it on."

Ping.

Lucas swerved hard to the right and I braced myself against the door and the dash. The air from the vents blew on my neck, making me shiver and instantly sending me into a flashback to the day Lucas and I killed Saul Roso. Roso had forced my surrender and threatened to make one of his wolves shoot me if I so much as tickled his brain with my ability. Then he sank his teeth into the back of my throat and started the humiliating process of changing me into a crossbreed against my will.

Panic rushed me and suddenly I wasn't just flashing back, I was *there*. My breath huffed out in puffing little gasps. All the fear, and all the rage, and all the hopelessness of that day poured into me and I reacted with pure instinct.

I pinched my eyes shut, let some of Lucas's energy flow into me. The witches had taught me how to let energy come to me rather than draining it from my environment. I wasn't perfect at it—I had a tendency to get impatient and pull—but I was learning.

In a whooshing rush, I pushed my ability into the car behind us. I wasn't good at spiking over long distances, but I didn't need to be. The wolves trying to kill us were riding our back bumper.

"Neely."

I pushed harder, all that delicious energy conveying my ability to the driver in an invisible line from my brain to his. I drank in the wolf shifter's shrieks of pain. The blast of endorphins coursing through me had me floating outside myself—a genuine out-of-body experience, no LSD required. The power was like nothing else.

Beautiful, thrilling, *addictive*.

"Sugar cookie, if you spike one of Malcolm's wolves dead, the rest of the pack will kill you. And me." He spoke softly as if he were trying not to spook me. "Seems like a waste of a good face mask, don't you think? I'm still dewy."

My voice trickled out in a whisper. "I don't have to kill him. I told you, I can spike without killing."

"Forgive me if I don't believe you. Look at you, crouched on the floorboard like a scared kid. There's no way you're in control right now."

I pushed harder into the wolf's brain, sliding over the ridges and bumps, stabbing through the twisting pale pink whorls...

"*Neely.*"

The wolf screamed again. I heard it in his mind the second before I heard another bullet hit our car.

"Put on your seatbelt. I've got this under control." Lucas reached over and pulled me by the back of my dress into the passenger seat, momentarily distracting me and breaking my connection with the shooter.

"Okay." I strapped myself in, reached for the wolf's brain again. "I can make him sleep." *Forever.*

"Me, too."

He thrust his arm across my chest and simultaneously slammed on the brakes.

In the center lane of a Southern California freeway.

The seatbelt tightened across my chest, knocking the air out of my lungs in one painful gust and ripping my consciousness completely out of the wolf shifter's head. The tires screeched and I smelled something burning. Lucas had likely taken an inch of rubber off his precious performance tires.

The driver of the blue Ford behind us slammed on his brakes at nearly the same time Lucas did, avoiding our back bumper by what had to be millimeters. Only a shifter could have pulled that off. No one else had reflexes that good.

Certainly not the driver of the semi-truck behind the Ford.

By the time the truck smashed into the shooters, Lucas had already hit the gas. I flipped around in my seat in time to see the driver of the semi hop down from his cab.

"Truck driver is ... okay." I puffed out a shallow sigh of relief.

"I know."

"Thank ... heavens." I took a few quick breaths to bring air into my lungs. "Traffic was ... light. What were ... you thinking?"

"I was thinking traffic was light, the semi wouldn't sustain much damage if it hit the Ford, and that shifters heal quickly."

"All that ... in seconds?"

"I'm fairly learned at this whole shifter-on-shifter violence thing. I'm not Chandra—the woman is a savant at this stuff—but I get by." He drove over three lanes to the next offramp, where he exited the freeway. "But you... *Spiking* him? What were you thinking? Are you trying to get yourself killed?"

"I was ... defending us."

"You were scared. Seems like that's the only time you use your ability. When you're scared, when you're hurt. Imagine what you might do if you used it *proactively* instead of *reactively*."

"R-Rules..." I coughed.

"Yeah, yeah. Your rules. Tell me this. Did you think about *reading* the wolves? Maybe find out who they work for, what they wanted with us?"

No, I hadn't. I hadn't been thinking at all.

I stared down at my hands. Blinked away the starbursts in the corners of my eyes and tried to draw in a deep breath.

"You have the gift of telepathy and you never considered using it. Because of your *rules*. But you sure spiked into that wolf's head fast, didn't you? So, is it really your rules that hold you back?"

Revulsion rolled over me. He was right. My rules hadn't entered into it.

"Start reading people. Now. Who knows? It might keep you from killing someone unintentionally."

———

"A week, Malcolm. Minimum."

"You do realize that Anne and Angelo Colombo are in a coma."

"Induced." Lucas rolled his eyes. "Dr. Penbright does that for all her shifter patients. We heal quicker that way. Unfortunately, my car can't be put into a coma. It's never going to be the same."

"*Oof.*" I sprawled in a wicker chair and tried not to breathe too deeply. I hadn't felt too bad earlier, but now my ribs were so painful I could identify them individually in my chest without touching them, my head throbbed, my back ached. Lucas hadn't offered to heal me, and I was feeling more than a little ticked off about that.

"Five bullet holes." He stomped across the solarium.

"And none hit you?" Malcolm asked.

"No. To be honest, your wolves could use some target practice. Pretty sure the female was aiming for my tires. Five fired bullets, yet all four tires are intact."

"At least she hit the car." Malcolm stretched his arms above his head, turned his neck from side to side.

We'd discovered the alpha leader meditating on a yoga mat behind a cluster of ferns when Lucas and I returned from the auto shop in a loaner BMW. In deference to the heat of the afternoon, Malcolm had eschewed the linen trousers and was dressed in gray cotton shorts and a white T-shirt. His muscled legs were as tanned as the rest of him.

"Did you take it to Pilar de Soto at the Pit Crew?"

"Yeah. With that many bullet holes I couldn't very well take it to the dealership, could I? She said it would be a day or so before they could even give me an estimate. Your reckless, inaccurate shifters may have ruined the integrity of my car."

"I'll buy you another." Malcolm sounded bored.

"They *shot* at us." Lucas stared straight into the other alpha's eyes. "If you think I'm going to let this slide, you are delusional."

"Not slide. The Colombos will pay restitution, but you aren't allowed to kill them."

Lucas's eyes flashed gold. His tiger's eyes. "You'll have no choice if I issue a challenge."

"You will not." Malcolm's eyes faded to the color of glacier ice, then glowed gold. "This is a wolf matter."

"Of course, it is. Wolves always get the benefit of the doubt. Even when the evidence against them is so damning it's embarrassing. Even if the not-wolf is a member of the pack."

Malcolm sighed. "You're never going to let it go, are you?"

"*Never.*" Lucas blinked, and his eyes returned to their normal whiskey shade.

The wolf alpha turned his attention to me. He too, had blinked his eyes back to normal. "Are you all right, Neely?"

"My chest is sore from the seatbelt, I have whiplash, and every time I take a breath my spine cracks, but other than that I feel … well, like I might barf, actually," I replied.

Malcolm slid fluidly to his feet, rolled up his mat. "We should have Dr. Penbright examine you. Come with me."

I looked to Lucas to tell me what I should do, but he'd crossed to the other side of the solarium with his cell phone at his ear. "Will you be able to match the paint, Pilar?"

"You're looking at him as if you need his permission." Malcolm cocked his head, showed me that deceptively casual grin. "Are you afraid of me?"

Deeply. To the marrow of my bones. I couldn't articulate why, but it was the same way I'd feel in the presence of a large, poisonous snake that hadn't yet bit me, but was in striking position.

"I'm afraid of getting shot at again."

"My wolves won't attack you in my presence."

"Forgive me for doubting you, Alpha Malcolm, but they shot at us after you commanded them not to."

He tipped his head to one side, regarded me. "Do you think I should step aside and let Blacke deal with Anne and Angelo? He's very angry, you know. He'll kill them both and they're kids. Twenty-two years old."

"That's old enough to know better."

"Wolves are passionate creatures. Remember, these two wolves thought you were a big enough threat that they risked pack punishment."

I didn't look him in the eyes—I wasn't stupid— but I stared at a point just below his eyes. "I *am* a threat, Alpha Malcolm. Pack or not, if someone shoots at me again, Lucas won't have to take care of them because I'll spike them dead before the second bullet leaves the gun."

Malcolm's mouth hardened. He didn't like that one bit. "Understood. Would you like to see the doctor now?"

"Yes, but I want a Kevlar jumpsuit and an armored car around me, please."

"I'll have my Rezvani Tank parked in front in five minutes," he replied.

CHAPTER TEN

"I thought you were kidding about the tank."

"Not me." Lucas regarded the black-on-black utility vehicle on steroids with pure avarice as we climbed inside. "I tried to get him to buy a Rezvani years ago."

Malcolm, who had exchanged his shorts for jeans and his white T-shirt for a blue button-up one, rested his head against the seat. "It's a *tactical urban vehicle*, not an actual tank."

I ran my hand over the handle, tempted to swing the door open wide and tuck and roll away from both alphas. I was happy that Lucas was keeping his word and sticking by me, but I wished he wasn't so hellbent on getting under Malcolm's skin. The fear it created in me was exhausting.

"Why do you need this type of vehicle?" I asked.

"Because a lot of people want him dead," Lucas said. "A *lot*."

Malcolm gunned the engine once before shifting into drive and pulling into the flow of traffic. "Your lover, for instance."

"Rude. I'm right here, you know," Lucas said from the back seat.

"Yes. I know," Malcolm drawled. "You're *always* right here lately."

I peered through the windshield. At six p.m. on a Saturday, it seemed as if the road would have fewer people on it, but traffic was thick enough to be down to forty miles per hour. I really missed Sundance's small-town non-traffic.

"I think that if Lucas wanted you dead, you'd be dead, tank or not," I said.

The wolf alpha glanced in the rearview mirror, then over at me before returning his eyes to the road. "Why do you say that?"

"I know him." That wasn't altogether true, but it felt like the right thing to say. And I meant what I said. If Lucas truly saw Malcolm as a threat, he'd take him out and Chandra and Amir would be right there with him. Dan, too.

"Maybe you don't know him as well as you think you do."

"She knows me *intimately*." Lucas hung a suggestive little laugh on the end of that statement and then patted the seat. "Leather come standard, or were these seats crafted from the hides of your enemies?"

"Genuine tiger-skin," Malcolm said with a grin. "Hope it wasn't a relative."

"There's a couple I'd be willing to trade in exchange for a Rezvani. This is a V-8, right? Did you get the thermal night vision package?"

"Of course." Malcolm glanced in the mirror at Lucas. "Otherwise, what's the point?"

"Truth. I saw the Rezvani Alpha Beast Blackbird at a car show not long ago. Beautiful machine. The perfect mid-life crisis car, if you're interested."

Malcolm set his jaw. "There's no crisis in my mid-life, Blacke."

I glared over my shoulder at the smug alpha in the backseat. He waggled his brows and gave me a perfect, pearly-toothed smile. Slowly, I turned to face the front. Any sort of twisting movement was liable to set off a chain reaction of muscle spasms, and the seatbelt snugged against my chest wasn't helping.

"Neely, do you know what Alpha Blacke used to do for me?"

Actually, I didn't, so I guessed. "He was your second?"

This earned a chuff from Lucas, but he said nothing.

Malcolm shook his head. "I have only wolves in my inner circle. Lucas was my ... *enforcer*."

"Oh." I spied the ocean through the spaces between more of the arrogantly constructed rich people houses and small stretches of public beach until we turned down a side street and the Pacific washed out of view.

"He was damn good at his job. I will admit that."

"I imagine he was. A waste, though." I adjusted my seatbelt, took a deep breath that made my vertebrae pop.

"What do you mean?"

"No offense, but you had a tremendously powerful shifter in your pack and you hamstrung him by making him into what amounts to a security guard? You seem like such a smart man, too." I pointed to a two-story white house with a three-car driveway at the end of a cul-de-sac, my eagerness to end this conversation coalescing with my eagerness to get some sort of pain medication inside my aching body. "This is the medical clinic you told me about? It looks like a regular house."

"It's supposed to." Malcolm pulled into the driveway. Switched off the engine and sat back in his seat. He looked at me, but I had the feeling he was talking to Lucas, too. "Most shifter groups are restricted to one animal, you know. I was a maverick for letting Blacke into my pack at all. Not everyone approved."

"So," I said.

"So?" Malcolm's forehead creased.

"Yeah, so what? You're the alpha. If they don't like your decision, they can take a hike."

His brow line dropped into his eyes. "What sort of alpha leader do you think I am?"

"The regular kind. One who does whatever he wants." I rolled my shoulders, gasped. "Oh, that hurts."

Malcolm ignored my cry of pain. Typical alpha leader. "I don't get to do whatever I want. I serve my wolves."

"Look, all I'm saying is that most people in the paranormal world fear you, and I don't think you got that reputation due to your diplomacy skills. The truth is, *you* didn't want a non-wolf that high up in your organization because *you* were uncomfortable with it." As soon as the words popped out of my mouth, I remembered who I was talking to and regretted them.

A low growl trickled out of the wolf alpha leader, the sound making all the hair on my arms and head stand on end. "We should go inside now," he snarled.

Careful, Neely. You don't have to defend me to him. It was the first thing Lucas had thought to me since yesterday and it startled me.

"Are you coming in with us?" I asked without turning around.

"I'll be in shortly. I've got a phone call to make."

"Fine." I shrugged, and another pain rocked me.

You'll be okay. Malcolm won't hurt you and he won't let anyone else hurt you in front of Dr. Penbright. It's neutral ground. She's protected by all the major shifter groups in the county, and is widely respected.

I climbed out of the SUV, wincing as I moved. My chest and shoulders were badly bruised. Malcolm shut the driver's side door and shook himself. It reminded me of something a wet Labrador might do.

I kept that observation to myself.

"Let's go." He ushered me to the front door and jabbed at the doorbell with his thumb.

"I think you'll regret it someday, you know," I said, because, apparently, I didn't know when to shut up. Also, because I really wanted Malcolm to see how wrong he had been about Lucas.

He glared at me through his wolf's eyes. "Was that a *threat?*"

My heart started beating three times faster and I had to go to the bathroom in an all-of-a-sudden sort of way. "Are you kidding?" I lifted my stiff arms and pointed at myself. "*Mírame.* Look at me. This is what a *seatbelt* did to my fragile body. Do you think I'm a *tonta?* Please. I'm not stupid enough to threaten an alpha leader who scares the pants off me. Not on purpose, anyway."

We stood there, both still, both one hundred percent focused on the other.

Lucas's voice drifted through my head and I realized he was watching me. *Look down, but not too far. His chin. No lower. That shows respect without fear.*

As scared as I was, looking at his toes wouldn't be far down enough to express my fear. But I did as Lucas instructed and stared at the solid line of Malcolm's jaw and chin. After one minute that felt like ten, the alpha's mouth curled into a reluctant grin.

"You lapse into Spanish when you're nervous."

"I lapse into unconscious Spanglish when I'm scared. Why? Did I just do it?" I honestly couldn't remember.

The grin widened. "It's impossible not to like you, Neely Costa MacLeod."

"Give me a couple days," I replied.

He chuckled with his wolf in his voice. The sound was low and rumbling, and surprisingly pleasant. "I don't think it's going to help. I'm already inclined to like you."

"Lucas knows me well and he's annoyed with me eighty percent of the time. Or I'm annoyed with him. Sometimes I get confused about that."

"Yet you sleep with him?"

I shrugged, then gasped in pain. Again. I'd had no idea how much I shrugged in a day. I needed to be more assertive. "Yes, I sleep with him."

"Are you in love with him?"

Oh, boy. Not going there. And why was he asking, anyway? Other than the fact that he was an alpha leader and instinctively nosy.

"Are you?" Malcolm smiled.

At the risk of injuring myself, I rose on my tiptoes to peer through the window in the door. "Where are these people? Is there a bathroom in there?"

"You should know Blacke doesn't get serious about anyone. It's just his way."

This again? Were Margaret Lentz and Malcolm in cahoots? If Malcolm referred to Lucas as a "manwhore," I was out of there.

"I mean, what's the hold up, am I right? What if we were dying out here?" I slapped the door this time and the pain reverberated in my bones. I sucked in a sharp breath. "This is just ... bad ... service."

"But *you* are the type to get serious, aren't you, Neely?" Malcolm persisted.

The man would not take the hint that I didn't want to talk about it. Or, he didn't care, which amounted to the same thing.

I jabbed the doorbell with my thumb. Leaned in.

The door swung open, revealing a beautiful, if disheveled, Japanese

American woman in her late thirties. She was small, had long black hair piled on top of her head in a somewhat messy bun, and wore black-framed glasses.

"Sorry for the delay, Alpha Malcolm. There was a fight tonight, so we're a bit shorthanded." She smiled at me. "You must be Cornelia Costa."

"Costa MacLeod. But you can call me Neely."

"I'm Dr. Rin Penbright. Please come in." She led us down a short hall into a bedroom that had been converted into an examination room. It looked exactly like a physician's office—examination table, pedal sink, sharps container—and somehow still managed to retain the indefinable quality of a bedroom in a suburban house.

"Which group was fighting?" Malcolm asked.

"Your wolves. The Cortez girls, Lupita and Ana, were involved. I can't tell you who they were fighting, because they were brought in unconscious by their mother Maria, who found them in their front yard. Apparently, Lupita drove them both home and then collapsed after exiting the car. Thank God their mother is a nurse or Ana might not have made it."

Malcolm's expression hardened. "How *exactly* were they hurt?"

I guess doctor patient privilege didn't extend to shifters, because Dr. Penbright answered him. "Internal bleeding, multiple contusions, concussion—Lupita had thirteen separate stab wounds. Ana only had two, but one nicked her heart." When Malcolm didn't change expression, she added, "There were no other signs of assault."

"You checked?"

"Yes."

"Definitely sounds like a Malcolm wolf shifter attack." Lucas drawled from the doorway of the examination room. "Let me guess, the Cortez's aren't wolves."

Malcolm ignored him and focused on Dr. Penbright. "Lupita protected Ana from their attackers?"

"We came to that conclusion. Many of the knife wounds were on her forearms, a few on her back."

Malcolm nodded at me. "See to Neely's injuries, please. I need to speak with Maria Cortez." He left the room.

Dr. Penbright watched him leave. "It'll make Maria feel better, to see the alpha."

"Will it?" Lucas's tone was guarded as he addressed the doctor.

"Better, I imagine, than it will make the parents of the Columbo kids feel to see you." She flung the comment over her shoulder as she picked up her stethoscope.

"Hello to you, too, doc." Lucas came into the room a couple of feet and leaned against the wall with his arms crossed.

"*Alpha* Blacke," she replied coldly with a tip of her head. "I see you've brought violence back to my medical clinic."

"Oh yes, I'm sure it's all me. Everything has been lemon candy and pink roses in the shifter groups until now, right?"

"Certainly, paranormal on paranormal violence dropped after you left." The bitterness in her tone startled me. I hadn't expected this sort of reaction from her. I recalled what Lucas said to me in the car this afternoon.

"You're going to hear about me.... They'll tell you I did some very bad things."

I wondered exactly what those things were.

"Yeah. Not buying it, doc."

"In under a day, I've had the Cortez sisters and the Columbo kids—"

"Why does everyone keep calling them kids?" I purposely interrupted her tirade against Lucas, and I wasn't apologizing for it. "They're *twenty-two* years old. Maybe part of the reason they do stupid things that get themselves hurt is because everyone keeps treating them like kids instead of the adults that they are."

"You know the twins?" Dr. Penbright frowned at me.

"Not personally. We've exchanged mayhem." It was a snarky answer, but I was really not in the mood to hash this out. The pain was kicking my butt and I needed to sit down.

"Not exchanged," Lucas said. "We didn't mayhem back."

I rolled my eyes at him, determined not to shrug. "We didn't *shoot* back at them, but we definitely mayhemed back."

"Shoot? They had *guns*?" The doctor looked at Lucas and then me. "You were both there today when the collision occurred?"

"Yes, yes, and yes," Lucas said.

"Alpha Malcolm didn't tell you?" I was a little taken aback. Malcolm said he'd called ahead. I figured he'd told the doctor everything that happened.

"All he said was that you were injured. He said nothing about a shooting."

Lucas shook his head, thought his next words at me. *Figures. Malcolm wouldn't want the doctor to think badly of the Columbos. He protects his damn wolves and to hell with the rest of us.*

I was starting to get that impression, too. "Those 'kids' were shooting a real gun with real bullets at Alpha Blacke and me. Now the alpha here is a shifter. He heals fast. But I'm not a shifter and I don't bounce back from bullet wounds. I can barely take a full breath at this point and that's just an injury from a seatbelt. Those 'kids' would have killed me if they'd gotten the chance, and they nearly did."

"That actually makes sense." The doctor seemed to be speaking to herself rather than to us. "The whole thing bothered me, to be honest." Then she seemed to realize what she was saying and clamped her mouth shut.

"I'm not Malcolm's shifter anymore," Lucas said. "Don't worry, Rin."

Dr. Penbright gave him a slight nod.

An accidental groan worked its way out of me. "Can I please sit down?"

"Yes, of course. Let's get you up on the table."

I managed to climb onto the examination table with a minimal amount of pain.

"Please exit the room or turn your back." Dr. Penbright said to Lucas.

He looked at me, winked, and faced the wall. I'd expected a smart-ass retort like, "It's not like I haven't seen it all before," so his immediate and silent compliance with Dr. Penbright's request was a shock, and a relief.

The doctor helped me slip off my top then gently prodded my ribs until I yelped in pain. "Nothing broken. I'll give you a human dose of morphine and send you home with something gentler on your stomach. I'm sorry, but you're going to be in tremendous pain tomorrow unless you can find a healer. We have one who visits twice a week, but he isn't due back until Tuesday."

"Oh, I'm sure I can find *someone*," I snapped.

Dr. Penbright didn't appear to notice my tone, but Lucas did. He met my gaze from across the room and slowly shook his head.

Don't tell her what I can do.

CHAPTER ELEVEN

DR. PENBRIGHT GAVE LUCAS AND ME A LIST OF LOCAL HEALERS AND WE took a seat in the waiting area. Malcolm stood in one corner of the room with a dark-haired woman in her late thirties who I assumed was Maria Cortez. His affection for the woman appeared to be real. He'd dropped that cold, calculating smile and adopted a softer, more genuine one.

Maria, however, was shooting nervous glances at the door. She was nodding too much, her shoulders were drawn up to her ears, and her arms were wrapped tightly around her middle. Dr. Penbright might have felt Malcolm was a comfort to Maria, but the woman's body language told a different story.

I turned away from them and surveyed the rest of the waiting room. It looked as though most of it had once been an enormous, open family room. Now it was divided into two parts, with a curtained triage station taking up one half of the room. The other half was dominated by a white brick fireplace. A jumble of mismatched furniture was arranged in four sections, each separated by utilitarian rice paper screens.

I wondered if that was a way to keep different shifter groups separated when things got busy here. In my somewhat limited experience with shifter politics, the only way I'd seen different groups get along was if they had created an alliance against another group, and even that was often fraught with distrust.

An elderly man and woman huddled together on a love seat in one section. A family was in another, the mother seated in an overstuffed chair holding a sleeping preschool-aged child on her lap, the father pacing in front of her. The family shot hateful looks in Lucas's direction, but didn't speak.

A shifter female, who looked to be in her mid-thirties, strode into the room and perched on the arm of the chair beside the woman holding the child. Immediately, the tension ratcheted up. The woman flipped her long auburn hair over her shoulder and muttered something under her breath. The male shushed her.

"I'll be in the tank." Lucas did an about-face and exited the room.

Once he was gone, the tension abated somewhat, though the auburn-haired woman was now staring daggers at me. I set my attention back on Maria and Malcolm and ignored her. I was getting used to people not liking me.

"Please call me tomorrow morning and let me know how the girls are doing." Malcolm patted Maria's trembling hand.

"Yes, Alpha Malcolm." There was a stiffness in her voice, an edge that told me she'd call because she had to, not because she wanted to. I considered reading her, even though I knew I'd only be doing so to satiate my own curiosity, not to help Lucas.

Malcolm rose to his feet. "Try to get some rest, Maria."

"Yes, Alpha." Again, that wooden tone. I couldn't be the only one who noticed.

Malcolm headed out of the room and I followed. We were almost through the waiting room doorway when the dagger-eyed woman's voice rang out over the waiting area. "Permission to issue a mortal challenge to the spiker, Alpha Malcolm."

He and I turned as one to face the woman. Malcolm sighed. "I understand you're upset about your niece and nephew, Simone, but this is unnecessary. And against Dr. Penbright's rules. Permission denied."

"*She's* the reason they're in a coma."

"No, their impulsive actions are the reason they're in a coma. Be thankful they aren't dead. You've been around long enough to know what happens to any shifter who crosses Lucas Blacke."

That felt more directed at me than at his shifter, and I wondered exactly what Malcolm was playing at. I was also surprised that he wasn't using his "stand down" alpha voice with Simone. In my opinion, he had every reason to.

"I know, sir. I don't care."

The woman in the chair hugged the sleeping child in her arms. The man wrung his hands and said, "We're upset, sir. Forgive my sister. She's alpha—it's in her blood to protect us."

For some reason my eye was drawn to Maria again. The look on her face told me everything this time. No need to read her. She did *not* like Simone.

Malcolm escorted me out of the waiting room, down the short hall, and out the front door. Simone followed.

"Alpha, I respectfully and formally request permission to challenge the spiker."

We moved away from the front door and into the driveway. I didn't see Lucas anywhere.

"Are you on any narcotics, Neely?" Malcolm put a hand to the small of my back and ushered me forward, past the Rezvani and into the street. Although the house was miles from the ocean, the faint scent of saltwater perfumed the cool night air.

"No." I'd refused the morphine for reasons I planned to berate Lucas about later. I'd taken some kind of herbal pain killer, but according to the doctor the tincture wasn't any stronger than a few hundred milligrams of ibuprofen. "Why?"

"All right, Simone." Malcolm stared down at the Rolex on his wrist. "I'll give you ten seconds."

"I'll only need two." A vicious grin twisted the wolf shifter's coral-painted lips.

I twisted around so I could face both shifters at once. Pain stabbed my upper chest and shot down my arms. "*What?*"

Malcolm held up his wrist. "On my word. In *five...*"

Panic joined the pain thrilling through me. "I can't fight her, she's an alpha. She'll kill me."

He stared directly into my eyes and smiled. It was a frightening echo of Simone's expression, bright humor with a vein of insanity running through it. "*Four...*"

Where the hell was Lucas?

Simone was bouncing on her toes now. "Permission to shift."

"*Three*—not until the count is complete—*two...*"

What the actual...? He was letting her *shift*?

Damn you, Lucas.

With no other choice available to me, I opened myself, drawing power from both alphas. I locked onto Simone's brainwaves, because once she changed it would be nearly impossible. And if I didn't spike her, she'd have my intestines on the floor half a second after shifting.

"*One. Begin.*"

My whole body felt sick. But as the energy from Malcolm and Simone filled me, that sickness faded into background noise. The pain, weakness, dropped away.

Malcolm began a new countdown, this one ticking off the seconds she had left to murder me. "*Ten.*"

Simone took off her shoes and chucked them into the front yard of the medical clinic, slipped out of her light jacket, unzipped her pants, and kicked them aside. As she stripped, she strolled across the asphalt about twenty feet from me, kicking loose rocks aside with her bare feet, acting like she had all the time in the world to rip my throat out.

She howled, high and loud.

Wasn't Malcolm worried about humans in the neighborhood seeing a shifting wolf in the middle of the street? What was *wrong* with these people?

"*Nine,*" Malcolm said, commencing the slowest countdown I'd ever witnessed in my life.

A now nude Simone took three steps more and leaned forward on her toes. She was preparing to lunge, and she wanted me to know it. She wanted me afraid.

To hell with her. I was done with being afraid.

"*Eight.*"

Raw power spooled inside me, wrapping around my heart and lungs, stitching through my muscles. Her brain was exquisitely active, delectably alive. Excitement sparked in my nerves and joints, tightening my body deliciously, the way it did in the seconds before an orgasm. The exhilaration I felt worried the side of me that held onto my humanity, but my body was infused with endorphins and that worry didn't last for long.

Neither did my humanity.

"*Seven.*"

From the other end of the street, she launched, changing as she ran, her brown eyes now golden-hued and glowing, her sinewy body furred, her muzzle elongated and bristling with long, pointed teeth.

Anticipation surged through me. I wanted this even more than she did now, and I was ready. I planted my feet and stared directly into her eyes. A slow smile crept across my lips. Damn, it felt good to let go, to let my ability do what came naturally. The feeling was like nothing else in the world and I was past ready to spike her straight to—

Don't do it.

Distracted by the sound of Lucas's voice in my head, I pulled back. She was nearly on top of me and I'd lost contact with her brain. I reached for her again, but she was too far gone, too much wolf.

"*Six.*"

I pushed energy at her, tried to grab hold...

"*Five.*"

A golden-orange and black-striped half-man, half-animal leapt over my head and landed in a pistol squat between Simone and me. Lucas had shifted to his Bengal tiger hybrid form and he was terrifying—golden eyes aglow, jaw slavering, hooked claws outstretched. He was a blur of teeth and fur and skin, moving faster than my eyes could track. With a ticking roar, he met the wolf shifter mid-jump and slashed her from ear to ear, splashing blood on the road, on Malcolm, and on me.

"*Four, three, two, one,*" Lucas rattled off, as he morphed from hybrid to human. "Challenge over."

"You can't interfere in a challenge," Malcolm said.

"According to Statute 5 of the Shifter Treaty of 1970, this isn't an official challenge." Lucas cleared his throat, stared dispassionately down at Simone, who was choking on her own blood. She would heal, but I'd bet it was going to hurt. "Shifters cannot challenge non-shifting paranormals without life-threatening provocation. Did Neely provoke Simone in any way? Threaten her life?"

Malcolm looked at me, then at Simone, and then at Lucas. "You've made your point, Blacke."

"Excellent." Without a glance back at Malcolm, he took my hand and dragged me off the street, down the sidewalk, and into an idling car.

Chandra smiled at me from the driver's seat. "Nice eyes."

I climbed into the back and peered up at the rearview mirror. My irises were glowing gold the way Lucas's did when he was getting ready to shift.

"Do they always do that when I spike?"

"As far as I know, no, they don't." Lucas got into the back seat beside me. "Get us out of here, Chandra."

"Got it." She flipped a U and sped out of the neighborhood.

"Then why are they doing it now?" My body filled with panic. "What's wrong with me?"

"Nothing is wrong. You probably just took in a little too much energy. Calm down." He stroked my head as he said these infuriating things. "You weren't supposed to spike. I told you that."

Emotion overwhelmed me. I was filled with rage and fear, and too much power. My vision blurred with unshed tears, and I had to grit my teeth against the urge to spike him.

"You left me alone with Malcolm."

Lucas's voice softened. "No, I didn't. I was in the front room listening the whole time. The last thing I heard was Malcolm declining Simone's challenge." He brushed my hair away from my face. "I stepped outside to make a call to Chandra out of Malcolm's earshot, and the next thing I know, you're in the middle of a challenge in the street. That situation escalated *fast.*"

"Malcolm pushed me into the street so I wouldn't be on Dr. Penbright's neutral ground." My breath was coming in pants. I made an effort to slow my respiration so I didn't pass out.

"He needs Neely," Chandra said to Lucas. "Why in the world would he let someone challenge her?"

"That's obvious," he replied. "The brain-haunted alpha wants to see the spiker in action."

"It's eleven o'clock. Where the hell did you and Chandra go?" Lucas grumbled when I walked into our room, heading straight for the bathroom.

"Nowhere," I snapped.

An hour before, Chandra had dropped Lucas off at the B&B, but I didn't go in. It had annoyed Lucas that I went with Chandra instead of going inside with him, but he didn't say anything, just slammed the car door and walked out without a look back.

"You obviously went somewhere."

He'd taken a shower and was dressed in a pair of white silky pajama bottoms and nothing else. I checked to see if they had an inappropriate word embroidered across the ass, but there was nothing but more white silk over smooth, curved muscle. They were nice, but as with the black pair, they weren't Lucas.

"We parked a few miles away. Talked." I motioned him into the bathroom, closed the door behind him. "I needed a moment to gather myself." To come down from my thwarted high. If I'd spiked that wolf, I'd be feeling much better. As it was, I felt like I was in the crossover hour of a tequila hangover, suspended between drunk and nauseated.

"Why couldn't you have had that moment with me?" He rested a hip against the sink, his gaze soft, almost vulnerable.

"I'm too angry with *you*." I leaned against the vanity countertop, unconsciously mimicking his position. The tincture Dr. Penbright gave me was rapidly wearing off and I was achy, tired, and wired. Sleep would not come easily tonight.

"Me? What did I do?"

"Why didn't you just heal me after the accident the way you always do when I get hurt?" I snapped. "You could have saved us both a lot of trouble."

He scowled, folded his arms over his bare chest. "Who am I, your personal Dr. Quinn Medicine Shifter?"

"No." But he had been a few months ago when he'd healed me of some terrible wounds caused by his people. He'd marched into the witches' tower where I was holed up and "took on" my wounds. Shifters healed quickly, so what would have taken weeks of recovery for me was healed in minutes once it was in and on his body.

"Did you tell Malcolm I can heal?" he asked.

"No. You didn't want me to."

Lucas eyed me as if he expected me to strike at him like a rattlesnake. Smart man. "He doesn't know that I can heal people—*some* people."

"Why not?"

"My healing ability originates from the prehistoric side of my nature. Malcolm doesn't know about that. If he did, he'd have had me killed long ago."

"I didn't say anything to him except that I like you, so let's be glad he didn't catch me in *that* lie." I flung a bottle of pills on the counter.

Lucas snatched them up, read the label. "Anti-inflammatories?"

"Exactly, you ass. I wouldn't let the doctor give me a morphine injection because I was afraid that I might relax and talk too much. So now all I have is a tincture that's nearly worn off, and these crappy pills. I'm in a lot of pain and I need to lie down, so will you kindly get out of my way and let me take a shower so I can drag my tired carcass to bed?"

"Should have known you wouldn't tell him anything." He was still looking at the pill bottle.

"What? Do you think I'm protecting you?"

"Maybe." He set the pills down. "But mostly I think keeping secrets is second nature to you."

One of my many endearing qualities. "I have to be that way. You of all people should understand that."

"Because of alpha leaders like Malcolm and Roso," he said.

And you. I didn't say it out loud, but I was sure he knew I was thinking it.

Toeing off my sneakers, I grabbed a hair tie off the counter and raised my arms to put my hair up. No way was I washing it tonight. I didn't have the energy.

Jabbing pains shot up and down my arms and into my neck and shoulders. I gasped and the elastic band dropped out of my hands and fell to the floor. "Forget the shower. I'm going to bed dirty."

Lucas kicked my shoes to the side and reached for me. "Come here. I can help."

"No, you had your chance to heal me and you were a giant jackass. Now you have to watch me hurt and feel guilty."

He rolled his eyes, tried to hide a smile. "Neely, come on."

"No."

"Like you could fight me even if you wanted to." He lowered his voice into a hypnotic purr. "And you don't want to fight me, do you?"

"You know what? Yes. Yes, I want to fight you. I want to punch you in your stupid head."

"The thing is—" He stepped into my space, his heated breath curling around my ear. "—I can't fix all the bruises."

"Because Malcolm will find out. Whatever. Stop doing that to my ear, you weirdo."

He kissed the top of my head. "I'll bring someone in tomorrow to heal you completely. But I can take the edge off the pain right now so you can shower, or bathe."

"Fine." I scrunched my nose at the kiss. "I want a bath and I want it with my vanilla ice cream bubbles you stole."

"There's still some left. Give me a second here."

He put his hands on my arms and let out a long, slow breath. Instantly, the pain lessened. When it was manageable, he released me and gasped a little as he bent down to pick up my discarded elastic band. He had my sore ribs now. Good.

Wordlessly, he ran his fingers through my hair and over my scalp. He didn't try to work out the tangles in my curls, which I appreciated, since I wasn't interested in a headache. He simply bunched it all into a serviceable ponytail and wrapped the elastic around it.

When he was finished, he tugged me against him, my back to his chest. We observed our reflection in the mirror. My russet brown skin was an appealing contrast to his white olive skin, dark curling tendrils of my hair grazed the dusting of blond hair on his arm. We looked good, as if we belonged together, and the way he was pulling me closer told me he saw it, too.

Beautiful. I wondered if he realized he'd thought the word at me. Knowing Lucas, he did.

"Lucas?"

"Mmm?"

"Tonight, when I was going to spike Simone, I scared myself."

"Because you wanted to kill her?" He bent to answer me, his voice humming against my ear.

"Because I wanted to kill *something.*" I opened my eyes. "I didn't care if it was her. I almost spiked you."

"I felt you losing control. It's not a good feeling, is it?"

He was probably thinking about his prehistoric side and his own fear of losing control of himself while in that state. I didn't read him to find out. He'd tell me if he wanted me to know.

"It's wonderful and horrific. Like the best drug in the world. But afterward I feel so … low. Like I'm losing my humanity."

"Maybe you are," he whispered. "Maybe you weren't ever supposed to have that humanity. Maybe it's time to leave the human side of you behind."

"It's the only thing holding me together," I whispered back to him. "My uncle is gone. The rules he taught me are my compass, and I need them so I don't lose my way."

"Maybe what you need is a new compass."

His movements sluggish, he dimmed the lights, ran a steamy bath with far too many bubbles, and fetched the candles from our night-stands. Once lit, they filled the room with the scent of vanilla. Of the bakery. Of home.

He left me to it. I stripped and slid into the stinging warm water. I must have dozed, because when I woke up Lucas was on the floor beside the tub with his hand on the back of my neck, keeping me from going under. Drowsily, I gazed up at his handsome face, so serious in the dim light of the bathroom.

"You're awake."

"Mmm-hmm," I mumbled.

He stared at me for a few seconds, his eyes sad. "I'm sorry I brought you here."

"I know you are." I really did know that. Regret radiated from him.

"Seems like no matter what I do, Malcolm always has a hold on me, and I can't seem to break free."

"He's not your alpha anymore."

"Yeah, but I protected him for so long that it's a part of me now. Written into my goddamned genetic code." Lucas touched his forehead to mine. It was nice, the skin contact. Even if I was still angry with him, I also cared deeply for him, and I'd be lying if I said I didn't like his touch.

"Would you kill him to protect your people?" I spoke softly so my words didn't echo off the shower walls.

"I'd do what I needed to." His voice matched mine. Soft, low. "Not only for my group, but for everyone I care about."

He was talking about me. I leaned into his hand as he massaged the back of my neck.

"Are you really going to spike him?" he asked.

"Yes." I hadn't been a hundred percent sure until that moment, but there seemed no way around it and I wanted to get this over with. I wanted to go home.

"If he dies when you do it, we'll have to move fast." Lucas gently turned my head so that I could see his face. His tiger-lightened eyes met mine. "I won't let them kill you. If anyone tries, they have to come through me first, and I will do everything in my power to protect you." His eyes went a shade lighter. The last time I'd seen them that color, he'd been changing into his prehistoric animal. "Nothing is off the table."

CHAPTER TWELVE

SLEEP CAME IN TWO-HOUR NIGHTMARE BURSTS. I DREAMED OF SAUL Roso, of another alpha I'd spiked years ago, of Julio, and of my uncle.

Whenever I spike someone, my brain processes the other person's thoughts, dreams, and visions of the future as if I had lived them. This sometimes causes confusion. Overwhelm. Sleep is where my mind reconciles the two, cleans up mental loose ends, so to speak. Unfortunately, this cerebral cleanup tends to occur during times of intense stress and usually manifests in dark and hideous nightmares. Mainly because I tended not to spike nice people with nice thoughts.

Several times I woke up gasping, panicked, sure that it was time to spike Malcolm, sure that I was going to end up killing him and then his wolves would kill Lucas and Chandra and everyone in Sundance and it would be my fault.

Twice I woke up sobbing. When that happened, Lucas tucked me against his warm body until I went to sleep again. He never initiated any other physical contact, but he didn't push me away, either. For my part, I clung to him like a drowning woman. And each time, he kept my head from sinking underwater.

God, did I love to complicate things.

I skipped breakfast and slept in, so at 11 o'clock Lucas brought me something to eat. Atop the silver tray he carried into the room, there was a bowl of fruit-topped Greek yogurt, a protein bar, a bowl of granola, three pieces of toast, and a pot of the best coffee I'd ever tasted.

"Thanks, but this is too much food. Here, have some." I poured a cup of coffee for myself and handed him a protein bar.

"Too *much?* I was worried it wasn't enough. You're going to be famished after the healer works on you." He was dressed in a T-shirt and running shorts, but I knew he hadn't been out for a run. He wouldn't have gone that far from the hotel. He wouldn't have gone that far from me. He'd promised.

The healer, an old woman in tattered clothing who smelled like chicken soup, showed up shortly after that and worked on me for half an hour. I felt better when she was finished, though not as good as I had when Lucas had healed me.

By the time one o'clock rolled around, I'd ordered a second pot of coffee, decaf this time, and eaten everything off the tray—except the protein bar, which Lucas ate. I was amazed I hadn't barfed it all up. Despite the decaf, my hands were shaking so badly I could barely tie my sneakers and zip up my cotton sundress. Green today, in case I accidentally murdered the San Diego wolf alpha leader with my spike and I needed to blend into the scenery to make my getaway.

"Take it slow with Malcolm." Lucas pulled on a black cotton T-shirt and shoved his feet into a pair of black hiking boots. The faded jeans he'd changed into hugged his muscled butt as he bent to tie the laces. I was working very hard not to notice, but I kept thinking about last night and how wonderful he'd been to me, and my disobedient eyes danced right back over to his backside.

"I know." I plopped down on the bed. "You've already told me this."

"There's no need to rush." He fastened a stainless-steel watch on his wrist. "Slow and easy."

I took my gaze off his ass and set it on his spine. Pretended I had a knife in my hand and mimed throwing it at him. "I *know.*"

"Molasses-in-January slow. Sunday-sermon-before-a-playoff-game slow. DMV line—"

"So help me, if you tell me to go slow one more time I'm going spike you into forgetting that word."

"An empty threat." He went around the bed to the nightstand where his wallet lay. Picked it up, slipped it into his back pocket. "You only spike people who attack you and alpha leaders who ask you to dig ghosts out of their brains."

"You are so not funny."

Using his shifter speed, he zipped around the bed and caged me in his arms, leaning over me mock-menacingly. "Take that back. I'm hilarious."

I smiled a little, and then let it fade away. "Lucas?"

"Yeah?" He straightened, strolled into the bathroom.

"What if I screw this up?"

"I'll be there with you the whole time." He stuck his head out of the bathroom door. "I promised, remember?"

"I know you did, but…" I cleared my throat. He wasn't going to like this. "I'm releasing you from your promise."

"Why?" He walked slowly back into the bedroom. "Because you don't think I can keep it?"

"Hardly. Not only do I know you *can* keep it, I know you *will* keep it, even if it costs you." I got up, met him halfway across the floor. We weren't touching, but we were so close to each other I could feel the heat of his body through his T-shirt.

"Then what's the problem?" The look on his face hovered somewhere between hurt and puzzled. For some reason, the combination made me sad.

"I don't want to be responsible for any more deaths."

He looked at me like he was trying to decide whether or not I was telling the truth. "Your uncle's death was the responsibility of the man who committed the murder, not you. I wonder when you're going to realize that."

Never. Because I knew in my heart of hearts that it wasn't true. Not completely. None of it would have happened if it weren't for me. Not one single death.

"I'm not leaving you, Neely."

"I've already released you from that obligation. You don't have to promise me anything."

A muscle pulsed in his cheek. He made a "that's enough" gesture with the flat of his hand and the muscles in his arm flexed. "This subject is closed."

"Yes," I said. "It is."

Cursing under his breath, Lucas glanced at my nightstand, where I'd left the sacks Bill Bill had given me. "Are you bringing a hex bag with you?"

"Well, yeah. I want to rule out a curse."

"I advise you not to show it to Malcolm."

"Why not?" I looked at the tiny velvet sacks. "It won't hurt him, and it might help."

"The question is, does he really want help, or is this some kind of game?"

I did an all-over sigh. It started at my knees and rushed out of me like a strong wind. "I can only address the information he's giving me. Once I'm in his brain, I'll know if he's lying."

"Will you?" He shook his head. "You'll do what you want, but don't say I didn't warn you."

"Damn it, Lucas, I don't need this from you right now. I need..."

"What?" He trailed his fingers down my throat. A light graze that made me shiver. "What do you need from me, Neely?"

I put both hands on his chest, clutched at his shirt. Tried to shake him, but he didn't move an inch. "Honestly? I don't know. I'm terrified. From my head to my shoes, one-hundred-percent afraid."

"Exactly."

"And..." I stepped back, fisted my hands at my sides. "It goes against everything I'm feeling to release you from your promise, but I'm doing it anyway."

He stepped into my space. "Sugar cookie, I don't give a damn if you release me from my promise. It changes nothing."

"Yes it does change things, and stop calling me that. Oh my God, you are *the* most infuriating, annoy—"

A knock on the door interrupted our argument.

Lucas sniffed the air. "It's Willa."

I darted to the nightstand and grabbed the items I'd picked up at Bill Bill's. Good thing I'd worn a dress with pockets. "How can you tell?"

"She wears the same perfume she's always worn. Right, Willa?"

"It's my favorite," came the muffled reply.

The door swung open and Willa Scott stood on the threshold.

"I'm here to escort you both to Alpha Malcolm's room." Her voice dropped into a whisper as she eyed the camera above the door. "And to warn you, Neely."

I nodded, indicating she should continue.

"If the alpha dies, the pack will kill you." Thank goodness Lucas had already told me that, because even hearing it a second time was scary. "There are those in the pack, old-school types, who think spikers should be put down the moment their powers manifest."

"Is that how you feel?" I asked.

She shook her head. "Lucas trusts you and that's enough for me."

"I don't want to hurt Malcolm. The idea is to help him, but I've never spiked anyone like this before and I'm not entirely sure what I'm doing."

Willa's gaze traveled from Lucas to me. "I understand. But there are wolves here who won't."

"Like the ones who came after us yesterday," I muttered.

"There will be more attempts like that before this is over. Be ready for them."

CHAPTER THIRTEEN

MALCOLM MET US IN A SUITE ON THE FLOOR ABOVE OURS, THOUGH I suspected this wasn't his main residence. It looked more like a real estate staging of a living space than it did a home. A bland blue fabric sofa, two matching wingback chairs, and a coffee table were nestled in an alcove near the door. They appeared to be brand new. A framed photo of a younger Malcolm and a man and woman I assumed were his parents was propped up on the coffee table, along with one of him with his shifters, and two where he was accepting plaques from human community figures. These were the only personal touches.

A desk, also new, was angled near an ocean-facing window. The window Lucas kept peering out of, as if watching for something.

Or someone.

Malcolm looked at me. "Did Willa properly frighten you?"

"No."

"You're saying she didn't warn you that the pack wants you dead?"

Malcolm seemed to be teasing me, but I didn't dare engage him in kind. It was bully teasing, the sort where you felt victimized by implied menace rather than actual brutality. If I turned the teasing back on him, it wouldn't be received well.

He was dressed like Lucas was today. Army green T-shirt, jeans, boots. It should have made him look sloppy, particularly when compared to his usual attire. It didn't. The clothes shaved ten years off him. Took him from handsome, dangerous, older guy to hot, dangerous, older guy.

"She did, but I already knew that, so I wasn't any more afraid than I had been before she issued the warning." I pulled one of the small black sachets I'd gotten from Bill Bill out of my dress pocket and set it on the table. The other one was tucked into my bra, something I'd done quickly before we left, after Lucas's warning.

Not that I believed I needed to, I just wanted to keep my options open.

"What's *that?*" Malcolm hit the last "t" hard. His jaw muscles were prominent in his face from clenching his teeth.

"Hex bag. I believe it's also called a spell bag."

"I know what a hex bag is." All remaining softness dropped from the alpha's face. "Why is it here?"

"I was concerned that you might have been cursed."

"*What?*" He gave the bag a baleful look, then transferred the look to me.

"I know it sounds a little wild, but I wanted to see if what we're dealing with here truly is from your connection with Suyin Chen. One way to do that is to rule out magic."

"I do not like magic." He pronounced each word with door-slamming finality.

Lucas chuckled in a "told you so" sort of way.

I stared hard at him until he stopped. "I think I hear William calling you in the hall, Lucas. Maybe you should go check it out." I ignored his scowl and returned my attention to Malcolm. "This isn't active magic. The witches assured me it will only activate in the instance of a curse. If you're curse-free, it just sits there."

"*Witches?*" His eyes glowed and his voice dropped into Alpha command zone. The atmosphere thickened and the scent of sweat and fur spiced the air.

"It's not danger—"

"*Get that thing out of here.*" He flew. There was no other explanation for how fast the wolf alpha crossed the ten feet separating us. His fingers dug into my shoulders as he yanked me close and breathed hotly into my face. "*Now.*"

Fear jetted through my veins like a drug, and I forced myself to stop pulling energy. I wanted to spike. Badly. "Malcolm, I—"

"*Let her go.*" Lucas went from the window to my side in under a second. His voice was deep and weighted with command, increasing the tension in the room so that I could barely breathe.

"Lucas, I'm okay." A lie, but I didn't want him to do anything both of us might regret.

"Get rid of it." Malcolm didn't yell. He didn't need to. The negative energy pulsing out of him made every syllable a promise of violence.

"Why?" Lucas asked. "Afraid it might tell us something?"

Malcolm growled, the sound hitting me like a punch to the solar plexus. I was barely holding onto myself, the urge to spike climbing ever higher. True, I'd intended to spike Malcolm all along, but with control and finesse, not while fearful and reactionary.

Lucas's mouth stretched into a parody of a smile. His eyes flashed gold, his canines extended and curved so that he looked less like a Bengal tiger and more like a Smilodon. Whatever he was up to, he was planning to do it in his prehistoric form, and with the wolves on the other side of Malcolm's door looking for an excuse to kill us, I was pretty sure that was a bad idea.

"Everyone, calm down." I swiped the spell bag off the table with numb fingers and ran to the nearest open window where I pitched it out. "Look. All gone."

"Don't touch her like that again, *wolf.*" Lucas pushed me behind him when I tried to walk back to Malcolm.

"Hey, it's okay." I ran my palm down Lucas's rigid spine, stroking from his neck to the small of his back until I felt his muscles relax. "I'm all right. Thank you."

Malcolm stared down at his hands for a long minute. They were covered with slowly receding fur, something I hadn't noticed before, focused as I was on Lucas not shifting into a form his ex-alpha didn't even know he possessed.

"Blacke is right. I was wrong for grabbing you like that, Neely. It was rude and I apologize—to you both." His voice was a mishmash of wolf and man. It reminded me of the voice modulation television reporters use to keep their interviewees anonymous.

I nodded. Lucas did nothing to indicate that he accepted Malcolm's apology.

The wolf alpha continued, his voice normalizing with every word. "Putting my hands on a woman, human or paranormal, is abhorrent to me. Outside of a direct challenge, of course."

"Why would you have to when you can sic one of your wolves on her?" Lucas stared at Malcolm with revulsion in his eyes.

"Can you blame me for wanting to see you in action?" His voice had returned to normal, silky-smooth and wryly condescending. "Neely, I would have stopped you before you killed Simone. Remember, I was married to a spiker. I know how long it takes them to kill someone."

"And how long is that?" Lucas asked.

"Certainly longer than the minute it would have taken me to grab Simone and run out of Neely's range." Malcolm smiled.

I could have killed her.

There was no way Malcolm could have outrun my spike. My uncle had been barely able to do it with me holding back and him throwing me into a car and driving with the gas pedal to the floorboard. And that was against a powerful alpha leader. I could have killed Simone in seconds. Less. And for no reason other than to satisfy a selfish alpha leader's curiosity.

Lucas very carefully didn't look my way, but Malcolm's gaze followed me as I fell into one of the chairs across from the sofa. The cushion was stiff, and smelled like dry-cleaning solvent.

He lowered himself onto the sofa with his gaze glued to mine. "My mother is a witch."

There was a lot of emotion loaded into that statement. The alpha leader had mommy issues.

"Hex bags may indeed be inert magic and harmless except to the curse, but I've seen too many magical double-crossings to trust that. So, I don't allow magic in my home."

I thought about the second spell bag I'd crammed into my bra. Something I'd done based on a warning from Lucas, who had likely known about Malcolm's strong aversion to magic and kept it to himself, the ass. Why did he keep doing things like that?

The hex bag in my bra, which had given me no trouble until now, began to feel scratchy and heavy. I shifted in my seat. Sweat pooled under my arms and my breasts. I swiped my forehead with the back of my hand.

"Fair enough," I said. "Okay. I won't cast any spells. Not that I know any, but you can't be sure, right?" Oh God, I needed to stop talking.

Malcolm's eyebrows shot up. "No, I can't."

I'll be right back. Lucas thought the words at me, then walked across the room and out the door, closing it behind him.

What? You said you wouldn't leave me, I thought back at him, but it was pointless. For one thing, Lucas couldn't hear my thoughts, and for another, I'd released him from his promise.

But he hadn't released himself. I immediately let the idea go. I had no cause to be angry with Lucas. I'd released him and had meant it.

I rolled my shoulders back and picked at the front of my dress in an attempt to shift the hex bag between my breasts without drawing Malcolm's attention to it. "Yeah, well, to be honest, I'm kind of with you on the hesitancy. I mean, I didn't even believe in the existence of witches until a few months ago."

"Why not?"

"I'm not a very good paranormal."

I gave him the sanitized, abridged version of my life, the running, the hiding from myself, the constant fear of dying or killing and not knowing which was worse. And all the while I blathered on, I twitched like a caffeine addict on a coffee bender. I was going to spike this man soon. I had no idea how it was going to work out, but my guess was, badly.

When I was finished, Malcolm patted my hand, his blue eyes softening with what appeared to be genuine tenderness. "Thank you for trusting me with your story."

"I thought I should give you something because when I read someone, I often see things you might not appreciate me seeing. That can leave people feeling extremely vulnerable." And sometimes murder-

112

ous. "So, I want to ask you one last time. Are you *sure* you want to do this?"

He was sure.

I, however, was having some doubts. "Let's wait for Lucas."

Damn that man. He wasn't back yet and I couldn't feel his brain in the hallway.

"No." Malcolm relaxed against the back of the sofa. Stretched out his legs. "Do it now."

"I prefer to wait for him."

"Why? Do you need his permission to proceed?" He was baiting me, and I wasn't falling for it.

"No. It's more that, in order to do this properly, I need to be centered." I flipped my hair behind my shoulders and lifted my chin. "I feel calmer when he's around."

My general philosophy on lying is, don't. Lying is one of those things that can backfire on you in an instant. It ruins reputations, sows the seeds of distrust, and is just plain rude.

However, if you are going to do it, do it audaciously.

Malcolm laughed. "Blacke calms you. *Lucas* Blacke."

"Yes, he makes me feel ... settled."

"Right." Malcolm crossed his ankles, sank deeper into the sofa, laughed a little more. "Neely, Blacke makes people feel a lot of things, but I guarantee centered, calm, and settled aren't on the list."

"You don't know him the way I do."

"I know him better than you think."

The door swung open and the devil we were speaking of sauntered back inside. Lucas's heated-whiskey gaze darted around the room, noted the exits, then the threat—Malcolm—and finally settled on me. The second his eyes met mine, the strangest thing happened.

I realized I hadn't lied.

With a half grin, Lucas strolled to my chair and positioned himself behind me. He twisted a strand of my hair around one finger, let it unravel, then massaged the back of my neck. It was obviously an act for the benefit of Malcolm, but his touch did something. If I was being honest, it did a lot of somethings to me, and one of those somethings was it made me feel settled.

"Are you *calmer* now?" Malcolm's lips curved in a languorous grin.

"Calmer?" Lucas asked.

"Apparently your presence calms her. Odd. I've always been told that your presence invokes a different reaction in most women—and some men."

Lucas's hand flexed on my neck. Not a threat to me, but a reaction to Malcolm's words. It was all I could do not to read him, but he wasn't projecting, and I needed to concentrate on Malcolm's spike.

"Perhaps it's because Neely and I have a deep connection."

"Is that right?" The wolf alpha stared into my eyes. I had the feeling he was surveying me with something more than his human, or even shifter, abilities, and that he'd know it if I lied.

"Yes."

It wasn't a lie. I lived in the town Lucas practically owned, we'd slept in the same bed for the last couple of nights, and we'd taken down a dangerous wolf alpha leader together.

We'd bonded.

"You believe that." Malcolm appeared surprised. "Are you in love with him?"

"If I am, I haven't told him. Shouldn't the first person I tell be the man I love?" Talk about tiptoeing around a bear trap. I hoped Malcolm wouldn't push me. I was already worked up about the spike and I didn't need this.

Malcolm gave Lucas a look I couldn't read. It was curiosity, admiration, and annoyance all rolled into one, and mixed with something unidentifiable.

The alpha uncrossed his ankles and sat up in the chair. "For your sake, Neely, I hope you don't. You're the type of woman who values loyalty. Love. Honor. Blacke here can give you some of those, but not all." He didn't specify which he felt Lucas couldn't handle, but I suspected loyalty was on the list.

Lucas's fingers tightened in my hair. It was just short of painful, in that sweet spot between too light and too much, and gave me noticeable goosebumps.

"Honey, maybe you should *spike* him now," Lucas said between clenched teeth.

Malcolm sat up straighter. "Now that you've *calmed* her, perhaps she should." I could practically hear the air quotations around the word "calmed."

This was going to be a long afternoon.

I inserted some cheer into my voice. "Okay then, let's begin."

Before I started working with the tower witches on controlling my ability, I used to always pull energy to me to prepare myself. I could draw it from anything with life in it, human, animal, insect, plant, but paranormals gave me the most power.

Dottie taught me that it was better to open myself and let the energy flow to me. That way I could regulate it as it entered my body, throttling when I needed less, revving when I needed more. I still pulled when I needed to, but that was only when I needed a lot of power in a short amount of time. Like last night with Simone.

Halfway through the exhale of a deep breath, I opened myself.

An unpleasant jolt, not unlike the hard snap of an electrical charge, rushed into me. Damn, I'd forgotten. Two alpha leaders in the same room? There was bound to be an overflow of energy.

I shoved the power back, throttling it the way Dottie had showed me. "Distract yourself, dear. Find something else to focus on for a moment until you've calmed."

As always, Dolores had had something to say, too. "Just don't stay distracted for too long or you'll lose it, kiddo."

So, I let my eyes drift over the room. There was nothing terribly interesting about the place, the pictures I'd seen, the desk was uncluttered, the floor was weathered oak, the ceiling and walls painted white. Desperately, I reached for something to distract me.

You okay? Lucas asked telepathically.

I tilted my head back until I could see him. Nodded.

Liar.

I responded with a partially suppressed grin.

Do I really calm you?

115

Huh? I said the word with a look.

What Malcolm said before. Is it true?

I was tempted to ignore him. The arrogant shifter deserved it.

Tell me.

The nod I gave him was so slight I was afraid he might not see it. Though I was kind of more afraid that he would.

I like that. I'd expected a self-satisfied grin from him, but what I got was a soft, happy smile.

"Is everything all right?" Malcolm asked.

Strangely, it was. The odd conversation with Lucas had done the trick. The energy was flowing into me at a measured rate now, no less powerful, but controlled.

I rose, took a seat beside the wolf alpha. Set my hand on top of his. I didn't require physical contact to delve into someone's mind, but it helped, and I'd already tried to telepathically read him twice since sitting down and had gotten nowhere.

"This might hurt."

It's difficult for me to spike someone without inflicting pain. Not impossible, but it takes a tremendous effort on my part, and is unnecessary anyway, because the person being spiked never remembers the pain afterward—unless I want them to. This wasn't a killing spike, but it was very close. Much more invasive than a telepathic read.

Still, I'd prefer to not hurt Malcolm with his wolves so close by. No sense courting danger, seeing as how I was already dating it exclusively.

With a measured pop of that delicious alpha energy that flowed hotly through my veins like a narcotic, I reached for his brainwaves. They were strong and sure, but slippery, which made perfect sense considering their source. I revved-throttled-*revved* the energy building up inside me as I locked onto the vibrations, held on for dear life as they threatened to shake me off. He was strong. It would have been far easier to full-on spike him and be done with it.

"Have you started?" Malcolm sounded peeved.

"Yes." My jaw was so tightly clamped I could barely speak.

"There's no point in being careful with me. I can take the pain. After all, I've been spiked before." He yawned. *Yawned.*

116

Arrogant bastard. Spike him, Neely.

I nodded at Lucas as I relaxed my hold and drilled into Malcolm's brain, all rev and no throttle, boring directly to the center of his consciousness. To his credit, Malcolm didn't scream. He spat a little, shook like a leaf in a windstorm, and went ice pale, but he didn't cry out.

Ignoring his discomfort, I pushed, seeking out the shadowed places in his mind. There were many. There were memories of Suyin —some good, most uncomfortable, some horrific. From what I could see, the end had been bad. Malcolm felt real sorrow at the loss, though that was open to interpretation. Had he missed Suyin the person or the weapon?

Surprisingly, Malcolm held no ill will toward Lucas for killing his wife. He'd understood there was nothing that could be done to help her at that point. In other remembrances, though, he had not been as charitable toward Lucas. In fact, he'd been downright brutal.

His cruelty toward Lucas made my heart ache. Young and eager to please his alpha, Lucas took punishments from Malcolm that would have killed most shifters. I drew back, gritting my teeth against the desire to spike the wolf alpha to Hell for what he'd done. It was not my battle to fight and Lucas wouldn't thank me for it, but the temptation was there all the same.

I concentrated on sifting through the wolf alpha's brain, looking for anything and everything pertaining to Suyin so I could get out of Malcolm's head before my euphoric response set in and I lost control. The energy humming through both of us was tempting me beyond my willpower. Only my fear of death by wolves and Lucas's distracting me had kept me in check so far.

Are you okay? Lucas asked.

I nodded.

Every person's mind was different. There were similarities, but because I wasn't exactly exploring the real brain, only the person's version of his or her own consciousness, I had to be flexible with my method of ferreting out information.

Unless I was in it to kill the person. That required zero finesse, just a whole lot of energy straight to the real brain.

It was tempting to spike deeper. The energy in Malcolm was strong and alluring and addictive. I took a shuddering breath. The euphoria twisted through me, spun me around like a fierce wind. If I let myself get caught up in it, I was screwed.

You still okay?

I nodded, but I was lying and we both knew it.

If you have to get out, do it. Don't risk killing him or yourself. Or me.

Lucas was right. I was losing control, and if I didn't pull out now, I'd get us all killed. Slowly, steadily, I began the process of extracting myself from Malcolm's brain.

And that's when I saw it.

A misshapen memory wedged into the forefront of Malcolm's thoughts. The colors were wrong, the sound was tinny, the vibrations of his brain were sluggish here.

The bedroom door creaked open.

A happily disheveled woman with long black hair in a white negligee reclined on a bed. An uncorked bottle of champagne stuck out of a bucket of ice, a bridal veil was draped over the back of a padded chair, and the shower was running in the next room.

"Suyin." The voice was breathy and formless, a verbal wraith.

Suyin flicked back her shoulder-length black hair, held out pale, delicate hands to the person. "It's business, love. Nothing more."

"Business means too much to you."

"You knew this when we started." She gracefully lowered her hands to her lap. "You said you understood."

"If only you had let this idea die." The voice faded out on the last word.

"I can't. You know why." The shower shut off. Suyin's face creased with fear. She mouthed, "He's coming back. Go. Hurry, or you'll ruin everything."

This was where it cut off and looped back. It played over and over until I thought I'd go insane from it, and I wasn't living it full-time.

Neely?

"I found it."

I let the memory twist away as I fought to get the unnatural euphoria in my brain to wind down. Thankfully, Lucas's voice in my head seemed to be helping me focus.

You're kidding. You actually found the memory?

118

"Yes, though it's less of a memory and more of a repetitive thought that someone has implanted."

Implanted?

"It can't be his thought. He's not the person experiencing it."

The wolf alpha let out a low growl. His eyes remained shut tight as he rolled his head back and forth and from shoulder to shoulder. The growl hadn't been in response to my words, but to the memory.

Don't touch it, Neely. Lucas eyed the other alpha warily. *Something feels wrong.*

Everything felt wrong to me, but I still had a job to do. "I-I'm going to try to disrupt it."

Be careful.

Yeah, because I hadn't thought of that.

A deep breath later, I reached for the memory again. When it reached the part where it cut off and circled back to the beginning, I opened myself wider, allowing even more power to course through me, and sledgehammered my ability into the loop. No aim, no artful subtlety, only blind brute force.

I swung at it, yanked and wrenched at it, but there was nothing in Malcolm's mind that connected to the memory, nothing to dislodge it from. It was an isolated thought floating in the aether of his brain, no relation to anything else. In essence, there was no breaking the loop by disconnecting the memory, because the memory was already disconnected.

I'd have to try something else.

Problem was, I didn't know what to do. The hex bag tucked against my breast was itchy and uncomfortable, but it wasn't doing anything magical, so it couldn't be the stone brain spell, as the witches had suspected. My disruption theory was a bust and I couldn't read him telepathically. Once again, the urge to spike deeper rose in me as hot, rapturous energy burned through my veins. I needed to do something, but I was running out of—

Malcolm screamed.

"What's happening?" I could barely hear Lucas's question over Malcolm's hoarse shrieks.

"I don't know. I didn't do anything." I concentrated on the loop, imagined a pair of scissors slicing through the ribbon of memory. It was a drastic move, but I was out of ideas.

The wolf alpha gurgled, then shrieked. I dropped the imaginary scissors and backed away from the memory.

"He bit his tongue." Lucas grabbed Malcolm's head and peered into his mouth. "It's not bad. It'll heal in a minute or so."

"What the hell is going on in here?" William Scott burst into the room.

"Put the guns away." Lucas's voice was low and growly. *Get out of his head. We've got company. With guns.*

"I can't just pull out. If I do, I could damage his brain," I said to the room at large. With my focus on Malcolm, I couldn't tell who all was in the room, but it felt crowded and overheated, and I could hear fast breathing.

"Stand down, wolves. The spiker isn't hurting Alpha Malcolm on purpose. He warned you this might happen." William again.

The alpha's throat-shredding screams died down the farther away from the memory I moved. Gingerly, I withdrew from his brain and glanced behind me.

Fourteen wolf shifters surrounded Malcolm, Lucas, and me. Thirteen had guns aimed at my head. The fourteenth, William, was trying to reason with the others. Lucas was watching me with undiluted concentration.

"You okay?" he asked.

Malcolm was sprawled on the sofa, head lolled to one side, bloody drool dribbling out of the side of his mouth. The guns were still pointed at me.

Nope. I definitely wasn't okay. Not by a long shot, so to speak.

"He was right, you know." I grabbed a tissue and dabbed at Malcolm's lip.

"About what?" William asked.

"Suyin. She really is haunting him."

CHAPTER FOURTEEN

"THERE'S NO WAY THAT COULD BE TRUE." LUCAS PACED THE LENGTH OF the room.

"I've certainly never heard of such a thing," William said.

We were alone, the four of us. The others had agreed to leave if William stayed behind.

I moved from the sofa to one of the chairs. "I'm not saying she's a ghost or anything. Just that a memory of her is stuck in his brain."

"Did he do it to himself? Guilt, perhaps?" William stood over Malcolm's slumped form on the sofa, his mouth cinched like a drawstring bag. The lines in William's face had deepened, and he'd lost a little of the ruddiness in his skin tone.

"Come on." Lucas ceased pacing, huffed out a mirthless laugh. "Do you honestly believe he feels even the slightest twinge of guilt for Suyin's death? As far as he's concerned, it was a gamble that didn't pay off."

"That's not how you feel about it, is it?" William stared straight at Lucas. Tension tightened between the two men and I was suddenly, exceedingly glad the thirteen armed wolves weren't in the room.

"No." Lucas's eyes flashed gold. That ozone scent, the one that proceeds rain, or an angry shifter's transformation, perfumed the air.

William shook his head as if to clear it, and took a step away from

Lucas. "How long does it take to recover from a spike? When will he wake up?"

"That's the thing," I crossed my arms high, rubbed my forehead with the heel of my hand. I needed rest. Holding onto my control for so long had drained me. "Malcolm shouldn't need to recover. After I read or spike someone, they might be tired, but they wake up." Unless they're dead.

I didn't think mentioning that was in my best interest.

"Then what's going on?" William gestured to the door. "I have a lot of wolves to keep at bay and 'usually they wake up' isn't going to work for them."

"I don't know what to tell you." I glanced at Lucas. His eyes were back to human, but only barely.

William exhaled loudly. "If Alpha Malcolm doesn't regain consciousness soon, you'll have to run."

Lucas dug a phone out of his pocket and began tapping on the screen. He must be desperate for communication, because he'd made it clear to anyone who would listen that he despised cell phones and that texting him was a good way to get bit. Him carrying one now was probably Chandra's idea. I couldn't imagine anyone else who could convince him to do something he hated so much.

"Christ, who would think a stupid memory could cause so much trouble?" Lucas muttered.

William frowned. "And why this particular memory?"

"I don't know." I bent over Malcolm and pressed two fingers against his throat. His pulse was bouncing around like a frog in a burlap sack, yet outwardly he appeared serene.

"Who could do something like this?" William asked.

"Warlock, witch, spiker, maybe a strong telepath? I don't know. I've never heard of it," Lucas said.

Gently, I prodded around the edges of Malcolm's mind, revving again, using a little of that alpha energy that was still coursing through my veins. Now that I knew where to look for the loop, I didn't have to go in far, and if I followed the same path and throttled back on my approach and retreat, he wouldn't feel any pain, wouldn't even know I was there.

That was the idea anyway.

Malcolm expelled a hissing breath as I entered his mind.

I really needed to work on that throttle.

"Neely, what the devil are you doing? There are thirteen wolves out there ready to tear you apart, you fool." William's sharp whisper cut into the air between us like knife slashes.

Lucas stepped in front of me. "Watch how you talk to her. She's your only hope of getting your alpha back."

"Seems she's the reason he's gone in the first place."

"She didn't plant that memory in Malcolm's head. It was here when we arrived. Besides, Neely wouldn't do anything to prolong her time here. She hates alpha leaders and does everything in her power to stay far away from them."

Plant that memory in Malcolm's head. An idea began to form in my mind.

"Except for you?" William asked.

Lucas's voice slid into the deep, low tones of arrogance and conceit, where it was most comfortable. "That's right. Except for me."

"Shh, you guys." I sat down on the sofa again, shut my eyes to better concentrate on Malcolm. "I want to try something."

Part of me wanted to just wrench the stupid thing out of Malcolm's head. But what if I did something wrong? What if forcing it out meant killing him? And me, by way of a thousand wolves?

So brute force was out. Finesse. I needed to employ finesse.

Plant a memory. I should be able to do it. If I was capable of reaching into a person's head for a memory and causing them to relive it, as I had with my mother, then I should be able to move a memory. If I couldn't remove Malcolm's mind loop, what if I looped a good memory and superimposed it over the bad one? That might take the edge off and slow the insanity-inducing power of the thing.

In theory.

I had to try something.

Within seconds, I'd stumbled across a memory from the day Malcolm took over the San Diego wolf pack. There had been weeks of violence and bloodshed, but it was still the best time of his life. Alphas had strange interpretations of happiness.

When I was done, I eased out of his head. There was no hiss of pain this time. His pulse had calmed, and a placid smile curved his lips.

William peered down at Malcolm. "He looks different. What did you do?"

"I took a good memory, looped it, and sort of set it on top of the other one. It didn't get rid of the other mind loop, but I'm hoping it will lessen the negative impact of it."

"You can do that? Move people's memories around?" William asked. "How?"

"I can't explain it. It's instinct." I scooted off the sofa and tumbled into my chair.

"Huh. It does appear to have calmed him," Lucas said.

"Yes, but why isn't he awake?" William's gaze flickered toward the door, reminding me about the wolves waiting behind it.

If they wanted my throat, they'd get it. I couldn't spike thirteen wolves at once.

Could I?

THE WOLVES MOVED Malcolm to his suite on the top floor. It was an uneasy trip, as the wolf carrying Malcolm was in hybrid form, covered in fur with sharpened teeth that protruded between his closed lips. The entire way up the stairs, he shot me menacing looks every time I peered over my shoulder at him. Eight of the other wolves had dispersed, leaving six to guard the hallway and room, including William Scott.

This set of rooms looked lived in. There was artwork and knick-knacks and framed snapshots. A comfortable sofa and two overstuffed chairs. The bedroom was elegant but relaxed, the California King bed in the center of the room was covered in a fluffy white duvet so sumptuous that Malcolm had practically melted into it when the wolf laid him down.

The hybrid wolf left soon after. Remaining in the room with Malcolm and me were William, Lucas, and Dr. Rin Penbright.

"He's still in there." The petite doctor perched on the edge of the bed and shone a light in Malcolm's pried-open eye. Her forehead was lined, and her mouth was a tight little slash in her face. "His vitals are all good. In fact, he seems very much at ease."

"I gave him a good memory to help mitigate the bad one."

"You say a memory is *haunting* him?" She pressed a stethoscope to his chest.

She didn't believe me. I didn't read her; it was the way she said "haunting" that tipped me off, though she seemed to be attempting to sound impartial.

I glanced at William, who was seated tensely on a sofa across the room, then at Lucas, who was in a more relaxed position beside him. I was standing against the wall by the bed to give the doctor room to examine Malcolm.

"Doctor, I know it sounds hard to believe—"

"It sounds like some sort of mystical dream garbage." She jerked the stethoscope from around her neck and stuffed it into a white canvas bag with a leather bottom.

"Fair enough." It wasn't like I hadn't had the same thought. "But it's what the alpha told me he believed and when I looked into his head, it was true. You're a physician, so you're familiar with the power of the placebo effect."

She nodded.

"Then we can agree that it is at least possible that Alpha Malcolm has convinced himself that his late wife is haunting him. Perhaps so much so that his brain is creating a scenario that makes it real."

"Placebo effect. An alpha leader of Xavier Malcolm's caliber." She blinked slowly. "It would be highly unlikely."

"Unlikely, yes. But still a possibility," Lucas said.

"Anything is a possibility at this point." Dr. Penbright stood, straightened the line of her white coat. "But it's far more likely you damaged his brain when you spiked him, isn't it?"

"I didn't spike him," I said. "Not the way you're thinking."

Lucas sat up straighter. "She didn't hurt Malcolm, Rin."

"However, I agree with you." I tipped my head to Dr. Penbright. "It is the more likely scenario. You have only my word that I did not harm him, and what's my word worth to someone who hardly knows me?"

"You also have a strong motive," she said to Lucas.

His eyes flashed gold. Dr. Penbright held her ground, but her lips tightened even more.

I leaned my head against the wall. I was tired enough to sleep in that position if need be. What I'd done had worn me out and I really, really wanted to go home.

"You're right about that, too." I yawned. "The thing is, Lucas didn't blame it all on me, which would make sense if he were behind the attack. He has a perfect scapegoat in me and he's still coming to my defense. What's more, neither of us have tried to leave. In fact, we've been doing everything we can to keep Alpha Malcolm comfortable." I shrugged. "It could be an act. I mean, you aren't wrong that it looks that way. All I can do is tell you that it's not, and ask for your help."

The doctor stared at me for a long second, as if assessing my integrity. I tried not to look as offended as I was.

Finally, she said, "I can call in a healer. See if they can do anything."

"You know he hates magic. All kinds," William said.

Plus, it won't work. Already tried it, Lucas thought to me.

"Well then, if it is the placebo effect, there's little I can do to help him. If he doesn't wake soon, we'll have to start an IV, a catheter, set him up on a monitor to keep track of his respiration. I should be doing that now."

"It might be better that he rests undisturbed," William said.

"Figured you would say that." The doctor dropped her penlight into the heavy canvas bag. "I can drug him, but I don't want to. One, he'll be furious when he wakes, and two, it's dangerous. It takes a tremendous amount of narcotic to subdue a shifter, and even more to knock out an alpha. Keeping a shifter drugged for hours would be detrimental to his nervous system. I don't recommend it."

I frowned. "Lucas said you put other shifters into medically-induced comas."

"*Magically*-induced, not medically. And we know how Alpha Malcolm feels about that." She zipped up her bag and slung it over her forearm. "He doesn't need to be put in a coma anyway, he appears to already be in one. He needs for you to figure out how to wake him up, spiker." Without a look at either Lucas or me, she headed for the door. "I'll check in tomorrow morning. If nothing has changed, he'll need fluids."

"I'll see you out, Doctor," William said.

When they were gone, I moved from the wall to the sofa where Lucas was, and asked the question that had been nagging at me since I watched Malcolm's dream unfold.

"Who was Suyin involved with while she was married to Malcolm?"

Lucas didn't seem shocked by the implication. "They had an open relationship. They both saw other people."

"Who did she date?"

"I can't say for sure that she dated them, but there were a couple of guys in the pack that were seen leaving her place now and again." He shrugged. "It wasn't a big deal."

"That's the thing. It is a big deal to someone." I described the dream in detail, leaving out nothing.

"That's odd. How would Malcolm even know her lover was there? The way you describe it, he wasn't in the room," Lucas said when I'd finished. "Unless he was faking being in the shower?"

"I can't be sure about that, but I can tell you that I was seeing the dream from Suyin's lover's perspective, not Malcolm's."

"We need to find out who the other person in Malcolm's dream was," Lucas said.

"Could it have been William?"

"Why?" Lucas sat up. "Did it sound like him?"

"It sounded garbled. Male, but garbled."

"Oh." Lucas leaned back against the sofa, stared up at the ceiling as if the answers he needed were written there. "It would be out of character. William is loyal to Malcolm."

"Love can make you do dumb things." My thoughts went to Julio and my own stupid mistake. I wondered if I'd ever get over the feeling of being duped when I remembered him.

Lucas dug his phone out of his pocket. "I'll make some inquiries.

I've still got a few contacts in the pack and around town, other shifter groups."

"Why would other groups be interested in Malcolm and Suyin's marriage?"

"An Alpha's mate cheating is the sort of thing that can destabilize a pack. The ensuing violence puts every paranormal in the city at risk of exposure."

"I thought they had an open marriage."

"They did, but not everyone knew it. Trust me on this, the shifters and other paranormals in San Diego keep close tabs on each other. Someone will know something."

CHAPTER FIFTEEN

"Don't get me wrong, I love the beach, but it's six a.m. and cold, and I haven't had any coffee, and what are we doing here?"

"Geez, you and Malcolm's coffee. Get a room."

"I would like to, but you dragged me out here. Also, you didn't answer me. What are we doing?"

"Waiting."

Lucas was playing the enigmatic card this morning. We'd spent most of the night in Malcolm's room, drinking his excellent coffee—the single bright spot of the evening—and standing watch over the wolf alpha while two of Malcolm's wolves stood watch over Lucas and me.

It had not been the most relaxing of evenings.

After a very short sleep, he'd shaken me awake half an hour ago with my pink and white polka dot bikini clutched in his fist and a request-order to follow him down to the beach across from the B&B. I'd added flip-flops and a cover-up to my ensemble since it was chilly this close to the water. I didn't bother with my hair, which had managed to simultaneously frizz and be flat at the same time, due to the dampness in the air. Lucas wore a pair of navy-blue board shorts, nothing else. He hadn't combed his hair or shaved, which made him look all-night-sex-party sleepy, while I looked alert-the-authorities-we're-out-of-coffee exhausted.

"I know that." I stretched my arms above my head and yawned. "What are we waiting for?"

"Not what. Whom." He pointed to a disturbance in the water a short distance away. "Him."

Lucas gripped my hand as we splashed through the surf. I shaded my eyes with my other hand as we waded deeper, only stopping when the water was up to my breasts and my teeth were chattering. "Is that a f-fin? That had better be F-Flipper." I tried to pull free to make a break for the shore. "Let g-go of me."

A god of a man erupted from the ocean in a shower of saltwater, flipped over our heads, and landed on webbed feet in the shallows behind us. He appeared to be around Lucas's age, brown-skinned and scruff-bearded, and built like he did hard labor for a living. His eyes were sea green rimmed with gold, and they sparkled with humor. If I had to guess at his heritage, I'd lean toward Latin American with Southern European ancestry—Italian, possibly Greek. He was entirely nude, his skin covered with thousands of silvery, tooth-like scales.

"Blacke." The man flipped his hair over his muscled shoulders. It ran in sun-bleached brown waves down his back—a look I'd seen people on TV shows try to copy with expensive salt spray product and scrunching.

"Mar," Lucas replied.

"What *are* you?" I asked.

Laughing, he hummed a few bars of the theme from the movie *Jaws*.

Oh God, he was a shark. Which was actually pretty obvious when you considered the giant freaking fin sticking out of his back and the three rows of very sharp teeth that I could clearly see.

"What kind?" I asked. "Not a Great White, right? Tell me you aren't a Great White."

Again, the man laughed.

I kind of wanted to be in on the joke, but I also didn't. I lifted both hands in a stop gesture. "Nope. Nope, nope, going to nope right on out of here, thankyouverymuch."

"Neely, trust me. It's okay." Lucas wrapped an arm around my waist to stop me.

"Trust you." I turned to the shark shifter, now on my left, who was suddenly a lot more man than shark, and still naked. "Do you know how often he says that and actually means it?"

He squinted down at me. "Blacke? I'd say a good forty, maybe fifty, percent of the time."

"You give him far too much credit. See you on the beach. You know, if that's something your kind do." I spun out of Lucas's grip and began trudging through the water toward the shore. I was freezing, my cover up was tangled around my legs making it hard to move, and *I hadn't had any coffee.*

Lucas called after me. "Neely, stop."

The shark shifter rolled in the surf now, swimming circles around me in the waist deep water. When he broke the surface again, his eyes had gone completely gold. The early morning sunlight glinted off the irises, giving them an unearthly glow. Panicked, I began to pull power.

"I'm Joaquin Mar. Nice to meet you." The sea god stuck out a wet hand. "Are you always this scared?"

Lucas's words ran through my mind. "*You were scared. Seems like that's the only time you use your ability. When you're scared, when you're hurt...* "

"I'm fine." Lucas was right. I hadn't thought of myself as fearful per se, but I was often scared about something, and it usually involved a shapeshifter alpha.

"Don't worry, I'm a nice guy."

I shook his hand. Mine was trembling. His was surprisingly warm. "Are you an alpha leader?"

"No. That's my older brother." He winked and offered me a sultry sideways grin. "I am an alpha, though."

Not an alpha *leader.* That was good.

"Do the sexy smile, the six pack abs, and the golden tan usually convince people that you're harmless?" I asked.

Lucas rolled his eyes. "Quit flirting, Neely."

"Ah, don't be too jealous, Blacke. The ladies just love my denticles."

Joaquin rubbed his palm over his sun-browned skin, raking up the tiny toothlike scales.

"Please. They're nowhere near as soft as fur."

It was clear the men were friends, but there was a cautious quality to their banter, as if they were sizing each other up while they teased.

"So, tiger, what brings you to my part of the ocean?" Joaquin asked. "Malcolm starting shit again?"

"Always. This time he involved my girl here."

My girl? Uh, no.

Lucas rolled his shoulders back. His thoughts flowed into my head. *I know what you're thinking. But trust me, it's best if they think you're not too sharp.*

My eyes narrowed and I opened my mouth to snap at him.

Go along with it and I will buy you a dozen bottles of that vanilla bubble bath you like, a hundred of those face masks, a case of that expensive coffee you've been guzzling down, and you can have the rest of the pillow chocolates.

I pitched my voice a little higher. "That's right, Alpha Malcolm involved me."

Yes. I can be bought, and my price is bubble bath, face masks, hotel pillow chocolates, and South American small batch artisan farm-to-cup coffee.

"Not cool." Joaquín made a hand motion in front of him, sort of like he was treading water, but different. "But it isn't like you haven't dealt with Malcolm's BS before. Why are you here?"

"I need information."

Joaquín's left brow shot up. "From the Mar shifters? What kind?"

"There's a rumor out there that Suyin Chen was cheating on Malcolm."

"What difference does it make now? She's dead."

Lucas stared hard at the other shifter. "It would have been valuable knowledge seven years ago."

"Gossip. I don't worry about that sort of thing." Joaquín stared hard right back at Lucas.

"Tauro does. And I know you just called to him, so don't act like you're alone."

I need you here when I talk to Tauro Mar. He's nearly as bad as Malcolm when it comes to sinister machinations, which means you'll have to read him.

"My older brother," Joaquín explained to me. "He's on his way. Dealing with a school issue at the moment."

"Your brother is in school?" Odd. Joaquín had to be at least thirty. Perhaps his brother was working on a post-graduate degree or had returned to school after a long hiatus.

"Not the kind of school you're thinking," Lucas said. "What's going on?"

"Dolphin pod being dicks again." Joaquín rolled his head around on his neck. "He won't let me beat any of their asses, says we have to use diplomacy."

Another very good-looking Latin-Euro male popped up in the water beside me and I nearly jumped out of my skin.

"Thanks for coming," Lucas said.

"Sorry, I'm late." He spoke to Lucas, but he was looking at me. "Hello there."

"Hi." My stomach dropped. I do not do well in the presence of powerful alpha leaders, and this man was very strong. Also, I was in the ocean, unable to make a fast getaway. I pulled a little energy from Lucas, just in case.

I felt that. He spoke to me inside my head again. *Do not spike. Calm down.*

"I could use some information, Mar."

"Happy to help anyone who hates Xavier Malcolm as much as I do. Who's this you've brought with you?" Tauro floated in the water, rode a gentle wave to a point a few feet away from us and then swam back.

"This is my girl, Neely."

"Nice to meet you, Neely. I'm Tauro Mar, alpha leader of the Pacific sea-shifters."

"Nice to meet you," I managed.

Joaquín spoke up. "Blacke wants to know if we heard any rumors about Suyin Chen cheating on Malcolm."

Lucas pushed two words at me. *Read them.*

Tauro's gaze narrowed. "What difference does it make? She's dead." *Of course, we know she cheated. What's his game?*

133

"There's talk." Lucas sidled up to me and played with the wet ends of my hair. It was drawn up almost to my shoulders in small, tight curls. Saltwater did that to it. "I'd like to lay some rumors to rest. Or not. The truth would be nice." *Does he know anything?*

"Yes," I said, answering Lucas's question, but directing my comment to Tauro Mar. "The truth would be helpful."

Don't tell him Malcolm is in a coma.

I'd already figured out that telling another alpha that Malcolm was out of commission would be a death sentence for the wolf alpha. I'd had enough experience with shifters to know that much. Then again, Tauro Mar killing Xavier Malcolm would definitely solve some of my problems.

Don't. It'll cause more problems than it will solve. Trust me and follow my lead.

"Helpful. Right. What's really going on?" the shark alpha leader asked. "The truth for the truth, Blacke."

"Mar, you wouldn't believe me if I told you."

We all jumped as a larger wave scrolled past, riding it closer to shore. I was glad for it, because my feet now touched bottom, and I had been getting tired of treading water. I took off my sodden cover-up and let it float behind me.

"Try me." Tauro ducked under the water, then shot up, spraying all of us with water.

The ocean created peaceful music as it rolled and flowed and lapped at us. People paid good money for sounds like this to help them sleep at night. Personally, I'd rather have the crackle of a campfire in the desert and the crunch of the wind blowing palm fronds any day of the week. I wished I was lying in the sand gazing up at a clear desert sky right now.

"Malcolm is being haunted by his late wife."

"What the hell, Blacke?" This from Joaquín, who was batting something away from him in the water. Seaweed. I was going with seaweed. "He thinks she's a ghost?"

Tauro ignored his brother and stared at me. "Some kind of curse? Spell?"

134

"Either one, or something else," Lucas replied. "We think it was an ex-lover, someone who hated Malcolm and loved Suyin."

Tauro Mar eyed Lucas like he wanted to say something but didn't. Instead he spoke to me. "Are you a witch?"

Tell them you're a telepath.

"No," I said. "I'm a ... telepath."

Both Mar men eyed me for a long minute. Then they did the same to Lucas.

Joaquín spoke first. "Wasn't Suyin Chen a telepath?"

"She was a spiker. That's different, isn't it?" Tauro brought his entire focus back to me.

Despite the chilly water, sweat trickled down my spine and my breathing quickened.

"Yes, it is. Anyway, Neely's not like Suyin was. She's ... softer."

Okay, I was getting tired of playing the part of the brainless little woman, even if it was only to serve some Lucas-hidden purpose with the Mar brothers.

"That's unfortunate," Joaquín said. "Alpha Chen was ruthless and mercenary. I liked that about her."

"I'm sure knowing that she had your approval for her lifestyle choices helped her sleep better at night," I muttered.

Tauro burst out laughing.

"*Soft* my ass, Blacke." Joaquín cocked a brow at me, smiled.

Lucas glared at me. *Nice job taking the bait. Didn't I ask you to follow my lead?*

I scowled at all three men and then rode another wave that took me into shallower water. The males followed.

"Malcolm and Suyin had an open marriage. We didn't keep track of the men in her life because it wasn't something we could use as leverage against Malcolm. I don't use information just to be an asshole. There has to be a reason behind it."

"You knew about their marriage?" Lucas asked.

"Everyone knew. It wasn't a secret."

"Can you tell us anything that might be helpful?"

"I know the three people who visited her most often. That was information I thought might prove to be valuable. In the end, it didn't, but it was a calculated risk and didn't cost me much."

Cost him much? I glanced at Lucas.

He purchased the information. That's good news. "You have a name for me?"

"I have a name." Tauro looked straight at me. "But I want something in return for it."

CHAPTER SIXTEEN

"A FAVOR FROM THE TELEPATH. AND FOR WHAT? WHAT INFORMATION did he give us? A lousy name. Why didn't you let me pluck it out of his brain? You're always going on about how I need to read everyone all the time."

Lucas watched me pace Malcolm's bedroom from his position by one of the windows overlooking the ocean. I was still in my damp bikini and cover up, and he was in his swim trunks and a white cotton T-shirt he took from Malcolm's dresser.

"Because he would have known you did it, and I deal fair with Tauro. Also, it's not just a name. It's the name of the trader who gave him the information. That trader will know much more than they told the sea shifters, and all it will take is some cold hard cash to get the information—*if* I can locate the person. You know how traders are."

"No, I don't. What's a trader?"

"How do you not know—never mind." He uncapped a bottle of water, tipped it into his mouth. When half of it was gone, he spoke again. "A trader is an information broker. Think gossip columnist meets private detective. Traders are usually, but not always, paranormals. They pride themselves on knowing all there is to know about our world. They work for information or money, and they aren't cheap or widely accessible. Traders tend to keep to the shadows for their own protection."

"Oh good. More creepy, dangerous stuff. I don't like this, Blacke, and I don't appreciate you using my ability to leverage a favor from that alpha leader."

"I had no choice. Besides, I got Mar to agree that the favor must be vetted by Chandra first. She'll keep you safe."

"Why can't it be vetted by you?" I paced past him and back to the bedroom door.

"He'd never have gone for that."

"Why not?"

"Because he thinks I won't be able to be objective."

"That's ridiculous." I turned on my heel and stomped back toward him.

"No, it's not. He's right." Lucas capped the water bottle and tossed it on the nearest chair. He reached for me as I paced past, and swung me around to face him. "Stop this."

"Damn it, I don't want to do favors for another alpha leader. That's what got me into this mess in the first place."

"I know." There was a tug on my hair, and I knew he'd twisted a lock of it around his finger again. He did it to soothe himself. I knew this because I'd read it in his thoughts the last time I was furious at him.

"I keep getting into trouble with you."

"Ditto," he said.

His sarcasm was starting to piss me off. "Why is it you make me want to hug you one second and pop you in the mouth the next?"

"I tend to have that effect on people," he replied. "Something we have in common."

"Only with you. Everyone else likes me." I rolled my shoulders, looked away. "If you don't count Dan Winters. And half the population of Sundance. Also, the shifters in Las Vegas, parts of Texas, and New Mexico..."

"But everyone else likes you, right?"

I waited for my hair to unravel from around his finger, then walked a brisk path across the room to another of Malcolm's windows. It also faced the Pacific, which was belying its name at the moment, sending roiling gray water slamming against the beach in foaming, dull-white waves. A storm had blown in over the last hour, and the shoreline was now littered with yellow-brown piles of kelp.

"Why do you keep walking away from me?" His words, and the low sultry way he spoke them, stroked into my ear.

"Why do *you* keep following me?"

"You want me to follow you."

"Arrogant son of a—" I spun around. He was so close my hip grazed the muscles of his thigh. Just that brush sent my heart racing— every pulse point in my body throbbed against my skin.

"It's true." He ducked his head, brushing his lips along the line of my jaw to my ear. "You like it when I'm pushy, you like it when I don't ask permission, and you like it when I run to you, because that means you can act on your attraction to me without feeling guilty."

"*Stupid.*"

One side of his handsome mouth crooked into a smile. "Name calling? Sugar cookie, I thought we were past that."

"That's not what I meant." I stepped away from him to catch my breath, shivered when my back pressed against the cold glass of the window. "I'm saying I don't feel guilty when I act on my attraction to you. I feel *stupid.*"

His smile faded. "What? Why?"

"Because you're an alpha leader and I know what you're capable of ... and I still ... I still *like you.*"

Lucas leaned in, those long-lashed amber eyes holding me captive, and brushed his lips over mine. It was the lightest of strokes, and it awakened every nerve ending I possessed. I shuddered and tried to hide it, but he saw me.

He *always* saw me.

"You have no idea what I'm capable of, Cornelia Costa MacLeod." He slid a hand beneath my hair and gripped the base of my head, holding tight. It walked the line between delicious pain and just plain hurt, but didn't cross it. And it wouldn't. Lucas might toe that pain line, but he'd never hurt me.

Not like that, anyway.

He used the hand on the back of my head to bring me closer as he deepened the kiss. His other hand parted the lapels of my damp cover up and he raked his knuckles over my bare belly in soft swipes that made my joints turn to liquid.

I pressed my palms to his chest. The idea was to push him away, but I stroked my hands up to his shoulders instead. "Lucas, this is impossible."

"What we do together has nothing to do with me being an alpha leader and you being a spiker. I'm not playing games with you. Read me and see."

I stroked my fingers over his cheekbones, his jaw, his lips. "You always play games. It's who you are."

"No, you mean it's *what* I am. An alpha leader." He drew his knuckles over my hipbone and played with the string securing my bikini bottoms. "And you're a spiker. You terrify people every bit as much as I do—maybe more."

"I'm no threat to you."

"How do I know that? It's not as if *I can read your mind.*"

I pushed at his shoulders, not moving him an inch. "I don't read yours. Much. A little. Not about this, though. Other things, I... Oh damn, that sounded bad."

"Well then..." He tugged at the string, making me very glad I'd knotted it before tying a bow. "I guess we're going to have to learn to trust each other the old-fashioned way. Honest communication and great sex."

That sounded pretty good to me, but I wasn't telling him that. "Malcolm is lying in a bed ten feet from us. If he doesn't wake up soon, we're going to be torn apart by about a thousand wolves. We can work on the communication, but I think we should back-burner any talk about sex between us."

"You have terrible ideas." He kissed me until I thought he made a pretty good point.

"*Su ... pl-ease.*"

"Lucas, Malcolm."

"It's fine. He won't mind. Look, he's sleeping."

"He's saying something. Listen." I pushed him away, and this time he went.

A thready sound, weak and watery, dribbled from Malcolm's lips. *"Su, no. Su, please..."*

"Is he calling for his late wife?"

We were on our way to his bedside when the suite door swung open and a young man in a lab coat scuttled into the room. The white coat was too long and too tight around the biceps. He looked like a kid playing doctor dress-up.

"Sounds like the alpha is in pain. I was down the hall when I heard his cries."

"You could hear him from the hall?" Lucas asked. "He barely made a sound."

"I'm trained to listen for signs of distress, sir."

Lucas stood up taller, planted his feet apart. "Who the hell are you and how'd you get here so fast, eagle ears?"

"I work for Dr. Penbright," the man replied icily. "I'm her assistant. She sent me here to give the alpha an injection for pain if he needed it, and he obviously does." He held up a syringe.

"Hang on." Suspicion bled into my voice. "Why would she expect him to be in pain? She didn't mention it to us earlier."

"She, uh, planned for the possibility." The man edged closer to the bed. *Just jab him and get it over with.*

"He's lying." I raced to the bed, but I'd never make it in time.

The man lunged for Malcolm.

"Kind of figured that out already." With practiced ease, Lucas vaulted over the bed, grabbed the man's arm and twisted it behind his back. He jabbed the syringe into the assailant's left butt cheek and pushed the plunger.

"Get it ... ooooout." The man began to wind down like a robot with a dying battery. "Please ... *pleasssse...*" *I'm dead. Dead for a lousy five grand...*

Lucas calmly yanked the syringe out of the man's backside, but it was already too late.

I was breathing like I'd just run a race. "That was close."

"Meh. Not really."

141

"What the heck? He nearly killed Malc—*damn it*, Lucas, get that syringe away from your nose. Here—" I grabbed a glass dish off Malcolm's dresser, dumped the contents into a drawer, and then handed it to him. "—put it in here before you give me a heart attack."

"Worried about me?" He grinned as he put the syringe in the dish.

"Yes, you dork." We both stared down at the dead man and tried to ignore the fact that he'd soiled himself. *I* did, anyway.

"At least he had a hearty last meal. Let's move. We're downwind from this guy." Lucas pulled me to the other side of the room. "Did you read him? Get anything useful?"

"He's a wolf shifter. *Was*, anyway. Someone paid him five thousand dollars to kill Malcolm."

"Sheez, that's cheap. Chandra charges twenty times that." He side-eyed me. "*Used to* charge that. And only for very, very bad people. Anything else?"

"No. Death was swift, as you witnessed. He didn't have time for lengthy inner monologues. Why did you stab him with the syringe?"

"So he wouldn't stick me with it."

"It would have been nice to interrogate the guy," I said through gritted teeth.

"Oh yeah. Sorry about that." He didn't sound sorry in the least.

The door flew open for the second time in ten minutes and William and Willa Scott tumbled into the room. "We heard screaming," Willa said.

I pointed at the body. "Someone tried to assassinate your alpha."

William ran to Malcolm, pressed his fingers to the alpha's neck. "Still breathing."

"Neely sensed the guy was up to something," Lucas said, "so I killed him before he could kill Malcolm. I'll file an invoice with accounting. You should know I charge a lot more for this sort of thing now that I'm an alpha leader."

I smacked him in the gut with the back of my hand. It was like slugging stone, and he didn't even flinch.

"Someone tried to assassinate Alpha?" Willa looked at her brother. "Why didn't anyone stop him before he made it this far?"

"Because the wolves guarding him either weren't paying attention or they're in on it," Lucas drawled.

All the breath whooshed out of Willa. "Oh God. This is worse than I thought."

"I'll call a security team meeting," William said.

"A *meeting*?" Lucas groaned. "Kill me now."

CHAPTER SEVENTEEN

"This should be a real shit show."

Lucas and I took our seats around Malcolm's enormous dining table. The other chairs were filled with wolf shifters, and most of them were scowling in Lucas's and my direction.

William cleared his throat. "I've asked you all to be here today because there was an attempt on our alpha's life this morning. As everyone in this room knows, Malcolm has slipped into a coma."

"Because of *her*." One of the wolves pointed a finger at me. I recognized him as the older wolf from dinner with Malcolm that first night, though the last time I saw him, he had a steak knife protruding from his arm. "*She's* the one who tried to kill him. Her ilk should be drowned at birth the way they did in the old days."

"Jesus, Richard." William dragged a hand over his face.

"Drowned at *birth*? That makes no sense." I scowled at the older wolf. "Spiker abilities don't manifest until childhood, usually later. Did your kind just go around drowning random babies?"

"They'd slit the throats of older ones," he snarled.

"Try it, wolf," I said.

Lucas locked gazes with the other shifter and shook his head. "I wouldn't."

"Everyone, please calm down." According to Lucas, William was filling in for Malcolm this evening. "While Alpha Malcolm did go *under* after Neely spiked him, it was his choice to be spiked and we must respect that."

"Yeah, take a seat, Dick." Lucas picked up the drink in front of him, peered into the glass with one eye shut, and then pushed it away. "Let the grownups talk."

"You aren't any better, Blacke." Simone, the wolf alpha who'd challenged me outside the medical clinic, strolled into the room and took a seat at the table. Her throat was healed, and she didn't appear to have any other lasting injuries from her run-in with Lucas's claws. "Maybe you're an alpha leader now, but I remember when you were nothing more than Malcolm's bitch. At his beck and call, doing all his dirty work."

Lucas flinched. On the inside, where only I could see it because he was projecting to me again.

"As I recall, you invited me into your bed several times, Simone. If I was nothing more than a bitch, why did you want me?"

"You're a pretty plaything." She looked him up and down, then laughed.

Another internal flinch. Simone's words bothered him on a subterranean level in his brain. His emotions toward her words were so strong they came at me like a blast of heat from a 450-degree bakery oven. I felt his revulsion at her words and tone.

I felt his *shame*.

"Do you really think I'm pretty?" He batted his eyes.

"Alpha Malcolm's dirty, pretty boy," Simone purred. "Does whatever or whoever he has to in order to get the job done."

On Lucas's third internal flinch, I lost it.

"You *shut up*." Fury built up in me until it was at a power level akin to what I used for spiking. "Or I'll finish the job I started when you attacked me in the street."

"As if you could."

"Are you absolutely sure I couldn't?" I put all the ugliness and rage I felt toward her into my smile. "Want to take that risk?"

She growled and her face began to elongate, sharp canine teeth pushing over her lips.

Lucas side-eyed me. *Stop it. What the hell are you doing?*

"Not taking her shit," I muttered, certain she and every other wolf at the table could hear me.

I'd had enough of listening to this wolf badmouth Lucas, and enough of the wolves who sat back and said nothing.

"Some of you have done much worse things," I said.

"Are you reading us, telepath?" Dick's face was flooded with color, so red it was nearly purple.

"Yes. So, think good thoughts." I smiled.

"*Bitch*," Simone said.

"Enough, Simone." William stood and placed both fists on the table. "If you shift, you are out of here. For good."

"Yes, Second." Simone retracted her wolf, threw herself back in her seat, and scowled at Lucas. "We all know what you are. You've killed."

"Do you mean today or when I was on his security team? You do know what a security team does, don't you?" Lucas drawled.

"Of course I do," she snarled.

"Then you realize that half the people in this room have done the same." Lucas turned away from Simone, addressed William. "I want it noted in the official meeting minutes that I killed to *protect* Alpha Malcolm, not harm him."

William sighed. "There aren't any minutes, Lucas. This is an informal meeting."

"Informal? I was told there would be cake. This is bullshit."

The more uncomfortable Lucas was, the more sarcastic he got. If his comments so far were any indication, I'd say he was dialed up to about a nine-point-five on the shifter discomfort scale.

"Ridiculous. You didn't kill for the alpha. You killed because you were born evil." A white-haired woman at the end of the table jabbed a gnarled finger at Lucas. If she was a wolf, she was a different sort from the rest. Droop-eyed and slightly hunched, the way she occupied the space around her made me think of an aging queen trying desperately to hold on to her throne. There was immense paranormal power in the woman, and she pulled it tight to her like a cold, dark cloak.

"Christ. Not this again, Agnes."

"Be nice, Lucas," I whispered. "She's got to be ninety years old."

That's an act. Agnes Romano couldn't be a day over seventy-five, and a shifter, so that's like forty-five in human years. Don't get sentimental and drop your guard, Neely. She's Malcolm's aunt and she reacts to tenderness the way a Mar brother reacts to a pool of injured fish.

His aunt? I nudged my chair closer to Lucas, farther from Agnes.

Malcolm's aunt continued, "It's in his blood, his family history. Demons and murderers, the lot."

"Not cool." Lucas jabbed his finger back at her. "If you're angry with my grandmother, take it up with her. Don't involve me in your vendetta."

Agnes's eyes glimmered gold. "Luciana Blacke is a godless woman."

"You're preaching to the choir, Agnes." Lucas sat forward in his chair, looked up and down the length of the table. "I'd love to hash this out with you, but time and place. We're here tonight to ferret out which one of you is trying to kill Malcolm, not to discuss my dysfunctional family."

"Exactly who here do you believe is trying to kill our alpha?" Agnes steepled her fingers, pressed them against her mouth.

"You, Dick, pretty much everyone, really."

"Soulless, demon, murderer," Agnes spat. "I'm his family."

"You act as if that's enough to stop you from killing him, when we both know it isn't." Lucas looked bored. "You were a Malcolm before you were a Romano. You're capable."

Her mouth twisted into a sneer. "You nasty *little*—"

"Kill our alpha? Ridiculous," Richard sputtered. "We're his pack leadership. We wouldn't—"

"Save it for someone who doesn't know you, Dick." Lucas leaned back in his seat and picked at his fingernails. "Still waiting on that cake, by the way." He voiced this in the general direction of the kitchen.

"There's no one in there, for God's sake." William frowned at Lucas. "Tell me why you suspect pack leadership is responsible for the hit on Malcolm earlier."

"Because it's a viper pit. Always has been. More than half of what I did in the old days was keep an eye on all of you under orders from your alpha."

147

Generalized grumbling ensued.

"Did the spiker read the assassin?" The wolf who said this had short hair dyed raspberry-red, wore black horn-rimmed glasses, and spoke with a slight southern accent.

"The spiker has a name. It's Neely." I looked at her expectantly.

"I'm Kim."

"Nice to meet you, Kim. To answer your question, the drug worked too fast for me to glean much. He was paid five thousand dollars for the hit. That's all I got."

"Five thousand isn't much." Kim pushed her glasses higher on her nose. "The killer either needed the money, owed the person who hired him a favor, or was being blackmailed in some way. Or it was personal."

"Finally, an intelligent comment." William paced behind Lucas and me. "Did you get the feeling it was personal, Neely?"

I shook my head. "I got the feeling it was for money."

"I think the spiker knows something she isn't telling us." Richard glared in my direction. "She should be considered a suspect."

"You could rule me out very quickly by taking a look at my bank account," I said. "I don't have five grand lying around."

"Your uncle was recently murdered. Surely he had an insurance policy—"

"Tread carefully, wolf." Lucas growled.

Dick's face infused with blood until even the tips of his ears were beet red. "Are you *threatening me?*"

"Yes," Lucas replied. "I was pretty clear about it. Pay attention, Dick."

"I will have your heart excised from your chest—"

"Let's do this, wolf." Lucas flung his chair back with his legs as he stood. A low growl rumbled deep in his chest, the barest hint of what the animal inside him was capable of.

Richard's grizzled face bled into his wolf's muzzle so subtly that, if I hadn't been watching, I'd barely have registered the change. He slammed a fist on the table. The surface cracked and two pictures fell off the wall behind me.

A wily smile curved Lucas's beautiful mouth. He remained

148

completely in human form as he retrieved his chair and lowered himself into it, looking every inch his usual arrogant self. The room quieted. I had the feeling something of significance had just occurred, but I wasn't sure what.

As Richard's countenance bled slowly back to human, I said, "I have a bakery and a small house left to me by my uncle, but few liquid assets. And besides all that, why would I want to kill Malcolm? Before he ordered me up here, I'd never met the man."

"So you say."

"I *say*." I was getting tired of defending myself to people I didn't respect or like. "Every time an alpha leader finds out what I am, they do one of two things: run away from me as fast as they can, or try to use me as a weapon. I don't like alpha leaders of any kind, and I do everything I can to stay away from them, Dick."

"My name is *Richard*."

"Alpha Blacke hasn't run from you," Kim said, completely ignoring Richard. "Is he using you as a weapon?"

"Alpha Blacke and I have an understanding." Sort of. What we had was more of a cautious friendship that occasionally crossed into something more. Understanding sounded better.

"I don't get it. If you don't like alphas, why did you come, spiker?" Simone folded her arms over her chest and leaned back in her chair.

"I told you. Alpha Malcolm requested my presence."

"So what?" She sniffed, rolled her head to the side as if trying to loosen her neck muscles.

"When was the last time you refused an alpha leader anything?" I looked at her, and at the other wolves at the table. Their gazes settled on me for a half-second, then skittered away. "What happened when you did?"

She didn't respond, only gave the barest hint of a nod.

Lucas spoke up. "Hey, I want Malcolm to recover. And soon. I have a pet cat and my own group to run, and I'd like to return to them both."

"Group." Richard's face evinced distaste. "Shifters are meant to be separated by breed. Your *group* is an abomination."

"As is your haircut, Dick. But I'm doing my best to live with it."

"Impudent, arrogant—"

"Dick, please." William hid a smile. "Lucas, can we keep to the—"

"It's *Richard*," the older man snarled.

"Of course, it is. My apologies." William didn't look the least bit apologetic. "Does anyone have anything constructive to add?"

"I have a question." Kim sat forward in her seat. "What's the best way to keep Alpha Malcolm safe until we find out how to help him?"

William addressed the group with his reply. "As second alpha and acting leader of the Malcolm pack, I've ordered twenty-four-hour security on our alpha. No one gets in or out of the house without my express permission. In the event I am unreachable, you will contact Willa for permission. Then Richard, if it gets that far.

"An attack on our alpha leader cannot happen again and *will not* on my watch." William's voice did that alpha thing where it gets louder without actually going up in volume.

Surprise, surprise. I hadn't realized he was that powerful an alpha, but I should have once I found out he was Malcolm's second. Malcolm wouldn't appoint a weak wolf to his inner circle. Every shifter in this room was a force to be reckoned with, whether through brains or brawn, and I would be smart to remember that.

"Yes, Second," Kim said politely. The others did the same.

"Good, fantastic, wonderful." Lucas jumped to his feet, clapped his hands together. "Now that we're all on the same page with house security, can someone here please tell me who was having a little 'adult naptime' with Suyin Chen while she was married to Malcolm? I think it might be important."

The room burst into indignant howling and name calling.

William sighed. "Damn it, Lucas."

"*Adult naptime*? Really?"

Lucas laughed. He was back in our room's tub again. He said he did his best thinking there.

"Not very respectful to your friend," I said.

"Are you kidding? I did it *for* her. Suyin loved shocking those

150

pompous, specist old wolves. We used to play a drinking game during pack meetings because neither of us were allowed to speak. It was called 'Apoplectic Dick.' Every time Richard made that huffing sound before he spoke, we did a shot of Patrón. The night Malcolm told the pack he intended to marry Suyin, we got hammered."

I'd known Lucas liked Suyin, but I still wasn't sure how far their relationship had gone.

"Were you in love with her?" I asked as I put toothpaste on my toothbrush and leaned over the sink.

"Suyin was smart, funny, and beautiful. Everyone loved her."

"You didn't answer my question."

He splashed water on the bubbles covering his chest. "No, I didn't." And yet, he had. In a way.

I finished brushing my teeth, set my toothbrush in my cosmetic bag, then rested my hip against the counter and listened to the swishing water echo off the sides of the porcelain tub. "What happened at that meeting tonight? When Richard shifted? Everything got weird for a minute."

"Dick lost control. I didn't." He smiled smugly. "It made him look weak."

"Great. So now he hates you even more."

"I'm not sure that's possible. That wolf has tried to have me killed at least ten times that I know of. Suyin tipped me off on the last one. Good thing, too. Dick got crafty with poison and some very fine scotch."

Suyin again. He'd definitely loved her. I wondered why I felt a little jealous about that. It wasn't as if I was in love with Lucas, and it certainly wasn't as if I didn't have a past myself.

Shaking the odd feeling aside, I knelt by the tub in exactly the way Lucas had when I'd needed him a couple nights ago. "I'm sorry you had to kill your friend."

Creases bracketed his eyes and mouth. "That's why I finally left Malcolm's pack, you know."

"I don't blame you."

"I hate it here among these wolves with their breed prejudices. Everywhere I turn, I'm reminded of how little I was valued by them and how desperately I wanted their approval." His voice was a hissing whisper that reverberated off the tile walls. "These people stripped me down. Made me feel less than human, less than paranormal, less than alive. I was humiliated and beaten, and not only physically. The worst part was, I allowed it."

And that was what tormented him. He felt responsible for his own abuse.

"Until you didn't," I said.

His vulnerability shone in his eyes. "I was weak. My own grandmother never missed an opportunity to tell me so. She thought I was squandering my power. That I should reveal my prehistoric side, challenge Malcolm, take over his pack with Suyin by my side. She hated that I hid behind my mother's animal, the Bengal tiger, which she considered inferior to her own."

"She was wrong about you. Controlling your ability does not make you a weak person. The opposite, in fact."

"Are we talking about me or you?" He picked up a clear bar of soap with bits of lavender and mint suspended inside it. Dunked it into the water.

"Both, I guess. I've certainly lost control. Too many times." I popped a bubble that had formed on his shoulder and he grabbed my hand.

"I shouldn't have said that. It was shitty. I take it back." He squeezed my hand and released me.

"Okay, I'll let you." I reached over and popped a bubble on his chest. "If you want to close your eyes and rest, I'll stay here and make sure you don't drown."

"I'm not sleepy." He scooped up a handful of bubbles and plopped them on my head. "Come in here with me."

I shook the bubbles out of my hair and onto his belly. "No."

"Why not?"

"I don't know."

My reasons for not jumping in the tub with him felt less and less important as he cradled my face with a wet hand and brushed his mouth over mine. Heat pooled in the lower half of my body, reminding me that it had been a long while since anyone but me had spent quality time down there.

I deepened the kiss, and he slid his fingers into my hair, massaging my scalp as he stroked his tongue into my mouth. I accidentally let out a soft little moan. It wasn't something I could help. The man kissed like he'd gone to school for it.

"Get in," he growled.

"This is a bad idea." So of course, it appealed to me in all the most delicious ways.

"Wrong. This is the best idea I've had in months."

"I shouldn't." I said this as I kicked off my shoes.

Lucas's cell phone vibrated, dancing across the vanity counter.

"Don't you dare answer that, Cornelia Costa MacLeod. Don't even look to see who's calling."

But I did the Lot's wife thing and peeked over my shoulder. Being turned into a pillar of salt would have been a step up from the way I felt when I saw who it was.

"I told you not to look." He tugged me back to him, kissed his way down my throat.

"We need to take this call."

"No, we don't."

I broke away and grabbed the cell, held it up.

Lucas glanced at the screen and let out a stream of curses. He snatched the phone from me, tapped the surface and held it up to his ear. "What is it?"

Joaquín Mar's voice floated out of the phone. "I have your trader."

"THIS TRADER HAD BETTER HAVE the greatest information anyone has ever possessed."

We stood under the lifeguard station and stared out at the line dividing ocean from sky, watching for Joaquín. The water smelled clean and sounded like thunder as it hit the beach. There wasn't much wind, but what there was of it was freezing, so I wrapped the sweatshirt I'd grabbed on the way out more tightly around myself.

Lucas looked as tense as I'd ever seen him, even more tense than when we first arrived in San Diego to meet with Malcolm.

I was feeling a little tense myself. Now that I'd had the phone call equivalent of a cold shower, I was doubting the wisdom of my decision to kiss Lucas. Again. Doubting, but not actually regretting, which really had me twisted in knots.

"Do you think Tauro will want me to do something dangerous for him when he calls in his favor?"

"No, he'll probably use you as a lie detector. Always good to have a lie detector in your back pocket."

"Can't alpha shifters detect lies?"

"Some can. But nothing like what you can do."

I suppose I could have read him for a better answer, but I didn't. He was likely telling some version of the truth. No one could wrap the truth in a lie better than Lucas—

"*Blacke.*"

We'd expected Joaquín to emerge from the ocean. Instead, he pulled up in a primer gray classic Ford truck, parked, got out. He wasn't alone.

The small woman accompanying him was dressed entirely in dark blue, from her hooded sweatshirt to her running shoes. Blue-framed glasses sat on a brown button nose, round umber eyes peered through the lenses, taking in everything.

The woman reminded me of Chandra in the way she assessed a place, checking for exits, threats, and allies. I had a feeling she didn't think there were any allies here. I didn't read her for that information. I didn't need to. It was evident in the way she hung back, balancing on her toes as if ready to take flight the second things went south.

"This is Diamond. Our resident trader." Joaquín leaned against the side of his truck. He was wearing jeans and a black long-sleeved T-shirt, and his wavy hair was loose around his shoulders. His sea-green eyes were fixed on the back of the woman standing between us and him.

"I'm not your resident anything." Her voice was soft and silky, even as she snapped at him. A grin spread across Joaquín's face. He liked it

154

when she snapped at him. Were all alphas weird like that? "The dealer sent me a message that you wanted to talk to me."

"The dealer is easier to find than Diamond, so I went through him," Joaquín said.

"That's by design, Mar." Diamond's grin was soft and pretty, though guarded. Her skin was dark brown, smooth, and unlined. She could have been anywhere from fifteen to forty.

"Diamond, dealer," Lucas drawled, "where's Heart, Club, and Spade? Where's poker and blackjack?"

"Around." Diamond thrust her hands on her hips. "You want to know who Alpha Malcolm's wife was sleeping with before she died. Why?"

"Long story," Lucas replied.

"I'm a trader. I like long stories."

"How about cash?"

"I like that, too." She negotiated what I thought was an insane price for such a small amount of information—the guy that tried to kill Malcolm only got half the amount she asked for—but Lucas agreed, and arrangements were made.

"Ordinarily, I'd require the money up front, but he's good for it." She up-and-downed Joaquín, scowled. "Pay him and he'll pay me."

"Deal. What can you tell me about Suyin?"

"I can tell you she slept with a lot of people. She wasn't only sleeping with shifters, either. Some were human, some were other paranormals. Suyin Chen was an open-minded, free woman. Very cool." Diamond nodded her head in approval. "There were people who visited her frequently. Not necessarily lovers. Malcolm's second was there often, sometimes with his sister. There were a couple of powerful old wolves that came by at least once a week. Richard Penn was one. Agnes Romano was another."

"Dick was meeting with Suyin? How did I not know this?" Lucas asked.

"You had your hands pretty full doing Malcolm's dirty work." Diamond shrugged, as though this was of little consequence. "Most nights you were at the clubs in Mexico."

"How do you know that? Never mind." Lucas shook his head. "Traders."

"It's what we do." She reached into her pocket, extracted a USB drive. "This is everything I have on Suyin Chen. As a bonus, I threw in most of what I have on you, too."

"I assume it's too much to ask that you give me the original footage."

"Not a chance," Diamond said.

"Has anyone else requested information on me?" Lucas asked.

"Yes."

"Don't suppose you'd tell me who it was."

"No. The anonymity thing is part of the information trader gig. But, rest assured, no one will know you have this information unless you tell them. Secrecy goes both ways."

"That's something to hold on to, I suppose." Lucas took the drive from her. "If you had to guess, who in this town would you say had the best reason to kill Xavier Malcolm?"

"His inner circle. Or one of the wolves he's thrown out of town. Or one of the poor people he's eighty-sixed from their homes in his East San Diego gentrification projects, or the family of one of the people he had murdered—you'd know some of those, right?"

Lucas let out a low, ticking growl, and every hair on my body stood at attention.

Joaquín gripped Diamond by the shoulder and spun her around to face his truck so that she was in profile to me. "Let's go before that mouth of yours pisses off this very strong tiger shifter."

"Don't manhandle me, shark." Her little nose scrunched up and her glasses slid lower. "I'm perfectly capable of walking by myself, thank you."

Joaquín made a hands-off gesture and they headed to the truck together. Before he got in, he yelled, "We even now, Blacke?"

Lucas stared hard at the USB drive. "Yeah."

CHAPTER EIGHTEEN

"What did Joaquín mean by 'even?'"

Lucas shoved the USB into his laptop. It was midnight and we were back in the bathroom at the B&B. This time he was fully clothed, and I wasn't trying to stick my tongue down his throat, so that was an improvement.

"I did him a favor once."

"What was the favor?" My shoulder brushed his as I leaned closer to see the screen better. He'd set it up on the vanity counter and was bent over it.

"I didn't kill his brother."

"Tauro?"

"No, Cristofer. The youngest."

"Why would you want to kill him?"

A folder named "Alpha Suyin Chen-Malcolm" appeared on the screen. Lucas clicked it and selected the first file. "Because he tried to kill me. After he stole from Malcolm, which isn't common knowledge."

I sat on the edge of the tub. "What did he steal?"

The file opened to a video of Suyin on a darkened porch, hugging a man I didn't recognize. It didn't seem to be important, because Lucas exited out of it and opened another. "He was working in one of our clubs downtown. Skimming a little off the top, not enough to flag accounting, but I noticed."

I watched his strong fingers flex as he moved the mouse from file to file. "If it wasn't enough for accounting to notice, how did you pick up on it?"

"It was my job." He squinted at the screen. "Cristofer was young. He wasn't a bad kid, just got in with some bad humans, is all."

"And you helped him out of it," I finished.

"I saw an opportunity," Lucas corrected. "He belonged to a powerful family of shifters. Doing them a favor meant they'd owe me."

He didn't say, and I didn't read him, but I was certain there was more to the story. "Did you use that favor just now?"

"I used that favor seven years ago, when I killed Suyin. After the pack trial, I needed to disappear for a while. Tauro's shifters lent me a fully stocked boat, no questions asked. I sailed the Pacific for two months and when I came back, I left Malcolm's pack and headed for the desert."

"So why did Joaquín say you were even?"

"He wasn't involved when Tauro lent me the boat. He felt he owed me separately, because when Cristofer jumped me after I accused him of stealing, I dragged him to Joaquín instead of beating the kid boneless." He cleared his throat. "Look, Neely, about what the trader said. I was naïve, and I thought I was doing the right thing carrying out Malcolm's orders. Sometimes I was. Sometimes I wasn't so sure."

"And sometimes, as with Cristofer Mar, you didn't follow orders at all."

He nodded without looking at me.

The video playing on the computer once again focused on that dark porch. "Where is that? It's not here."

Lucas stared hard at the screen. "Suyin's house in Solana Beach. She and Malcolm lived separately most of the—*what the hell?*"

The camera focused in on a slender figure dressed in black. The person didn't look in the direction of the camera before being let inside the house, but I recognized her. And if I recognized her...

"*Chandra.*"

158

WE DROVE twenty minutes to a Del Mar breakfast place where Lucas knew the owners so we could be assured of privacy. Chandra was sipping coffee at a secluded table overlooking the street when we arrived.

Like Lucas, she was dressed in blue jeans and a casual white T-shirt, normal attire for some people, but not quite right for her. I supposed she was trying to blend in with the tourists, but she looked like a stingray among sardines.

We sat. Lucas opened the laptop and played her the video.

"Damn. I had a feeling someone was out there that night. I warned Suyin, but I honestly don't think she cared." Chandra leaned back in her chair.

Lucas said nothing so loudly my ears rang.

"I told you everything that mattered, Alpha." Chandra bowed her head, stared into her coffee cup.

"What were you doing with her that night? Were you lovers?" I asked.

"No." Chandra picked up her cup, took a sip. "This was business. I don't mix business and personal." She glanced out the window. "Usually."

"*Chandra, goddamnit, tell me—*" Lucas yelled the first part of the sentence, but ended it in a guttural whisper. "—what you were doing there."

"Respectfully, no." Chandra looked away when Lucas's tiger showed in his face. Literally. His animal shadowed across his face like a mask and disappeared. "I'm sorry."

"Tell me *now*."

"No."

Lucas faced me, snarled, "Read her."

I really didn't want to tell him no. It wasn't that I was afraid of him, even with the furrowed brow and the lengthened teeth. It was the pain in those golden eyes that made me want to do anything he asked, anything, just to see that hurt gone.

Instead of responding to his order, I appealed to Chandra. "I know how close you are to Lucas. How loyal. I know it better than most, because I've read you. Help me understand why you would keep something like this from him because it's hurting him, and I know you don't want that."

A muscle pulsed in Chandra's cheek. She looked so hostile I thought she might backhand me if I didn't stop talking.

Lucas stared at the computer screen where he'd paused the video. His entire body was vibrating as he attempted to keep from shifting. It was rare for him to experience any loss of control, rarer still for him to show it. After all, he'd been furious with Richard Penn at the meeting last night and still kept his animal under control.

Chandra knew all that, and she was still sitting there staring down at her coffee like it was an oracle of divination and would give her the answers she needed.

And then it hit me.

There was no way Chandra would lie or deceive Lucas. They were best friends. She wouldn't keep anything from him. Unless…

"The omission is better than the truth."

"What did you say?" Chandra's mouth flattened into a harsh line. "Did you read me?"

"No. I don't need to read you. I only need to focus on what I know about you."

"Don't," she said.

Lucas closed the laptop. "'The omission is better than the truth.' What are you saying, Neely?"

"Think about it. What would be the only reason Chandra wouldn't have told you about her visit to Suyin's house?"

The second he stopped being angry and started thinking, Lucas got it. "You're *protecting* me?"

Chandra drummed her fingernails on the table, gave me a look that would have scared the bejeezus out of me if I didn't trust her.

"I didn't read you."

"Oh, I believe you. You're guessing based on what you think you know about me." She rolled her shoulders back, bounced her foot on the floor. Kept drumming her nails.

Lucas's gaze darted from me, to the computer, to Chandra. The second time around, they fixed on her.

"Holy shit, Suyin hired you to kill me."

Chandra slouched in her seat. A server appeared on the other side of the room, two mugs and a pot of coffee in her hands. Lucas glanced at her and nodded. The woman hurriedly set the mugs on the table in front of Lucas and me, filled them, and then refilled Chandra's.

When she was gone, we continued the conversation.

"She *tried* to hire me," Chandra said. "And it wasn't only you she wanted taken out. Malcolm, too."

Lucas's tiger regressed, but he still seemed unsteady. "Did she tell you why?"

"She wanted Malcolm dead and she wanted it badly. She said you would protect him, that it was your job and the only way to get to Malcolm was to kill you first." Chandra glanced at me and then at Lucas. "I didn't know what she was back then, but I could tell something wasn't right because her behavior changed so fast, I got whiplash. One minute she was begging me to take the job, the next she was threatening me, saying if I hurt you, she'd kill me. She'd cry, then laugh, and then snarl. Not being familiar with crossbreed spikershifters, I figured she was on drugs."

Lucas eyed Chandra. "Why didn't you take the job? Your targets were bad people and I certainly qualify as one. Suyin was wealthy. She would have paid you well."

"You think you *qualify*?" Her mouth turned down and her voice softened. "You have no idea how wrong you are."

"Then why?"

"Because I knew you. Back then, by reputation only, but given the information I had on you, I figured you'd kill me. The risk-return ratio was skewed sharply in favor of you. I'm a businesswoman and, strictly speaking, it was a bad investment."

Lucas chewed on that for a little while. "Why did you find me in Sundance?"

"Because I wanted out of the business," Chandra replied. "Because I needed a fresh start. Mostly because of what I said—that you could kill me. And if it ever becomes necessary, you will."

161

"I apologize for doubting you, Chandra." He let out a long-held breath, picked up his mug, and then set it down without taking a drink. "Know that it was a reflection of my own weakness and had nothing to do with my faith in you, my friend."

"Forgiven, forgotten. I apologize for doubting you, too, Lucas. For thinking I couldn't tell you the truth."

I'd never heard Chandra refer to Lucas by his first name before. My being here, in this relationship-defining moment between two close friends, felt like an intrusion. I stared down at my hands wrapped around my mug and tried to fade into the background.

"Forgiven, forgotten." He took a drink of his coffee, swallowed. "Christ, I hate it here."

Chandra stirred her coffee, rested the spoon on an empty sugar packet. "You've become accustomed to small-town life."

"I've become accustomed to not having all this insidious scheming bullshit in my life. We need to find out what's going on with Malcolm so we can get back to Sundance."

"You're homesick?" I nudged him, smiled.

"Yeah." He took a gulp of coffee, set the mug down. "At this point, I'd even be happy to see that power-siphoning witch with the repulsive T-shirts."

"I APOLOGIZE for demanding you read Chandra. It was the assholery cherry on top of the assholery sundae I was responsible for back there."

Instead of heading straight back to Malcolm's place, Lucas and I put the laptop in the trunk of his loaner car and walked a block down to the beach. It was mostly deserted due to the overcast skies and the accompanying drop in temperature. A yoga class was wrapping up and a couple people were sitting around on chairs and blankets, watching the ocean.

"Okay. Or should I say, Forgiven, forgotten?"

He shrugged. "Chandra and I piss each other off a lot. It's just something we say."

"It's nice." We walked a little farther down the beach before I spoke again. "She was mentally ill, Lucas."

"I know."

"If Suyin had been herself, she wouldn't have—"

"You didn't know her, Neely. She wasn't only smart and funny, she was merciless."

I slipped off my sneakers and sank my toes in the squishy, cool sand. He was right. I didn't know Suyin. I did know what betrayal felt like, though, and I knew he was feeling it right now.

He toed off his running shoes and kicked them to the side. "She wasn't wrong to target me. It was a smart move."

"No, it wasn't." I threw up my hands. "Why do I have to keep explaining this to people here? Having you as a trusted ally is much better than treating you as an enemy combatant."

He stared out at the horizon. A breeze swept over the ocean and into us, rustling his hair and blowing mine into my mouth.

"You think you know me."

I spat my hair out, tried to tuck it behind my ears. "Not one hundred percent, no. But I've seen you under pressure. I've seen you with murder in your eyes. I don't know it all, but I have a good idea." I took his hand in mine and tugged him down the sloping beach toward the water.

He allowed me to lead him. "Good idea?"

"Yes. You aren't perfect, not by a long shot, but you are essentially you. I can't think you've changed that much in the last few years."

"I was Malcolm's thug. I've done things for him that I deeply regret." He threaded his fingers through mine. "Things I wouldn't even ask Chandra to do, and she was once an assassin-for-hire."

"She has regrets, too. Everyone does."

We waded into the water. Lucas didn't even roll up his pant legs, just let the water drench his jeans. I was back in one of my sundresses —a yellow one Lucas had once told me he liked.

"What are your regrets, Neely?"

I shook a piece of seaweed off my leg. "I've killed. You know that."

"Yes, but do you regret it?"

"I wish there had been another way, but, no, I mostly don't regret what I did."

"Because your kills were justified. If you hadn't done what you did, those people would have hurt you or others."

"Maybe." I lifted one shoulder. "Still wish I'd found another way."

"That's because you're a good person."

"You are, too."

He shook his head. "I'm morally ambiguous at best. I've killed when I could have allowed the person to live. Under Malcolm's orders, but it doesn't matter, does it? I did those things."

I turned his logic around on him. "If you had allowed those people to live, would you or others have been hurt?"

He didn't answer, so I read him. Just a brush over his brain.

"I feel you," he said.

He shouldn't have, and that worried me. Was I getting sloppy, or was Lucas getting better at detecting me? Whatever the reason, I didn't apologize for reading him. I wasn't sorry.

"It's as I suspected. If you had allowed them to live, they would have hurt others." The tide rushed out, revealing a wad of green-gold seaweed. I pushed on a rubbery pod with my toe and it popped. "Circumstances matter, Lucas. You really don't see yourself as a good person?"

"As I said, morally ambiguous."

I disagreed, but I didn't pursue the subject. "You have to admit, some of my moves sit in the moral gray areas, too. For instance, I just read your mind without permission."

"True."

"I don't do that to any of my other friends." We backed up as a wave broke in front of us, drenching my dress and Lucas's jeans.

"Why do you do it to me? I'm an alpha leader. Aren't you afraid of what I'll do?" He asked this lightly, obviously not affronted or angry, but puzzled, amused.

I shook another string of seaweed off my foot. "To be honest, I don't know why I'm not more afraid. You're the most powerful alpha I've ever encountered, and it makes sense that I would run far and fast away from you, but here I am. Our relationship is unlike anything else in my life. The rules aren't the same for you."

"Relationship?" One blond-brown, perfectly shaped brow shot up.

"You would pull that word out of my sentence. You know what I mean. Our relation-friendship."

He tugged me close, my back to his front, slung an arm around my waist. His warm body was a welcome contrast to the frigid water now lapping at my knees.

"Why don't we have a relationship? We want each other."

"As I said before, because we're still figuring out the friendship side. Besides, you don't do them, Blanche." I leaned back, rested my head on his chest. His arms automatically drew me closer. Lucas wasn't the only one this town was getting to. I craved comfort and, as unlikely as it seemed, this man gave it to me.

"I don't do them?"

"No, and I doubt you'd start with me."

"You think so?" He turned me to face him, slipped one hand beneath my chin to tip it up, and rested his forehead on mine. "Read my mind."

"Not a chance."

"Scared of what you might see?" He grinned, showing me the strong lines of his jaw, the creases around his amber eyes, all of his perfect white teeth.

"Terrified." I played with the front of his shirt. "Lucas, why did you come to my place the night I had that nightmare and got my ring tangled in my hair?"

He replied without hesitation. "I was home, getting ready for bed, when I felt you struggling."

"*Felt* me?"

"Yeah." He sighed. 'I don't get it either."

"Does it have something to do with why you're able to push your thoughts into my head?"

"Good question. I—"

There was a sudden crack, followed by a sort of thumping sound, then another crack-thump, crack-thump. In the half-second between the first thump and the second crack, Lucas shoved me into the water

165

and stood in front of me. Red blossoms appeared on the back side of his T-shirt and I felt, rather than heard, myself scream.

"Stay down."

"Lucas?"

He sprinted up to the street. One moment he was bleeding in front of me, the next, I was alone.

CHAPTER NINETEEN

I TRUDGED OUT OF THE WATER AND UP THE BEACH. TRIED TO RUN, BUT fear dragged at me, made me feel as if I were running against hurricane force winds. On my slog through the sand, I gathered power, prepared myself for what I might have to do once I reached Lucas. The sight of blood drenching the back of his shirt stayed with me as I moved, as I gathered energy, as I armed myself.

When I crested the slope and planted my bare feet on the sidewalk, the casual posture of Lucas's shoulders told me that spiking the shooter would not be required.

I breathed a sigh of relief.

There was no urgency in the scene, only Amir—in human form and wearing nylon shorts that barely contained him—shuttling between two vehicles, and Chandra scowling down at her thigh.

"Where's the shooter?" I puffed as I bent over to catch my breath, hands on my knees. I let my power spin out until I was empty again. It was becoming easier to do. I'd have to mention that to the witches if I ever made it out of San Diego.

Lucas winced as he gestured toward the car. The driver's hands were clasped to the steering wheel, but his head had been twisted around until it faced the back seat. The white flesh on the man's neck was stretched like taffy on an old-fashioned pulling machine. I slapped my hand to my mouth, tried not to gag.

"Oh my God." I craned my neck, rolled it around in that automatic empathetic way. Not that I felt any empathy for this shooter—or any public shooter, for that matter.

When I had my gag reflex under control, I peered closer. There was neither fur nor fangs evident, but that didn't mean the person wasn't a shifter. It just meant he had been in human form when he died.

"Was he a wolf shifter?"

Amir shook his head. "Fox."

So not one of Malcolm's people then. "Did he hurt anyone else?" I stared at the bloody holes in Lucas's shirt. One bullet had hit his lungs, one had struck near his heart. There was no way he'd have survived if he were human. No way.

"He shot Chandra in the leg," Amir replied. "Poor bastard didn't stand a chance after that." Which told me exactly who the taffy puller had been.

The eagle shifter reclined the driver's seat all the way back and shoved the driver into the rear of the car before sliding behind the wheel himself. "Let's get out of here. I don't want to have to deal with the local police."

"Take it to the Pit Crew in North County for disposal. I've got a tab going," Lucas drawled.

Chandra limped to the SUV. She'd be fine, but I asked anyway. "'You okay?"

"I'm good. *You* be careful."

Amir cocked his head to one side like a puppy hearing a strange sound. "Sirens. Eight miles out."

I couldn't hear them, but I didn't doubt his shifter hearing. Neither did Lucas, because he grabbed me by the elbow and started fast walking across the street.

"Why did Chandra say, '*You* be careful' to me like that?"

"Because she cares about your safety?"

"Is something going on that I should know about?"

Lucas ushered me around the restaurant and out to the rear

168

parking lot before answering. "They might be referencing the fact that there's a hit out on you, but I can't be sure."

"What? A *hit*? As in *hitman*?"

"Don't be sexist, Neely. Hit*person*."

"Damn it, Lucas." I was going to poke him right in the bullet wounds, first chance I got. "How long have you known about this?"

"About four days."

"*Four days?*" Guess that meant we could rule out anyone who thought I'd put Malcolm in a coma. The contract would have already been active by the time I spiked him.

"Give or take a day." Lucas appeared unperturbed.

"Why. Didn't. You. Tell. Me?" Fury, cold and sudden, gripped me. I was so pissed I could hardly breathe. "Don't you think I deserve to know if someone's trying to kill me?"

"Take it easy. We don't know this shooter was here for you. Plenty of people in this town hate me enough to take me out. Of course, they would have been packing silver if they intended to kill me, but maybe it was meant to be a warning or—"

"You have had countless opportunities to tell me," I said through gritted teeth.

"Are you still on that?" He looked at me and reared back, then winced and put his hand over the wound to the right of his heart. "Yeesh. Okay. I didn't tell you, but it's not like I did nothing about it. I took care of it."

"How?" His casual attitude was starting to get to me. I was seething by the time we got to the loaner BMW, so angry I could have spiked him and not felt an ounce of guilt for it.

"I brought in Amir. He's here to watch you since Chandra refuses to watch anyone but me."

"So where was Amir the night Simone tried to gut me in the street?" I demanded.

"He has to sleep sometime." Reacting to the murder in my eyes, Lucas reared back again. Winced again. "Fine. I was with you. I didn't think he needed to be there, too."

"You had no right to keep something like this from me." My

shaking hands fumbled the car door open and I threw myself into the passenger seat. "No right."

Lucas got in on his side, watching me from the corner of his eye as he started the car. With the ease of an innocent man, he pulled out of the parking lot and onto the main road, passing the police cars parked in a disorderly jumble where the shooter's car had been minutes ago.

"I would have thought you'd have picked it out of my head by now. It's been on my mind enough. But you were following your rules again."

"I already told you I don't follow the rules where you're concerned," I snapped.

"Not always, but most of the time."

"That's sure as shit going to change." I crossed my arms and stared out the passenger window, my brain spiraling through death scenarios involving faceless assassins, Lucas, and me.

"Good." His mouth tightened into a frown. "It should have changed a long time ago. You don't live in a world where those rules of yours make sense. You live in a world where people try to shoot you while you're wading through the waves on the beach. You're following rules that no one else gives a damn about, and it's going to get you killed."

He had a point, but I didn't like it. "My rules are there for a reason. I don't like breaking them."

"So-the-fuck-what?"

"*What did you say?*" I gaped at him. Lucas had never spoken to me with disgust, something I only realized because he was doing it now.

"So. The." With one arm wrapped around his chest, he wrenched the steering wheel to the left, jerking the rental BMW over to the side of the road. Slammed it into park and cut the ignition. "Fuck. What. That's what I said."

We were parked on a gritty stretch of asphalt beside a mile expanse of beach that was bookended by residences and restaurants. No one was around except for a few surfers on the water. The shooting scene was a couple of miles behind us.

"Who cares what you *like*?" He ran his hand through his hair, then winced and lowered his arm to his side. The bullet wounds had to have been serious to still be hurting him. "You could have been killed

170

today, you know. If you had moved a few inches to the right, you would have taken one directly through the heart. If one of your human boyfriends was with you instead of me, do you think he would have survived?"

"I don't have a human boyfriend. And that's not fair."

"Fair? Tell me, Neely, how many people have to die before you get it through your head that the paranormal world doesn't screw around? It's a dangerous place and, like it or not, by virtue of your ability, *you live in it.*"

I sucked in a shallow breath. Another. My pulse was thundering in my ears, and I felt sick to my stomach. "Thanks a lot for that. For the reminder of all the death I'm responsible for."

"Is this the part where I'm supposed to feel sorry for you?" Lucas unlatched his seatbelt and turned in his seat, staring at what had to have been a washed-out, stricken look on my face. "Their deaths were the fault of the bastard who murdered them, not you. But, yes, if you had been proactive instead of reactive, fewer people would have died. *That's* something you have to live with. As you said, we've all got regrets. Thing is, most of us face them. You hide from yours and pretend you're better than the rest of us paranormals because you're part human."

"Not true." I was trying hard to swallow the burning at the back of my throat. I would not angry cry. Not now, in front of him.

"It's in the way you say you're not a wolf shifter even though your mother is one. You constantly suppress and deny your paranormal side, but have no trouble embracing the human side of yourself."

"I don't shift. I don't have a wolf." I thrust out my arms. "See? No fur. No super strength. Nothing."

"There is such a thing as a latent shifter, you know."

"I know. And people with latent animals know there's an animal inside of them, they just don't shift. There's nothing inside of me." I crossed my arms low over my belly, looked out the side window. "I know exactly what I am, what I'm capable of. *That's why I have rules.*"

"Please. You have no clue what you're capable of because you've never let yourself find out. The closest you've come was the day José died. Why do you think I asked you to help me with my prehistoric side, Neely? I saw what you could do that day. Not all of it, but I saw the potential in you."

My next words were drenched in spiteful fear. "So, because I said no to helping you, you're punishing me?"

He leaned over the console, stuck his face in mine. "You didn't say no to me that day, you said no to yourself. You don't want to find out what you can do because you're still playing human."

"Not playing. I am half—"

"*Bullshit*. I don't know exactly what you are, but there is no way you're human. If your father says he's human, he's in as much denial as you are."

I bit back a retort. That conversational detour would get us nowhere.

"When I spike someone to kill, when I completely let go, I get a rush out of it. A thrill. I *love* it, Lucas. Is that what you want to hear? That I lust for it? Well, I do. It's the best drug I've ever tried, better than any narcotic or hallucinogen, and once I have it, I want more." I drew in a shaky breath. "You wouldn't understand."

"*I* wouldn't understand?" His eyes, normally irreverent but mostly kind, narrowed into angry slashes, as did his mouth. "You have no idea what I feel when I'm in prehistoric form. Why do you think I lose control when I go too far? *Why do you think I asked for your help to control it?*"

I hadn't considered that, and now the signs that had all along pointed to that truth seemed massive. Lucas was as much a slave to his prehistoric form as I was to my killing spike ability. We were addicts, desperately trying to hold on to our sobriety.

"Then you understand why I have rules. You must have them, too."

"Yes. Rules I'd break in a heartbeat for you, but I don't have faith that you'd do the same for me." His mouth was so close to mine I was sure he'd either bite me or kiss me. He did neither.

"Yes, I would."

"If you were afraid, right? Reactive?"

"If you were being attacked, I'd be scared and reactive, so it's the same difference."

"Then what happened today?" He was still staring into my eyes. Still too close.

"Today? But ... I was too slow. By the time I reached you all, the shooter was dead. You didn't need me to spike him."

His voice lowered. "And how relieved were you by that?"

I opened and closed my mouth.

Lucas was right. I *had* been relieved when someone else had taken care of the killer for me. I'd happily foisted that man's death onto Chandra's soul. Even if I was too late to do anything, I shouldn't have been so relieved to not have had to act. That was immature and unfair.

"You say you have rules, but you break them, don't you? You broke them when that medic tried to kill Malcolm yesterday. You broke them when that poacher came into your bakery to kidnap a shifter boy. You smashed right through them when José was killed and read any brain that came within ten feet of you. Seems like those telepath-spiker rules of yours are more arbitrary than you say they are."

I shuddered in remembrance of the day I walked in on my uncle lying on his kitchen table in a pool of blood. "I had to find out who killed him. I had to."

"Exactly." Lucas lifted my chin with the edge of his hand. The anger in him had lessened, the disgust in his face had disappeared. "You break your rules when it's necessary, right?"

"Yes."

"Well, sugar cookie, with enemies on all sides of us, it has become goddamn necessary."

I COLLAPSED into a chair beside Malcolm's bed and stared at his face. The lines of tension around his mouth and eyes had softened. Nice that he was getting some sleep, because I sure wasn't. My head ached and I was so tired I could barely keep my eyes open.

Someone wanted me dead badly enough to pay a lot of money to someone else to kill me, and that wasn't even the worst of my problems. If I didn't find a way to fix Malcolm, a whole bunch of wolf shifters were going to murder me.

Every time I come into contact with an alpha leader, something awful happens.

Every single time.

"Take a break. It's nearly midnight and you're exhausted." Lucas was slouched against the back of the sofa watching me. He'd spent most of the evening patrolling the room in Bengal tiger form to heal his gunshot wounds. Also, I think he got a thrill out of scaring the hell out of the wolf shifters who walked into the room.

"I read every person in here tonight," I said dully. "Nothing."

"Did you spike anyone?"

"No, just read them. A quick glance over their thoughts."

"What about Dick and Agnes? Did you see the way they shoved us out of the way to get to him? I was sure those two were up to something. They're always scheming—not usually together, but stranger things..."

"I got nothing from either one."

"Damn." Lucas almost seemed disappointed they weren't trying to kill Malcolm.

"That doesn't mean they aren't up to something. It only means they weren't thinking about it when I read them. As I told you, I didn't spike."

"Maybe you should have."

"The shifters that visited tonight were all genuinely concerned for him. Most believe I tried to kill him. Roughly a third intend to kill me if he dies. Most don't trust you. None trust me. Call me crazy, but I didn't want to delve any deeper into their brains after that."

"If you were in their shoes, how would you feel?" He rolled to his feet, stopped behind my chair. "I'm the bastard they know and hate. The only thing they know about you is that you could kill them with your mind."

"Yeah, and thanks for announcing that to everyone the first night," I muttered.

"I wasn't telling them anything they didn't already know. Malcolm has spies in my group, remember?" He set his hands on my shoulders, squeezed, rubbed my upper back with his thumbs. My body relaxed into his touch. I hated that he could do that to me so easily, even when I was angry with him.

"Why?"

"Seriously? You've met him, dealt with him. Does he seem like the sort of alpha who would let someone like me get completely out from under his control? He'll always keep tabs on me. It's the way he is."

"No, I mean, why are we doing this?" I turned in the chair so he could see me mouth the words. There were guards outside the door with shifter hearing and guns. "Why are we saving him?"

He pointed at his head, so I read him. *Because you spiked him, and if we don't, his shifters will make it their life's work to see you dead.*

"Is that the only reason?"

Lucas spun me back around. His hands were a warm weight on my shoulders. "No."

"Are you trying to tell me that it's complicated?"

He sighed. "It's labyrinthine."

My eyelids drooped as he slid his fingers down my spine and pressed out the knots in the muscles on my lower back. "Mmm."

"Nice?" As usual, he sounded a little too pleased with himself.

"Yes, but I'm still really, really angry with you."

"Why? Because I yelled at you in the car? You had that coming, Costa-MacLeod."

"No, you ass, because you didn't tell me about the hit." My shoulders drew up to my ears, all the work his magic fingers had done to calm me gone in an instant.

Someone wants me dead badly enough to pay another someone to kill me.

He worked on my newly tightened muscles with the heel of his hand. "I won't let anything happen to you."

I scowled up at him. "Don't worry about me. I'm a telepath and a spiker. A paranormal. I can take care of myself."

"Turning over a new leaf, are we?"

"That, or I'm BS-ing you to keep you massaging me. A little to the left, please. That's where it hurts. Yes, right *there*."

He laughed, the sound a deep rumble in his chest. I let my head fall back against him and he wrapped both arms around me.

175

"I feel ... lost." My voice shook.

"That's normal when you're trying to figure things out." He pressed a kiss to the top of my head, moved down to my ear. "Are you human or paranormal? Fighter or flighter? A baker or a baker's niece?"

"Fighter or *flighter*?" I closed my eyes, smiled a little. "Here I am, nearly thirty, and I don't know a thing about who I really am. That's sad, isn't it?"

He bent down in front of me, put his hands on my knees. "Life took a hard left turn on you a couple months ago and now you're having to reevaluate things. But you know who you are. Deep down, here." He tapped my chest and stood, bringing me to my feet as he rose. "Get some sleep. I'll keep an eye on Malcolm—and you."

"You aren't telepathic." I yawned. "What if someone comes in?"

"I'll play it safe and bite everyone who visits."

"No biting." I stumbled from the chair to the sofa, where I collapsed against the stiff pillows. Dazed from exhaustion, I stared up at the ceiling, jaw slack, eyelids drooped. "Lucas, do you know who put the hit out on me?"

"No, but I'll find out."

I read him to be sure he was being straight with me, as I had told him I would.

I'll find out. And when I do, I am going to unleash hell on them.

It was with that assurance that I drifted off. My dreams were hideous, slashing and stabbing, red splashes, screams. Fear and hate and pain. It wasn't uncommon for me to have nightmares after poking around in someone's head, but these were especially bleak.

After a particularly bad one that ended with me sobbing myself awake, Lucas bent down beside me, brushed my hair behind my ear. "Go back to sleep. You're safe."

"Tell that to my subconscious."

"Neely." He clicked his tongue at me. "I can't believe you'd even have bad dreams after having seen me naked. Your dreams should all be happy. Very happy." He beetled his brows.

"God, you're gross." I flopped onto my side and promptly dropped off to sleep again.

176

CHAPTER TWENTY

I woke with tears on my face. Thanks for the nightmares, shifters. I wiped the wetness away, sat up on the sofa, peered around the darkened room.

Lucas was gone. Seated at Malcolm's bedside was a young woman who couldn't have been older than nineteen or twenty. She had straight black hair that hung to the middle of her back, brown skin, and large hazel eyes with thick lashes. She was dressed in jeans and a stretchy green sweater.

"Hi spiker, I'm Lupita Cortez. Alpha Blacke said to tell you that so you didn't have to read my mind because you're tired. Are you really telepathic?"

Cortez. She was the young woman from Dr. Penbright's clinic. The one who had protected her sister from the specist wolves that had tried to kill them.

Despite Lupita's assurance that I didn't need to, I brushed over her mind to make certain she was who she claimed to be. I was doing that now, taking zero chances. Lucas had said a lot of things after the shooting at the beach yesterday, but my mind kept cycling back to one thing in particular.

You break your rules when it's necessary ... with enemies on all sides of us, it has become goddamn necessary.

"I am telepathic—and a spiker, but my name's Neely. Nice to meet you, Lupita."

She nodded, gave me a shy smile that didn't match what I thought of as her personality, which was anything but shy.

"What are you doing here?" I stood, stretched my arms above my head. Listened to my vertebrae snap back into place.

"I wanted to see Alpha Malcolm. Alpha Scott gave me permission. He's in the hall talking to your alpha right now."

Not my alpha, I thought, but I didn't correct her.

After another few stretches, I shuffled across the room to sit on Malcolm's bed beside Lupita. She was still visibly bruised. For a shifter to carry injuries for this long... God, the beating must have been brutal.

"How's your sister?"

"Better. Did you do this to Alpha Malcolm?" Her gaze remained on the man while she spoke.

I sighed. "Yes and no. Someone put a memory loop in his head. When I disrupted it, he collapsed."

"His dead wife? The other spiker?"

"That's what Malcolm thought. I'm not so sure."

She clasped her hands in her lap. "Alpha is not a good man, but he's been trying to do better. It used to be whenever my sister or I were called 'half-breed,' or my mother was pushed around, he'd turn a blind eye to what his shifters were doing. He ignored it. But when the beatings began, he stood up for us."

What a saint. "You're still getting beaten."

"Alpha Malcolm waited too long." She sighed. "The wolves who hate us feel empowered, righteous. They see Alpha's former hesitation to condemn them as affirmation that what they're doing is right. Now that he's standing up to them, they see him as weak."

She stood, and I did, too. Lupita was an inch taller than me and about twenty pounds thinner. Too thin. The more I looked at her, the more I wanted to make her something fattening to eat. A fresh *concha*, a hot *mantecada* slathered with butter, or a *conejo* filled with pastry cream.

"Why don't you leave the pack?" I asked.

"We have nowhere else to go." She took one last look at Malcolm and stood. "I agree with you. That ex-wife of his couldn't have done this. She's dead, and the dead can't hurt us. My mother believes in curses from beyond the grave, but I know better. It's the living you have to watch out for." She shoved her hands into her sweater pockets. "I should get home. I don't like leaving my family unprotected."

"Nice meeting you, Lupita."

I meant it, which was a pleasant change from how I normally felt about meeting Malcolm's wolves. It was hard not to admire the way she had protected her sister—was still protecting her and their mother. It reminded me a little of my uncle and me, though he'd done most of the protecting.

"Yeah, it was cool meeting you, too." She lifted one shoulder. "Honestly, I thought you'd be weird, but you seem pretty normal."

"Give me time."

We both laughed. She'd crossed the room and was nearly to the door when it swung open, slamming hard against the wall. A white-skinned, bearded giant of a man stomped inside. He was dressed in boots, jeans, and a red and black plaid lumberjack shirt. All he needed was a beanie and an ax over his shoulder and his Paul Bunyan costume would be complete.

His voice was low and coarse, and peppered with meanness. "We heard you were here, coyote-wolf. Your kind doesn't belong near the alpha of the San Diego wolf pack." He bared his teeth, snarled at her.

"I'm leaving." Lupita stuck up her chin and made to walk past him.

A beefy hand shot out, and the slap of his palm on her skin as he gripped her arm set my back teeth on edge.

"*Half-breed,*" he growled.

"Let go of her or you will regret it for the three seconds that you live before I spike you straight to the grave." The words flew out of me without my consent, but it was the truth, so I didn't retract them.

"Like you did the Alpha?" The man sneered at me. "I didn't come alone, spiker. You really think you can take us all on?"

Three men crowded into the bedroom behind the first one. I immediately categorized them as tall, medium, and squat.

The tall one went first. His words were flavored with a slight

Portuguese accent, as if he used the language at home, but spoke English everywhere else. "Rick's right. I remember when Alpha Malcolm wouldn't be caught dead around creatures like this."

As I had with everyone who had entered Malcolm's room, I did a telepathic sweep of the man's brain. Not much independent thinking going on there. I needed to find the leader.

"Huh," I said, to keep them talking. "You don't like anyone but wolves? Seems limiting."

"We get along with other shifters fine," the squat one said, his thin lip curling. He was short and white with red cheeks and a bulbous red nose. He would have made a good Santa Claus if he wasn't such a jackass. "We just don't want to share a pack with half-breeds and freaks. There was a time Alpha Malcolm felt the same. Guess my buddy here is right. Time's up for Alpha."

"And you're here to kill him?" I knew the answer before I asked. I'd already read them all. They were all thinking three things.

1. Kill the spiker.
2. Kill the half-breed.
3. Kill the alpha.

A squeak of pain bubbled out of Lupita. The sound sent rage screaming through me, and I instinctively opened myself up to the energy in the room.

"I told you to let her go."

"Or what?" He laughed. "You going to kill every one of us, *spiker*?"

If I had to, but I didn't think it would come to that. "I don't need to kill you all. Four wolf shifters against two women and a comatose man? You're cowards. I kill one of you and the others will be halfway to Mexico before their buddy's body hits the ground."

"If you're asking for volunteers, I nominate this one." Lupita gasped as the man twisted her arm behind her back.

"Shut up, half-*bitch*."

I locked onto the lumberjack's thick, clumsy brainwaves and spiked right to the core of his brain. It was so easy I was embarrassed for him—usually people offered token resistance. Not this guy. He screamed like a banshee and went down like a big, sweaty bag of rancid potatoes.

When she was free, Lupita swiveled around, fists up. I'd though she might run out of the room then. It would have been the smart move. Instead, she kicked Lumberjack in the gut and backed closer to me.

"You should run," I said.

"No, I shouldn't," she said. "I'm not leaving you alone with these fools. You aren't a shifter."

True. But I *was* a spiker. "One down, three to go. Who's next?"

Tall and Squat appeared to be thinking it over, but the third shifter was made of braver stuff. He had light black skin and round glasses, was average height, average build, average handsome. The shifter looked like the personification of the word "medium." I hadn't expected resistance from him. I'd barely noticed he was in the room.

"What did you do to Rick, spiker?" Medium kept touching the center of his chest. It was as if he'd tucked a worry stone inside his button-up white shirt.

"Turned his brain into a plate of scrambled eggs. Would you like the same?" I spoke evenly, though my head was pounding like a bass drum in a rock band. The spike had been effortless, but stopping was always a pain.

Not usually *this* big of a pain, though.

"You going to scramble all our eggs?" He gestured to the other two shifters. "At once?"

God, I hoped not. My head was light and heavy at the same time. I thought I might throw up. "If I do, you won't come out of this nearly as well as Lumberjack Rick did."

Medium looked from me to Lupita to Malcolm. Settled on Malcolm, patted his chest again. "Not worried."

I glanced at the other two. "How about you?"

Tall eased out of the room without saying anything.

"Nah, man." Squat shook his head, backed out through the open doorway into the hall. "We'll get another chance. Let's go."

Medium spat on the floor, once again touching his chest. Was the guy crossing himself? Did he truly think God would approve of his specism? Deluded, devoted, and dumb. A pathetic combination.

"You better get out of here," Lupita said.

"Shut up, half-breed." He took a step closer to the bed, but he didn't look sure about it.

Power continued to flow through me. I hoped I wouldn't need to use it. Hoped this shifter would decide it wasn't worth it and would leave without challenging me, as his two cohorts had.

I hoped he wasn't as dumb as he looked.

HE WAS.

"Neely?" I heard Lupita's voice from far away. "Are you okay?"

No. "Yes." I tried to focus on Medium's brainwaves, but my concentration was off. My head ached and my vision was blurry. "Is he down?"

"Yeah, I think he's dead. I think they both are."

"What?" I'd held back. How could they be dead? It made no sense.

Something was wrong.

Icy-hot pain rocketed through my head. My knees buckled and I collapsed on the bed beside Malcolm, my head buzzing like a beehive. I shouldn't be hurting this badly after two spikes, especially if I really had killed those men.

"Neely? Oh my God, your face..." Lupita's voice went up two octaves. "What do I do?"

"Get Alpha Blacke. Please," I murmured.

"Sure. Will you be okay while I'm gone?"

I gave her a thumbs-up.

The door opened and closed, and the world went gray around the edges. Dampness spilled from my eyes and nose. As much as I'd rather it not be snot for vanity's sake, I really didn't want it to be blood. I liked this sundress. Also, Malcolm had a white bedspread.

"Neely? What did you do?" Lucas flipped me onto my back and cursed. "For shit's sake, how do you get into so much trouble? I leave the room for ten minutes to talk to William and two people are dead and you're bleeding all over the place."

"She hurt herself protecting me," Lupita said, "and the Alpha."

"Yeah. She does that." Lucas took a box of tissues from the nightstand and dabbed my face with a handful. "This is a mess. I mean, this comforter is never going to come clean, no matter how much club soda Malcolm pours on it. Serves him right for buying a white comforter. How arrogant is that anyway? White comforter. It's like he thinks he's better than the rest of us crumb-dropping bed dwellers."

I cough-laughed and tried to sit up. "You're worried. You always get more sarcastic when you're upset." Again, the world grayed around the edges.

Fine lines webbed his forehead. "I've never seen you like this after a spike. You're usually tired, but fine. Tweedle Dick and Tweedle Head shouldn't have been much trouble for you. They couldn't have had more than a dozen brain cells between them."

"I tried hard not to kill them. They shouldn't have died."

"It's all right." He swabbed at my mouth. "They were bad people."

From the corner of my eye, I saw Lupita go from one unconscious man on the floor to the other. "Alpha Blacke, I think I know what's wrong. Maybe."

"What is it?"

She held up two long silver chains with matching silver globe charms hanging from them. "These were around their necks. I've seen similar ones before. When my mother went to see a—"

"Witch." Lucas shook his head. "Damn it."

That must have been what Medium kept touching. "He'd thought it would protect him from me."

Lucas cursed.

"Witch, yes." Lupita eyed the silver starred charms. "These things come with spells attached. Curses. I've even heard that demons use them when crafting their contracts."

"You read a lot of fantasy fiction, don't you?" Lucas asked the young woman.

She cocked an eyebrow. "I'm a half-breed in the Malcolm wolf pack. My family and I don't exactly get invited to the community barbecues. What else am I supposed to do with my time?"

Lucas nodded. "Point taken."

"L-Lupita helped me. She s-stayed when she could have r-run." My voice was as weak as water. "Remember that."

"I remember everything. Lupita, will you do me a favor?"

She shrugged. "Depends on what it is."

Lucas grinned. "I like this kid."

"Young woman," I said.

"*Young woman*, I want you to find William Scott and only him." Lucas pointed toward the hallway. "Then I need you to..."

The rest was low and inaudible. When Lupita had gone, Lucas sat beside me on the bed. "What do you think is in the charms? Spiker resistance spells?"

"If so, they didn't work."

"Could that have been the point? Someone told them they were protection charms, so they'd come in here and piss you off, get spiked, then bring the rest of the pack in to take you out?"

"Don't know." I rolled to my side so I could see him better. The lines on his forehead had extended to his eyes. "You look tired."

"Worried. This is what worried looks like." He picked up my hand, brushed his lips over the knuckles. "I've mentioned that I hate this town, right?"

"Couple hundred times. It's not a bad town, though. Jus' a lot of bad guys right now."

He glanced at Malcolm behind me. "Sleeping like the innocent. That wolf doesn't know you've saved his life twice. He *has* to live now. He's beholden to you. I can't wait to see what it looks like to have Xavier Malcolm in your debt. I wonder if he'll grovel? I bet he'll grovel."

"Head hurts," I rasped.

"Fine, I'll shut up," he said. "But headache or not, we're about to take this carnival of horrors on the road."

"We're leaving?" I couldn't believe Lucas would abandon Malcolm at this point, even if he was worried about me.

"More like we're taking. I'll explain on the way." He shot me that sexy, charming, up-to-something smile of his. It chased away a few of his worry lines, but most of them remained.

"HE's my alpha and my closest friend, but the man has finally lost it."

The next thing I knew, Chandra was jostling me awake. She scooped me off Malcolm's bed, jogged out of the room and down the stairs, and outside to where Amir was waiting in yet another SUV.

"You mean Lucas?"

"Who else?" Chandra pushed the seat back all the way down until I was lying as flat as possible, buckled my seatbelt, and tucked a blanket around me. I recognized it as one from Malcolm's bedroom. "Wait until I give the signal. Stay close." She shut the door.

Amir started the SUV and pulled onto the street. It had only been a couple of hours since I'd spiked the two men in Malcolm's room. I stared out the passenger window at the gray and pinkening predawn sky, and wished I was in a bed in a cabin in the middle of the desert where no one would bother me.

"You look like hell," Amir said.

"You say the most romantic things, dear," I croaked.

He chuckled. "Keep your head down."

"Bullets kill shifters, too, you know."

"Only if they're loaded with silver. Regular bullets just piss us off." The click of the turn signal and the rhythmic whine beneath the tires told me he'd merged onto the freeway.

"What's going on? Where's Lucas?"

"Behind us. We've got a convoy going. Chandra took point; we're behind her; Blacke and Malcolm are in the SUV behind us; Malcolm's second is bringing up the rear. There are a couple other Blacke shifters here, too. And some other Malcolm shifters. I don't know them."

"Lucas moved *Malcolm*?"

"I believe the word he used was 'stole.'"

"*Oh my God, he's kidnapped Xavier Malcolm.* If the San Diego shifters didn't have plans to kill us before, they're loading up the big guns now." My head hurt too badly to consider the full ramifications of what Lucas had done.

"You aren't wrong." Amir grinned, revealing a row of perfect teeth.

"You're happy about this. Why?"

His smile widened. "Because soon we'll be home and those bigot

185

wolves will be following *our* lead. I'm tired of playing by their rules. If shit is going down, I want it to go down where we're surrounded by our own people."

"That's not super reassuring." I yawned. I was almost too tired to worry about it. Almost.

"We can talk about it later. Rest now. I have a feeling you're going to need your strength."

I fell asleep five minutes later, and woke two hours after that.

"We're here."

Amir's voice floated to me through a storm cloud of nightmares and I woke on a gasp. "What happened? Are we dead? Where's Lucas?"

"Nothing. No. There." He indicated the SUV parked in front of us. Lucas and William were pulling the wolf alpha leader's limp body out of the back.

"We're at Lucas's house?" I sat up in my seat.

"Yeah." Amir squinted out the windshield. "I feel better already. This is a good place to withstand a siege."

If a Swiss chalet had mated with a mountain cabin and an Arizona ranch, the result would be Lucas's house. It had the security measures of an underground missile silo, and that was when the Blacke shifters *weren't* on guard duty. The fence surrounding the property had an anti-crash cable barrier approved by United States Homeland Security.

"Are you expecting a siege?" I asked.

"Aren't you? You don't think the people who tried to murder Malcolm are going to give up that easily, do you? This is a powerful alpha we're talking about here. If they had the guts to attack him in the first place, they aren't going to stop until he's dead."

In truth, I'd already figured that out. Evidently Lucas had too, or he wouldn't have moved Malcolm out of San Diego and away from his wolves.

"The charms, the booby-trapped mind loop, everything about it makes me think it's one person," I said. "Or one very organized group of persons."

"Conducting a coordinated attack?"

"Yeah." I watched a desert breeze ruffle the palm fronds on the trees bordering the road. It was hot out. I could feel the heat baking through the window even this early in the morning.

"It's not those specists you dealt with last night in Malcolm's room. People like that don't have the brains or the courage to pull off a surgical attack. They go for messy and loud and stupid."

I frowned at him. "Lucas told you about the specists?"

"The young woman told everyone." He pointed out the passenger window to where Lupita Cortez was standing with two other women —her mother, whom I recognized from the medical clinic, while the other appeared to be her younger sister. "I think you've got yourself a fan."

"Lucas brought them with us?"

"The mother is a nurse, and we need one for Malcolm. Also, she agreed to come."

It occurred to me that I was finally home. Things were far from resolved, but I felt a surge of relief all the same. "I need to check on the bakery." I patted myself. "Damn. My keys are with my things back at Malcolm's B&B."

"Alpha probably got them," Amir said.

Lucas walked out the front door and beelined to Amir and me. He was wearing his alert face, his tiger showing through his human facade.

"Thanks for driving her." Lucas helped me out of the car.

Amir smiled. "It was an easy drive. She slept the whole way, so I got to pick the radio stations."

"Do you have my purse?" I asked Lucas.

"It's inside. Your clothes, too. Sorry for the bad packing. I was in a hurry."

"Thanks. And thanks for the ride, Amir." I took two steps toward the house and my legs gave out. I would have hit the dirt if Lucas hadn't caught me.

"Take it easy." The lines in his forehead were back. He was worried again.

That made two of us.

"There's something wrong with me." I flopped my arms around his neck to keep myself upright.

"I called someone I think might be able to help."

The sound of a distant car engine told me we had company. Amir spun around to face the road and Lucas's human ears reshaped into tiger ears. The Bengal, not the prehistoric one.

He lifted me high in his arms and cradled my sore body against his chest. It felt so good and so safe, I didn't want him to ever put me down, which worried me because I did not need to get attached to Lucas Blacke.

"You know who that is?" Amir asked.

"No," I replied.

"I have a bad feeling about this." Lucas stared hard at the road. "Let's get inside."

"WHAT IS *THAT*?" Lucas recoiled from the window, his upper lip curled.

Once we determined that the vehicle approaching Lucas's house wasn't a pack of pissed-off wolf shifters or an assassin death squad, but two elderly witches in a 1977 AMC Hornet, Amir got into the SUV and left.

"Dolores bought a car." Dottie flitted like a large, nervous bird to where I was lying on the sofa in Lucas's sunken living room. She smelled like lavender and exhaust. "Alpha Blacke left us a message that you aren't well, dear."

Lucas continued staring out the window. "There's black smoke coming out of your car and it's been turned off for five minutes."

Dolores' brows dropped down over her eyes. "Yeah. It needs work."

"It needs to be put out of its misery."

"Listen here, tiger, we came over as a favor to you. If you're just going to insult my car, we'll go." She crossed her arms over her chest and lifted her nose in the air.

"Take that thing to King Jones at Sundance Auto Repair. Tell him to send me the bill. Consider it repayment of the favor you did me by coming over so quickly." He turned away from the window and walked with Dolores to where Dottie and I were. "And consider it a favor to the environment."

"You had to add that last bit, didn't you?" Dolores snapped.

"It needed to be said."

"No, it didn't," Dolores and I said at the same time. She peered down at me. "You look like hell, kiddo."

Lucas took the two silver globe charms out of his pocket and gave them to Dottie. "She spiked two wolf shifter males wearing these."

"They're from Bill Bill's shop." Dottie rolled them in her palm. "Nasty magic attached."

"Hey, they look like our charms." Dolores took the necklaces from her sister, squeezed them in her palm, whispered something. I caught the words *infernum* and *hoc* but heard nothing else.

"What did she say?" Lucas asked Dottie.

"It's Latin. Loosely translated, it means, 'What in the hell is this?'"

Without so much as a mutter more, Dolores threw the charms into Lucas's cold fireplace and yelled, "*Caeruleum igne.*" Jeweled blue flames swallowed the necklaces, charring and then melting them into liquid.

"*What did you do that for?*" Lucas yelled.

"That's the best way to deal with demon magic. Send it back where it came from." Dolores rubbed her hands on her purple sweatpants. "Sis, we've got to give Bill a call. He doesn't need to be selling witch charms to demons. It makes us witches look bad."

"*What were you thinking?*" Lucas glared at Dolores. "*You destroyed the only evidence we had.*"

"Evidence that you're too dumb not to recognize demon magic when it's right in front of you?" she asked.

Teeth gritted, he said, "That's it. Outside. You and me, witch."

"Try it, you overgrown house cat."

A ticking, like the sound of a bomb rapidly escalating toward detonation, emanated from Lucas.

Dolores backed away from him. "Changed my mind. Don't try it. I take it back."

"Uh, guys?" A rush of cool, clean energy filled me, and I sat up. I was still tired, but it was a normal sort of fatigue, without the weakness in my limbs and the fogginess in my brain.

Lucas stopped ticking, whipped his head around to look at me. "Neely? Are you ... okay?"

"Yes. I-I feel better." I blinked up at him, smiled. "Much better."

He stared at me so hard my smile began to dip, and my heart beat faster in my chest. Without breaking eye contact, he addressed Dolores. "Tell King to keep the Hornet and give you the keys to the new Toyota with the dented fender I brought him last week. It's yours."

"Uh, actually..." Dolores scratched the back of her neck. "If you're handing out rewards, I'd like to talk to you about some plans I've got for the tower."

Lucas closed his eyes. "I'm not going to like this, am I?"

CHAPTER TWENTY-ONE

AFTER A FEW MINUTES OF FUSSING OVER ME, THE WITCHES GOT INTO their smoking car and left, Dolores grumbling about charms and Bill Bill and betrayal.

Dottie, though, had looked decidedly happier after Lucas gave them the new car. She thanked him several times.

And I was alone with Lucas, once again.

Alone, except for Malcolm, William, and the Cortez family, but they were at the other end of Lucas's enormous house.

"Where's Lestat?" It had occurred to me that I hadn't seen the cat in a while.

"Probably napping in one of his ten beds around the house," Lucas replied.

I grinned. "You love that cat, don't you?"

"Love is a strong word." He kept staring at me, and I kept being confused by it.

After a half-minute of silence, I said, "I should get home."

Lucas shook his head. He grabbed my hand and dragged me out of the living room, down the hall, and into his bedroom. I'd been here a few times before, and each time our interactions had fallen on the platonic side of affectionate.

"The window is, uh, dark." Apparently, the best way to fill awkward silence was with awkward talk.

"It's dark because it's bright out."

One entire wall in the bedroom was a window made from some super-secret special glass that wasn't on the market yet. It probably cost more than everything I owned multiplied by three. I wasn't entirely clear on what Lucas did for a living, but whatever it was, he was good at it. The man was not hurting for money.

"Oh, that makes sense," I said.

He glared at me.

"Why are you frowning like that? It's not like *I* made it bright."

"Didn't you?" He picked up one of my curls, shifted his gaze to it. "You have no idea what you've done to me, do you?"

Because I wasn't quite ready to go down that path with him, I changed the subject. "I can't stay here. I need shoes. You left mine on the beach."

"I left *our* shoes on the beach and yes, you can stay here. You have another pair in your suitcase." He went into the adjacent bathroom and turned on the light. "There are clean towels and a robe in here."

"Lucas, I can't—"

"Don't fight me on this. Please." He looked at the floor, the ceiling, a point beyond my right shoulder. Shoved his hands in the front pockets of his jeans. I'd never seen him so plainly uncomfortable.

"You're worried about me?"

"Neely, I don't know what's going to happen next—I mean, I'm anticipating an attack, but it's hard to say from whom or from where. There's so much more to this than we're seeing right now. Malcolm's wolves have gone batshit since he went *Rip Van Winkle* on us, and they weren't exactly stable to begin with. I'd like for you to be where I can protect you." He hurriedly added, "And yes, I'm fully aware that you're a spiker and can protect yourself, so don't get mad at me for saying that."

"I'm not mad." Blood rushed to my cheeks and my eyes felt itchy. Either I was having an allergy attack, or it meant something that he was worried about my safety. Maybe it meant more than it should. "Thank you for caring about me."

He stared hard into my eyes. I really wanted to know what he was thinking, but I didn't read him. Not for this.

Finally, he said, "You'll stay here? You promise?"

"Yes."

AFTER A FITFUL, solitary sleep in Lucas's bed, I woke at noon with a cat curled up on my head.

"Guess I was less solitary than I thought."

Lestat meowed in response, then kitten-swatted—no claws—my nose for daring to move him to the other pillow.

After I properly snuggled the cat, I left him to his after-nap nap and took a shower to wake up. I half-fixed my hair, then threw on a sundress I'd dug out of my suitcase before padding barefoot into the kitchen. I was starving.

Lucas and the Cortez women were nowhere to be seen. William Scott was standing in front of the stove in jeans and a gray T-shirt, a black apron tied around his waist. His red hair was shower damp and he smelled like soap and sage.

"Whatever you're cooking, I want some."

William tilted his head back so I could see his grin. "I thought I heard you sneaking up to pilfer my biscuits and sausage."

The man was a wolf shifter. He'd probably heard the first yawn I'd let out upon awakening.

I looked around. "I'm shocked that Lestat isn't in here. He's a food thief, you know."

"The cat? Oh, he was. He meowed aggressively until I fed him. After he finished his food, he left."

When I'd come out of the bathroom, the white tabby was in the exact same position on the bed as before. I'd honestly thought he hadn't moved a muscle. Sneaky cat. Just like his owner.

"Eggs, too?" I pointed at the carton on the counter.

"Fresh ones. How do you take them?"

"Scrambled with cheese and some of that sausage mixed in."

"Now, that sounds quite nice. I think I'll have the same." He dropped some cooked sausage into the pan and added the entire carton of eggs. "The Cortez ladies have all eaten. Alpha Blacke put them in the room down the hall from Alpha Malcolm." He stirred the egg mixture. "Do you suppose they'll stay here when this is all over with?"

"I think they probably should."

"Why? They live well enough in San Diego."

"You can't really think that, William. You know as well as anyone that Malcolm's pack is unwelcoming to any shifter who isn't a pure-blood wolf. I think they'll not only be safer here but happier among people who accept them as they are."

Steam issued from the pan as he stirred the eggs. "Is that why you stay here?"

"Most of Lucas's group is afraid of me. Some of the ones who are afraid have let their fear turn to hate." I strolled over to the refriger-ator and grabbed a bag of shredded Colby-Jack. "I might not be fully accepted here, but the Cortez women will be. They're shifters."

He sprinkled cheese over the eggs and sausage. "There's all kinds of prejudice in the world, isn't there?"

I nodded. He wasn't facing me, but he probably heard my neck creak.

When the eggs were cooked, William pulled biscuits out of the oven, placed two each on our plates. We sat beside each other at Lucas's breakfast bar and ate.

"Soda biscuits. I haven't had these since I was a kid in Texas."

"They soak up the butter nicely, don't they? I'm not overly fond of a sweet biscuit. I like mine savory."

"I like them in all their biscuity manifestations." I bit into my second one for emphasis and butter ran down my chin.

William laughed and handed me a napkin. "It's easy to see why he likes you."

"Who, Lucas? You know, I've heard that before, and I'm not sure I believe it."

"No. My alpha. He's quite fond of you, you know."

"Malcolm. Fond of me." I barked out a laugh.

"He is. We spoke about it before you, well, before you..." He cleared his throat.

"Before I spiked him into a coma?"

William cocked his head to one side. "Is that what you did?"

"Yes and no. But you already knew that, William." I loaded some of the egg mixture into the last bite of my biscuit. "We told you what happened."

"Yes, you did. It all seems so far-fetched when you really think about it, reading people's thoughts and spiking into a person's brain. Like something out of a speculative fiction novel."

"You mean like human beings who shift into wolves?" I waggled my eyebrows at him as I took a bite of sausage.

He chuckled. "Touché."

We finished our meals and I took our plates to the sink and began cleaning up. Felt it was the least I could do since he'd done the cooking.

William ate the last of the eggs, sausage, and cheese straight from the pan, then handed it to me to wash and finished off the other eight biscuits.

"You're better than a garbage disposal," I joked.

"That's what my sister says."

He grabbed a towel and dried the dishes I'd set in the drainer by the sink. We lapsed into a comfortable silence until I broke it.

"Who do you think is trying to kill Malcolm?"

"Someone who hates him. This isn't a power play. It's too—" He grappled for the word. "—too passionate for a power play."

"Jilted ex-lover maybe?"

"Malcolm doesn't jilt. His ex-lovers are treated well, and they enter into the relationship with their eyes wide open. He makes certain of that. Similar to our Lucas, Malcolm tends to remain friends with his mistresses after it ends. Good thing, or they'd have half the world after them, the way those men go through lovers."

I pulled the plug and watched the soapy water swirl down the drain. "That sounded like a warning."

"If you're as smart as Malcolm and Lucas think you are, you don't need a warning. You'll have read them both, the way you're likely reading me right now."

"Nope."

His brows lowered. "Nope?"

"I haven't been reading you. I've been talking with you."

William's mouth fell open. "You don't read everyone?"

"Not unless I'm looking for something."

"For the love of Pete, why not?" He tossed the dish towel on the counter. "We live in a dangerous world and you don't have the speed, strength, or reflexes of a shifter. You must use all weapons at your disposal at all times in order to keep yourself safe."

After he said that, I read him, a quick pass over his thoughts.

Good gracious, woman. Take care of yourself.

"'Good *gracious*?'" I laughed.

He threw up his hands. "*Now* she reads me."

Two hours later, William and I were standing over Malcolm's bed. The alpha was thinner now, and he'd lost his suntan. The coma was taking a toll on his body.

"I'd like to try spiking him again."

"*What?*" William gaped at me.

"He's in a weakened state," Maria Cortez slipped into the room behind us. She lifted Malcolm's wrist and stared down at her watch. "His pulse is steady, but it's far weaker than it should be."

"If he gets too distressed, I'll pull out of his head. Right away."

"What if you send him deeper into the coma?" Maria asked. "I don't know that we should risk it. He's holding on, but even Dr. Penbright isn't sure for how much longer."

"Then what have you got to lose?" I touched Malcolm's palm. It was as cold and dry as the hand of a corpse.

"His sanity?"

"Look, I don't want to hurt him, Maria. I honestly don't. However, I don't think intravenous feedings and antibiotics are going to do the trick. He needs release from the thing in his head, and I'm the only one here who can do that."

"What is in there, exactly?" she asked.

"A curse." I recalled what Lupita had said about her mother's beliefs and instantly wished I'd phrased it differently. "I mean, a very *human* sort of curse. Not a demon or witch or anything. Well, maybe a witch, but definitely not a demon. I don't think."

I kept thinking about how Dolores had thrown the charms into the fireplace and burned them with blue fire until they liquefied. She certainly believed in demon magic.

Ignoring Maria's horrified look, I said, "I need to look around his head. I won't poke at the loop unless I one hundred percent believe I can fix it. It's his memories I need. I'm almost certain he trusted his attacker."

"Why do you say that?" William asked.

"Because he either didn't notice them poking around in his head or he didn't care. We're talking about Xavier Malcolm. The most suspicious shifter in Southern California let his guard down to the extent that someone got into his head."

"What if that's because they wiped the memory away? I've heard demons can do that," William said.

Maria crossed herself. I had the strangest urge to do the same, and I'm not religious.

"I suppose that's possible, but I didn't see any evidence of it." I released Malcolm's hand, laid it gently by his side. "We should bring in a healer. Or a witch."

"No. Absolutely not." William thrust out his hand like a karate chop, palm down. "I've already pissed off my entire pack. If my alpha found out you involved witches in his treatment, he'd have you and me murdered, then he'd find Lucas and murder him twice. Malcolm hates witchcraft."

"I know. Because of his mother. But desperate times call for desperate measures. We aren't getting anywhere with the current treatment. If I can't figure out a way to break the loop, we'll have no choice but to call in a witch. It's either that or watch him slowly die."

William let his hand drop. His face paled, making his dark red hair stand out in marked contrast.

"We're running out of options, William."

"I know."

"His condition is weakening, and I'm not only talking about physically. His mind is giving off a strange vibration."

"You've been in his head again?" William's shoulders went up and his brows went down.

"No. I don't have to. I can feel it from here." I decided it was time to say what I'd been thinking. "I think his brain is dying."

CHAPTER TWENTY-TWO

"Shouldn't we wait for Lucas?" William stood by the only window in the room, peered out through the curtains.

"We've waited all afternoon. He said he'd be home four hours ago and he keeps making excuses for being late. Where is he now?" I crossed the room to Malcolm's bedside, straightened the blankets. Maria had gone to her room to rest with her girls after showing William how to care for the IV in the bend of Malcolm's elbow.

"Last I heard, he and his second, the eagle, and a couple of his shifters were setting up lookout points all over Sundance."

"How long will that take?" I asked.

"It could take hours if they've never been established." He turned away from the window. "But knowing the violently paranoid Blacke security team, they've prepared for something like this."

That sounded about right. Chandra was violent and Lucas was paranoid. They made a scary efficient team.

"Let's hope they show up soon." I took the extra black velvet spell bag out of my dress pocket.

He groaned. "Is that what I think it is?"

"Depends. What do you think it is?"

"A hex bag. Neely, you can't use witchcraft. Malcolm wouldn't approve."

"Fine. If it'll make you feel better, I'll ask permission." I held up the bag and shook it at the alpha. "Is it okay if I use this hex bag to determine if you've been magically cursed, Alpha Malcolm?" I waited a beat, then said, "He doesn't seem to have any objections."

"Christ. I cannot see this."

I tossed the bag and caught it in the palm of my hand. "Then you'd better cover those pretty green eyes, Mr. Scott, because this is happening."

The bedroom door swung open.

"Stop flirting, Neely. We have work to do."

Lucas strode into the room. Black smudges circled his eyes, his color was off, and so was his mood. He didn't seem like a person who was currently angry so much as someone who'd been recently annoyed and was feeling prickly.

"You finally made it," I said dryly.

"It would seem so." He looked at my hand. "Another hex bag? Are we really that desperate?"

"It's the same bag I had before," I said, but I was drowned out by Dolores, who entered the room with Dottie on her heels.

"Nothing desperate about it, tiger. Hex bags might not be sexy magic, but they work." She dropped her scowl and gave Lucas a wide, crafty smile. "Now about my new bar, my plan is to work around the gift shop, since the tower won't let me put the displays into another room."

"Won't *let* you?" I asked.

"Yeah. The place has got its own ideas about how furniture should be arranged. A pain in the patoot, but I can work around it."

Lucas groaned. "I told you I'd talk to you about that later. We need to concentrate on the multitude of problems facing us right now."

"Fair enough, Tiger." Dolores nodded brusquely, then faced the room. "How's Sleeping Bastard doing?"

"Don't talk about my alpha like that." William's eyes flashed gold.

"Well, he's no Sleeping Beauty," she said.

"He's weakening," I answered.

Dottie flitted to my side and rested the back of her hand to my cheek. "No fever. Good. You're a strong young woman to have recovered so quickly from that terrible spell."

"Spell?" William let his head fall back. "Merciful heavens. These aren't witches. They aren't."

I ignored William and took a closer look at Lucas's exhausted face. "What's wrong with you? You look terrible."

"I told you to stop flirting."

"Drop the sarcasm, Lucas, and tell me what's going—"

"You bet your pale white heinie we're witches, wolf." Dolores pointed at herself and Dottie.

"Oh Lord, the ball's on the slates now." William wore the look of a kid whose ball had indeed been kicked up on a roof. "I'm done for."

Dolores's anger visibly subsided. "Well now, fella, you look like you just walked off the moors. Whereabouts in Scotland are your people? We've got an aunt—"

"Come with me." I exchanged positions on the bed with Dottie and took Lucas's hand, dragging him out of the bedroom, down the short hall, and into the kitchen. "Sit."

He must have been tired, because he obeyed me—sans snark, for once. He dropped onto the same stool I'd sat on when William fed me brunch.

I took some frozen vegetables out of the freezer, grabbed salad fixings and two sirloin steaks out of the fridge. While the meat warmed to room temperature, I threw the vegetables into a pot with a can of broth and stewed tomatoes. Brought it to a boil, then set it to simmer.

"What are you making?"

"A quick meatless *caldo*. It would be better with fresh vegetables, but you need food now. I think you lost five pounds on the trip from the bedroom to the kitchen."

"I forgot to eat today." He frowned. "No, wait. I had an apple."

"You have a shifter metabolism. You need to eat regularly." I poured the makeshift soup into a bowl and some red wine I'd taken from the wine cooler under the counter into a glass and set both in front of him. "Don't be stupid."

"You say the nicest things." He ate half the soup in one big slurp.

201

"Here. Eat this, too." I handed him an over-sized bowl of salad I'd poured a quickie olive oil and red wine vinegar dressing over, and took away the empty soup bowl. He fell upon the salad like a man starving, which is what he was.

His lips were slick with vinaigrette when he smiled up at me. "Whoa. I didn't know you could cook like this."

"I opened a two-pound bag of salad greens and threw in some grape tomatoes you had on the counter. As my *tío* would say, 'this isn't cooking, it's fixing.'" I gestured to his salad. "Finish the rest."

I tossed the steaks on Lucas's fancy stovetop grill. While they cooked, I whipped up butter, lemon juice, rosemary, basil, and a couple other spices I found in the cabinet. I slapped the barely seared steaks on a plate, slathered them with the herb butter, and got them in front of Lucas just as he'd speared the last piece of lettuce in his salad with his fork.

"Marry me."

My left eyebrow shot up. "I might take your proposal more seriously if you said it to me instead of the steaks."

"I was *talking* to the steaks."

While he ate, I located the ingredients for Tío José's famous snickerdoodles and whipped up a batch. It had been a while since I'd made the little cinnamon-dusted treats, but I never forgot a recipe.

"I smell vanilla. Are you making cookies?"

"Snickerdoodles. You need calories."

He lifted his head as high as he could without standing up, tried to peek over my shoulder. "If those really are snickerdoodles, I take back my proposal to the steaks."

"Good thing, since you ate one of the steaks right after you proposed."

I dropped sugar-and-cinnamon-dusted dough onto a cookie sheet and slid it into the perfectly preheated convection oven. Everything in Lucas's kitchen was high-end. The Viking professional gas range had to have cost at least twelve thousand dollars. Cooking on it was a religious experience.

"You have Nielson-Massey Madagascar vanilla, unsalted grass-fed butter, and Ceylon cinnamon. I own a bakery and I don't have this grade of ingredients."

"I like nice things."

"You don't cook. Who does your shopping?"

"I cook a little." He looked at me sideways. "Okay, fine. Dan. He's a great cook. Really knows his stuff."

Dan Winters. Oh joy. "Great. I used his ingredients. He'll hate me even more now."

"You used *my* ingredients and Dan doesn't hate you. He fears you. There's a difference."

"Not so's you'd notice, though, right?" I flicked on the oven light.

"Dan needs to pull his shit together. You aren't going anywhere, and he can't keep acting like an ass. He can either get over it or move on."

"What? Why?" I stopped looking through the oven window and looked at him instead.

"It's disruptive," he grumbled.

"No, I mean why do you say I'm not going anywhere?"

"Because you aren't." He shoved a piece of steak into his mouth. Chewed and swallowed, drained the wineglass. "And if Dan can't deal, he can find another group."

"But you've known him longer than you've known me."

"It's not about that. If I let Dan chase you away because you're a spiker, it sets a bad precedent. It tells my group that I'm only good with some types of paranormals, not all. That gets people thinking, makes them wonder where they stand with me. Makes them fearful."

I wanted to read him so badly. Wanted to see if he meant that, or if, perhaps, there was another reason he didn't want Dan to run me out of Sundance. I suppressed the temptation. Yes, I was reading him more now, but only during times where the information I gleaned from him was important to my physical and mental wellbeing.

Not because I was wondering if the cute boy in class really liked me.

"Makes them fearful?" I poured him another glass of wine.

Nodding, he chewed and swallowed the last bite of steak and downed the wine I'd just poured him. "What if this week it's spikers, but next week it's reptile shifters? Who won't be accepted next?" He came around the bar with his dishes and set them in the sink. "I don't want what's happening in Malcolm's pack to happen in my group. I've never wanted that."

He washed the dishes, finishing up just as the cookies came out of the oven.

"That smells the way a hug feels."

I grinned. "You sound like a TV commercial. *'Folks, these cookies are like a hug from Grandma.'*"

"From Grandma? No, not what I meant at all." He wrapped both arms around my waist and squeezed, resting his chin on my shoulder. "Thanks for all this."

His body was a comforting weight against mine and I leaned into him because, even though he was a bad idea waiting to happen, he was also the one solid thing I could hold onto right now.

"You're welcome."

I prodded one of the fragrant cookies with a finger. Not quite cool enough for eating, but Lucas didn't seem to care. He let go of me with one arm and snatched up a warm cookie, shoveling it into his mouth.

"Mmm." He chewed, swallowed, then grabbed another.

"Good to see I still have some baking skills left." It really hadn't been that long since I'd baked, but every day I spent away from La Buena Suerte Panaderia felt like too long.

"Have you decided to keep the bakery open?"

"No. I haven't decided anything." I hadn't had time to think beyond the moment since leaving San Diego.

"Understandable. It's a big decision." He grabbed another warm cookie off the pan. "I know you probably won't marry me if I ask, since I did propose to the steaks a few minutes ago, but how about being my friend?"

I laughed. "I think I can manage that."

"Stay out of this, Neely. I'm talking to the cookie."

204

"Spiking Malcolm again, huh? Well, it's not a terrible idea," Lucas said.

"Wow. Thanks for the enthusiasm." We were sprawled on the floor cushions in the living room, gorging on snickerdoodles and arguing about how to proceed with the comatose alpha leader in the guest room down the hall.

"Then tell me. What are you going to do this time that you didn't attempt to do last time? Because it sounds like nothing."

I wrinkled my nose at his condescending tone. "For starters, I'm not going to touch the memory loop. I'm going to look for Malcolm's memories leading up to the loop. If I can pinpoint the moment the person put that thing in his head, I should be able to tell you who did it."

"Why didn't you try this before?"

"Because it's a delicate process. Because it might make things worse. Because the last time I was in Malcolm's head there were a bunch of guns pointed at me. I wasn't going to try something I wasn't a hundred percent sure would work."

Lucas looked at me. "Are you a hundred percent sure now?"

"No." I sighed.

"Then don't do it."

"I have to try something. His brain is getting less and less responsive. Do we just leave him to rot in this mental coma?"

"For now? Yes." Lucas leaned back against the pillows and closed his eyes. The lines in his face had deepened since this morning. I'd thought he needed food, but it looked like he needed sleep even more.

"You're exhausted. When did you last sleep?"

"I don't know. I told you, I don't trust Malcolm."

Yet he'd made sure I slept, even holding me in my sleep when things got bad. The man annoyed me six ways from Sunday, but he confused me even more.

"Lucas Blacke, I really don't understand you sometimes."

Though his eyes remained closed, his mouth curled into a smile. "Good. I like to keep you on your toes."

"You keep me on my heels," I retorted. Then I adjusted the pillows around him, so he'd be more comfortable.

"Too soft," he whispered.

I looked around. "Do you want firmer ones? Are there any here?"

"Not the pillows. You."

"I'm not soft. I'm just concerned about you."

"Soft and sweet and warm, like a sugar cookie fresh from the oven."

Maybe I really was destined to be a baker after all, because I kind of liked the comparison. Obviously, I couldn't let him know that or he'd never let up.

"Soft? Ha! I'm as hard as they come. I'm Bruce Willis in *Die Hard*, I'm Sigourney Weaver in *Alien 2*, I'm John Wick and Thor and Wonder Woman all rolled into one. Do you want the rest of this snickerdoodle?"

He laughed and opened one eye, snatched the cookie out of my hand, and ate it.

Behind us, sneakers squeaked on the kitchen floor. "Neely? Is that you, dear? I need to speak to you—and Alpha Blacke, if possible." Dottie peered into the darkened living room. "If you aren't, *erm*, well, busy."

"I'm eating Neely's cookies," Lucas said.

I smacked his leg. "Don't be gross."

"Oh dear. Oh well, you know ... I can come back later, although I really shouldn't, because this is quite important."

"*Snickerdoodles*, Dottie. It's not a euphemism, I really did make cookies. Don't you smell them?"

The elderly woman looked relieved. "Yes. Now that you mention it, I can. In that case, finish eating quickly, because I have something quite unpalatable to discuss with you."

Lucas blew out a long sigh, closed his eyes again. "More good news? Bring it on."

"Sorry, Alpha Blacke, it's not good news." Dottie scuttled into the room, clutching the black velvet hex bag. She knelt by one of the cushions and dumped the contents onto the fabric surface. "You say you got this from Bill Bill, Neely?"

"Yes."

"Impossible." She indicated the ingredients with a wave of her hand. "There's no wintergreen."

"Possible, and you never mentioned wintergreen to me," I said.

"Not to you, no, but I did tell Bill. Not that I needed to, he'd have known it was a requirement. Why didn't he include it in the hex bag?"

Lucas's eyes popped open and he sat up. "What does the wintergreen do?"

"Breaks hexes. Well, along with the other ingredients. But without a wintergreen base, this spell bag is useless."

"Harmful?" I asked.

"Not in any active way. It simply doesn't work."

"So, we have a useless hex bag and cursed globe charms and the one thing both have in common is Bill Bill," Lucas said.

Chandra strolled through the front door, catching the last of our conversation.

"Come on, Alpha. Not another enemy. At this point, I need a spreadsheet to keep track." She started toward the kitchen, then did a full stop. "Wait. Bill Bill? Didn't we just get a shipment of ammunition from him?"

"Oh dear." Dottie hustled out of the room. "I'd better get Dolores."

"It's not as if I knew he was double-crossing us. He's neutral. He's not supposed to be able to." Lucas sank back into the cushions. "He gave me a great price."

"Didn't you read him?" Chandra asked.

I shook my head.

She squeezed her eyes shut and massaged the top of her head.

Wincing, I said, "I'm sorry. I should have."

"Yeah." She turned away from me and faced Lucas. "Alpha, we need to check that ammo."

"Put Earp on it," Lucas croaked. He sounded weaker than he had the moment before, and it was starting to seriously worry me.

"Got it." Chandra slid her cell phone out of her pocket and tapped on it. When she was finished, she looked at me and asked, "Where's the cat?"

"Lestat? Last I saw, he was on Lucas's bed."

"He might be in the Kosta Boda bowl on the top of the refrigerator," Lucas mumbled. "Those are his two favorite spots."

"He sleeps in an art glass bowl?" Chandra asked.

"Lestat is a cat of refined tastes." Lucas's eyes slid shut. He was entirely too exhausted, even considering his lack of sleep. Shifters required substantial amounts of food and good rest to function at their best, but they had stamina for days if they didn't mind dialing back the shapeshifting.

"How many times did you shift today?" I asked him.

"Once or twice. Hybrid form three times."

For another shifter that might be a lot. For Lucas, it was a slow morning.

Chandra made a kissy sound and rubbed her fingers together. "Here, cat."

My surprise must have shown on my face, because she scowled at me.

"Chandra likes Lestat. They've bonded," Lucas murmured. "Isn't that right, Second?"

"He's tolerable. Also, his fur is soft to touch, and his purr makes my pulse slow down." She cocked an eyebrow at me. "So, how did you know he was in Alpha Blacke's *bed*?"

"Because she slept there," Lucas replied, "which makes one of us."

Chandra clicked her tongue. "You two are slow."

I started to reply when I noticed Lucas's eyelids fluttering as if he were dreaming. His skin, washed out before eating, had faded to a worrisome gray color.

"Lucas?" I touched his arm.

No response.

"Lucas?" This time I shook his arm.

Chandra looked from me to her alpha. In a booming voice that made my teeth hurt, she said, "*Alpha Blacke.*"

When he didn't respond to that either, I started yelling at him, shaking him. "Lucas? What's wrong? *Lucas?*"

Nothing.

Her expression stark, Chandra said, "I can't reach him through the pack bonds. Read him."

"I am. His thoughts are running in these ... I don't know, these sluggish circles."

"What's he thinking about?"

I shook my head. "It's too personal."

Chandra's eyes narrowed to slits. "This man is not only my alpha, he's my friend. I have very few of those. Understand that there is nothing I would not do to keep him alive. If you can trust anyone with his personal thoughts, you can trust me. Read me, spike me, whatever you have to do to convince yourself of that, because you're going to tell me what he's thinking *right fucking now.*"

"Okay." I pressed my hand to his cheek. His skin was dry and cold, corpse-like—same as Malcolm's. "He watched me this morning. Stood over his bed and watched me sleeping in it. It's what he's picturing. He stroked my hair. I think he likes to touch it—touch me." I swallowed, tried to keep my voice from shaking. "I'm feeling what he feels." Which amounted to confusion. Lucas cared for me, but he was conflicted. I could definitely understand that.

"What else?" Chandra asked.

"That's it. Me sleeping, him touching my hair. Repeating in a slow circle."

Chandra's mouth flattened into a grim little line. "He's in distress."

"Why do you say that?"

"Because he's comforting himself."

Comforting himself. With thoughts of me. My heart squeezed in my chest and tears sprang to my eyes. "Lucas, wake up, *please.*"

Dolores trotted into the room, followed by Dottie and William. "We heard yelling. Where's the fire?"

"We can't wake him." I sniffed, wiped my eyes with the outer edge of my hand. "Can you do anything?"

"Let me take a look." Dolores muscled her way around the sofa and kicked through the floor pillows. Dottie followed. Both witches crouched beside Lucas, closed their eyes, chanted under their breath. William stood over all of us, watching intently.

Dolores's eyes popped open. "Sis, what's this feel like to you?"

"Could be a succubus." Dottie said this between chants and without opening her eyes.

"Makes perfect sense," Dolores said. "If anyone was going to get caught up with a succubus, it would be this one."

"Show some respect, witch," Chandra snarled.

Dottie finally opened her eyes. "My sister's insult to the alpha aside, we're not talking about an actual female sex demon. It's a spell."

"Another fucking spell." Chandra looked like she had something bitter in her mouth. "Who did it, what does it do, and how do we break it?"

"I can't tell you who cast it without a blood sacrifice. Dolores and I stay far away from dark magic. Dangerous stuff. As far as what it is, it's a wasting spell. Usually, it's connected to a cursed object. A potion, a hex bag, a crystal, a stone."

"Check his right front pocket. He had a pink rock in there earlier. Said he wanted to have it made into a necklace." Chandra made an obvious effort to not look at me. "For someone."

Dolores patted Lucas down like a police officer. She pulled out the quartz he'd purchased at Bill Bill's shop and immediately tossed it on the pillow by Dottie. "I don't have to guess where he picked this up. It's got dark magic all over it."

"Can't you call that blue flame again?" I asked. "Burn it?"

"No." She'd paled, which wasn't easy to do, since her skin was already the color of a bag of flour in a snowstorm. "It won't work. Dot and I'll do what we can to break the spell, kiddo, but for now, the alpha needs to rest."

Dottie fashioned a white handkerchief into a sling and rolled the rock into it by moving the pillow. "This looks awful."

It looked like a pretty rock to me.

Dolores shook her head. "I can't believe Bill would double-cross us like that."

"I can. People are always doing stupid shit when power, money, or love is involved." Chandra stood, stared down at Lucas, but spoke to me. "Hey, Neely?"

"Y-Yes?" I wiped my cheeks with the heel of my hand before looking at her.

"You up for a road trip?"

"Dot and I are." Dolores slapped her leg as she tottered to her feet. "Just need to stop by the tower first for supplies."

CHAPTER TWENTY-THREE

"I THOUGHT YOUR JOB WAS TO PROTECT LUCAS."

It was eight p.m. and the sky was just starting to darken. We were sitting in Chandra's silver Jeep Wrangler, parked in the lot at the witches' tower, waiting for Dolores and Dottie. I'd changed into jeans, a green T-shirt, and a black hoodie. Not exactly clandestine gear, but the best I could do.

Chandra gave me a hard look. "It is."

"Then why are you leaving him?" I admit, the question came out a little whiny. I'd been stifling a sob since leaving Lucas's house twenty minutes ago.

"Amir is there."

"But—"

Chandra held up her hand. "Dan Winters and Amir Gamal are Alpha Blacke's third and fourth for a reason. Amir is absolutely the shifter I'd want at my back in a fight. He's loyal, brave, and smart. Dan's those things, too, he just doesn't have the killer instinct the rest of us do. You know that's why Alpha made him his third, right? Dan is a good guy. He keeps the leadership of the group balanced."

Good guy? That hadn't been my experience, but I was willing to go along with it for argument's sake.

She continued, "Dan's good, but he can't do the things necessary to keep Alpha safe. Dan will die for his Alpha, but Amir? Amir will kill for him, indiscriminately and without hesitation. Like me."

I'd seen inside all three of their heads and knew this to be true.

"Neither of them has my experience with tracking, and that's what we need right now. We need to track down who put that spell on Alpha, and then we need to kill him. Or her. Or them. In case it isn't Bill Bill."

"I don't like leaving him when he's this vulnerable." I swallowed the acrid taste of tears at the back of my throat.

Chandra did a very un-Chandra-like thing then. She reached over and squeezed and released my hand. She did it so quickly I had to wonder if I'd imagined it.

"Same here. As I told you before, Lucas Blacke is not only my alpha, he's my friend. Possibly the only true one I've got. I wouldn't leave him like this unless I had to, and I wouldn't leave him with anyone I didn't believe could protect him."

"I trust you, Chandra. I'm just worried."

"Yeah. I know." A squirrel scuttled past us, disappearing into an arroyo beside an ironwood tree with gray shaggy bark and no leaves. Chandra and I both tracked the squirrel's progress, though I was pretty sure for different reasons, considering the momentary amber glow in her eyes.

"You're wrong, you know," I said, after a while.

"I'm not. He'll be safe with Amir."

"No, not about that. About Lucas being your only friend."

I smiled to myself as she opened and closed her mouth several times, clearly having no clue how to respond. For some reason, that cheered me.

"Sweet pepper salsa, what's the hold up?" The tower door swung open and Dolores sped out, Dottie trundling along behind her.

"I'm coming."

"About time. I could have been killed waiting for you to get ready, Dot. Let's get this show on the road before Malcolm's wolves turn up flashing teeth and guns and subpar IQs. Or Bill Bill sends a demon curse our way. Not sure which would be worse. Dead is dead, after

213

all." She opened the rear door of the Jeep, and she and Dottie slid into the back seat.

"Piffle. You think everyone is out to get you."

"It's only considered paranoia if I'm wrong."

"Well, you're wrong about Bill." Dottie shook her head as she fumbled with her seatbelt. "I've known that man since he was an infant. I knew his parents and grandparents. He would never do such a thing as this. He's a neutral party—in fact, the Williams family has been neutral since the Dark Ages. I find it hard to believe he would risk the reputation of his ancestors and his descendants."

Dolores scowled. "You've got a point. He didn't kill the alpha, just put him in a coma. He didn't sabotage the bag to kill Alpha Malcolm, just left the wintergreen out so it wouldn't work. Seems like if he was set on betraying not only the trust of his loyal customer base, but centuries of his family, he'd have at least made it bloodier."

Bloodier? I shook my head. "Not where I thought you were going with that, Dolores."

"Exactly where *I* thought you were going." Chandra pulled onto Interstate 8 and headed west. "You know, witch, I think you and I might get along fine."

"Thanks, hyena." Dolores held up an insulated bag with a picture of a cartoon tiger wearing rhinestone spandex on it. The sound of bottles clinking inside the bag drowned out the radio. "Brought wine for the trip. And some snacks."

"Good thinking. We might need the extra sugar for our magic." Dottie grabbed a bottle out of the bag and proceeded to take a hefty slug.

I relaxed into the passenger seat and tried to trace back to the origins of how I'd ended up on a late-night road trip with a homicidal hyena shifter and two wine-soaked witches. It started the first time I plonked a sneaker down on Sundance dirt, I concluded. It was destiny. Karma. Fate.

Staring out the window, I watched the desert scrub turn to mountain scrub, then green-topped pines. The gentle bounce of the road, coupled with the low music and the humming of tires against asphalt, succeeded in lulling me to sleep just as we crossed the line between Smokethorn and San Diego counties.

I was soon awakened by the sweet, soothing voice of a witch.

"Wake up, kiddo. Time to kick some ass."

My eyelids popped open and I jerked up in my seat. We were parked in Bill Bill's back lot. Chandra was gone, Dolores was in the driver's seat, and Dottie was passed out in the back.

"Dropped the hyena off a mile from here. Been waiting half an hour and nobody's come or gone. How do you feel about going in?"

I rubbed my eyes, yawned. "The lights are out. Is he there?"

"Yeah. He lives under the shop." Dolores opened her door. "I suggest we leave Dottie here for now. We might need her on the outside. In case we get into trouble."

A quick look in the back seat told me Dottie wasn't going to be playing the part of the cavalry anytime soon. "She's drunk."

"Nah, she's taking a nap. Takes more than two bottles to bring down a Fairfield witch. If we need her, she'll come."

Two *bottles*? I got out of the car and reached my arms above my head, relishing the feel of my muscles stretching and my back popping. "Do you think he'll answer the door?"

Dolores laughed. It wasn't a cackle, but it was close. "Nope. But it doesn't matter. I've got a key."

She laughed again, and this time it was definitely a cackle.

"Your foot is not a key."

"It opened the door, didn't it?" Dolores shouldered her way into the shop, making no effort to stay quiet. She took down the wards surrounding Bill's place with a few Latin phrases and told me to follow.

"That and your magic."

"You saw that?" She made a face. "I wanted you to think I was like one of those action heroes from a movie. Like Jet Li or that Stallone fella."

I rolled my eyes. "Let's get this over with."

215

"Fine." She smacked the light switch and cupped her hands around her mouth. *"William Williams, you haul your sorry hide over here right now before I blast your inventory of dragon eggshells to smithereens,"* she yelled.

Blinking to acclimate my eyes to the bright light, I muttered, "Subtle."

"The Fairfield witches don't do subtle." She made a so-so gesture. "Sometimes Dot can be subtle."

"When she's not passed out from drinking too much homemade wine in the back seat of a Jeep?"

"Humph. A little judgy for someone who drank a bottle and a half the last time she came over."

"We weren't on an investigation then." I closed my eyes to concentrate, reaching out with my telepathy. "I think he's over there." I pointed to a darkened corner about fifteen feet to the right of where we stood. Stacked cardboard boxes partitioned the area off from us and the overhead light.

"You think? You can't tell for sure?"

"His brain is very quiet." I opened myself to the energy around me, tried again. "There's barely a life force present in his head."

"Is he asleep? Drunk?" She sniffed the air. "Do you smell wine? I don't smell wine."

"Not everyone gets drunk on wine, Dolores. Proceed with caution. I don't know what's going on with him, but it doesn't feel natural."

"I knew it. He's cursed." Dolores reached into her pocket and pulled out one of the globe charm necklaces. "Here, this should help soften the damage from any demon spells. Won't last for long, but it's better than nothing. I made it after that whole demon curse thing. I used one of the charms I stole from the tiger."

"Okay." I took it from her and slung it over my head, but then I questioned why I was constantly trusting a witch who got me into trouble every time we were together. "Wait a minute. The charms you *stole* from Lucas? I saw you throw them into blue fire."

"See, back in my twenties, I was a magician's assistant."

"You're telling a story *now?*"

"What? Bill's not doing anything." Her mouth curved in a faraway smile. "Boy, I thought Myron the Magnificent was the one for me. The man didn't have an ounce of magic in him, but he was excellent at sleight of hand tricks and he was hung like a bull."

Oh God. "Dolores, there's a time and—"

"Sadly, his wife found out exactly how good he'd been at sleight of hand with his assistants. She broke his fingers with a sledgehammer. After he recovered, he went to work for her father's insurance agency, and I went back to my witchcraft practice. But I never forgot the tricks he showed me." She waggled her brows. "Not a single one."

"Hey, thanks for the visual, but can we concentrate on the man we came here to confront?" I continued staring into the dark corner. As far as I could tell, Bill Bill hadn't moved.

"Sure thing. You're the one who asked about the necklaces."

I scowled at the charm resting against my sternum. "Hang on, if you didn't destroy the charms, why did I feel better?"

"Lavender-based hex bag. Dot had it in her pocket. The fire stuff was a show for the alpha. A little Latin, a little blue flame—"

"Why?"

"Because those blasted charms were very dangerous and very specific—to *you*. If the tiger had them, he'd have power over you, could potentially control you. After that Roso guy, I figured you'd rather not let that happen."

"You were *protecting* me?" A little burst of warmth spread through my chest. I knew Dolores liked me, but I hadn't realized how much. Lying to an alpha was no small thing—even for a witch.

"Of course, kiddo. Who else is going to bring the cookies to margarita night at the hot springs?"

"Thanks." I smiled. "You know Lucas is going to murder you if he finds out."

"*Pfft*. He'll have to get in line." Her brow dropped over her eyes. "Shh. Someone's coming. Use your telepathy and see who it is."

I had just reached out with my ability when a thickly muscled arm wrapped around my throat and cinched tight. "Tell me where that bastard Bill Bill is, or I'll snap your neck."

"Joaquín Mar?" I rasped.

The shark shifter whirled me around. "Neely? What the hell are you doing here?"

A low, gravelly voice in the corner answered for me. "*Dying.*"

The lights went out.

Joaquín shoved me to the right and I crashed into what I feared were the dragon eggshells Dolores had threatened to break. Whatever it was felt crunchy beneath my palms and knees and emitted a stench that reminded me of cat urine.

"Get him," Dolores grunted. I didn't know what she was doing, but it sounded like she was working hard at it. "He's going after Neely."

"I'm trying—*ouch.*" Furniture scraped across the floor. "It's too damn dark."

"Huh. Could have sworn you were a shifter. The Mar family I used to know were shark alphas—*for crying out loud, you stepped on my blasted foot.*"

"Sorry. I *am* a Mar shifter."

"Well, can't you people see in the dark?"

"Really? 'You people?'" Something ceramic hit the floor and shattered.

"Oh, don't get precious on me, fish boy."

"Yes, you pain in the ass, I can see in the dark—usually. I can't see in *this* darkness."

Dolores halted. "Must be a spell. Let's see what I can do."

Bill's beefy hands wrapped around my throat. I coughed to signal to the really strong shifter in the room that I needed help, when I remembered that I was a force to be reckoned with myself.

Why was I always having to remind myself of that?

I did my best to block out the pain from Bill's fingers crushing my windpipe as I pulled energy into me. Once I clamped onto his brainwaves, which were as jangly as an off-tune piano, I drove into his head.

Empty. The best way to describe the inside of his head was to picture a dusty desert plain with tumbleweeds rolling past.

His grip tightened, and panic took hold as I struggled to draw in air. My consciousness began to fade. Desperate, I drove as deep as I dared. I finally located a frantic little spark of life caged in a seldom-used part of his brain. It was fighting for its freedom—and losing badly.

Getting to the cage was the easy part. Once I was there, I pulled on the bars, rattled the door. Nothing. I focused on the locking mechanism, blasting it with the last of the energy and power and strength I had. It was a gamble. If it didn't work, I was dead. The air in my lungs was already gone. I had nothing else left.

The cage door exploded open and Bill Bill's consciousness flowed out of it, filling his skull with what felt like a rush of warm, placid water.

"There. That ought to take care of it," Dolores said. The overhead lights flickered on.

Bill Bill cried out and immediately released me.

I dropped to the floor like a stone and everything went dark.

CHAPTER TWENTY-FOUR

"Are you healing her or killing her?"

"Shut it, shark. I'm trying to concentrate. She pulled some of my energy back there and I'm not as strong as I usually am."

"Is that what that was? I felt it too," Joaquín Mar said.

"Yeah, well, apparently she needed it. Now quit hovering and go talk to Bill. See what he knows."

"Fine. Bossy witch," Mar grumbled.

Healing energy, vibrant and electric, cooled the burning in my throat. I awoke in increments of senses—first hearing, then touch, then *scent*.

My eyes flew open. "What is that godawful smell?" I coughed. My throat felt like someone had taken a cheese grater to it.

"You." Dolores had her hands on my throat and her face was twisted into a scowl. "You fell into a carton of boggart-treated stink bait. Now shut up and let me heal you. I'm not as good as Dottie is with choking wounds, and she's still three sheets to the wind in the back of the car."

"Told you she was drunk," I wheezed.

"Is this really the time for I-told-you-so's, bakery girl?"

Deciding I wanted the pain to stop more than I wanted to be right, I shut my mouth.

"You say it was a woman?" Joaquín asked.

"Woman? I don't know. Female, yes. I'm certain of that much." Bill Bill sounded pretty drunk himself, but I knew that he hadn't been drinking. He leaned against the wall across from Joaquín and rubbed his eyes with the heels of his hands. "Mr. Mar, I'm telling you the truth. She came into the store and bought some quartz and an elf tooth. That's all I remember. It's all pain and fear after that."

"When did she come in?" I asked. Dolores released my throat and I sat up, attempted to blink away the fuzziness in my brain.

Bill's forehead wrinkled. "Right after I did your tattoo. The same day, in fact. What was that, a couple days ago?"

"No." I showed him my healed tattoo.

"But you aren't a shifter, there's no way you could have healed so … quickly." Bill's face bled out its color as a look of horrific realization set in. "How long did I lose?"

"You gave me the tattoo at the beginning of August."

"I know," he said.

"It's the middle of September."

Bill sank heavily to the floor.

Joaquín looked at me, then back at Bill. "You don't remember her face?"

"No."

"Then how do you know she's female?" The shark shifter paced away from him.

"I-I don't know, but … I do."

I read Bill Bill. Just a quick whisk over his mind was all that was necessary. He was broadcasting his distress loud and clear. "He's telling the truth as he believes it."

Dolores knelt beside a badly shaken Bill Bill and spoke softly to him. I could tell she was worried. The witch was cantankerous and brusque, but she had a tender heart when it came to her friends. She'd proven that even before she stole the charms from Lucas to protect me.

"Dot, you booze hound, get in here." She called this out in a voice not nearly loud enough to reach the back seat of the car in the parking lot.

"We meet again." Joaquín held out a hand to me. I took it and he hauled me to my feet, waiting until I was steady before he let go.

"Thanks. What are you doing here?"

"We bought something from Bill Bill and it didn't work as planned. I came here to find out what was going on."

"It wasn't ammunition, was it?"

"I cannot confirm or deny that," he said, while nodding his head. Then he grinned. "The bullets won't fire. They fall apart in the chamber. It's the damnedest thing I've ever seen."

"Speaking of bullets, where's Chandra?"

"She'll be here when she gets here," Dolores said. "At least, that's what she told me."

"Lucas Blacke's assassin came with you?" Joaquín backed away from me. "You know what? I've got to go. I'll, uh, catch up with Bill later."

"*You're* afraid of Chandra? Chandra *Smith*?" I had to laugh. It was so absurd, this six-foot-two, two-hundred-twenty pounds of pure muscle shark shifter afraid of a hundred-twenty-pound woman.

"Yes, Chandra Smith." Joaquín leaned close and lowered his voice. "We went out once."

"Only once?"

"I forgot my wallet and didn't realize it until after the meal. She paid for dinner and then, as we were exiting the restaurant, she broke every bone in my right hand. No weapon, just a strategically placed punch. Hurt like a bastard."

"I bet you remember your wallet when you ask someone out on a date now," a voice behind me drawled.

Joaquín spun around. "I told you it was an accident. I left it in my duffel with my change of clothes." He flexed his hand into a fist. "It took weeks to heal, Smith. Dr. Penbright had to re-break it three times."

"If it had healed easily, it wouldn't have been a good lesson." Chandra leaned against the wall by the door and gave him a bored look. "Your dates should write me a thank you note."

"*Three* goddamned times," he snarled.

"So, where have you been?" I moved in front of Joaquín lest he make the stupid mistake of challenging Chandra.

"Outside. Watching the watchers, of course." Chandra snapped her head and a slender figure in a dark blue hoodie and glasses walked into the room.

Joaquín's mouth fell open. "*Diamond?*"

"WHAT ARE YOU DOING HERE?" I asked.

"My job." Diamond's face screwed into a frown. "Oh my God, what is that *smell?*"

"Me, apparently. I fell into some boggart stink bait. I can't imagine why anyone would want to catch one if they have to use this stuff to do it." I sniffed my arm and gagged.

"It's not for catching a boggart, dear. It's used in invoking ceremonies, to lure demons and ghouls into a circle." Dottie had finally shown up, and after Dolores chewed her out for being late, both witches perched on either side of Bill Bill, talking to him, offering comfort and sips of water from a plastic bottle.

"If she didn't know that, guarantee she doesn't know how boggart stink bait is made." The devious glint in Dolores's eye told me I didn't want to know. "Give you a hint. The harvesting occurs after the boggart has eaten a big meal."

"Oh God, that's so gross." I dry-heaved.

Chandra let out a long-suffering sigh. "Everyone shut up, please. Except you." She pointed at Diamond. "You start talking."

"Don't hurt her, hyena," Joaquín said, in that loud-without-yelling alpha tone.

A wicked smile spread across Chandra's face. "Means something to you, does she, Mar?"

"I am not screwing around."

He meant it. I didn't need to read him, either. Given the glowing, gilded eyes and the enormous gray fin that burst out of his back, there wasn't a soul in the room who didn't know he meant it.

Chandra appeared unimpressed. "All she has to do is answer my questions and I won't."

"I don't have answers." Diamond tucked her hands in the pockets of her blue hoodie. "I was watching. I'm a trader. It's what I do."

"No, see, traders don't watch just anything." Chandra slowly circled Diamond. "They watch the things that they've been paid or tipped off to watch."

Diamond didn't deny it. "You can hurt me all you want. I won't talk."

"Hurt you? You mean physically?" Chandra asked. "Why would you force me to do that?" She zipped across the room and grabbed a stool, zipped back. Slammed it on the floor in front of Diamond and motioned for her to sit.

Diamond was no fool. She sat.

"Smith..." Joaquín shook his head and gills erupted on the sides of his face.

"All I want is a name."

Diamond said nothing.

"Okay then. I'll give you some." Chandra backed up until she was against the wall. She leaned against it, arms crossed. "Herman Louis Shetland."

Diamond said nothing, but she didn't look comfortable.

"Marjorie Breckman Shetland. Jonathon William Breckman. Terri—"

"What do you think you're doing, assassin?" Diamond snapped.

"Showing you what I want, trader. By example. Terri Monroe. Jacquelin Reed. Norma Walker. Ellen Claymore."

"Whose names are those?" Joaquín asked.

"Stephania Reed Watson."

Diamond flinched. She narrowed her eyes at me. "You told her this, spiker?"

Now it was my turn to flinch. "Who told you I was a spiker?"

Joaquín Mar's head flew around. "You're a *spiker*? I thought you were a telepath."

"She's that, too." Diamond glared at me. "I'm a trader. It's my business to know."

"*Hole-lee* shit. When my brother finds out he had a spiker in front of him and all he negotiated for was a telepathic read?" Joaquín practically hooted with laughter. "This is going to be so good."

I ignored him, concentrated on Diamond. "I don't know what Chandra's talking about. I haven't read or spiked you."

She rolled her eyes. "Right."

"Unfortunately, she's telling the truth." Dolores called this out from the other side of the room. "Neely here abuses her ability. Rarely uses it unless a situation falls in line with her 'rules.' Can you imagine?"

"No way." Diamond frowned at me. "Knowledge is everything in our world. If I were a telepath-spiker, I'd use it all the time."

I rubbed the back of my head. It wasn't sore, thanks to Dolores, but I remembered falling and kept thinking it ought to be. "No, you wouldn't."

Diamond laughed, a little meanly, I thought. "Hell yes, I would. If I could spike, I'd be using it now, on all of you."

"What a jerk," Dolores muttered.

I said nothing, simply glossed over Diamond's brain. Telepathy only, no spiking. For now.

"They're *your* names," I said. "Chandra was rattling off your aliases. Except that last one. That one was your—"

"I told you. I was watching the watchers," Diamond snapped.

That last name was her daughter's, and she obviously wanted to protect it. Fine by me. I wasn't about bringing kids into an adult situation if it wasn't necessary. As Dolores had lamented, I had my rules.

"*Herman Louis* Shetland?" Joaquín laughed. "I'd pay to see that alias."

Diamond's responding smile was accompanied by an eyebrow raise. "You already have. You just didn't know it."

Joaquín stopped laughing.

"Were you paid to watch whoever was watching Bill Bill?" Chandra asked.

"Yeah, I was paid for it. Can you honestly imagine me doing it out of the kindness of my heart, assassin?"

"Drop the sarcasm. I want the name of who hired you and whatever watcher you were supposed to be watching."

"All of them, and I won't tell you my employer's name."

Chandra stared unblinkingly at her. "Tell me who the watchers are. Now."

"That I can do. It's not proprietary information. However, it'll cost you."

Her teeth tightly clenched, Chandra nodded. "*Fine.*"

Diamond ticked them off on her fingers. "Richard Penn."

"And?" Chandra made a hurry-up gesture with her hand. Apparently, Dick's name hadn't surprised her. It hadn't surprised me, either.

"And a shifter from your pack. Female. Latinx. Lisa Cesar."

"Fucking rattlesnake." Chandra dragged her hand through her hair. "She was here tonight?"

"No. Tonight it was only Penn. I've been watching this place for weeks." Diamond stood, dusted off her clothing. She cleaned her blue-framed glasses with a cloth she removed from her hoodie pocket.

"I want your employer's name," Chandra growled.

Joaquín made a threatening clicking sound. He was half-way into his hybrid form now.

Diamond blinked. "No." I wasn't sure if she was talking to Joaquín or answering the question.

Chandra persisted. "Local?"

The information trader shook her head. "I said I won't tell you who my employer is. You can shout out every name that means something to me and I won't tell you. This is about my honor."

"A trader with honor? They exist?" Chandra laughed.

"They do."

The way Diamond said it wiped the smirk off Chandra's face. She looked at the trader, looked at me, then gave a nod in the direction of the exit. "Fine. Go."

Diamond strolled to the door, halting beside Chandra. "I'll send you my bill."

Chandra examined her nails as she replied, "I'm sure you have the address."

"Wait." I held up a hand. I knew what Chandra wanted me to do, but I needed a few seconds more. "I have to know. Is it your employer's intention to hurt Luc—Alpha Blacke?"

"Spiker, you ask a lot of questions." Diamond locked gazes with me for a long moment, her wide brown eyes glimmering in the unflattering fluorescent lights. "I've already made it clear that I won't tell you anything about who I work for."

Because she knew she didn't have to. She could use me to tell us what we wanted to know and still keep her honor because she hadn't willingly given up her employer. My personal rules were once again starting to seem more like light suggestions in the face of cold reality.

I skimmed her brain. She was purposely thinking about her employer, making it easy for me. In case she'd conjured up this person to throw me off track, I drove deeper into her head to get the whole truth—as best I could, anyway. Telepathy was open to interpretation, even when blended with spiking.

Power flowed into me—*from Joaquin, Chandra, the witches*—and I used it to push into Diamond's head. She would feel this, but I didn't care. We both knew what I was doing.

A minute passed. Diamond gritted her teeth. Shook her head as if to clear it.

"What's going on?" Joaquin Mar's voice echoed in the silent room. "Why do you look like that, Di?"

"Neely," Chandra said.

Diamond's brain was strong and vibrant and delicious. The longer I spent there, the harder it was to leave. I wanted to crawl all the way inside her head and devour her.

Chandra called to me again. "Hey, Neely?"

The trader's energy felt so good. *I* felt so good. My head rolled back. "Mmm?"

"Her nose is bleeding. Stop, spiker. Get out of her head." Joaquín's voice rose in volume. "Make her stop, Smith, or I will."

This time I felt Chandra's hands on my shoulders, but in a removed way, as if I were wearing a heavy coat. "Get out of her head. You're done."

"Not yet. Not done," I murmured as I drove deeper, swimming through the gray whorls, rolling through her memories, drinking in the energy and the pleasure and the pain.

"That's it."

"Hang on a sec, fish face. I've got an idea."

Diamond grunted, let out a squeak of pain. I swallowed it whole and smiled as the energy behind it warmly worked its way through my body.

"This might sting a little, kiddo."

Cold metal wrapped around my shoulders. All the air rushed out of my lungs in one painful whoosh and I dropped like a stone, landing on my ass on the floor. A ferocious scream ripped from my throat as my consciousness was torn from Diamond's brain and crammed back into my own. My eyes flew open to find Dolores holding the ends of a seven-foot chain with links the size of handcuff bracelets.

"Enchanted chain. It disrupts paranormal energy and renders the person powerless—or less powerful, anyway. Short term spell. Works on all magical beings, including us witches, hence the rubber gloves." She dropped the chain at my feet and snapped the gloves. "Sorry to have to do that, but you were unreachable."

I nodded. Tried to stop shivering. "Th-thank you. For bringing me back." I glanced at Diamond, who was dabbing her nose with her fist. Joaquín stood over her fussing and she kept shooing him away. "I'm s-sorry." I clenched my teeth to stop them from chattering. "I apologize, Diamond."

"I'll send you my bill." She didn't look nearly as cool as she sounded. After one last distrustful glance at me, she turned on her heel and walked out, closely followed by Joaquín.

I coughed. "My throat. So dry."

Dottie hustled over, handed me a water bottle. "It's the magic in the chains. Dries you right out. Drink up, dear."

I downed the entire bottle in one long drink and the witches went off with Bill to his apartment to grab me another. Chandra hunkered down next to me. "This is why you don't like spiking. It's not about your rules, is it?"

"This is a big part of the reason I have rules."

"Does Alpha know how hard it is for you?" She helped me to my feet.

"Yes."

She nodded, saying nothing, her expression carefully blank.

I was still thirsty, but otherwise I felt okay. Slight headache, sore butt, nothing serious. And Diamond had walked away alive, thank God.

Diamond.

"Why do you look like that?" Chandra asked.

"Like what?"

"Like someone stole the filling from your cookie." Dolores strolled into the room with a water bottle and tossed it to me. I immediately unscrewed the lid and downed half of it.

"I got something from Diamond's mind," I said, between gulps.

"Who's the employer?" Chandra felt around in her pockets as if searching for a weapon, as if she herself wasn't enough of one.

"According to Diamond, it's Willa Scott," I replied.

"Never liked that wolf. Bit off her fingers once." Chandra located what she had been patting for. A pack of gum. She popped a piece in her mouth, offered one to Dolores and me. We declined.

"She was only hugging him."

"Couldn't be sure of that, could I?" Chandra frowned. "So, Willa is the one who hired Diamond?"

"Not. At least, I don't think so." I poured the rest of the water down my throat.

"But you saw it in the trader's mind. You plucked it out of her brain."

"The problem isn't my plucking." I grappled with the challenge of explaining what I'd seen. "It's Diamond's brain. It's missing things. Only in the part where she carried the memories of this job, though. I didn't see it until I spiked in." I wrapped my arms around myself. This whole thing kept getting creepier and creepier.

Dottie strolled through the doorway with two more water bottles. "What'd I miss?"

Dolores replied, "Neely says the trader's brain was missing stuff."

"A spell?" Dottie handed me the water and took the bottle I'd just drained.

"Could be." Dolores frowned. "There have got to be a hundred spells out there in different variations on making someone forget. You've got two in that crying book on your nightstand, Dot."

"It gets worse," I said.

The witches quieted.

"Diamond didn't tell us everything, because she couldn't, but I saw something. There was a third watcher—one she caught a glimpse of here, around the time Bill Bill was brainwashed."

"Who was it?" Chandra asked.

"William Scott."

CHAPTER TWENTY-FIVE

"WHERE'S BILL?"

I walked into the shop through the front door, dabbing at my wet hair with one of Bill Bill's beach towels. I'd only been gone fifteen minutes, but every second away from Lucas felt like wasted time.

"Resting downstairs. He's doing better. It took Dottie, me, a healer, and our entire supply of wine, but we brought him back."

"Who locked him in that brain cage thing?" Chandra was playing with a box of organic tea bags. Meanwhile, I turned my telepathic ability toward the bottom floor. Only Bill, and he was indeed sleeping.

"He still doesn't know, and Dot and me sure couldn't figure it out. Maybe Neely can give him a once-over when we're done with this other stuff."

"Already did it." I picked up a deck of Rider-Waite tarot cards, scanned the back of the package. "Same as before. Nothing. I don't see either Willa or William in his head—not in any negative way, anyway."

"You smell much better now." Dottie smiled at me.

"I took some of Bill's shampoo and bathed in the ocean like you told me to."

"Good, because you stank real bad," Dolores said. "The drive home would have been awful."

I glared at her.

She continued, indifferent to my annoyance, as usual. "The salt in the ocean water neutralizes the magic and the odor—on skin, anyway. Not coming out of those clothes and shoes, though."

"Already threw them out. Another pair of sneakers bites the dust." I stepped out from behind the display of tarot cards. "I picked up this batik sundress and these sandals at that overpriced beach boutique two places down." The gradient copper and teal pattern on the dress reflected the early morning sunlight shining dustily through the glass on the front door.

"Pretty," Dottie said.

Dolores eyed the material. "They have anything with sequins appliqué?"

"All right, let's lock up here and head out." Chandra dropped the box of tea bags and headed for the door.

I followed on her heels. "You called Amir to check on Lucas, right?"

Chandra rolled her eyes. "As if you haven't called him three times in the last half hour."

"I'll run down and tell Bill we're leaving." Dolores whistled. "This is sure going to be bad for someone."

Chandra and I paused by the door. "Why do you say that?" I asked.

"Because no one screws around with Bill Bill's head and gets away unscathed. He's a neutral. No one would dare."

Dottie nodded her agreement. "There will be retribution and it will be swift and final."

"Are you saying Bill Bill is going to *kill* the person who did this?" That didn't line up with what I knew about the man, what I'd seen in his head. He was tough, sure, but he was also fair and kind. There was zero hatred in him. Everyone had hatred for someone, but I hadn't seen any in him at all.

"No. He's a neutral. They don't deal in retribution," Dolores said. "He doesn't have to. The universe does it for him."

"*What?*"

Dottie tried to help. "It's a bit like karma, dear. Bill Bill just whispers into the ear of fate and the universe takes care of the rest."

I suppose that should have comforted me, that there was some metaphysical referee out there keeping us following the rules and regulations of our world, but it didn't. I kept wondering when the universe was coming to even things up with me.

"Do you really think it's the Scot?" Dolores asked a few minutes later, as we gathered our things and headed back out to Chandra's Jeep.

"William Scott," I said, "and he's American, not Scottish."

"Yeah, yeah. Whatever. Did he do it? Is he the one who put the spells on the tiger and the wolf alpha?"

"We don't know," Chandra said.

"Well, this was a fat waste of time then." Dolores picked up her empty wine bag and stomped to the car.

"It's not a total waste. We know there are a lot of those anti-spiker charms around." Dottie patted my shoulder. "Now that Bill Bill is feeling better, he's remembering things."

My gut clenched. "Bill made more anti-me charms?"

She nodded. "With the help of the witch who spelled him, though he still can't recall who that person is. It's not a simple thing to spell a neutral. Dolores and I could do it, but not without accessing some very dark magic."

Chandra lifted one shoulder. "I don't get it. They're necklaces, right? I can just rip them off the neck of the person wearing it."

"*Never* do that." Dottie's eyes widened and she shook her head in a slow sweep. "If the spell is done correctly, there will be backlash and it will be severe."

"How severe we talking?" Chandra asked.

"Have you ever been struck by lightning?"

"Once. The pain was excruciating." At my stunned look, Chandra said, "I dated a woman who was really into camping."

"Compared to what the magical backlash will do to you, being struck by lightning is a like a kiss on the cheek from your mother." Dottie shuffled off to join Dolores at the Jeep.

"Damn. Magic doesn't mess around," Chandra said.

I said nothing. I'd had a taste of magical backlash and I was starting to think I'd been very lucky.

We'd loaded up the Jeep and were pulling away from the curb, when Bill Bill lumbered outside in a neon green bathrobe. His eyes were glazed, his beard and hair were tangled, and there was a piece of paper crumpled in his hand.

"I did some thinking." Bill cleared his throat. "There aren't many paranormals in the western U.S. and Mexico that could do something like what was done—" He cleared it again. "—to me. And even fewer who could do it *to me.*"

"But you have some ideas?" I asked this gently, because he seemed so fragile and confused.

He thrust the paper through the passenger window. There were twenty names on it and I only recognized four. My own, Dolores Fairfield, Dottie Fairfield, and the surname of a man called Harry Romano.

"Is Harry Romano related to Agnes Romano?"

"Her brother," Bill said. "Xavier Malcolm's uncle. Mother's side. He lives in Seattle most of the year but maintains a residence here. I've never had a run-in with him, but he's certainly powerful enough, as are you and the witches here."

"Aw, thanks for saying so, Bill." Dottie beamed.

"Not that I think it was any of you. I'm only saying. And the witches have worked with the charms a lot, so they know how to use them."

Hell. I was afraid to ask, but I didn't see any way around it. "Bill, exactly how many of those charms do you think are out there?"

"Far as I can tell from my orders and past inventory," Bill's voice went soft and small, "hundreds."

A spot just above my right eye began to throb. *Hundreds.* I couldn't take on hundreds of shifters anyway, but hundreds of shifters with anti-*me* charms? My only intelligent course of action was to run, fast and far and now. Put myself on a plane to anywhere that wasn't here and never return.

The second I considered it, my thoughts zinged back to Lucas, sprawled on the cushions on his living room floor, his strong, vibrant body a lifeless shell. Even bringing the image to mind made my heart ache.

I was wrong. I had one course of action, no choices at all.

Because, somewhere down the line, running away from Lucas Blacke and Sundance had stopped being an option for me.

———

WE MADE it home in record time, but it was still after ten o'clock in the morning before I was able to see Lucas again. The second we parked, I exited the car and ran to the front door. I pushed past Amir and Dan, my own personal hater, and let myself into Lucas's bedroom.

He looked asleep. But isn't that what people always say dead people look like?

I checked his pulse, dipped into his thoughts. His pulse wasn't as strong as before. Visually, his mind was blank. Like a swirly gray fog bank. Aurally, his thoughts were loud, jangly and jumbled, like a drawer full of silverware being tossed onto a tile floor.

With a washcloth I'd dampened in the bathroom sink, I dabbed at his face and neck. He didn't have a fever, but he was warmer than usual, and I thought it might feel nice. As the cloth cooled his skin, I told him about what we'd done. I left out nothing, not even how I had to throw my clothes out after falling into boggart stink bait.

As I talked, I realized that it felt natural, sharing things with Lucas. That somewhere between my fear of him and my annoyance with him, I'd grown to think of him as a friend. If I was being sincere, more than a friend. I'd never talked to anyone the way I did with Lucas. It was special. Honest—or at least, honestly dishonest.

"Neely."

Amir's voice woke me up. I'd crawled under the comforter and fallen asleep with my head on Lucas's chest without realizing I'd done either.

"Yes?"

"Chandra is talking to William Scott. You should hear this."

As I pushed out of Lucas's bed, I felt myself being pulled back. By my own feelings or by his, it didn't matter. It was equally hard to resist. As I slid my feet into my sneakers and followed Amir out of the room, I gave Lucas one last over-the-shoulder glance.

"Start talking, Scott."

Chandra's face was flushed and shiny with sweat. Fur bristled on her arms and her ears kept elongating and shrinking as she worked to contain both her fury and her hyena. She paced in front of the sofa where William sat in human form, tight-lipped and stiff-backed. Around his neck hung a charm like the one the specist wolf shifters had worn.

An anti-me charm.

"What do you want to hear? That Malcolm wants another cross-breed in his pack, and he doesn't care who he has to take out to get one? Would I be telling you something you hadn't already figured out?"

"You're saying that your comatose alpha put some kind of spell on my alpha?" Chandra's pacing grew increasingly frenetic. She kicked cushions out of her path and cursed to herself on every third step.

"Are *you* saying you don't think he's capable of engineering this whole scenario—including having that *spiker* put him into a coma?" He opened his hands, leaned forward on the sofa. "Come on, we're on the same side here."

"If that's true," Chandra came to a stop just past his feet, "why are you wearing one of those anti-spiker charms? That *is* what's hanging around your neck, isn't it?"

"It doesn't mean anything. I just don't want that *spiker* in my head."

"And here I thought we were breakfast buddies, *shifter*." I took a seat on the stone fireplace mantle a few feet away from him.

William paled. "Oh, uh, Neely, hey, I didn't mean anything by that. I just—"

"Don't trust me." I glanced over to the sliding glass door where Dan shuffled his feet. "Yeah, I get that a lot. Are you working with Malcolm against Lucas?"

"As I told Blacke's assassin, I'm trying to protect him."

"Ex-assassin." Chandra resumed pacing. "Scott, I need you to tell me how to wake up Malcolm. Once he's awake, I'll beat him until he tells us what he did to my alpha. Problem solved if *we're on the same side*."

William shook his head. "I don't—"

"What is it? Some kind of drug, poison, what?" Chandra halted and stood over the wolf shifter with her hands fisted at her sides. She was barely hanging on.

"I don't know," William said.

"*Bullshit.*"

"Don't you think I'd help if I could?"

"No, I don't." Chandra started pacing again. "But then I've never trusted your smarmy little ass."

William sat up as tall as he could on the sofa. "You don't trust anyone. You bit off my sister's fingers for hugging Lucas."

"That's *Alpha Blacke* to you," she snapped.

"It's a spell, isn't it?" Dottie trotted into the living room from the kitchen and stood in front of William. "But not one of ours. No self-respecting practitioner of the natural arts would perform this sort of spell. Witches have scruples."

"Larry would do it." Dolores plopped onto the end of the sofa opposite William and munched on one of the leftover snickerdoodles.

"Larry is dead," Dottie replied.

"Not Larry Carob, Larry Dustman."

Dolores was right. Larry Dustman had been one of the names on Bill Bill's list.

"Oh." Dottie nodded. "Yes, Larry would do it, the weasel. But he's not in California anymore. He moved a few months ago."

"Far as you know." Dolores shook her cookie at her sister. "Guy that slippery could be anywhere. I'll bet he—"

"*It's not Larry,*" William yelled. He made to stand up, caught Chandra's expression, and sat back down. "Not every spell has to be cast by a witch, you know."

A crafty smile curved Dolores's lips. "So, it *was* a spell."

William scowled. "That's not what I meant."

It was exactly what he'd meant. It didn't take a telepath to see that. I had to hand it to Dolores, the woman was an expert at provoking people. Lucas could certainly attest to that.

"Warlock then. The only practicing warlock in the lower quadrant of the United States is Francine Steadman." Dolores chuckled. "This should be a hoot. Right, Dot?"

Francine Steadman had also been on Bill's list. This was getting interesting.

Dottie's mouth cinched into a frown. "No, it most certainly will not be a 'hoot,' sister."

Chandra said, "I'm afraid to ask, but I'm strangely compelled to. Who's Francine Steadman?"

Dolores grinned. "Dottie and Francine went to school together. Old rivals. It's what the kids call, what is it? When your friend is also your enemy?"

"Frenemy." I was still feeling pulled into Lucas's room. It was getting harder and harder to resist the temptation to run back in there.

"That's it. Francine stole Dottie's first boyfriend, so Dottie stole Francine's favorite enchanted cloak. Do you still have that thing, sis?"

Dottie's gaze slid sideways. "Maybe."

"Well, at least you kept it longer than she kept your boyfriend."

"What does the cloak do?" Since talking to the witches, Chandra's animal had calmed down and she was completely human again. Not a normal response to the Fairfield witches. "Make you invisible?"

"No. It's a protection garment. It's not actually a cloak, not the way most people would think a—"

"*It wasn't a blasted warlock*," William yelled. "Cripes, how would a person even find one?"

Dolores flapped her hand at William. "Please. You've got a trader on the payroll, every high-ranking shifter does. And any trader worth their salt knows about Francine Steadman. The woman is a legend."

"Meh," Dottie said.

Enough. I'd had enough. I had an idea, but I was going to pay dearly for it. In for a *centavo*, in for a *peso*, as my uncle would say.

My eyes slid shut as I opened myself and let energy flow into me. There was a lot of it in the room and in the shifters all around Lucas's house, which helped.

I reached for William's brain.

The pain was like taking a hatchet to the skull, but I managed to spit out some words. "It was ... a d-demon." I pulled out of his head and opened my eyes.

Dolores and Dottie looked at each other, then at me.

"How do you know it was demon magic?" Dottie asked.

My chest was so heavy I could barely draw breath. "I read him."

William held up his necklace. "You can't read me, the charm—"

"Worked like ... a charm." Pain ice-picked into the top of my head and burned down my spine. "Don't have ... long." I stood and began backing out of the room, tiny explosions bursting in my head. "Witches ... help ... demon..."

"Malcolm or Alpha Blacke?" Chandra asked. "Which one was cursed?"

"Cursed." Agony ripped into me. Thinking straight was a challenge. There was a disconnect between my brain and my vocal cords, and keeping my mouth shut was imperative if I didn't want to ruin everything.

"Neely?" Chandra called out from the other end of a mile-long hallway. Impossible, as logically I knew she was only about ten feet away.

"Kiddo?" Dolores set aside her cookie and charged toward me.

The world went an ever-darkening shade of gray and my mouth tasted like I'd been chewing aluminum foil. "Need ... check ... Lucas."

Dolores took my arm as I stumbled down the hall into his room. "What are you up to?"

I didn't have much time left. I huffed out a short version of my idea to the witch and hoped she understood me, because the pain pulsing in my head soon took over, filled my entire body. I slipped out of her grip, dropped to my knees on the floor, and flopped over on my side.

The room spun for a few seconds, then everything went black.

"Only three major problems?" A melodious male voice, it sounded like Amir Gamal's, floated into my dreams.

Well, into my reality. I hadn't opened my eyes, but I was awake. I could feel Lestat curled in a ball against the small of my back. I smelled lavender near my head. Lucas was breathing softly beside me.

I reached for him with my ability, and got a wall of fog and a sharp pain to the temple for my trouble.

"Yeah. Alpha Blacke is still out." Chandra sounded exhausted and angry.

"That's one," Dan Winters said.

"We have William Scott and his son-of-a-bastard alpha."

"That's two—well, three."

"Really, Dan?" Chandra snapped.

"Eh, sorry, just trying to help."

"And *three*, members of Malcolm's pack are headed this way." Amir sounded sterner than I'd ever heard him.

"To kill him or save him?" Dan asked.

"They're going to kill one of the alphas," Chandra replied. "Not that it matters. One way or another, we'll have a fight on our hands."

"I still say it's too soon to assume it wasn't an inside job," Dan muttered.

That comment had probably been directed toward me. I opened my eyes, keeping my lids lowered, and watched the shifters from beneath my lashes. Both men were staring at Chandra, waiting for her orders. It was obvious they deferred to her authority.

"We've done what we can. Alpha Blacke and I set up lookout and ambush points before he..." She cleared her throat. "We're armed, though according to Bill Bill, we can't use the ammunition he sold us while under that spell."

"Maybe we can talk to the Malcolm pack. Reason with them." Dan ran a hand through his short brown hair. He looked like a banker or an accountant, not a shifter group third.

"Sure, we can do that. Who should I send as emissary? In other words, which of our shifters should I sacrifice?" Chandra held up a hand when Dan made to argue. "Think it through, Winters."

"Do we have enough ammunition in the house for this sort of a siege?" Amir asked.

"No. At least, not the kind we'll need. Alpha is a fair fighter. He knows we'd need weapons as a show of force, but he'd expect the battle to be fairly fought. Hand to hand, paw to talon."

"With honor." Dan obviously agreed with his alpha.

"Yeah. That's why I'm here. I always expect treachery." She pulled a revolver out of the holster on her shoulder, popped it on the side so the chamber opened, and shook the bullets into her hand, smiling when they began to smoke against her skin. "Coin silver coated with six layers of fine silver."

"Chandra, you can't." Dan took a step back. "It goes against the treaty."

"The treaty is a joke. The only one who worries about it is you." She reloaded her gun, tucked it into the holster. "I have enough silver stockpiled around town to take down Malcolm's entire pack."

"I won't use it," Dan said.

"We know," Amir and Chandra replied in unison.

"I'm not apologizing for my stance on this. It's not weak to have morals."

"No, it's not." Amir patted Dan on the shoulder. "But they're a liability when you're fighting enemies who don't have any."

Dan shook Amir's hand off and stomped out of the room. I wasn't ready to announce that I was awake to the others, so I closed my eyes again.

"It must be hard to be Dan," Chandra said. "Trying to reconcile his need to serve the group with his own misguided morality."

"And you don't have that problem?" Amir asked.

"Nope. I serve the group, starting with Alpha Blacke and ending with the last shifter. I will always do it to the best of my ability using every weapon at my disposal."

"I hope I never piss you off," Amir said.

"You piss me off plenty. I just have a high tolerance for people who value Alpha as much as I do."

Amir spoke quietly, reverently. "I will never betray Lucas Blacke. I owe him too much."

"Same. We're friends and I don't make friends. It's a proven fact that I suck at it."

"Yes, you do."

"There you go, pissing me off again, Gamal."

Amir chuckled. "You've got a friend in that one." I had a feeling he

241

meant me, but I didn't open my eyes to check. "She seems pretty fond of you."

"Who? Neely the faker? She's all right."

"Faker?" Amir asked.

"Yeah. She's been awake this whole time, listening to us. Didn't you hear her breathing change when she surfaced? Shame on you, eagle."

My eyelids wouldn't stay shut after that, so there was no more faking it. "I didn't want to interrupt."

"Bullshit. You wanted to wait until Dan left the room. Wuss."

"That too. My head feels like someone used it for a kickball. How long have I been asleep?"

"Day and a half. I bet you have to pee like a racehorse." Dolores strolled into the room, followed by Dottie. They were dressed in cotton capri pants and T-shirts and sneakers. Dolores's were denim with rhinestones. Dottie's were hot pink with glittery shoelaces. They didn't look like witches at all. In fact, they looked a lot like someone's grandmothers visiting from Florida.

"How'd you two get in here?" Amir asked. "There's a guard at the door."

"He's sleepy." Dolores laughed. "I mean, he is now."

"Irwin? Hey, are you all right?" Amir stomped out of the room.

"It'll wear off in twenty minutes and he'll feel great. He'll be thanking me." Dolores plopped down on my side of the bed. "How are you doing? Did the lavender hex bag help?"

"Is that what I keep smelling?" I yawned.

"Yeah, I stuffed it into your pillowcase."

"Thanks, it helped." I yawned again. "Dolores, did you understand what I said to you before I passed out? I mean about William and—"

"Good news. We found the demon that Scott fella must have gotten the curse from." She patted my arm and nodded. "Don't worry about a thing."

"There are thousands of demons in the underworld." Chandra crossed her arms over her chest. I hadn't had a chance to talk to her yet, and obviously Dolores hadn't told her anything. Honestly, I wasn't sure Dolores had even heard me.

I tried again. "Look, I'm not sure I was clear—"

"You were crystal clear, dear," Dottie said, and then turned to Chandra. "You are correct, but there are only a few demons who will deal with a human and follow through. Contrary to popular belief, most demons are quite happy in Hell and have no desire to leave. They don't mind making the odd soul deal, but they aren't terribly motivated to get involved in human problems."

While Dottie explained this to Chandra, I nudged Lestat off my back and went to use the facilities. When I returned, Dottie shuttled to Lucas's door and hung what appeared to be a hex bag from the doorknob.

"There now. That should keep things in this room for the next five minutes. Go ahead, sister."

"All righty. While you people were futzing around with Malcolm and the tiger, Dot and I got to work on a spell." She smiled smugly. "Actually, Tim found it in my least favorite grimoire. The one that cries if you don't open it at least once a day. What a baby."

Dottie said, "She means the grimoire, not Tim."

"Do I?" Dolores shrugged.

Tim Carver was a water witch who occasionally worked for the witches. His husband, Fred, was one of Lucas's shifters. Tim and Dolores had a slightly less antagonistic relationship than Dolores and Lucas did.

"So, what does this spell do?" Chandra stood near Lucas, studied the rise and fall of his chest.

Someone had washed his face while I was sleeping. Probably Dan. That seemed like a Dan thing to do. I should be happy the coyote shifter had morals. The way he hated me, if he had Chandra's moral outlook, he'd have snuffed me out with a pillow while I slept beside his alpha.

"It should give us full access to his brain." Dottie sat on the other side of me. "But we'll need a little help once things are in place."

"What do you need?" Chandra asked.

"Brute strength." Dolores grinned. "Anyway, Dot and I are ready to go whenever you are. I brought a few bags of salt and a vial of blood from an of-age virgin. We figure a summoning spell should take care of the problem."

"Wait. 'Summoning' spell? An 'of-age virgin'?" I looked to Dottie for an explanation. I felt there were nuances of this conversation that I wasn't picking up on, and I couldn't decide if it was my grogginess or the witches being their usual selves.

"Above the age of consent, which is 18, in our world." Dottie replied. "Bill Bill said he mostly tracks down Internet trolls and offers them pizza, and something called bitcoin to lure them out of their parents' basements. The price has really gone down since the advent of social media."

That made a strange sort of sense. "These are *human* trolls, right? A jerk who goes out of their way to make an offensive comment on a social media post, something like that? Not the sort of trolls who live under a bridge. Right?" I desperately hoped real trolls weren't a thing.

"Ask Bill." Dolores clapped her hands and bounced off the bed and onto her feet. "Now, let's go summon up some trouble."

CHAPTER TWENTY-SIX

A WATCHFUL WILLIAM, TWO VERY EXCITED WITCHES, CHANDRA, AND I gathered behind Lucas's house on a cement patio that wound around the back and south end of the house, abutting a low, stilted deck. This was where the Blacke group held important shifter meetings, called convocations. Tonight, it was the scene of a summoning.

"It's not an actual summoning, you know." Dottie emptied the last bag of rock salt. "We're looking for residual demonic energy. From that energy, we should be able to extrapolate the type of curse the demon used."

"How?" The way William asked this, with humor underlying his tone, told me he thought he had the upper hand.

"You'll see." Dolores showed us her wickedest smile, the one that made the hair on the back of my neck stand on end. "Hand me that bag of salt, Dot—oh, and the boggart stink bait."

The witches poured a five-foot diameter circle with the rock salt. Then they poured another, larger one around that, and set five black pillar candles of varying heights around the exterior. The sealed box of stink bait was placed beside the tallest candle, where I hoped it would remain unopened.

Chandra was sighing, William standing beside her, was watchful and unconcerned, while I was saying a silent prayer that the witches didn't somehow bring down Armageddon on our heads.

"It would help a lot if you'd tell us the demon's name," Dottie said to William.

"It won't help you," he said.

"Why not?" I asked.

William looked away.

"You know, I get that you don't like or trust me. Who am I to you? But Lucas is your friend. He trusted you and you betrayed him. How could you do this, you worthless *cobarde?*"

William's face screwed into a frown. "What does that mean?"

"Coward," Chandra spat. Literally. She spat on his shoe. "That's exactly what it means, you sack of *mierda.*"

"I may not know Spanish, but I know that was an insult. You shut your mouth, *spiker.*" He held up his globe charm as he made a beeline in my direction. Adrenaline washed hotly through my veins as I opened myself to the energy surrounding me, gathering enough to defend myself.

"Nope." Chandra zipped across the patio, coming to a halt between the wolf shifter and me.

William tried to push past her. "I'm not going to attack her, hyena. Alpha Malcolm's orders. He wants her alive."

Chandra stared him down. "Do I have to explain to you why I don't trust that?"

"No, you don't, assassin. *Who would expect you to trust a traitor?*" The male voice floated out of the dusky evening light. Although it was almost sultry in its smoothness, the sound grated on my nerves.

The wolf who followed the voice onto the patio wasn't the same bombastic old man Lucas and I had encountered in William's pack meeting. He wasn't even the same wolf Malcolm had flung a steak knife into at dinner.

He was worse.

"Good evening, Blacke shifters." He raked his gaze over me. "Spiker."

Dressed in a gray business suit and tie, his white hair slicked back, Richard Penn looked like a mafia crime lord headed into court. Triumph was scrawled into every line of his weathered, white face.

Chandra threw up her hands—which was better than what I did, which was to throw up in my mouth. "Just what we needed to round out this fun-filled family evening."

"I'm not a traitor, Dick," William said. "I moved Alpha Malcolm because he was in danger at home and, as pack second, I had every right to do so."

"*My name is Richard.*" The older wolf stood on the other side of the patio flanked by two fully shifted wolves I didn't recognize, and one rattlesnake shifter in human form I did.

"How long have you been Malcolm's spy, Lisa?" I hadn't read her, yet there was no surprise in learning that Lisa Cesar was working for Xavier Malcolm. It fit.

"Ever since you came to town, *spiker.*"

"*I'm going to kill you.*"

When Chandra said this, Lisa shuddered and backed behind one of the enormous, snarling wolves. The wolf snapped at Chandra, its jaw dripping with foamy saliva, and I opened myself up again, letting the energy of the shifters flow into me.

I wasn't letting Chandra fight this battle alone.

"Now, now, assassin. Ms. Cesar has sworn loyalty to the Malcolm pack. She's at the bottom of pack order, of course, as she's not wolf. According to the treaty, you cannot harm her in any way, except in self-defense. We have declared her a refuge-seeker, and as such she is immune from all formal challenges for one year, with some caveats. In order to get to her, you'll have to fight every alpha who ranks above her first." Smug looked at home on Dick's face, as if the emotion had been created especially for him.

But smug was never a good choice when dealing with Chandra.

"*Every* one?" She appeared to be thinking this over.

"Every single one." Smug made a second appearance.

The shifters standing in front of Lisa howled, their slavering maws dribbling as they growled and snapped, and crept threateningly toward Chandra. They seemed to be spoiling for a fight.

"Challenge accepted."

In the pause between one breath and the next, Chandra changed. Her clothes ripped as her enormous, furred form emerged from her human one. She lunged at one of the wolves, moving so fast I could barely track her, and ripped out his trachea with her teeth.

She spat out the bloodied cartilage tube and cackled as the wolf shifter lay twitching at her feet. The second wolf was ready for the throat attack, which Chandra turned to her advantage, diving low as he lunged for her head. She slid beneath him, unzipping his torso with her extended claws and pouring his organs out in a steaming heap onto the body of the other wolf, then crushing them beneath her feet.

Chandra was furious, vicious, but also in complete control. For her, the attacks were a sort of barbaric ballet, with deadly *jetés*, merciless *entendres*, and murderous *arabesques*. Her performance wound to a close, and instead of roses at her feet, there was steaming viscera and cascades of blood.

The shifters were dead. Wolves could heal wounds that could easily kill a human, but there was no coming back from having vital organs stomped into paste.

Her compact muscled, speckled body slowly turned to face Lisa Cesar. Since Chandra had taken care of the wolf shifters so efficiently, I hadn't needed to use the energy I'd let flow into my body. Now it was spooling through me, coiled and crackling, and I was ready to use it.

"Only six hundred seventy-two more alphas to go," Dick said, and laughed.

Two of his wolves were lying a few feet away in a blood-soaked wad of fur and organs, and he was *laughing*?

I'd known alphas like that my whole life. Recently, I was almost dragged into a pack headed by an alpha like him. Everyone was disposable, all lives but their own meaningless—except in service to the pack.

"Have some respect, Penn." William's eyes narrowed. "Those wolves were our pack mates."

Chandra cackled again. Her muzzle and rounded ears were soaked in wolf blood, her eyes moving wildly in their sockets. She seemed one hundred percent capable of ripping through every wolf in the

Malcolm pack at that moment, and would likely have done so to get to Lisa Cesar.

The witches had backed up all the way to a corner of the porch, Dottie clutching a box of stick matches in front of her like a talisman. William bent over the bloodied wolves. Dick stared at Chandra, slack-jawed and overtly fascinated.

"You should go," I said to Lisa. My voice was sluggish, dragging out my vowels as I worked to hold on to the power coursing through me. "Noooow."

She lifted her chin. "I'm not sorry."

It felt like an epidemic, all these people who weren't sorry for the awful things they'd done. Too bad there wasn't a vaccine for assholes, because I'd have ordered a truck-full for this town.

Chandra cackled again. The sound of her rage made me shiver.

Lisa glared at her ex-alpha second. "Since this spiker and her cur uncle got here, the Sundance group hasn't been the same. Alpha has weakened and the group is fractured. I'm glad to finally be in a pack with a strong alpha."

"You mean the guy wasting away in Alpha Blacke's guest room? That *strong* alpha?" I asked.

"It's not as if *your* alpha is doing any better." The rattlesnake looked so pleased with herself, I wanted to rip her face off. And if I felt that way, Chandra had to be barely hanging on to her temper.

Chandra slowly morphed into a humanoid-hyena creature—her hybrid form. It took powerful control to shift like that, and even more to say in a husky voice, "Neely's right. You should go now. We'll have our reckoning after I kill off all the wolves between me and you."

Lisa nodded, took a solemn step back.

The moment Chandra stepped out of her way, Lisa shifted to hybrid form. Her head flattened and elongated, and her skin thickened. Her smile widened until she looked like a child's drawing of a happy face, and as she opened her comically wide mouth, her ropy pink tongue flicked out. When she was fully in hybrid form, she squatted into what would have been a coil if she'd been fully shifted.

And struck.

Without a second's hesitation—because I'd lived in the desert with rattlesnakes long enough to know I didn't have even half that much time—I latched onto her brain and drove into her head, arrowing straight to the core of her consciousness.

She screamed and dropped to the ground in front of me, drumming her feet on the cement. As she gurgled her last breath, I switched gears, digging into her mind for any information about Lucas and the Blacke shifters and Xavier Malcolm.

The only helpful bit of information I found was that Lisa had hired the assassin to kill me. She'd paid a lot of money to make me dead, and even if she died tonight, the attempts would continue.

More good news.

Peripherally, I became aware that Chandra had slid further into her hybrid form. She watched me, not Lisa, as I rampaged through the rattlesnake's memories. I was slip-sliding into the ecstasy that threatened to engulf me every time I spiked. Losing myself.

It wasn't about information now. It wasn't about Lucas, Malcolm, or the group. It was about me and the euphoria that erupted within me, body and soul, when I threw control and all my rules out the window and fully unleashed my ability.

It was the first warm wind of summer after a cruel winter. That beautiful surprise that grips your body during lovemaking as waves of pleasure break over you. It was like flying with my feet on the ground, and even as I reveled in the thrill of it, I hated myself for needing it.

"What's going on?" Dan burst through the back door, closely followed by Amir. The coyote shifter looked at the pile of blood and wolf parts, at Chandra, at Lisa Cesar's half-shifted, still body, and then he looked at me.

Chandra held up a hand. "Dan. Neely. Ah *shit.*"

His shift was faster than Lisa's, though not as fast as Chandra's. He charged me, and that was a mistake, because I was brimming with power, and the instant I was kicked out of Lisa Cesar's dead brain, I set my entire focus on the man-sized coyote trying to kill me.

I drilled straight into his head.

The howl Dan let out as he hit the cement went straight to my bones. It was pain and it was fear and it was awful, because I barely cared.

"Stop now, Neely. Stop," Chandra whispered. "You're killing him."

Her whisper reached me in a way yelling would never have. It took all my strength, but I pulled out of Dan's head. Slowly, carefully, so as not to harm him further.

When I opened my eyes, Dick Penn was smiling at me.

I didn't like it. Not one bit.

Exhausted, I sank to my knees, then to my hands and knees, and then I dropped my forehead to the cold, rough cement. It took a few minutes, but the energy inside me finally ebbed, leaving a hollow, empty feeling in its place.

I rolled onto my side and opened my eyes. Dolores was crouched beside me. Her shirt had a sequined wolf on it. I hadn't noticed that earlier. Now I seemed to notice all sorts of things, like the way the wind was blowing hot gusts of air over my face, how blindingly bright the stars were in the sky, the ozone scent of water from the humid atmosphere and from the watering hole Lucas had built for his shifters. My every sense was on high alert.

"Your eyes are all gold and glowy, kiddo. Like a shifter's."

Uh oh, not again. "Dolores, what did I do?"

"It's all right. You did what you had to do."

"Did I h-hurt him bad?"

"Whatever you did, it was less than that fool coyote deserved for coming at you like that." She brushed my hair out of my face. "They're back to their normal brown now. Your eyes, I mean."

My senses had lessened, too. I'd have to explore that with the witches at some point. Not tonight, though.

"Is Dan okay? Tell me."

"You scrambled his eggs a little, but he'll recover. Pretty sure the rattlesnake has kicked the breathing habit, though."

Lisa Cesar was slumped on the ground a few feet away, still in hybrid form. I felt ill seeing her lying there motionless. Guilty, too—though I knew that if I hadn't spiked her, she'd be looking down at my dead body on the cement and probably doing a celebratory dance. Or jumping on her cell phone to get her assassination money back.

"She hired someone to kill me."

"Not surprised." Still in hybrid form, Chandra crouched between

251

Dan's furred form and me. "She was pretty vocal about you in the last meeting, so Alpha and I figured she was up to something. I, for one, am glad you spiked the living shit out of her because it saved me a lot of trouble."

"The assassin isn't going to stop because she's dead." Panic threaded my voice.

Chandra put her clawed hand on my shoulder. "No. But we'll find her or him. Don't worry." We both looked at Dan. "Neely, he isn't a bad guy. I mean, he doesn't mean to—"

"He means it." I turned to look at her. "I would know that better than anyone."

"Yeah. Guess you would."

With Dolores' help, I sat up. Dick Penn and William were arguing on the far side of the patio and Dan was sprawled on the cement with his eyes closed, so only Chandra, Dolores, and I saw Dottie light the rest of the candles and begin to chant.

Chandra got to her feet and stalked over to where William stood with his back to her, then gave Dottie a quick nod. "Say when."

Dottie chanted louder and Dolores joined in.

Dick scowled at the witches. "What's with all the racket?"

"They're summoning a demon," William drawled, a grin lifting the corner of his mouth.

The arrogant wolf still assumed he held all the power in this situation. Thought he had it all figured out. He'd figured Chandra wouldn't hurt him because he was the key to saving Lucas. He'd figured he had one up on the spiker, that he must be some kind of strong alpha for me to have gotten things so horribly wrong.

He'd figured the witches *were actually summoning a demon*.

"*Now*," they yelled.

Chandra grabbed William by the back of the neck, spun him around, and, with a mighty shove, pushed him straight into the center of the salt circle.

DOTTIE HURRIEDLY FILLED in the broken part of the circle with a small bag of salt she'd pulled out of the back pocket of her capri pants.

"What did you do to me?" William flung himself at the salt lines but found himself unable to cross them.

"Won't do you any good, Scott." Dolores walked around the second salt line, out of her quarry's reach. "You're stuck in there until we let you out."

Dottie continued chanting under her breath.

"That should nullify the charm—at least for a few minutes." Dolores made a hurry up motion. "If you're going to spike him, do it fast."

"Now, see here." Dick wagged his finger and puffed out his chest as he stormed toward me. "This is uncalled for. William is a Malcolm shifter and, as such, should not be subjected to—"

Slam. Dick hit the cement, face first. Amir crept out of the shadows, a plastic straw and a small drawstring bag in his hand.

"Nice job, eagle." Dolores took the straw and bag from Amir. "Ol' Dick here will be out for a half hour, maybe less. The tincture in the dart isn't exact."

"When he wakes up with a broken nose and—" Amir used his foot to turn Dick over. "—jaw, he's going to be pissed." He glanced at Dan, and then at me. Shook his head. "I'm going back to Alpha's room. Something's happening with Malcolm, and I don't like it. I suggest you hurry."

After Amir left, Chandra opened a teak storage box shoved against the far wall. It was the sort of thing used to store patio furniture cushions, BBQ accessories, things like that. She put on a pair of gloves, then dragged out the chains Dolores had used on me at Bill Bill's.

"Just in case," Chandra said.

That was fair. I'd killed Lisa Cesar and nearly killed Dan. As much as I'd like to spike William to Hell, I couldn't kill the guy. We needed him.

"What do you think is going to happen here?" William had given up ramming the invisible salt line barrier. He gave us all a superior grin and rocked back on his heels. "Look, I hate to tell you, but you're wrong, spiker. I didn't summon a demon." He laughed. "I wouldn't know how to."

I rose to my feet, slowly walked the perimeter of the second circle. "I know. But inside that head of yours is the name of the witch—and it *was* a witch, I saw that much in your brain—who put the spells on Malcolm and Lucas."

William's face clouded with confusion. "But you said it was a demon."

I cupped my hand around my mouth like a child imparting a secret. "I lied."

Obviously nonplussed, he tried to argue. "There's no way. I-I had the charm."

"It worked. I wasn't able to get everything I needed. Hence Plan B." I spread my arms wide to encompass the entire scenario. As we bantered, I let energy roll into me, this time not pulling, but simply acting as a vessel.

"Neely." Chandra turned a worried look to the back door, where there was some kind of commotion. "Do it now. Something's going down in there."

William ran to the edge of the salt circle. "No, wait. Please, Neely. Look, I... I'll tell you what you want to know, just don't spike me."

"Oh, we're way past negotiating, William."

"Wait. *Please*, don't—"

I spiked, finessing my entry into his brain instead of heading straight for the off button. This wasn't a light's-out mission, and I kept reminding myself of that as I wound through his mind. This was a fact-finding mission. A save Lucas mission.

William fell to his knees, screamed, then quieted. I opened my eyes, trying hard to keep one foot in the now and the other inside William's thoughts. It *hurt*. The effort it took drained me.

To my left, Dan had shifted to hybrid form and climbed to his feet, eyes narrowed with hatred. Chandra stepped up to block his path to me. Meanwhile, the witches' chanting reached a crescendo and the hypnotic harmony of their voices had me swaying back and forth.

"What do you see, Neely?" Dolores stopped chanting long enough to ask.

"Spell." It was the only answer in William's brain, so it had to be right. Unlike the others, his brain hadn't been tampered with. He'd known what was going on. He'd *helped*.

"It's a spell?"

"Yes. *Somnio-infernum?*"

Dolores whistled. "The dream hell spell. Takes a powerful witch to pull that one off."

"I can't see the witch. Only..." My head was beginning to pound. "I think your spell is wearing off."

"Please, Neely." Chandra's voice cracked with emotion. "Who did this to him?"

Dottie grabbed Dolores and shook her head, all the while continuing to chant.

"Get out, kiddo. Dot's losing control of the spell. No telling what it will do to you if you're still in there when it breaks."

I ignored her and burrowed deeper into William's brain, my focus lasered to a fine point and one question on my mind. It shouldn't be this hard to find, but William was protecting the person responsible, erecting barriers in his head. I could bust through them all eventually, but we were running out of time.

Who did this to Lucas? Who?

"Why is she bleeding like that? It's like the day José died—Neely, *stop.*" Chandra sounded panicked.

"Did you hear me? It's not safe. Get out." Dolores sounded as worried as Chandra.

"*Don't you dare* come out until you have some answers," Dan snapped.

"She could end up brain damaged, you horse's ass," Dolores said. "Or dead."

"Two birds, one stone."

"Shut up, Dan," Chandra said. "Neely, get out."

The chanting slowed. Dottie's voice seemed to be coming from far away.

"This is bad." Dolores was closer to me. I felt her breath on my cheek as she yelled directly into my ear. "*Are you going to get out, or am I going to have to kick your skinny rear end?*"

"It's okay, Neely," Chandra said. "We'll find another way."

"Can't." My voice sounded faraway, even to me. "There is no other way."

"*Get the chains, hyena,*" Dolores yelled.

"There's always another way," Chandra said. "Don't make me do this."

"Don't you hear her? There's no other way. Let her finish it." Dan's voice trembled, with rage or excitement, I couldn't tell.

"Shut your mouth, or I will shut it for you," Chandra snarled at him.

"*Now,*" Dolores yelled. The chanting stopped.

I wrenched out of William's head as the spell broke, powering through the vise-like pain that gripped my head. William screamed and slumped to the ground, dazed, but not unconscious. His nose was bleeding. It felt like my entire head was bleeding, so I didn't have much sympathy for the guy.

"Neely?" Chandra cocked her head to one side. "Are you okay?"

"*Who did this to Alpha Blacke?*" Dan demanded through clenched teeth.

I was shaking so badly I couldn't speak. Pulling out that fast hadn't only hurt William.

Chandra let the chains drop to the cement and came to my side. "Hey, it's okay. We'll find another way."

I blinked up at her. Was I crying? It seemed so.

"Kiddo?" Dolores crouched on my other side and dabbed at my face with a handkerchief she'd pulled from her pocket. It came away red. "Are you okay?"

"Malcolm," I blurted. "All of it. It's Malcolm."

CHAPTER TWENTY-SEVEN

"How can it be Malcolm? He's been in a coma for the past few days." Once I'd stopped shaking, Chandra left my side. She returned the chains to the teak box and laid the gloves on top of them. "It makes no logical sense."

I stood still while Dolores cleaned the blood off my face. Thankfully, my nose and ears had stopped bleeding.

"Because it's bullshit. The *spiker* didn't see a thing." Dan's upper lip curled, and his voice had a distinct growl running beneath it. "Right?"

"Why don't you take a long walk off a short pier, coyote?" Dolores snapped.

I ignored Dan. "Come on, Chandra, think about it. *It makes no logical sense.* That's what makes it the perfect plan."

At that moment, a snarling growl thundered inside the house, making the windows quake and sending my heart rate into the stratosphere.

"Shit." Chandra swung her head around. Her gaze moved from Dan to where William was slumped on the concrete, and back to Dan. "Grab him." She threw a worried look over her shoulder. "Lock him down in Earp's stronghold. Malcolm can't know we have him. It's the only advantage we have."

"Can't *she* just spike him again?"

"Dial down the bullshit, Dan. Alpha won't like it."

I rubbed my temples with the pads of my fingers. "What are you going to do about Dick? He knows William's here."

"I've got this." Chandra went very quiet. Her eyes slid closed.

Dan cocked his head to one side, as if listening to something none of us could hear. Then he nodded. "Good idea."

"*Where is Lucas Blacke?*" The voice came from the living room. Something crashed to the floor and someone yelped.

Xavier Malcolm was awake.

"Umm, Chandra?" I cleared my throat.

Her expression didn't change. It was as if she hadn't heard a thing.

A deep voice called to us out of the darkness. "*I'm here.*"

Chandra's eyelids popped open. "Thank you."

A shifter with moonless midnight dark skin, deep brown eyes, and a full black mane, leapt onto the patio wearing only a pair of minuscule black nylon shorts. He was an enormous man, well over six foot, with the body of a powerlifter and the bone structure of a deity. I'd spoken to him a few times, but they were always short, brusque conversations. He was a "get to the point" kind of guy.

"Whatcha know, King?" Dolores waved.

He inclined his head. "Dolores. Dottie." His voice was low, but not bass deep. More like a honeyed baritone.

King Jones was the introverted proprietor of the Sundance Auto gas station and auto repair shop. Other than Chandra, he was the most alpha shifter I'd ever met that wasn't an alpha leader. King had been out of town when my presence had drawn Saul Roso to Sundance, so he was one of the few shifters who didn't actively hate me.

Chandra ran her hand through her hair. "Hate to ask, but I need your help."

"Shit's gotten that bad already?"

"Yeah."

He nodded respectfully at her and shifted further into his lion form. The blue undertones of his skin blended into the pure blackness of his mane. His fists widened, his feet lengthened and widened. His ears shifted to the top of his head and human teeth gave way to lion teeth as his nose became a snout. Lions were beautiful, but lion shifters were in a completely different class of beauty.

"Which one?"

"This one." Chandra indicated Dick's unconscious form. "Earp's panic room."

"The cave. Got it." King swung Dick onto his shoulder and was gone.

"*Move.*" Chandra slapped Dan on the back, jerking him into action. The witches had stopped chanting and the candles had snuffed themselves out. The spell was broken, which meant William could leave the circle and he was already climbing to his feet.

"Yes, Second." Dan shifted further into coyote hybrid form and ran full speed at William, hitting him so hard I was surprised the wolf didn't break in half. He swung the groaning man over his shoulder. Like King, he was there one second, gone the next.

"*Who has done this to Alpha Blacke?*" The booming voice inside was much closer now. "*I will not tolerate it.*"

"How did you get King here so fast?" I whispered to Chandra.

"Group bonds." The smile she gave me had zero humor in it. "Also, I always have a backup plan—and a backup plan in case that one fails. Also, a failsafe in the event that everything completely goes to shit. And for unforeseen complications, I—"

"Jeez Louise, we get it. You're a control freak." Dolores took Dottie's hand and climbed off the patio. "Sounds like the sleeping wolf is up and at 'em again. We're going to head home and start working on countering the *somnio-infernum* spell. Dot'll text you, Neely."

"Watch yourselves." Chandra tipped her head to indicate she was listening to something in the house. "Go slowly. Mask your scent."

"This ain't our first rodeo, hyena."

Dolores opened the box of boggart stink bait and dumped it over her and Dottie's heads. She pulled her sister close to her and hustled around the side of the house.

"*Where is the spiker?*" Once again, the windows rattled with the force of his fury-infused voice.

Fear soaked hotly into my muscles, my bones. "He's going to kill me."

"Probably going to try." Chandra lifted her shoulder, looked at me. "What's new about that? Alphas are always trying to either own or kill you."

I started breathing too shallowly, too quickly. "It's not something you get u-used to."

Chandra marched straight up to me. She used her shifter speed, so it took her half an eye blink to reach me on the other side of the patio. "If you don't start getting used to it—hell, *anticipating* it with every single alpha leader you meet—you may as well let me kill you. I'll make it fast, at least."

"What?" Rage replaced fear, leaving me no less likely to throw up, but at least the shivering stopped. "Why would you say that to me?"

"I say it because no one else seems to want to lay out the truth for you. I say it because I need you to help Alpha and me, not cower like a scared little bitch. I say it because we're friends, Neely. *It's time for you sack up and start acting like the goddamn lethal predator you are.*"

The rage fled, taking some of the fear with it. "We're friends?"

"*That's* what you... God, you're weird." She rolled her eyes. "Yes. We are. Now pull it together, because Malcolm is going to get tired of posturing soon. He doesn't give a tin shit about Lucas, he knows you're out here, and he's got a plan he intends to see through. Our only advantage is that we know the plan, kind of—oh, and we have a spiker and an assassin on our side."

"*Ex*-assassin," I said.

Chandra's responding smile had too many teeth.

"*Neely Costa MacLeod.*"

Malcolm flung open the sliding glass door and strode barefoot onto the patio. He was dressed in a pair of Lucas's jeans and a white T-shirt, and looked a great deal healthier than he had a right to. His cheeks were no longer hollowed, and his shoulders were no longer bowed and weak. Even his tan had returned, the sallowness of his skin fading into a healthy pink glow.

"Right here." I did my best to keep my voice steady. "You're awake, Alpha Malcolm. That's ... good news. How did you wake up?"

"Slowly." His gaze swept over the mangled bodies of his wolves, and I thought I saw real regret, but I wasn't sure it was genuine. Even after crawling through his mind, I didn't know him at all.

Jaw set, he stared at me for a moment, then directed his gaze at Chandra.

"You've been busy, assassin." He gestured toward his dead wolves. "This *is* your work, isn't it?"

I opened my mouth to tell him that I had killed Lisa, but Chandra gave a short shake of her head and I swallowed the words.

"It is." Chandra circled away from the Alpha, keeping her distance while also keeping her gaze glued to him.

"Brutality is your specialty," Malcolm said.

"Brutality is in the eye of the beholder," she replied.

Malcolm almost smiled. "Touché." He stepped up to the edge of the salt circle, kicked over an unlit candle. "I smell boggart bait. Summon any demons tonight?"

"One," Chandra replied.

This time Malcolm did smile.

"It's good that you're awake." I tried to infuse the words with upbeat emotion rather than the dark dread I felt. "Is the dream gone now? The one with Suyin?"

Malcolm nodded slowly. "You seem to have healed me, spiker."

"I don't think it was me. When I tried to help you, I put you in a coma."

"Yes. And now Alpha Blacke is in one. You really don't like alpha leaders, do you?"

So that was his game. He was going to pin this all on me. Now that he'd tipped his hand, I saw it all so clearly. This had been his big plan from the beginning. Frame me for Lucas's murder, figuring that the Blacke group would happily kick my ass to the curb, at which time he could scoop me up and make me his little pet crossbreed.

"I would never hurt Lucas," I whispered.

Two vaguely familiar wolves, one male, one female, leapt onto the patio behind Malcolm, landing about a foot from his back. Both were of a similar build—tall and muscular, thick and strong.

"Neely, you've met the Colombos." The look on Malcolm's face

261

reminded me of William's expression right before Chandra shoved him into the salt circle. Unbridled arrogance.

"We were never formally introduced." The female wolf said this with a smile that showed all her teeth. "Anne and Angelo Colombo." She didn't hold out her hand.

Unbelievable. These were the shifters who'd tried to shoot Lucas and me on the freeway.

"Charmed," I muttered.

Angelo grasped his wrist in front of him and stood with his shoulders thrust back in a typical bodyguard posture. His sister assumed an identical stance. They both wore the same silver globe charms William wore. Angelo handed Malcolm one of the charms. The alpha stared straight at me as he put it on.

I hoped Chandra had a plan B, C, D, and E, because I could spike one person wearing the charm, maybe two if the charms were weak enough, but it would leave me vulnerable. Spiking three people, including an alpha leader, wearing those things was out of the question.

It struck me that I hadn't seen a charm on Dick Penn, but it would have been easy enough to hide under his shirt. The two wolves and Lisa Cesar hadn't been wearing them, though. Guess they had been considered expendable.

"It's nice to have pack members you can rely on to protect you. Seems to be a waning quality in most groups." Malcolm picked up the silver charm on the end of his necklace, rolled it around his palm. "Wouldn't you say so, assassin?"

"It is hard to find good help these days." Chandra stood on the other side of the patio looking bored.

The air thickened. Malcolm's grin tightened, and his breathing quickened. There was some weird alpha mojo going on, but I couldn't pick up on exactly what. Chandra's expression remained impassive and her breathing even.

"Ever the professional," Malcolm drawled.

She said nothing, merely stared at him impassively.

I swept over her brain, a light read, and nearly gasped out loud at the pain she was in. Pain Malcolm was causing her somehow. Pain she didn't dare show him.

"Who will serve as alpha leader of the Blacke group while Alpha Blacke is incapacitated?" He asked this as if he didn't know the answer.

"Me." Chandra stood her ground. She was elegance in throttled violence, a work of art in constrained rage. I had never admired her more than I did at that moment.

"Only until your alpha awakens, correct?" Malcolm smiled, as if he knew something we didn't. "This isn't some sort of coup, is it?"

"I am the second of the Blacke group. I will serve as Alpha leader until Alpha Blacke is able to reassume leadership."

Malcolm gestured to the Columbos. "In the meantime, I'll leave some of my people here to help guard your territory."

"Thank you for your generosity, Alpha Malcolm," Chandra said, "but we are fully fortified against attack."

"With you at the helm, I'm certain you are. But, all the same, I feel it's my duty as Blacke's alpha leader to keep a close eye on things while he's out of commission."

"*Ex*-alpha leader," I said.

Malcolm chuckled. "Of course. *Ex*-alpha leader."

IT WAS two hours past midnight and I was back in Lucas's bedroom. Amir stood over the bed, arms crossed. He looked like an avenging angel in his most basic hybrid form, a beautifully muscled man with heavy black brows, deep brown eyes, and golden feathers threaded through his thick, black hair.

"Did you get anything from William Scott about Alpha Blacke's condition?" he asked.

"Only the name of the spell and that Malcolm orchestrated the whole thing. He's got a pet witch somewhere. Probably his uncle." I blew out an exasperated sigh. "And now he's wearing that damned charm. I could spike him again, but you saw what happens when I do. I'd be incapacitated. I'd like to leave it as a last resort."

"Aren't we at the last resort stage?"

Yes. "Almost."

263

"What a mess." Amir leaned his head back, rolled it from shoulder to shoulder. "Chandra will be challenged soon. You can bet Malcolm is gearing up for it."

"If you can get him to take off the necklace, I can spike him dead. I'm becoming something of an expert at murder." The bitterness in my voice must have caught Amir's attention, because his head popped back up.

"The traitor snake would have killed you," he said, "and Dan was an accident."

I nodded. I knew that, but it didn't change how I felt about taking a life—and nearly taking another.

Amir returned to his neck stretches. "The Malcolm shifters took the bodies off the back porch. Probably sending them to the crematorium in his area."

All shifters were cremated upon death to destroy any evidence of their existence. A shapeshifter corpse in the wrong hands would be a disaster—a dangerous disaster. This was the one mandate in the Shifter Treaty that all shifters seemed to adhere to.

"Yeah," I said.

"A damned witch. This makes no sense." Amir paced from the bed to the window and back. "Everyone knows Malcolm hates magic."

"That's what I've been told, too. But his whole family practices it, including his own mother. I hear demons are master liars, but I think most of them would have a run for their money trying to out-lie Xavier Malcolm."

Amir paced back and forth again.

"And what's the deal with holding us prisoner here?" I sat on the bed, tucked the comforter around Lucas. "Not that's he's come out and said it, but the Malcolm wolf bodyguards by the front door lead me to believe leaving might be a challenge."

"Did you question him about their presence here?"

"Yes. He told me that's how the Colombos are paying restitution to Lucas and me. That they're here for our *protection*." I smirked. "As if I believe that."

Amir studied me. "Do you think you could spike him into a coma again if he wasn't wearing the charm?"

"No. Doubt I did it in the first place." I suspected Malcolm had made it look like I'd put him in that coma. Not that it had been fake. I'd have known if it was.

"But you could kill him?"

"Yes—even with the charm. It will hurt me, but I can do it." I kept my voice low. "He'll be expecting me to try, though. He'll have planned for it."

"What makes you say that?"

"Because he's controlled everything from the minute we arrived in San Diego. Probably before that. He's miles ahead of us, and the only person capable of going toe-to-toe with him in Machiavellianism is lying in this bed."

"We need Alpha, and he needs us." Amir paced across the room, stopped in front of the floor-to-ceiling glass wall. "He's weakening, Neely. His heart is slowing. If we don't do something soon, he's going to die."

As I watched, Lucas took a shallow, uneven breath. He looked exposed and vulnerable, and everything within me wanted to protect him. This man was important to me in ways even I didn't fully comprehend.

I would not let him die.

"What do I do?" I whispered.

"Honestly? I don't know. But then, I'm not sure what all you're capable of, Neely Costa MacLeod." Amir quietly exited the room, leaving me alone with Lucas.

My cell phone buzzed in my pocket. A text message from Dottie explaining more about the "dream hell" spell and possible reversals. Nothing definite yet.

The basic idea was that Lucas was trapped inside his own head, stuck in a REM cycle loop, dreaming himself to death. Looped memory, looped dream. Whoever was doing this was definitely a one-trick magic pony.

I stared at Lucas's eyes. There was activity behind them. They darted from side to side, jumping and twitching behind his eyelids.

Spiking him the way I had tried to with Malcolm wouldn't work. I didn't know how I knew that, but I did. My next move had to be unexpected. Something Malcolm had no idea I could do. Something *I* didn't know I could do.

Something different.

An idea had been percolating in the back of my brain since Malcolm's grand awakening. It wasn't a great idea. In fact, it was risky and might not help, even if I was able to pull it off. It could leave us in an even worse position.

On the plus side, it was different.

And Malcolm would never see it coming.

Mentally battered and bruised, though, I was in no shape to take on a powerful alpha. I wasn't a shifter with unlimited energy and heightened healing abilities. I needed time to recover from the thwarted spike on Dan. I needed time to plan.

Unfortunately, Lucas had next to no time left.

CHAPTER TWENTY-EIGHT

THE A TEAM WAS OUT.

I couldn't involve Chandra, Dan, or Amir–couldn't have them acting suspiciously around Malcolm or anyone else in the house, which was slowly filling up with wolf shifters. My plan hinged on the element of surprise.

So, I called in the B Team.

An hour later, two witches and a Gila monster shifter in hybrid form stood on the other side of Lucas's window wall. It was a quarter past 3 a.m. and dark out, with only half the moon showing and the stars bright and clear in the sky.

Dottie and Dolores took a long swig from a green wine bottle they passed between them, handed it to Earp, who set it aside, and pressed their palms to the glass. Each witch wore a starred globe charm on a silver chain.

"*Bathroom*." Earp mouthed this and pointed. He, too, was wearing a silver witch charm.

In hybrid form, the shifter's flesh was pearly, sunburn-white, and he had a wide, heavy tail that pushed his dusty jeans down past socially acceptable. He was most comfortable in fully shifted form and spent his days in various desert and mountain hideaways.

It was to one of his mountain hideaways that we were headed. A place that even Lucas didn't know about, miles from Sundance.

I ran into Lucas's bathroom and flicked the lock on the largest window. The other windows in the bedroom and bath didn't open, but this one did—however, all Lucas's windows were alarmed. If the witches spell hadn't disabled the security system, we were sunk.

Weighted with fear, I blew out a sharp breath and shoved open the window.

Silence.

Holy moly, they'd done it.

I didn't have time to marvel over their success, because Earp immediately dove through the window and ran to get Lucas. I shimmied out, landing with a thud in the dirt, rocks jabbing into my back and ass as I scrambled to my feet. A half minute later, Earp climbed out with Lucas's sheet-wrapped, lifeless body flung over his shoulder.

The three of us made it to Earp's old truck in record time. Earp lowered Lucas into the truck bed, and I climbed in after him and peeled back the sheet. Pushing my fingers through his scruffy dark-blond hair, I carefully lifted his head and lowered my ear to his mouth, relieved when his warm breath washed over my jaw.

Earp reached over and whisked off Lucas's sheet. He ripped it in half lengthwise and threw one section across the road, where it was snatched out of the air by someone I hadn't noticed was standing there because it was still dark out and I was one hundred percent focused on the man lying in front of me.

King Jones wrapped the torn sheet around himself, gave me his patented brusque nod, then took off running in the direction opposite of the one we'd be going in. Earp started the truck while the witches said a quick incantation which I figured had something to do with cloaking us. Then they too got into the cab and we drove off.

As the old truck bounced and jerked and jostled, I snuggled down beside Lucas and took his hand in mine. It was cold and limp. His whole body felt ... empty.

"I'm going to save you. I won't let you die." As I said this, I recalled the last person I'd tried to save, my uncle, and how that had ended. I wanted to burst into tears, but I didn't have time for self-pity.

"Hold on. Please." I plugged one ear and pressed the other to Lucas's chest to listen to his heartbeat. It was slow, and so faint I could barely hear it.

He wasn't going to make it to Earp's cave hideout.

I banged on the window and told Earp we needed to change the plan, that we didn't have a half hour, and I told him where to go.

IN THE END, it made the most sense, though it was an obvious place to hide and the very last place I would have chosen.

We went to my uncle's house.

Thankfully, the spare key was still in the fake rock under the bougainvillea bush. I jumped out of the truck and raced to open the front door. Earp carried Lucas into the house. When he returned to the doorway empty-handed, I figured he'd put Lucas on the sofa in the darkened living room as we'd discussed through the rear truck window on the drive over.

"You can save him, Neely. I know you can."

I wished I had his confidence. "Thanks."

"Jones and I'll do what we can to buy you time." He wrapped one of his skinny strong arms around my shoulders, gave me a side hug, and left.

Inside the house, the curtains were drawn over the windows, suffocating the living room in darkness. I felt my way to the wall switch and flicked it on. The light flickered once then held, but it was weak.

Crossbreed.

Although it had been cleaned and repainted, every time I closed my eyes, I saw that accusatory bloody word scrawled in blood on my uncle's dining room wall. I remembered the violence that had happened here was because of me, because I was a spiker.

"Neely?" Dolores called out as she walked through the front door. "You okay?"

"Goodness, I can't see a thing in here." Dottie murmured something under her breath and the weak light brightened.

269

"This isn't the same thing." I stood in the center of the living room, arms dangling at my sides. "Lucas isn't Tío José."

"No, he's not." Dolores's voice softened. "And you're not the same, either. You're stronger."

Was I? Because it sure didn't feel that way.

"With a will like his, Alpha Blacke has likely bent the dream to suit him by now." Dottie pulled some bundled herbs from a grocery store bag and set them on the wood coffee table. The scents of sage, thyme, and mint wafted up to me. "So, while it may begin with the spellcaster's dreamscape, with images they assumed would keep him locked in the dream, it will have evolved."

Dolores set a fist-sized white crystal next to the herbs. "Yeah, and knowing that tiger, it probably won't be rated G."

We had discussed the plan via text. I knew I had to come up with a solution that didn't involve traditional spiking or magic. Malcolm was aware of my relationship with the tower witches, and would assume Dolores and Dottie would be among the first people whose help I'd seek out. He was too smart not to plan for that.

So, no spikes, no spells, no hex bags, no magic.

My plan was straightforward, almost simple, but there were a lot of moving parts. It was also a little "out there," but I figured everything about the situation was ten miles past Jupiter anyway. There were no guarantees for either of us—if it even worked.

I stood beside Lucas's unnaturally sleeping form. He was barefoot and shirtless, in black cotton sweatpants. Amir had probably changed his clothes. Dan would have added a shirt and socks. Chandra would have outfitted him in body armor.

"Are you sure you want to risk this?" Dolores asked.

"Yes."

"Listen here. I know you've got a connection with this alpha, and even though the tiger and I have had our differences, I don't want him to die. But this is dangerous. We know nothing about this witch, other than it's someone connected to that double-crossing alpha leader. It could be a warlock, or it could be more than one witch. If a spell has been fed enough magic, it can continue even when the caster is dead."

"We've seen it before, dear." Dottie examined a craggy oyster shell the size of her palm.

"My point is, you've never done anything like this before. There are a hundred ways it won't work and only one way that it will." The tall, sturdy witch looked small and tired. "No one will blame you if you don't do it."

"I know why you're saying this." My voice, like the rest of me, shivered to the point of breaking. "But, right now, I need you and Dottie to be with me on this. To believe in me, because I'm having a really hard time believing in myself."

"We believe in you," Dottie said.

"You're damn tootin' we believe in you. I'm just a natural worrier is all." Dolores nodded sharply, then squeezed and released my hand. "All right then. Do what you have to. Dot and I'll get things ready on our end. We're going to put up a low energy cloaking spell to buy us some time, but we can't give it much juice because we're going to need all our energy for the shielding spell. Still, with the cloaking, and with Earp and King doing their things, we should have an hour before the shifters come knocking down the door. Maybe more."

The Blacke and Malcolm shifters would find us, there was no question about that even with the cloaking spell and the scent diversion. If anyone thought twice about it, they'd probably figure I'd take him somewhere familiar. However, our choices had been narrowed to the point of choking, and time was not on our side.

"You both do whatever it takes to get out of here if Malcolm shows up. He'll make an example of you in order to deflect his guilt."

Dolores scowled. "Don't you worry about us. The Fairfield witches can handle ourselves."

I went to my knees on the carpet beside Lucas. Stroked my hand down the side of that too-handsome-for-his-own-good face. The sarcastic tilt of his mouth remained, even in sleep. Or, maybe I was only seeing what I wanted to see.

"If you were awake, you'd lose your mind over what I'm about to do. So would your shifters. Frankly, I'm a little freaked out about it myself. But I'm going to do it because it's the only way I think I can save you, and Lucas, I really need to save you." I took a long, shivery breath. "For both of our sakes."

I climbed onto the sofa with him, crawled on top of his strong, but disturbingly lifeless, body. He was freezing cold. Lucas was *never* cold.

It was the quiet in his brain that scared me most, though. This was an alpha shifter whose inner machinations had inner machinations. He was always scheming, always two steps ahead of everyone else. As a result, he had one of the busiest brains I'd ever encountered.

"Put up the barrier now."

"You got it." Dolores wrapped her hands around the crystal while Dottie took a lighter to the sage, blew the flame out, then set the smoking bundle on the halved oyster shell.

I drew Lucas's head against my chest, snugging him into me. My eyes slipped shut as I pulled energy. The witches had taught me to let the energy come to me rather than draining it from my environment, but they had also told me there were going to be times when I might need more than would willingly come to me.

This was one of those times.

"The safety net is in place, dear. Go ahead and take what you need."

Once I knew the witches and the rest of the people and animals in the neighborhood were safe, I began. I didn't pull energy from my environment, I wrested it, bled it out, more even than I'd managed when trying to save my uncle's life. I squeezed it from every blade of grass, pressed it out of every flower, drew it out of the air itself. Every inch of me was alive and crackling, like the dancing end of a cut electric wire. If the witches hadn't put barriers around the house and themselves, I'd have drained the life forces of every living being within a mile radius.

"Focus on the core of the spell. There's always a weak spot. You find that spot, then do what you do," Dolores's voice was steady and firm, and I drew strength from it the same way I'd drawn power from the living things around me. "It's going to be personal. Spells like this always are. What works for the tiger won't work for you."

"Look for the knot," Dottie added. "That snarled, tangled part of you that you don't want to face. Find the knot."

Pleasure, warm and liquid, sank into my bones. Although I'd taken more energy than I could ever use, I wanted more. I wanted to feel it surging through my veins. I wanted that jump-off-a-cliff, stomach-gripping, heart-stopping, delicious rush.

Before starting the spell, I'd settled on a focus phrase, something that would pull me out of my euphoria, something that was harder to resist than even my own addiction.

I won't let you die.

The energy inside me calmed, and while it was still powerful, it was controllable.

The interior of Lucas's mind was dark. I had no way of knowing if the place where I was standing, sitting, lying, was the size of a closet or a football field. There was no ground beneath my feet, bottom, or back, no wind in my face, nothing to indicate direction or place. For lack of anything else to do, I began to walk, hands held out in front of me, all the while anticipating a wall or beam to the face.

An overhead light flickered on in the nothingness and a wooden cart popped into view. It was red and gold, and looked like a carnival rollercoaster car.

A square door on golden hinges swung open and I climbed inside. With a jiggering snap, the cart creaked forward. Rusty squeals accompanied the movement, along with the sense that this ride, like this idea, was not entirely safe. A sensation of misty damp pressed in as the cart began to climb upward in ratcheting jerks and jolts.

Click-click-click.

Fear crowded in, and I reached for the euphoria again. When it threatened to drag me under, I brought my focus phrase to mind. Held tight to the emotion behind it.

I will not let you die.

Lucas, I'm coming for you.

I'm on my way.

Click-click-click.

My breath jammed in my throat as the cart ascended. It crested and hung there, leaving me trapped in a moment of breath-held suspension.

*Click-click-*stop.

The cart tipped forward, then plunged into a breakneck descent, as I spiked deeper into Lucas's head. This was not a traditional spike. I wasn't trying to hurt him or read him, and I wasn't pulling anything out of his brain. Quite the opposite, in fact.

Lucas, I'm coming for you.

So, get ready.

As the cart raced downward, I pushed the entirety of my consciousness into his. At that moment we were so intrinsically joined that if someone were to shoot Lucas in the heart, I'd feel the bullet tear into my chest. And if he died, I'd go right along with him.

I was falling, my stomach told me so. My breath lodged in my lungs, and a sterile, tepid wind whipped at my clothes and my hair. None of it was true, but it didn't feel like a lie.

The cart rolled to a stop. I jumped out and ran to where the spell was wrapped around his brain. It had taken the form of a snapping, snarling, writhing nest of onyx serpents with five-foot pearlescent fangs and twenty-foot forked golden tongues.

I will not let you die.

I backed up, crouched, and sprinted toward the nest as fast as I could.

The largest, fattest serpent hissed, tried to grab me with its enormous split tongue and missed. Not that it mattered, because we were both after the same thing.

I dove headfirst into its mouth, narrowly avoiding the poison oozing from its fangs, and the bottom dropped out of my world.

It was disconcerting, sliding down the throat of what my brain told me was a thirty-foot serpent, but was, in actuality, just an image in Lucas's mind. I slip-slid twenty feet or so, finally emerging into a scene out of an LSD trip.

It was the desert, but it was also the city. It was noon, but also midnight. The street was narrow and dusty, the sidewalks crafted out of clear glass bricks. A marching band comprised of human-goat hybrids in red uniforms, played a flawless version of AC/DC's "You Shook Me All Night Long," on vest-supported snare drums.

Lions and wolf-shifter hybrids dined on moonlit patios straight out of a Van Gogh painting. Giant bronze elephants with howdahs strapped to their backs carried smaller elephants who likewise wore howdahs on their backs. None seemed happy with the arrangement.

As I wandered farther into Lucas's bizarre dream world, I encountered more hybrid shifters. Some waved to me, some scowled. One tried to bite me. I didn't know where I was going, but I figured it was the right direction, because everyone else was headed away from it.

It took me hours. Or was it days? Seconds? I macheted my way through a half-mile of jungle, I dodged freeway traffic like a pixelated frog in a video game, I waded through a shallow lake. I was drenched and scared and exhausted, but when I finally reached my destination, my heart squeezed in my chest.

Before me was a two-story building, pale gold stucco, the veranda over the entrance brilliant pink, the exterior windows bright purple, the glass front door frame fire engine red.

La Buena Suerte Panaderia.

Lucas had chosen my bakery as his safe place.

"Lucas?" My *bisabuela*'s bell rang against the glass as I swung open the door and stepped inside. It was cleaner than my place, brighter. My great-grandmother's bell sounded louder, clearer. It smelled the same, though. Fresh bread, coffee, vanilla, and the faint odor of soap and cleanser. At least it smelled the way it used to, when the bakery was still open full-time.

Neely?

His voice echoed in my head. I sprinted through the cafe and the kitchen, and up the stairs to where my apartment should be.

Lying in my bed wearing a pair of tan khaki cargo shorts and his *Golden Girls* T-shirt, bare ankles crossed, was Lucas. His hair was shower damp, there was a half-eaten plate of pink *conchas* on the nightstand, and he was reading the romantic suspense story he'd teased me about the night before we went to see Malcolm. Lestat was perched on the other pillow, tail wrapped around his front paws.

I was so relieved to see him alive and awake that tears sprang to my eyes. "You're okay."

"Of course I'm okay." He set the romance book aside and frowned up at me. "I've been waiting for hours. What took you so long?"

CHAPTER TWENTY-NINE

I WAS GOING TO CHOKE HIM.

"Saving me?" Lucas rolled his eyes. "I don't need saving. Look at me, I'm fine. I'm superfine. In the dictionary? Under the word 'fine?' Yep, that's my picture. Right, Lestat?"

"*Meow*," the cat responded.

For the last five minutes I'd been trying to explain to him that I hadn't just been downstairs working, that he was in an unnatural coma, and that we were both in his head.

Or at least for what felt like five minutes. It could have been milliseconds or days, years. Time was elastic here, which made me worry that we were stretching it thin enough to snap.

"For the last time, you are trapped inside your own head."

He winked. "I'll try to be more communicative in the future, sugar cookie."

I groaned. "What's with the elephants and howdahs anyway? It seems a strange choice—not that anything is normal here."

"Howdahs? You mean those things humans strap to the backs of elephants to carry them around? I saw one in a parade when I was a kid and the cruelty of it has always stayed with me." He gestured toward my kitchen. "Have you eaten yet? I'm hungry."

And so it went. It was like talking to a brick wall, which wasn't unusual in my dealings with Lucas, but this was different. He truly believed he was in my apartment at the bakery.

"We think Malcolm had a witch put a spell on you."

"Nah. He hates witches—except for his uncle and an aunt or two."

"I know. I was shocked, too—*what?*" My mouth fell open. "You *knew* about that?"

"Everyone knows about it." He picked at the half-finished *concha* on my nightstand. "He hates his mom, but still talks to the rest of them."

I took several short, shallow breaths. "Okay. He's got magical contacts and we know he's not above using anyone and anything to get what he wants. Think, Lucas. Think hard."

He shoved the pink *concha* into his mouth. Chewed.

"*Why would I lie to you about this?*"

"Because you hate Malcolm?" He chewed some more and swallowed.

"Well, yes, but I'm more the running away type, not the lying type."

He set the plate on the nightstand and picked up a bottle of water that hadn't been there two seconds before. Took a drink, then capped it. "You lied to the whole town about your ability. A lie of omission."

"I had my reasons. *Think*, Lucas. Malcolm called us up to his home, his place of power, makes a show of dominance at dinner by stabbing Dick Penn—"

"That was hilarious—"

"—*and then* fakes a bizarre brain affliction that only my spiking him can cure. Finally, all hell breaks loose and you fall into a—*unconscious*. You fell unconscious."

"Were you going to say a *coma?*" He set the water back on the nightstand and it immediately disappeared.

"Uh, well, I..." I shifted from foot to foot. "Yeah. I was."

"He put me in a coma." Lucas said this thoughtfully, with no surprise behind the words. "The bastard is making a power grab, isn't he?"

I nodded excitedly. I was sure I had him now. "*Yes.*"

"This is really bad news."

"Yes, it is, but I have a plan—"

"I'm never getting my glacier silver metallic M6 back, am I?"

I was taking a baseball bat to that damned car when we got home. "*Listen to me.* You've been out for too long. If you don't wake up, you're going to die."

He gave me a speculative look. "How long have I been out?"

"Two days, but the witches said there's probably something connected to the spell. A metabolic accelerant. In short, your body is cannibalizing itself. You're wasting away."

"*Our* witches? Please." He threw up his hands. "Why would I trust anything they'd say?"

"They're helping me save your life, so you might want to be nicer to them."

Lucas eyed me with a mixture of pity and annoyance, as if I were a misbehaving pet. "Neely, honey, this is crazy."

"It probably feels that way to you, *honey*, but I can prove it."

He sighed. "How?"

"Stay in that bed. Do not get up."

He shrugged and lay back on my pillows. "I wasn't going to. I'm tired."

"I'm trying to prove a point about you being trapped here. Try to get up—but you won't be able to."

He shook his head. Picked up the book and began reading again.

Desperate times, Neely.

I lowered myself to the floor about six feet from the bed. Well out of his current reach. Crooked a beckoning finger in his direction and tried to sound seductive instead of frustrated.

"Come here, Alpha Blacke. If you can, which you can't."

"Leave me alone. I'm at the best part of the story." He peered at me over the top of the book but didn't lower it.

Slowly, I reached up and unfastened the yellow ribbon wrapped around my ponytail. My hair tumbled down my back in a frothy mass of tight curls. I dropped the ribbon in a pool on the floor and stared at it for a beat. It wasn't something I'd imagined myself wearing. The ribbon was Lucas's fantasy.

I made a mental note to pick up some yellow ribbon when I got home.

If I got home.

"What are you doing?"

"Enticing you into getting out of that bed." I slid my hands down the front of my body until I reached the hem of my yellow sundress. Again, this wasn't what I'd been wearing when I entered his mind. Another Lucas fantasy. I half-dreaded, half-excitedly anticipated what was underneath the dress.

He gave up all pretense of reading and gripped the book in his hands, squeezing until the binding cracked.

"Come here, Neely."

"No. You come here—if you can." I whisked the sundress up and over my head. I was left wearing a white lace bra and panties, both dotted with tiny yellow roses, and a pair of pearly thigh-high stockings with a yellow ribbon threaded through the white lace tops.

Lucas, you naughty man.

"What are you doing?"

I scowled at him. "For heaven's sake, will you pay attention? I told you already. I'm enticing you." I squinted up at him. "Is it working?"

"Let me put it to you this way: I could hammer a nail in the wall with no hands."

"Oh my God, why are you so gross?"

"What?" He grinned. "It's a compliment."

Even trapped inside his own head, the man found ways to annoy me. Sighing, I rose to my feet. Took a step back and slowly rolled the first stocking down my thigh. I snagged it with my fingernail, of course. Stockings and I were always a risky proposition.

"Don't move away from me again." Lucas growled. "That's a hateful thing to do."

"Tell you what. I'll do anything you ask me to if you get out of that bed right now and come over here. But I'm telling you now that you can't."

"Anything?"

"*Anything.*"

He tossed the book aside. "Start humming the theme to *Bonanza*. How do you feel about spanking? Me, of course, not you. I prefer soft restraints, but if you're into metal, I'm down for stainless steel. No silver for obvious reasons."

I thought about it. "I'm okay with the spanking, but I don't care for restraints, soft or hard. And I don't know the theme to *Bonanza*."

"Ooo, that's very close to a deal breaker." His admiring gaze drifted over me, turning his words into a lie. "What about *The Fresh Prince of Bel Air*?"

That one I knew. I sang the first few lines as I pushed the other stocking to my ankle and kicked it off.

"I am so turned on right now." He grunted as he tried to sit up. Wrenched himself around on the bed so hard I was surprised the mattress didn't tear in half.

"You can't move, can you?"

His face suffused with blood. He was going to dislocate his shoulders if he didn't settle down. "N-no. What the hell?"

"I told you that you can't get off the bed. You're trapped here, Lucas. That's why you can't move."

"No way." He grunted and jerked around some more.

"Do you believe me now?"

He didn't. It took another few minutes of him trying to get out of bed for him to admit defeat. I stood and watched, hands on hips, foot tapping impatiently.

"Hell. A spell, huh?" he gasped, having finally exhausted himself.

"Yes."

He glared at the ceiling. "Xavier Malcolm is a double-crossing bag of dicks."

"Speaking of betrayal..." I told him about William, which meant I had to break the news about Lisa Cesar.

Quietly, he said, "I'm sorry you had to kill her."

"Me, too. Lucas, I lost control again." My voice tapered to a whisper. "I attacked Dan. I was lost in it, in the euphoria, and I nearly killed your third—your friend."

"But you didn't." His expression was kind, which wasn't what I'd expected.

"Only because Chandra stopped me. Lucas, I was *gone*. I can't do that anymore. I'm afraid one of these days I'll get so lost I won't find my way home again."

"You didn't have a choice. It seems to me that you rarely do."

"I'm dangerous."

"Everyone is dangerous. Even humans. The strong control it. The weak lean into that side of their nature and end up spraying a shopping mall with bullets. *You* are not weak, Cornelia." He gave me a stern look. "What's your middle name?"

"Costa. It's my mother's maiden name. I don't have another one."

"Come here. Sit by me, Cornelia Costa MacLeod." He patted the mattress beside him. "Sorry I can't scoot over, but my ass is apparently glued to the mattress."

I gave him a sad smile, sat down. "Dan hates me even worse than before. He thinks the world would be better off if I were dead."

"Does he?" A muscle pulsed in Lucas's jaw. "And what do you think? Because that's all that really matters here."

"I think he's right. What I can do, no one should have this ability."

"Yet you do. Ever think that maybe the universe knows what it's doing?" He nudged my shoulder with his. "It could have given this ability to anyone, and it chose you. A woman with a power that could murder the world, who hamstrings herself with overly strict rules—"

"My rules are important. They keep people safe."

He nudged me again. "Exactly. The universe knows what it's doing."

I leaned closer to him, rested my head against his bicep. We sat quietly beside each other, thinking private thoughts.

"Is William dead?" he asked after a moment.

"No. Chandra said you'd want to handle it yourself."

"She's right." Lucas dragged his hand over his head. "Why are all my old friends assholes?"

"Not all of them. Chandra's pretty cool. Amir, too." I elbowed him. "And there's me."

"There's you." His eyes briefly glowed amber. "You're a new friend."

"Old enough."

"True." His gaze raked over me and I realized I was still in my underwear.

I shot to my feet beside the bed, pointed at the lingerie. "This is your fantasy, not mine, Alpha Blacke."

"Say I bought it for you in real life. Would you wear it?" He waggled his eyebrows and I couldn't help but laugh.

"Yes, but I wouldn't let you see it."

"Punishment. I'm into it. But let me memorize you so I'll have a mental image."

"That's what this is, you dork." I smiled at his unrepentant perusal of my underwear. "It's your mental image. Trust me. My thighs don't look nearly this good."

"Yes, they do." Lucas's eyes slid closed and he released a drawn-out sigh. "I'm going to kill Malcolm. It's going to be carnage. A blood bath."

I said nothing. I certainly wouldn't mourn the loss.

"So, you're inside my head. You spiked your image in?"

"Yes. No." I wrinkled my nose. "Well, kind of. Not exactly."

"Thanks. You've totally cleared that up."

I hunched my shoulders, stared at the floor. "This is different from my usual way of spiking."

"How did you know it would work?"

"Um, about that…"

"You didn't know." He covered his eyes with his hand. "I'm doomed."

"I did know. It's just … the last time I tried something similar, it didn't work."

"The *last time* it didn't work?" Lucas stared at me. "Are you talking about José?"

"Yes." The word came out as a pained whisper. I'd failed my uncle, but I wouldn't fail Lucas.

"What did you do differently, Neely? Because you almost killed yourself last time." His jaw tightened and his voice dropped into alpha leader zone. "What *exactly* did you do?"

"Will you hold me?" I asked. "Please?"

His nostrils flared and I got a peek of his tiger. If he was letting it slip, he was upset. Furious, more like. And yet … he opened his arms to me.

I crawled right into his lap. His body hardened beneath me, but he didn't touch me in a way I'd deem even remotely sexual. Instead, he hugged me and buried his face in my throat.

"Tell me. *What did you do?*"

Time to come clean. "Instead of spiking power into your brain the way I did with my uncle, I spiked myself in. My consciousness." I sipped a nervous breath. "My lifeforce."

"How do you even know how to do that?"

"Instinct. Guesswork. The witches helped."

"Damn you." His arms tightened around me until I could hardly move. "You're risking your life to be here, aren't you?"

"You were going to die."

His tone hardened. "Then you should have let me."

"I couldn't." I didn't mean to cry. But this moment was too big, too much. What I felt for Lucas was too heavy for it not to drop out somehow. "I couldn't let you go."

"Ah, sugar cookie." He kissed my neck, then pulled his head back and searched my tear-stained face with that heated whiskey gaze.

"I hate that nickname."

"No, you don't."

"Yes, I do, you ass." I sniffed.

He hugged me tighter. "What do we do now? Is the spell broken, since I know about it, or—"

I saw it in his eyes, the moment everything fell into place, the instant it all clicked for him and he realized what I was going to do.

"No. No, no." Tremors shook his body and his eyes went tiger-gold. "Don't you *dare*—"

"Why yellow?" I blurted.

"*What?*"

"Yellow ribbons, my dress, the flowers on the lingerie—why yellow?"

He looked distinctly uncomfortable. "It's corny."

"Tell me anyway."

When he looked back, it wasn't at me, but my hair. He wrapped a curl around his finger. "It's the way I see you—the way I've always seen you. You're like this ray of sunshine in the gray darkness of my existence. When you look at me, I feel ... I don't know, warmer."

I smiled. "You infuriate me, Lucas Blacke. And annoy me and aggravate me, and yet I care about you. So much."

"How much?" He was trying to tease me, but he couldn't quite pull it off. The terror in his voice ruined the effect.

"You'll see."

I began gathering power the same way I'd done when entering Lucas's mind, only slower this time, as a warning to the witches to get the protective barrier up again if they'd brought it down. I had no idea how long I'd been here, and Dottie had explained that it would take a lot of power to keep the thing up for any length of time, so they would lower it once I was in and raise it when I needed it again.

"Stop it, Neely."

The room shimmered, and items began popping out of existence. First the romance book, then Lestat, then the floor, until we were floating on my bed in the middle of nothing at all. I pushed Lucas flat on his back on the bed and wrapped myself around him.

"Time to wake up. Your group needs you."

"I'm not leaving you alone." His golden eyes were joined by a wide, orange-brown nose and black-striped ocher fur as he shifted into one of his hybrid forms. "I won't go."

I rolled over, taking Lucas by surprise so that he rolled with me. When his body was on top of mine, I looped my legs around his thickening waist, my arms around his furred neck, and pressed my mouth to his. It was the only part of him still one-hundred-percent human.

"Neely, *please*."

"Wake up." I accessed the power I'd been throttling inside me and forced it into him. He whipped his head back and roared, though I didn't know if it was in pain or fury. Spikes hurt, but he was also very angry. I sensed it thrumming though him.

"No. Won't ... leave you," he grunted.

His words and the resistance behind them meant everything, even though they were making things harder for us both.

"You have to."

"Don't you do this to me."

284

The fur covering him rippled, black stripes transformed into sandy brown. He was changing, a full shift, from Bengal tiger to his truest form, the prehistoric Smilodon. His cranium expanded, nose and jaw lengthening, as he coiled his enormous arms around my waist, claws punching into the mattress beneath us.

He threw back his head and roared. "You will *not* stay here. You will come home with me."

"Please." My voice shook, tears clouded my vision. "Please let me go. I need to save you—because I couldn't save him."

Lucas had been with me when my uncle died, and afterward. He knew what it had done to me to fail Tío José, and he had to know what it would do to me to fail him, too.

He grunted his reply, having lost the ability to speak. Blade-like canine teeth burst from either side of his massive upper jaw, curving slightly back as they extended well past his lower lip.

"It's okay." I reached up to stroke his head and he leaned into my touch, probably sensing my lie. It wasn't okay and we both knew it.

Figuring the witches had had enough time to shield by now, I inhaled, drawing in every atom of energy in the atmosphere. I was inside the dream, reaching out, overflowing with power. The surface of my skin sent off blinding white sparks as electrical energy blazed through me.

When I'd looked like this before, like a human Tesla coil, I'd scared the hell out of Dan Winters. He'd recoiled, moved as far from me as he could get without actually running away.

Lucas pulled me closer.

My heart broke a little as I threw every drop of power I had left into my next words. "*LUCAS BLACKE, WAKE UP.*"

I tumbled face down on the bed, arms empty, energy depleted. Lucas was safe.

And I was alone.

CHAPTER THIRTY

I HADN'T EXPECTED TO FEEL SO BEREFT WHEN LUCAS WAS GONE. SO immediately and monstrously lonely.

The bed disappeared a second after he did and my body jerked—once, twice—and then I was yanked backward as if on a string, through the water and road and jungle, through the town with the goat band and the unhappy elephants, up the snake's throat and out its mouth, down the tracks of the roller coaster, *click-click-click*, and *slam* —into a concrete cell.

At least I wasn't in underwear only anymore. Lucas had taken the lingerie with him and I was in jeans and an oversized T-shirt. Lucas's *Golden Girls* shirt.

I lifted the hem and buried my face in the fabric, comforted because it smelled like him, and took a moment to relax in the knowledge he was safe. That I hadn't failed him, that maybe, just once, this ability of mine had done something good for someone else.

I'd freed Lucas from the witch's spell. The next step was freeing myself. I pushed against the four cement walls constraining me, but only managed to open a window the size of a photograph and a narrow prison door with thick iron bars. Within the cell, I had total imaginative freedom, though nothing I conjured up—*solvents, demolition tools, explosives*—put a dent in the prison bars or walls.

I took a second and made myself a little more comfortable. When I was finished, the room, though cramped and cold, now had a rug covering the floor, a bed with a down comforter, and soft music playing at a low volume.

"Wow, Neels, you really Al Capone-d this cell."

"Who the heck?" I spun around. "*Julio?*"

"It's me." My ex-fiancé looked the way he had the last time I'd seen him. Just under six foot and lean, with shoulder-length brown hair, twinkling green eyes, and a radiant, inviting smile.

I scowled. "What are you doing here?"

"Why wouldn't I come? I love you. You've always been the one for me, baby."

Of all the distractions my mean little brain could conjure up, it had to be Julio Roso.

"Neely." He stood outside the room, gripping the iron bars with slender brown fingers. They were musician's fingers, nimble and talented, and I recalled the way they'd strummed over his acoustic guitar while we lounged in bed after making love, dreaming out loud about our future.

I'd loved those beautiful hands so much—right up until the day they picked up a figurative knife and stabbed me in the back.

"Go away, distraction. I have to figure out how to escape this spell before it drains me dry the way it tried to do with Lucas. I'm not a shifter. I don't have his kind of time."

Julio strolled past the barred door and popped up in the window. "I don't like that alpha."

"Yeah, a lot of people feel that way. He can be a smidgen abrasive." I shooed him aside and peered out at the vast nothingness that surrounded me. "If I concentrate on this window, I might be able to widen it enough—"

"You can't trust alpha leaders. You know that."

"—to climb through, but that's only going to dump me into all that nothingness. Maybe it would be better to—"

"He's using you. It's been his plan all along. Get you to trust him and then he takes you over. Or maybe you go willingly. Either way, he gets his weapon, doesn't he?"

"—sit tight and focus on the core of the spell. Find its weak spot and spike into it.'"

Julio threw up his hands. "You aren't listening to me."

"You aren't real," I snapped. "You're nothing but a figment of my imagination, echoing my innermost fears about Lucas."

"That ought to tell you something." He *poofed* out of existence.

"It tells me I have questionable taste in men, so nothing new there. Which won't matter anyway if I don't get myself out of here."

Panic began to rise in me as I searched for an exit. My hands shook, my pulse jackhammered, and I was drenched in sweat.

"*Calmate*, Nelia." My uncle's voice floated into my head. "Calm down and think. What was it Dottie said? Look for the noose—no, look for the *knot*."

I walked my cell from corner to corner, diagonally, and in circles starting at the center. I got rid of the furnishings and walked it again. No rope, no knot, no way out.

Hours passed. Or, again, what felt like hours, given the elasticity of time in this mental-spiritual dreamscape trap.

I crawled over the floor, examined the walls of my prison, even lowered the ceiling to run my hands over its cold, rough surface. I brought the walls in until they were snugged against me, until I felt like I was in the trash compactor scene from *Star Wars*, albeit a less stinky version. Examined them. Pushed them out again when claustrophobia gripped me tighter than the walls and I needed to breathe.

Finally, exhausted from searching, not to mention my recent trek through Lucas's weird dream world, I sprawled out on the concrete floor and fell asleep.

"Mama, who was that man?"

I watched in the mirror as my mom worked a fat-toothed comb coated with watered down conditioner through my waist-length curls. They were dry and frizzy again. Everything was dry in Texas—especially in August.

"What man, mija? We need more of that good conditioner. This stuff is garbage. Remind me to pick up some in town."

That damn dream. Of course I'd have it now, when I was feeling helpless and alone.

"Sometimes I have to leave. I always come back, don't I?" She snagged the comb on a knot. "Darn these tangles."

The dream took on a decidedly surreal quality. It played in my brain like an old movie shown on a black and white television set.

I picked up a loose curl, glared at it. "Is my hair bad?"

"Bad?" Mama laughed along with a studio audience laugh track. "Hair is just hair. It's not good or bad." Her silver and turquoise bracelets jingled as she worked the comb through another section. The long braid she always wore slid over her shoulder. Her hair was silky black, thick, and straight. Unlike me, she hardly ever got tangles.

This time when I awoke, I crawled to the door and shook the bars. Frustrated tears sprang to my eyes when they didn't move, didn't make a sound, even when I kicked them.

I'd thought I was so clever, thought I could fight the spell better than Lucas because I was a spiker. I'd figured that if I was such a great weapon, why not use myself? So, I jumped into Lucas's head and took on this witch's spell that I didn't completely understand.

Dolores hadn't believed I could do it. Lucas didn't believe it, either. Even Earp had seemed worried. No one really believed I could do this.

No one but me.

And now, even I didn't believe it.

TIME ISN'T ELASTIC. It's mud. Thick mud that sticks to your feet and makes it impossible to run away from your own thoughts. Away from the lies your brain tells itself.

Away from the nightmares.

It was a struggle to stay awake. I was in a near-constant dream state, surfacing periodically to again search the cell for a weak spot in the spell.

"What do you think about cutting it?" Mama asked.

"Daddy will say no."

"Not much he could do if we decided we wanted to cut it, is there?" Waggling her eyebrows at me, she took hold of a handful, pulled it up. "We

could trim it to your shoulders. It would be easier to manage. Your curls would be even bouncier."

"Daddy will still say no."

"Yeah. He will." Mama's slender shoulders slumped. She reminded me of a soccer ball with the air let out. "Another knot." She sank nimble fingers into my hair, worked at the snarl until it was gone, then resumed combing.

How long had I been asleep?

Hunger gnawed at my insides. I was thirsty, too, and my head ached. It was difficult to stay awake, and fighting it seemed less and less worth the effort.

But I dutifully searched my prison, dragged myself from corner to corner, inch by inch, until I collapsed on the cold stone floor again.

Lucas tsked at me and moved my head to the side. "You've really got yourself knotted up in here."

"It's my ring. I wore it to bed."

"Don't wear rings to bed anymore."

I reached for him and got a handful of cold air instead. I whimpered and tumbled into another dream.

A man stood over a huddled little girl with straight black hair and my brown eyes, a thick leather belt doubled over in his hands. His whole body smelled like my daddy's breath after he watched football with my tío.

"Mentirosa. Bruja." Liar. Witch.

"Por favor, I won't tell. I promise. Please, Papa," she cried as the belt cut into her skin.

Though I couldn't feel the actual pain of the lashes, I saw them as if they were aimed at me, and I sensed her fear.

My stomach tightened into a hard ball in my gut. How long had I been out this time?

"Mama, what's happening?"

"Y-you." Her voice was so small I had to bend close to hear it.

"Mama?"

"Please. It ... hurts."

I was doing this. Somehow, I was hurting her. Making the memory come alive in her head, too.

My eyes flicked open. This time I didn't look for the weak spot in the spell. There was no weak spot. It had all been a terrible miscalculation and I had no one to blame but myself.

I lay on my back in the middle of the cold concrete floor and stared at the rough gray ceiling of my cell, too tired to cry.

"Get up, Nelia."

My gut clenched at the sound of that familiar voice. My uncle, whom I'd loved so much and ultimately failed. But this time his voice was closer, as if he were standing in the room with me.

"No, please. Don't use him. Anyone else—send me Julio, even that bastard Saul Roso himself, but not *mi tío.*"

"Use who, *mija*?" Tío José stepped into my sight. He wore a white apron dusted with flour over gray trousers and blue button-down plaid shirt.

It seared my soul to look at him. The guilt I felt at having been unable to save his life blindsided me and tears pricked my eyes.

"Lo siento."

"You're sorry? About what? Get off the floor. *Estas sucia.*"

Four sentences out of his mouth and I was thirteen again. "I'm dying, Tío. Do you really think I care that I'm dirty?"

"Dramática." My uncle perched on a green and pink-painted chair that would have looked at home in our bakery. The chair hadn't been there the moment before.

"Looks like my brain's sending in the big guns now," I muttered.

"Sí. As you said, you are dying." He hummed the tune to *"Amor Eterno,"* the Juan Gabriel song he'd liked so much. It reminded me of baking *bolillos* in the bakery. I could almost smell the yeasty, bread scent.

Loss and guilt and fatigue slammed me. "I'm so tired. That dream with my mom. It haunts me."

"Why do you think that is?"

"Because the inside of my head is a mean and nasty place?"

He shook his head. *"Tonta."*

"I'm not a fool. It's not as if I can help any of this. I can't control my thoughts."

"Tonta. You're a spiker. Controlling thoughts is exactly what you do."

"No, I don't—"

"That's right. You don't. You follow those rules I taught you, exactly the way you were conditioned to. But these rules no longer serve you, and if you don't start using your ability the way you know you can, you will not live out the year."

"What?"

"I taught you rules that meant something when you could hide what you are. You cannot hide any longer, and you are vulnerable. To bullets, to poison, to witchcraft and demon charms, to all the things that kill humans and other paranormals. The only way you will survive in this world is by using the tools you have."

"Become my own weapon," I said.

He smiled. "Exactly."

"I killed Lisa Cesar, Tío. You remember? The rattlesnake teacher. She attacked me and I spiked her dead. I don't like who I am when I access that side of my ability."

"The snake tried to kill you. You killed her first. There is no dishonor in defending yourself."

"But—"

"You will kill, or you will die. *Es fácil.*"

"*Es fácil* for you to say," I muttered.

"Perhaps that was the wrong word. It is not easy, but it is very, very simple."

I was fading. It was so hard to keep my eyes open. But I didn't want to have that dream again.

"Why don't you just tell me how to break the spell?"

"Because you don't know the answer yet." He smiled, and the kindness was back in his eyes. "One last thing. Your head is not a mean or nasty place, it's a good place and it's trying to protect you."

"By making me relive the day my own mother abandoned me?"

"By getting your attention the only way that it can. Remember. You are a spiker. Thoughts don't control you. You control them. Be strong and think." He stood. The colorful chair disappeared. "The answer is with you, *mija*. It has been there the whole time."

"Please don't leave."

"If I don't, you won't figure it out and you need to. Fast. *Estás muriendo.*"

"I'm dying? No. Tío, I don't want to die alone."

"No one does, but we all do. *Te amo.*" He popped out of existence.

"I love you, too." My eyelids were weighted with sleep. I closed them, and the dream dragged me under once again.

"Sometimes I have to leave. I always come back, don't I?" She snagged the comb on a knot. "Darn these tangles."

I surfaced, gasped, went back under.

"Another knot." She sank nimble fingers into my hair, worked at the snarl until it was gone, and then resumed combing.

Again, I surfaced. Again, I went back under.

Though I couldn't feel the actual pain of the lashes, I saw them as if they were aimed at me and I sensed her fear.

I was doing this. Somehow, I was hurting her. Making the memory come alive in her head, too.

My eyes popped open.

Making the memory come alive in her head...

The answer is with you, mija.

It was right in front of me the entire time and I couldn't see it. I was supposed to *look for the knot.*

I laughed like a fool then, like a *tonta*, and pushed myself upright. I was dizzy and I was weak, but I was not finished, and I was not going to die.

In the dream, as in my childhood, I'd spiked into my mother's mind and not only experienced the memory of her father, but forced her to relive it, too.

But that wasn't all I'd done.

The reality was that I had unintentionally pulled power from my alpha wolf mother, which I then used to spike her, accidentally making her re-experience the memory foremost in her brain at that moment. I had used the power I'd siphoned to viscerally *connect* her to that memory, essentially *attacking her brain using her own energy.*

Finding my way out of this spell wasn't about discovering some trap door in the floor of my cell. It was about *connection.* There were all kinds of connections, but they all had one thing in common.

They were a link between things.

The link between my mother and the memory of her father; the link between my mother and me; the link between Tío Jose and me; the link between Lucas and me.

The link between a witch and his or her spell.

The witches said that a spell could outlive its caster. I was sure that was true, but I was equally sure that wasn't the case with this witch and this spell, because when I stopped panicking and started focusing, I could feel the link.

All I had to do now was find a way to follow it.

I was breathing heavily by the time I got myself seated tailor-style, hands grasping my knees, but I was awake, and I was alive, and I was *angry.*

"You messed with the wrong spiker, witch." I didn't dare close my eyes. I was so exhausted it had transmuted from sleepiness to physical agony, but I was focused, and I was desperate.

Look for the knot, Dottie said. *That snarled, tangled part of you that you don't want to face. Find the knot. Face it.*

And my mother: *"Another knot."* She sank nimble fingers into my hair, worked at the snarl until it was gone.

Lucas's fingers digging the ring out of my knotted hair. *"You've really got yourself knotted up in here."*

Imaginary Tío José had been telling the truth. My head *was* trying to protect me.

My hair. I reached into the curly strands, fingers tunneling underneath until I happened upon a knot. With curly hair, it's never a problem to find one, and I nearly always had one behind my left ear for some reason. I worked at the knot, gently untangling the strands. Getting the snarl out the way my mother had failed to the day she left me.

That snarled, tangled part of you that you don't want to face.

It was important not to rip or tear, but to patiently unravel.

Unravel the knot.

Unravel the knot and follow the strands. The strands will lead to the head, to the brain.

Unravel the knot and follow the strands and find the brain and—

Spike.

As the knot fell apart in my fingers, my prison broke open, concrete walls splitting into pieces, chunks, powder. I was suspended in nothing for a half-second, and then I was back in the little red and gold cart, climbing up the lift hill. *Click-click-click.* I climbed the steep rise to the summit where I hung for seconds, suspended in time and space.

Thousands of tightly woven strands webbed at the bottom of the drop. The hair-like threads were tangible filaments that linked the spellcaster to the spelled, and since Lucas was gone, the spelled was now me. I was now linked to the witch.

And the witch was linked to me.

I lunged, sped down the slope of the roller coaster at full speed, charging straight into the brain of whoever waited there. At the last moment, Agnes Romano, Malcolm's shifter aunt, lifted her silver head and stared up at me with glowing gold and onyx eyes. *Witch* eyes.

I'd been expecting Harry Romano, Malcolm's witch uncle. Not that it mattered.

Agnes shrieked at me and began to mutter under her breath, her white hair streaming in cottony wild rivulets over her shoulders and back.

She didn't look like an aging queen now. Her appearance was reminiscent of a wraith, a ghostly apparition, as insubstantial and as distant as she bodily was. But even that was magic. An illusion. Agnes Romano was as real as everything else in this nightmare world she'd created. She was palpable, she was corporeal, and she was *mortal*.

I spiked everything I had inside me—*energy, rage, magic*—straight into the witch-shifter's brain.

CHAPTER THIRTY-ONE

"My magical prowess is wasted on you, Blacke." Dolores huffed. "Like putting diamonds on a duck. No, wait. Pearls on a pig."

"Christ," Lucas muttered.

"I think you mean, 'Don't cast pearls before swine, sister.'"

"Oh, yeah. Thanks, Dot. That is probably what I mean. Is that from the Christian Bible?"

"Perhaps. Or is it the Martinus Tome?" Dottie asked. "I get these things confused sometimes."

Chandra said, "Christian Bible. The full verse is: 'Don't give that which is holy to the dogs, neither throw your pearls before the pigs, lest perhaps they trample them under their feet, and turn and tear you to pieces.'"

"Ooo, someone went to Vacation Bible School before they became an assassin." Dan snickered.

"I will choke you until you are dead, coyote."

"I'd believe the hyena if I were you." Dolores said. "She doesn't sound like she's kidding."

"This conversation is what would happen if a fun house mirror was granted the gift of speech," Lucas said. "Would you all kindly shut your pie holes?"

"A little moody, aren't we, tiger?"

"Witch, so help me, I will..."

Home. Joy bubbled up in me. I'd done it. I'd broken the spell and I was finally home. "Lucas, be nice."

Dolores huffed. "Will what? Exactly what do you think you—"

"Quiet, witch. I heard my name."

"Good gravy, you're arrogant. No one is saying your name."

"*Quiet,*" Lucas growled.

I opened my eyes, peered around. "Oh no, not again."

Indeed, I was in the witches' tower on a mattress in the main room, in exactly the same position I'd been in after being attacked by Dan Winters and Della Bates a couple months ago. Only this time Dan and Chandra were inside the room, not outside trying to claw their way to the second floor to murder me.

"Neely?" Lucas dropped to the mattress, stroked my hair away from my face. He looked awful—drained, too thin, and gray around the edges. "Are you awake?"

"Yes. What's wrong with you?" I asked.

"He's been keeping you alive." Dottie bustled over and sank down on the other side of me. She touched my face with the back of her hand. I didn't have a fever. I felt fine. Weak, and a little gross, but nothing food and a shower wouldn't fix.

"Keeping me alive? How long was I out?"

"Two days." Chandra scowled down at me. She was in her fighting clothes, all black leather and heavy, thick-soled boots. "You would have been dead in six hours if the witches and Alpha hadn't kept you going. You aren't a shifter, you know. Exactly what the hell were you thinking?"

"Thank you," I said, because I knew her snapping at me was her way of telling me she cared.

"Don't ever do that again," she replied, expression softening.

"Hey kiddo," Dolores said, "You found the weak spot, huh? You broke the spell."

I nodded. "I unraveled the knot."

Dottie's smile was grandmotherly sweet. "I knew you could do it, dear."

"Thanks. Also, I have never had to go to the bathroom so badly in my entire life."

"Yes, well, Dolores and I put you in a physical stasis spell to slow your bodily functions and to keep the other spell from killing you." Again, Dottie smiled. I wished she wouldn't look so perky when she was talking about things killing me. "You broke it when you woke up, so your needs came rushing back, so to speak."

"How did you escape, Neely?" Lucas's eyes, hooded and deep-set with fatigue, stared straight through me. "I was holding you and then you were gone."

"I found Malcolm's witch."

"Who?" Chandra asked.

"Agnes Romano."

"*Agnes is a witch*? So many things make sense now. How did I miss it? She even has a witch name, which is a huge clue." Lucas sobered and set his disapproving stare on me. "Where is that lying wolf-witch?"

"Dead. I traced back to her through the energy of the spell and spiked her." Sort of.

"Good," Chandra said.

"That was dangerous." Lucas cursed and pushed to his feet. His mouth was pressed into a flat line, his fists were clenched at his sides. "Taking on a witch powerful enough to hide her magic from a pack she'd been a part of for twenty years. You could have been killed."

Dan looked at me with even more distrust than before, and I hadn't thought he could get any worse. The witches were more positive overall.

"Holy smokes, I didn't know you could do that," Dolores said. "Dot and I will have to look into this new ability of yours."

It wasn't new, but I didn't want to explain that in front of everyone.

"We've got company." Amir flew in through the window, shifting into his hybrid form as he landed on his feet. "Some of Malcolm's wolves are headed this way. Oh good, you're awake."

I waved at him from my position on the floor.

"How many?" Chandra asked.

298

"You shouldn't have gone after me." Lucas pronounced every word as if it were its own sentence.

"Don't do this." I sat up slowly. My head felt both heavy and light at once. "Not right now."

Without responding, he took a step back, arms crossed over his chest, and watched me with cold eyes.

I tottered drunkenly to my feet. "If you'll all excuse me, I need to use the facilities."

When I returned from the bathroom, Lucas was standing in the same spot. Again, he looked through rather than at me, and the ice in him chilled me.

"What's that noise?" Dan leaned his head to the side like a dog listening for the mail carrier. "Sounds like scratching."

"Sounds like twenty wolves trying to shimmy up the side of the tower." Dolores hooted a laugh and stuck her head out the window. *"Begone from my sight. The Fairfield Witches' Interdimensional Tower and Watering Hole will tolerate your insolence no more,"* she yelled.

"The Fairfield Witches' Interdimensional Tower and Watering Hole?" Lucas scowled at Dolores. *"That's* the name you're going with?"

"Well, no. We shortened it a little. Now it's: *The Fairfield Witches' Interdimensional Watering Hole.* It's catchier. Also, the neon sign guy couldn't fit the whole name on the size sign I wanted."

"You're really opening a bar?"

"As soon as you okay my liquor license, Alpha Blacke," Dolores said, almost politely. Almost. "Like you said you would."

"Do I look like the Department of Alcoholic Beverage Control? Besides, I've seen what you witches do here. I seriously doubt you need a license to liquor up."

"True, I could fake it, but I wanted to be respectful to you as the alpha leader of Sundance." She crossed her arms, covering the silver sequin tiger on her shirt.

"That would be a first." Lucas rolled his eyes.

Dolores directed her attention back to the window. *"Hoo-hoo-hoo,* look at that. The tower iced itself up. An oldie but a goodie." She patted the window frame as if giving the building a high-five. "Wolfie

299

there isn't coming back from that fall anytime soon. Normally, femurs belong on the *inside* of the body. Skulls, too."

Lucas poked his head out the window. "That's handy. Can you put a spell on my house to make it do that?"

"Perhaps, Alpha Blacke. Of course, I'd be more inclined to do it if I'm licensed up, liquorly speaking," Dolores said.

"I'll have my people look into it."

"Where's Malcolm?" I directed the question to Lucas, but, surprisingly, Dan answered me instead.

"After you kidnapped Alpha Blacke, he lost it and left Sundance. Said you were a traitor and that you were going to kill Alpha and *how could we all just stand around and let it happen?*"

"And you believed him, of course," I muttered.

Dan shook his head, one quick snap. "No. If you'd wanted our alpha dead, you could have done it while you were sleeping beside him, or when he was in a coma, or any of the times you both were alone."

"I'd have done it when they were in the ocean together," Chandra said. "Spike him and let him sink to the bottom of the deep blue sea. No body, no crime."

"I'd have poisoned him in San Diego. Made it look like Malcolm did it," Amir said. "Pillow chocolates would make a good vehicle for poison."

"Very true," Dottie said. "The sweet flavor would mask any bitterness."

"I'd have shanked him the first time he called me 'sugar cookie,'" Dolores said, and everyone nodded.

A muscle pulsed in Lucas's jaw. "Will you all shut the hell up?"

Amir winked at me. "Good thinking using Earp and the witches. Malcolm never saw it coming."

Chandra crossed her arms over her chest and walked to the window. I'd done some damage to our friendship by not confiding in her. I was going to have to fix that.

"I would have told you all, but I had to move fast once Lucas started declining. I didn't know if you'd believe me, and I didn't have time to deal with group politics."

With a thunderous meow, Lestat strolled into the room, tail puffed out and raised high. He looked affronted in the way only a cat can, and stalked in front of Lucas to meow again.

"Looks like he's met Charlie." Dolores wagged her finger at the cat. "Do not eat him, tuna breath. He's cute and sweet, unlike you."

"Baby desert tortoise," Dottie explained. "Dolores found him on a walk last week. The mother was killed by an ATV who'd gone into protected land. Charlie was the only tortoise left alive."

"An ATV, huh?" Lucas scratched his chin. "Did you curse the killer?"

"Let's just say that driver will never get another off-road vehicle to work for him again," Dottie said.

"Or another zipper." Dolores stuck up her hand in a Napoleon *Crossing the Alps* gesture. "Let the sexual harassment suits begin."

Whomp!

Dottie blinked. "Dolores, was that you?"

"No, sis. That was outside and it sounded like a—"

"*Grenade*," Chandra yelled.

Lucas pulled me to the back of the room, away from the window.

"Don't worry," Dottie said, "the tower won't let it—"

THE TOWER LET IT.

The explosion was earsplitting for all of one second. Then there was no sound at all, nothing but a low keening whine. I think I lost consciousness for a few minutes, because when I awoke, coughing and blinking the smoke out of my eyes, everyone was yelling. I could tell this by the way their mouths were stretched, but I wasn't coherent enough to read their lips.

You back with us? Lucas thought to me.

I nodded. Coughed.

I know it hurts. Sorry. Took me out for a few seconds, too. My ears are more sensitive than yours, but I heal faster than you, so it evens out.

Did it? Because it didn't feel very even to me.

Energy, not my own, flowed into me, and the pain broke loose and

301

floated away. My ears were still plugged, but that might not be a bad thing if the wolves decided to hit us again.

"Thank you," I mouthed.

Welcome. So, good news is, it wasn't a grenade. It was some sort of magic-infused smoke bomb meant to disorient us. It worked, by the way, because we were disoriented as hell for a few minutes, but it wasn't an explosive and no one was hurt.

"Why didn't the tower protect us?" It was odd, not being able to hear myself in my own head. But Lucas heard me, and understanding that I couldn't hear him, continued thinking his side of the conversation at me.

It did, in a way. It didn't let the wolves swarm in after the smoke bomb hit. The witches claim the tower isn't at full power, so it missed the first bomb. It blocked the second and third ones, though. The witches say it's learning. I say it's pissed off. Look what it's doing now.

I peered through the dissipating smoke to the window, out of which Dolores was leaning and shaking her fist. The window frame was aflame, but it didn't appear to be affecting the witch at all.

Chandra jogged up to Lucas, whispered something in his ear. He glanced at each member of his security team, nodding in apparent dismissal. Amir dove out the fiery window, shifting to eagle form in midair. Dan pulled off his clothes, shifted into coyote form, and Chandra did the same with her hyena form. The two land shifters bolted out of the room.

"What's going on?" I blinked at Lucas.

He yelled something to Dolores, who nodded. Damn, I wished I could hear. I also wished I could see better. My eyes were watering fiercely.

"What's happening? Where did everyone go?"

Instead of responding, Lucas stripped down and shifted into hybrid form. When his hands and feet had shifted to paws, and black-striped golden-orange fur lightly covered his body, he loped to me on two legs, flung me over his shoulder, and raced out of the room, down the stairs, and into the surrounding mountains.

BY THE TIME I had my bearings, we were on the roof of the bakery. Lucas set me on my feet and pried open a metal vent, revealing a hole that led straight into a sectioned off part of the attic I hadn't seen before. He lowered me through the hole and followed me inside, closing the vent behind him and locking it.

"So that's how you've been getting in."

He said and thought nothing, only scooped me up and carried me the rest of the way into my apartment. On the threshold of my bathroom door, while still in hybrid form, he pressed the padded palms of his hands against my ears. That delicious energy of his again flowed into me and, with a gentle *pop*, my hearing returned. He spun me around and nudged me into the bathroom.

"Geez, I can take a hint."

"If I could make it a command, I would." Although he whispered, his voice still hurt my ears. As if he sensed this, he spoke to me in my head. *Give it a few minutes. The sensitivity will fade.*

"Lucas." I turned to say *thank you, I'm sorry, I need you, please stay.*

He closed the door before I could get the words out.

My shower was long and warm, a Neely-renovation, where I soaped and shampooed and shaved and exfoliated and just stood under the water and got clean. I applied gel and used a microfiber towel to scrunch-dry my hair, forgoing the blow-dryer and instead leaving it hanging down my back in damp curls. Then I brushed my teeth, applied lavender moisturizer all over myself, threw on my yellow fuzzy robe, and called it a day.

When I opened the door, the scent of soup cooking reminded me that I was starving. Lucas, in human form, stood at the stove wearing one of my white cotton aprons tied around his front, and another tied around his back, like a skirt. He'd left his clothes at the tower when he shifted to hybrid.

I'd never realized how many muscles it took to cook until I watched a nearly naked Lucas stir a pot of soup. His back muscles contracted and released, his biceps flexed, his thighs and calves tensed as he moved to the side cabinet for salt and pepper. His color was better, though he was dusty from the smoke bomb, and black soot

303

streaked down his back. He'd scrubbed his hands and nails clean, something I noticed when he set a bowl of *caldo de res* in front of me, along with a sleeve of crackers.

"I found this beef soup in your freezer and heated it up. There's nothing else to eat in this place and I don't know how to bake."

"Thank you." I sat, picked up my spoon. "Aren't you going to eat?"

"I ate. I'm going to take a shower. It's been a long couple of days for me, too." He tossed a dishtowel on the counter and headed for the bathroom.

"Lucas?"

He halted but didn't turn around. "We'll talk when you finish eating."

"Why not now?"

"Because I'm very angry with you and I need to cool off." He stalked into the bathroom and firmly closed the door.

I finished my soup and washed up, then went downstairs for a minute and grabbed some things. When I came back up, Lucas was still in the shower. Either he was exfoliating and shampooing and soaping away—or he was so pissed at me he couldn't leave the bathroom yet. I read him, briefly and shallowly, and was depressed to discover that it was the latter.

When he finally emerged, it was with his hair sticking up in damp spikes all over his head and my towel knotted around his slim waist, hanging low enough to accentuate that wonderful V-shaped muscle above his groin.

I stared at him. It was hard not to. He was perfectly formed, all defined muscles and smooth light-olive skin. The kind of perfect that usually scared me off from a guy because I assumed that he was either a narcissist or way too into the gym for my taste. It wasn't a fair assumption, but it had been my experience, so it was the way I automatically thought.

Lucas Blacke was neither a narcissist nor a gym rat.

He was simply … Lucas.

I was lying on my bed pretending to be relaxed, holding a book I was pretending to read, playing music on a radio I was pretending to listen to. "There's a toothbrush, a pair of sweatpants, and a T-shirt on the kitchen table. My uncle kept supplies in the kitchen closet for himself and other shifters."

"Thanks." He swiped the items off the table and went into the bathroom. Usually he didn't bother leaving the room to change. He was a shifter and none of them cared two figs about modesty.

Obviously, he was still angry with me.

Well, I'd had enough.

I gave him five minutes alone, then I tossed my book onto the nightstand, scooted off the bed, and stomped into the bathroom. The door wasn't locked.

"Fine. I know you're mad that I disobeyed you in that dreamscape nightmare world, but I did it to save your life. Now I'm not saying you have to throw me a parade, but you could at least be a tiny bit grateful to the woman who saved your..."

Although he'd had plenty of time to do so, Lucas hadn't gotten dressed. The toothbrush had been used, but the clothes were on the countertop and he was leaning against the wall by the door, wearing the towel. There was something fragile in the way he looked at me, something soft about the way he picked up one of my curls and coiled it around his finger, something that arrowed straight to my heart as he pulled me close and kissed the top of my head.

"Thank you for saving my life."

"You sound angry." I scowled at him. "You can't say thank you and mean it when you're angry."

"I can and I did."

"Lucas, I want you to stop being angry with me." I tipped my head up and stared into those mellowed amber eyes.

"Why?" He released my curl and put his hands behind his back.

"Because I don't like it."

"Why?"

"Seriously? Are you two years old?" I huffed out a sigh. "Who likes it when someone is mad at them?"

The left side of his mouth lifted in a half grin. "You don't mind that Dan is angry with you."

I stuck my hands on my hips. "I don't *like* it."

"Okay, but would you burst in on him in the bathroom?"

305

I let my arms drop to my sides. He had a point. I'd never chase down Dan in a bathroom because I didn't care enough about what he thought of me to bother. "Well, no."

Lucas came off the wall in that hips first way I found so sexy. "I'm going to ask you again. Why, Neely? Why don't you like it when I'm angry with you?"

He was so close I could feel heated alpha energy emanating from him. His skin smelled like my soap, his hair like my shampoo, his mouth like my toothpaste. A powerful burst of possessiveness jolted through me. Not of my things, of *him*.

"Because you're *mine*." I blurted it out, instantly regretting it. "Mine friend, I mean. My friend."

"Smooth save. Not." A predatory smile curved his lips and he edged toward me.

"I-I don't know why I said that." I backed out of the bathroom, continuing until the backs of my heels hit the platform my bed rested on. "I must be confused from the smoke bomb. That thing sounded like a gunshot and scared—"

"Say it again." His voice dropped low. It soaked into my skin, sent a blast of heat through my body.

"No. It was—wasn't what I meant, I..."

He ambled out of the bathroom, taking his time as he stalked me up onto the platform and to the edge of my bed.

The smile dropped off his face. "Do you have any idea how scared I was?"

I shook my head. I didn't trust myself to speak anymore. I kept saying stupid things.

"We couldn't wake you up for *two days*, Neely. Halfway through the second day, you had a seizure. I thought I was going to lose you then."

A seizure? That damn witch. "I didn't know that."

"After that, you went downhill fast. If the witches hadn't been there, I don't know that I could have saved you. For all their half-assery magic, they did right by you." He grabbed my chin when I tried to look away. "Chandra lent me her strength. She and half the group. You have no idea how close you were to dying, do you?"

I'd known.

"Your breathing was shallow and slow. I listened to every single one thinking it would be the last, my entire universe narrowed to the next sip of a breath—" His thumb stroked over my mouth. "—from those beautiful lips."

"And you think I didn't feel the same way? I kept my head on your chest because I was afraid every weakening heartbeat would be the last. I couldn't stand to leave you. It was a physical pain. So, damn you." I pushed at his shoulders and he stepped back. "Because you made me care about you and then you tried to leave me, and then you got mad at me when I went after you. Nothing I do is right."

He made a slashing motion with his arm. "You should have obeyed me. Should have left me to die. You had no right to sacrifice yourself—"

"*I had every right*," I screamed, "it's my life, and if I want to forfeit it so that the man I..." I clamped my mouth shut and tried to slow my breathing.

"The man you what?" For the first time, I noticed that he was breathing hard, too.

"Nothing. I was just making a point."

"The man you what?" His voice deepened. "*Finish it.*"

I folded my arms over my chest, looked away. "The man I'm going to kick in the male parts if he uses his alpha voice with me again."

"*Coward.*" He stared straight into my eyes. "You are a coward and I am out of here. Stay inside and don't answer the door."

"You're leaving?"

"You'll be fine. As Dan said, Malcolm is back in San Diego. Stay away from the windows and don't make it obvious that you're here." He stomped off the platform.

I followed him. "Oh, so just because I won't say what you want me to say, you're throwing a fit and leaving."

"What I *want* you to say? Neely—" He dragged a hand over his face. "—all I want from you is the truth about why you saved my life. And a promise that you'll never do it again, but I know I won't get that." He inhaled deeply, blew it out slowly. "I just want the truth, and since I'm not telepathic, I can't read your mind to find the answer the way you can mine."

"I'm not reading you."

"How do I know that?" He crossed his arms over his chest, tucked his hands behind his biceps.

"Fine. You want the truth? The *real truth*?"

He arched his eyebrows, nodded.

"The truth is, I'm not entirely sure why." I walked back to my bed to put some distance between us. "When I'm with you I feel … ambivalent. Safe and in danger at the same time. I want you with me —even when you annoy me, and you annoy me often. I don't trust you all the way yet. I'm still not one hundred percent sure this isn't some elaborate plan to make me your crossbreed. It's ingrained in me not to trust alpha leaders, to run from them, yet I find myself always running to you. Always *wanting* to run to you." I stopped, took a breath. "I could not let you die, Lucas Blacke. You want a clear reason why, but I don't have one. It was partly about my failure to save my uncle, partly because I couldn't bear to lose another person I cared about, but that wasn't all of it. I just knew that if you died—" I closed my eyes against the pain the thought evoked in me. "—something inside me would have died, too."

From one second to the next, he went from several feet away to standing in front of me. "*Now* you get why I'm angry with you."

He cupped my face in his hands and kissed me.

CHAPTER THIRTY-TWO

THAT KISS WAS THE IGNITION POINT THAT INCITED THE INFERNO.

I wound my arms around his neck and brushed my tongue over his, drew his lower lip into my mouth, then let it slide out. He tasted like mint from the toothpaste and he tasted like Lucas. Like home.

Tears filled my eyes and I swiped them away. "That's how you feel, too?"

He pressed his forehead to mine. "Yeah, sugar cookie. That's how I feel, too."

For the first time ever, the nickname made me smile.

We'd almost lost each other, and the desperation we felt was revealed in the way he wrapped his hands around my waist, holding me against him, squeezing just a little too tightly. It was in the way I grabbed a fistful of his hair, pushed his face closer, and kissed him just a little too deeply.

"Are you still angry?" I whispered into his mouth.

"Furious." He feathered my face with his lips, coasting over my jaw and down my throat. He pulled me close and inhaled, one long, deep draw of air. "*Livid.*"

He pushed my robe off my shoulders, and I unknotted his towel. Both fell to the floor and I climbed up his body, his hands cupping my ass and hoisting me up to twine my legs around his hips, his erection hard and hot against me. Then we were falling, Lucas making sure he didn't crush me as we dropped onto the bed together. He tried to kiss my jaw, my throat, but I kept redirecting his mouth to mine, needing to taste him, needing to never stop tasting him.

"I'm sorry," he said against my mouth, "I should have known what Malcolm was up to. If I'd been thinking straight, I'd have seen this coming and you wouldn't have had to—"

"Come for you?" I arched my eyebrow.

"Pervert." He grinned down at me. "At least this time when you come for me, there won't be any weird parades or elephants wearing howdahs."

"Then what even is the point?" I pulled his mouth to mine again. "Please stop being angry. I don't like it."

"Then why are you so good at making me that way?" He stared hard at me. I wasn't kidding anymore, and he picked up on my mood the way he often seemed to. "I'll try. I think—" He kissed the corner of my mouth. "—I'm more scared than anything. Saying I'm angry makes me sound more badass."

Deflection via humor. The man could give a class on the subject. "You're badass enough without anger. Be honest."

He raked his fingers down my neck and chest and over my breast. Then he did it again, opposite direction. Such a light touch to create such a firestorm inside me. "I want you, Neely. Every part of me wants you—and that should probably scare the hell out of you. It terrifies me."

Maybe it should have. But it didn't.

I ran my palms over him, up his shoulders, down his arms, over his chest and groin. I took him into my hands and gently squeezed, my gaze locked on his, and then released him, sliding down on the bed to reach his thighs, his calves. Twisting around him, I slipped my palms over his muscled ass, relishing the feel of his overheated skin against my hips and breasts.

"I can't stop touching you," I whispered. "You're here. You're safe."

"Come back here." He rolled over to face me. "Stop squirming around. You're always doing that. Always holding yourself just out of my reach."

In response, I twined my arms and legs around him, ground my pelvis against his. "I'm right here."

"Christ, Neely." He thrust against me, teasing, gliding over that delicate bundle of nerves between my legs and sending me skyrocketing toward orgasm.

Blindly, I reached for my nightstand drawer, my radio and book crashing to the floor as I rifled through it. The radio volume went up and Lucas chuckled.

"*Air Supply?*"

"It's that new oldies station. Hang on." I found the condoms I'd been searching for, tossed them on the bed, then reached for the radio. "We are *not* doing it for the first time to 'I'm All Out of Love.' *Damn it, Lucas—*"

Before I could turn off the radio, he rolled me over on top of him, kissed me again. When we came up for air, he snagged a condom and tore it open with his teeth. He put it on one-handed while the other hand slid beneath my hair, gripping it in his fist as he yanked my head back to gain access to my throat. He rained kisses from my jaw to my collar bone while he adjusted himself. The man had obviously had a lot of practice putting on condoms, which reassured me.

He hummed the song as he licked his way down to my breasts. "It's not *Bonanza*, but it'll have to do. We need a sex theme."

"We do *not* need a sex theme."

He flipped me on my back, and I moaned as he licked, kissed, nuzzled his way down between my thighs. When he hummed the chorus to the Air Supply song against a very sensitive part of my anatomy, I had to bite my lip to keep from screaming out his name.

"Okay, yes, *yes* ... I was wrong. We *definitely* need a sex theme."

My body began to tingle in that familiar, anticipatory way, so I pulled on his shoulders. "Come here." I looped my legs around his waist and tilted my hips. He thrust into me as our mouths met, and the tingling sensation evolved into back-arching, delicious convulsions.

"*Lucas.*"

He didn't try to slow me down, didn't do that thing where the guy worries he's going too fast—*thank God*. He pistoned his hips, plunging into me, giving me exactly what I wanted, exactly the way I wanted it. I didn't need slow and sweet, I needed what this man could give me as fast as he could give it to me, and he seemed to know that instinctively.

I was starting to think he might be a telepath after all.

He angled his hips and rolled them, and I cried out and dug my fingernails into his shoulders.

"Neely, Neely, *Neely*..." He whispered my name over and over as he found his own release, the look on his face one of delight and surprise and ... peace.

WE WENT SLOWER the second time.

Right before the third time, I turned off the radio, bought the Air Supply song online, and loaded it to my iPod. Lucas put it on repeat.

After a nap, we ate the rest of the *caldo de res*, the crackers, and a gallon of Rocky Road ice cream I'd hidden in the bakery kitchen freezer. We took a shower together and spent a lot of time touching, kissing and caressing, reassuring each other that we were alive and well and here.

Finally, we exited the safe, intimate cocoon we'd created, got dressed, and addressed our immediate problem.

"I killed his aunt. He's definitely going to come for me."

"I still can't believe that old witch actually was a witch. I've known her for twelve years." Lucas put on the sweatpants and T-shirt I'd provided for him. "You're sure you got her?"

"Yes. I saw the light in her eyes go out." I slipped on a pair of faded jeans and a thin black cotton T-shirt.

"It's just that she's a witch—a powerful one, if no one suspected it —I'm concerned she could have faked it."

"That's valid. If anyone could have done it, I imagine it would be her." I went into the living area to put on my sneakers. "The thing is, when I spike someone, I feel their life-force while I'm with them, I, uh, feed on it, in a way. It's part of the energy that drives that terrible, uncontrollable euphoria."

I hated admitting that out loud. It was tantamount to confessing I was some kind of addict who couldn't control her own mind and body—which wasn't far from the truth, I supposed.

Lucas seemed unfazed by my revelation. "So, she *could* have faked it?"

"No. See, the stronger the life force is, the harder I'm ejected from the person's consciousness when it's snuffed out. When hers went out, I was thrown from her head hard enough to wake me from that spell."

"I thought killing her took care of the spell." He joined me in the living area.

"According to the witches, if a spell has been fed enough magic, it can continue even when the caster is dead."

He paled. "Are you saying you *knew* that when you went in after me?"

Damn. I should have been more careful. I'd just reminded him of why he was so angry with me. "Yes. Dolores made sure I knew all the risks, so don't be mad at her."

"Hell." He fell into the chair across from me, his mouth hanging open. "You really didn't know if you could get out of there, did you?"

I tied my shoes, staring at my laces instead of him. "No."

"You went in anyway."

"Yes."

"Goddamn you." He flopped back in his seat, ran his hand through his hair. "Thank you and damn you. You went in anyway. My God."

"Yes. Just like I'm going to go in and take down your ex-alpha."

Lucas jerked up in the chair. "We should talk about this."

"Not a chance." I rose to my feet. "No matter what happened here today, I make my own decisions, Blacke. And I've decided that I'm going to spike that manipulative, murderous bastard—and this time it won't be to heal him."

Lucas rose to his feet. "*No matter what happened here today*, Costa MacLeod, I'm going to tell you when I think you're being unreasonable. I'm going to freak out when you put yourself in dangerous situations."

Because I liked that he cared, I lowered my voice. "I have to finish this."

"You're exhausted. You spiked a witch dead and just woke from a two-day coma."

I tried to think of how to explain without sounding like even more of an addict. "Spiking does take a lot out of me. But it's not actually the spike. It's the holding back, it's the stopping myself from going too far. When don't hold back, when I ... when I spike someone dead, it's the opposite of exhausting. It's exhilarating. I've explained this to you."

"But you only slept a couple of hours."

"I slept a lot when I was in the dream world—look, there's nothing you can do to stop me from going after Malcolm."

"Oh yeah?" He scowled down at me. "What if I kissed you senseless, threw you back on that bed, and did that thing with my tongue that makes you scream and curl your toes?"

"Nope." I pursed my lips. Glanced from side to side. Shuffled my feet. Cleared my throat. "I mean, you could always *try* that to see if it would work."

"But it won't?"

The sexy smile on his face made it very hard not to smile back, but I held strong.

"No. I'm going."

Lucas stood toe-to-toe with me, frowned into my upturned face. "Good. I hate traveling alone. Let's stop at my place first so I can change. We'll take your Mini." He kissed me, then leaned down to swipe my car keys out of the bowl on my coffee table.

"That is not what I thought you were going to say. And we're not stopping at your place. It's surrounded by pissed-off Malcolm wolves."

"Oh yeah. Well, we'll stop by the tower for my clothes, then." He twitched his brows at me and headed for the stairs. "Grab your iPod, too. We'll need music."

"We are *not* listening to our sex theme on the way there."

BACK AT THE TOWER, Lucas alerted Chandra to our plans and left her in charge of the Blacke group. She yelled at him, apologized, then yelled at me. I got no apology, just an earful of worried hyena shifter.

Lucas changed back into his other clothing and, uncharacteristically, thanked the witches for their help, politely promising Dolores that he'd approve their liquor license if they went through the proper channels. I think he was grateful that they'd tried to stop me from saving him, though he didn't say anything about it.

Neither of the witches tried to dissuade us from going. They knew what had to be done.

On the way out, Dottie draped a navy-blue garment over my shoulders. When I tried to tell her I didn't need it, she winked and told me it was cold up on the coast and that this cloak might come in handy in the absence of protective salt circles and witch chants.

Dolores patted me on the back. "Trust yourself and that power inside you. It's big, kiddo. Bigger than even you know."

Lucas and I didn't end up listening to our sex theme on the ride up to San Diego. In fact, we didn't listen to anything. We were one hundred percent focused on taking out Xavier Malcolm, and we spoke of nothing else.

"Will he have reinforcements, do you think?" I asked. "I can spike two or three, but I've never tried doing any more than that at once. And if they're wearing those charms..."

"He won't have reinforcements. Not at the house." Lucas appeared to mull that over. "He might call some in. I have a plan in place for that."

I frowned. "You really think that's where he is?"

"If he operates the way he did when I worked for him, then yes. Malcolm is arrogant, and when no one is around to check that arrogance, he does dumb shit. Seeing as we're holding the two advisors with any sense in their heads and Agnes is out of the picture, he'll revert to arrogance—but be ready for tricks. He's always been good at those."

I parked my Mini in front of the Victorian B&B and we walked up to the front door and rang the bell. Malcolm answered, wearing a cream linen pantsuit and no shoes. He looked like a hipster groom at a beach wedding. His hair was combed, and he was cosmetically put together, but there was something dark lurking underneath it all. Something ugly that the linen and the broad smile and the sparkling silver starred charm around his neck couldn't hide.

Alpha Xavier Malcolm was coming undone.

"Hello, Neely. Lucas. You're looking well."

"Hello, Malcolm," Lucas replied.

"May we come in?" I asked.

The wolf alpha's smile tightened, then he did a flamboyant gesture with his arm like a game show host, inviting us inside. The door closed with a firm finality, and I suddenly felt cold all over. My heart was beating so hard I knew he could hear it, and my toes were numb in my sneakers. Malcolm scared the hell out of me on a good day, and this was not a good day.

"You're all bundled up, Neely. Are you really wearing a sweater in San Diego?"

"More of a cloak, actually. I'm a desert rat. I was a bit chilled."

"Aren't we all?" He didn't offer to take my cloak, simply motioned us to follow him down the hall.

"It's quiet here today." There was no one around, paranormal or human. It felt like a house the day after a funeral.

"It's been a busy couple of days for the Malcolm Pack."

"What a coincidence. We're experiencing a similar situation in the Blacke Group." Lucas tucked his hands into the front pockets of his jeans, rocked back on his heels. They were playing the "everything's cool" game, an alpha tactic I'd witnessed many times, and both Malcolm and Lucas were experts at it. Though Lucas had a slight edge, in my opinion.

We strolled into the solarium together.

The first thing I noticed was a disturbingly large succulent in a clay pot big enough for me to swim in. It reminded me of the plant from *Little Shop of Horrors*. I only hoped it wasn't carnivorous.

The second thing I noticed were the two bodies hanging from the ceiling on meat hooks. I recognized them both, despite the missing limbs and internal organs. It was the two remaining shifters who had harassed Ana Cortez and me in Malcolm's bedroom. Tall, the Portuguese wolf shifter, and Squat, the wolf shifter who had resembled Santa Claus, which made his gruesome death even more disturbing.

"What is that?" I blurted.

"It's a bromeliad," Malcolm said. "*Hechtia melanocarpa*, native to Mexico. It arrived last night."

"You think *that's* what I'm freaking out about? A *plant*?" I put my hand over my mouth. The combined scents of flowers, soil, and rotting corpses was making me ill.

"Personally, I'm more interested in your new chandeliers," Lucas indicated the two mangled bodies with a nod. "I always thought you were more of a crystal and gilt guy, something that could have hung in a Victorian ballroom."

"They tried to kill me. Neely and Ana Cortez, too. Was I to supposed to let that go?" Malcolm led us away from the bodies to an area populated by what had to be fifty potted ferns.

"No." Lucas moved away from the bodies. "I wouldn't have expected you to turn them into an art project, though."

"They were people," I said.

"Bad ones," Malcolm replied impassively.

My knees wobbled. I sat down on one of the cement benches artfully arranged around the solarium. Malcolm leaned against the wall a few feet away. Lucas stood between us.

Let the subject of the bodies go. Lucas sent the words directly into my head. *It's not what we're here about and if we push, Malcolm will balk.*

I nodded, though I didn't see how I was going to ignore two bodies hanging from the ceiling. To anchor myself, I touched the fern next to me, ran my fingers over its lacy fronds.

"Appropriate that we'd meet in here, isn't it, Neely?" Malcolm's smile was unhinged. "This is where we had our first heart-to-heart."

First lie-to-heart, more like. "Full circle." I let my hand fall away from the plant and into my lap. "Why, Malcolm?"

The wolf alpha chuckled. "That's a vague question. Why what?"

"You don't need the Blacke group. You're a wolf pack and you don't like outsiders. So why go after Lucas?"

He drew in a sharp breath through his nose. "Different reasons, actually. I want to expand, and Los Angeles is a dead end. Too many

317

factions, too much to clean up. Branching out to the southeast made the most sense."

"Bullshit," Lucas said.

Malcolm scowled at Lucas. "What exactly about that is bullshit?"

"If you'd wanted to expand, the most logical direction to go would be south. You have a heavy presence on the Mexican-American border already, and run six dance clubs in Tijuana. The groups down there are spread out, and there's been a leadership vacuum at the top since Maria Hernandez died. No one has come close to her in power. But you could."

Malcolm gave the idea a dismissive wave of his hand. "I have no interest in taking over Tijuana. Too much of a mess. I'd have to send in my wolves to slaughter at least five wolf packs. We could do it, as you said, they're spread out and small, but it would be a hassle."

"A hassle you've undertaken before."

"Yes, but it's a bother."

"It's really not. You wouldn't have to kill them all. Just the alpha leaders." Lucas laughed without humor. "No wonder your own wolves are trying to kill you. The things you do make no fucking sense."

"Killing you makes perfect sense and you know it," Malcolm snapped.

Lucas did that grim laugh again but said nothing.

"The way you speak about killing…" I shivered and pulled Dottie's cloak closer around me. "You sound almost bored."

"I am bored. With this subject. I didn't let you in here to talk pack business."

"No, you let me in here to convince me to become your personal crossbreed. You let Lucas in because you think it will be easier with his cooperation, and because you think you have the upper hand."

"I don't think it, I know." Malcolm approached me, keeping the fern between us. "It would be the smart move for you both."

I tilted my head. "Would it?"

"This way, you both live." He directed that disconcerting smile at me. "Come on Neely, there's nothing holding you in Sundance. You aren't in Blacke's group, and you have no family there anymore."

That one hit me in a low place.

"You're wrong. There are a lot of things holding me in Sundance. The most important one is that no one there is trying to turn me into a weapon."

"You're a fool if you think that's not on Blacke's to-do list," Malcolm rolled back his shoulders. "But he's gotten you into bed and convinced you otherwise, so you won't listen to me."

I rolled my eyes. "Maybe *I* got *him* into bed and convinced *him* otherwise."

"It's true. You made a persuasive argument." Lucas clasped his hands behind his back. "I was helpless to resist."

"Thank you, Alpha Blacke."

"No, thank *you*, Spiker Costa MacLeod."

Malcolm's expression tightened. "*Regardless*, you're here, ostensibly to kill me, but I'm sure you've figured out that I've got a witch charm to protect me from you." He dangled the charm around his neck. "This isn't like the weak necklaces the other wolves wore. This one won't just hurt you—if you spike hard enough, it'll fry your beautiful brain."

Not unexpected, but not welcome, either. "Then what will you do? Your new pet spiker will be dead."

"I'd prefer not to have to use it. But if you attack..." He shrugged. "Let's just say, better you dead than me."

"And what about me?" Lucas asked. "Did you pick up a charm to protect yourself from me?"

"*Charm?*" Malcolm laughed. "I've always been stronger than you, Blacke. We both know that. I'll rip out your throat the way I should have done when you left the pack." Malcolm slipped out of his jacket, hung it on a hook next to a rhododendron bush in a large clay pot.

"You made me kill Suyin. How the hell was I supposed to stay after that?" Lucas glanced at me as he spoke to Malcolm, his voice fading into a whisper. "You knew how I felt about her."

I'd suspected Lucas was in love with Suyin, but it was upsetting to hear him admit it. I can't imagine what it had done to him to have to kill the woman he'd loved.

"I knew you loved her."

"And I was loyal to you." Lucas's jaw tightened. "Once she made the choice to be yours, it was done."

"I know," Malcolm said. "You could have had her from time to time, if you wanted. Suyin and I were all about power with a little sex thrown in for fun. We made that clear from the beginning."

He says that, but he would have seen it as a betrayal and would have had grounds to execute me without a challenge. Lucas thought this to me without taking his eyes off his old alpha. *Not that it mattered. She made her choice.*

That gave me an idea. "Malcolm." I stood, tugged the cable-knit cloak tighter around me and wished to heaven that I could read his devious mind. "Tell me something."

"Shoot." His smug grin was fingernails-on-blackboard irritating.

"When you found out William was sleeping with your wife, why didn't you have him executed? You would have had the grounds to do it, right? Without a challenge?"

Lucas's head jerked around. He hadn't known about William. But I'd bet Malcolm had.

Self-satisfied smile in place, the wolf alpha leader turned his back to me and weaved through the plants to the back of the solarium. "Figured it out, did you?"

More like guessed.

Be careful. Lucas sent me this thought as we trailed Malcolm. *He's leading us back there for a reason.*

"William was the man in the dream loop. He was the one who visited your bedroom the night you married Suyin."

"Yes. I caught it on film," he said, "I film everything that goes on in my private rooms."

Gross. "And your aunt planted it in your brain to trick me."

"The spell wasn't supposed to go the way it did. You really did put me in a coma, you know. It wasn't until Aunt Agnes was allowed in to see me that the spell was lifted, and I awoke. After that, it was easy to fake. Agnes did the hard work of making me look as if I was wasting away. William kept you out of the room long enough for me to use the facilities and eat." He shrugged as if the whole thing was no big deal. "To answer your question about William, why would I execute my most loyal wolf for something so unimportant? You're aware that

Suyin and I had an open marriage. As long as she performed her duties to the pack, she could see anyone she liked."

Unless that someone was Lucas Blacke, of course.

"Where is Scott, anyway? Did you kill him, Blacke?"

One corner of Lucas's mouth lifted. "The question isn't, 'Where is Scott?' It's, 'Where are William Scott *and* Dick Penn?'"

"You captured my second *and* my third?" He chuckled. "I admit, I'm kind of proud of you, Blacke." Malcolm said this, but he didn't look proud. In fact, he looked profoundly irritated. "You've been busy since Neely broke you free of my aunt's spell."

"It wasn't easy. Your aunt *was* powerful. A wolf-witch who managed to hide her magic." I put the emphasis on *was* to see how he'd react.

He stiffened. "Agnes wasn't powerful. Not alone, anyway. What she was, was smart. The spell she put on Blacke was pure genius." He laughed and the sound emerged jarring and loud. Like someone hitting all the keys on a piano at once.

"The spell failed," I said.

"Because of *you*." Malcolm spun around to face me. His eyes shone gold and his teeth had lengthened. I felt the air change behind me, and knew Lucas was shifting, too. Into his hybrid, Bengal tiger, or prehistoric form, I wasn't sure which, but he was doing something.

"I knew you were powerful the first moment I saw you, serving coffee to Blacke's ungrateful shifters in your bakery."

"You were watching me in Sundance?"

It's not that I was surprised he would do that. What surprised me, was he had done it and I hadn't known. I was sensitive to alphas, particularly sensitive to alpha leaders, and yet I hadn't noticed him.

"Of course." He didn't retract his teeth when he smiled, instead allowing fur to sprout on the edges of his face. "It sparks off you, you know. Power. It's like an inextinguishable flame that engulfs your entire being. Blacke knows it. That's why he wants you."

Behind me, Lucas growled.

"I wouldn't fit into your pack, Malcolm. I'm not a wolf."

"Your mother was, and it's in you. I know, because she calls to me, your wolf. I want her." In an instant, Malcolm was inches from my face and Lucas was the same distance away behind me. His breath heated my left ear. I was crushed between them, barely able to breathe, shivering with fear.

Malcolm twisted his finger around a lock of my hair that had loosened from my ponytail. I hate it when people touch my hair without permission—except Lucas. "With my help, we could bring her to the surface. Think about how powerful you would be as a shifter-spiker."

"That crossbreed thing didn't work so well for Suyin Chen."

"Suyin wasn't part shifter. She was a spiker-human. It was a mistake to change her, and I paid dearly for it."

He paid dearly? God, this man and his hubris. "I'm also a spiker and a human, Malcolm."

"You seem to think that, but you can't be. There's no way."

I didn't bother arguing with him. I didn't care what he believed.

"Come to me, wolf," Malcolm growled the words into my ear.

Something loosened inside me then. It was as if a weight that had lodged in my chest broke free. "Stop it," I gasped.

Lucas snarled and snapped at Malcolm. He wrapped his furred arm around my chest and pulled me against him. The fur was orange and black, the arm human, so he'd landed on hybrid Bengal with his shifting choices, which was probably a good thing.

"Is that how it is then, tiger?" Malcolm laughed and released my hair, walking deeper into the solarium. "The spiker isn't enough? Even the wolf must be yours?"

I belonged to no one, and was pretty sure I hadn't inherited my mother's wolf. But it served me not to argue, so I stayed quiet.

Lucas released me as we followed Malcolm through the plants.

When the wolf alpha arrived at a wall covered with dense, twisty green vines, he pushed on a section in the center. A hidden door. It creaked open and he went inside. Lucas and I trailed behind him.

"What is this?" I asked. "Where are you taking us?"

"To my secret room. No one sees it."

"Then why bring us?"

"To show you how powerful you are, spiker. I truly don't believe you know." We walked past a plant with furled leaves large enough to wrap around my waist. "See for yourself."

"What the hell, Malcolm?" Lucas covered his nose and mouth when Malcolm pushed open the door. "How many wolf meat chandeliers do you have hanging in this place?"

"Not chandeliers," I whispered.

Agnes Romano was strapped to a chair and pushed into a corner between a fern with fuzzy leaves and a fragrant star jasmine, the older woman's white hair tangled in sticky vines. To her left was a woman similar to Agnes in age and appearance, while to her right was a man who looked like an older Malcolm.

All three were dead.

"What's going on?" I took a step back, and smacked into Lucas's chest.

"Meet the family." Malcolm did that awful laugh again. "Neely, this is my mother Adele, my uncle Harry, and of course you already know my aunt Agnes."

"Malcolm?" Lucas wrapped his arm around my waist, tugged me closer. "Why haven't you properly disposed of the bodies?"

"I wanted you both to see exactly what she's capable of." He went to stand between his mother and Agnes, and smiled aggressively at me. His teeth were clenched, and his eyes glowed a sickly green-gold. "She killed them all. Every one of them a powerful witch." He jabbed his finger at me. "She killed them all with her mind and *she wasn't even in the room with them.*"

"I never... Lucas, I never saw them. I only saw Agnes." I leaned into him and he squeezed me tighter.

"Now you see why I want her so badly." Malcolm's smile was too wide for his face. "If she's powerful enough to take out three witches long-distance, there's no limit to what she can do."

CHAPTER THIRTY-THREE

"THAT'S WHY THEY WERE ABLE TO DO SO MUCH DAMAGE." LUCAS sounded awed. "Three related witches working together. A blood coven."

"The coven should have been unstoppable." Malcolm began pacing. He moved like a wind-up toy, his steps uneven and herky-jerky. "They even took down the neutral, Bill Bill. They cleansed the minds of anyone I asked them to, then patched them up. No one could stop them when they were together."

"*When* they were together?" Lucas asked.

Malcolm waved his arm around in a "never mind" gesture. "They fought at times. Siblings do that. When they were in agreement, they were pure power."

"And they were in agreement when I killed Agnes?"

"No." Malcolm shook his head a little too hard. Pulled his hand through it, leaving it mussed and standing at odd angles on his head. "That's what I don't understand. They fought that entire day. Something petty and stupid, as usual. Neither my mother nor my uncle should have been here when you killed Aunt Agnes. It was a terrible coincidence that they were."

I thought of Bill Bill's connection with the universe. Was it coincidence? Or was it karma? Maybe I owed both the man and the universe a thank you.

"Something has been bothering me," I said.

"*Has it?*" Malcolm snarled the words.

"Yes." It had been far too easy to jump into Agnes's brain, too easy to kill her. I was good, but I was fairly certain I wasn't good enough to take down three shielded witches. "The witches had all that power, yet they didn't put up any shields to protect themselves. Why not?"

Malcolm glared at me. "Why would they bother? Who could stop them?"

"*Hypoxia,*" I whispered.

"What?" He gave me a tight-lipped scowl. "What are you talking about?"

"They protected you with charms and cast spells on your enemies, but they neglected to do the one thing they should have done to protect themselves. This is why airlines tell parents to put their oxygen masks on first, before their children. If they don't protect themselves from the effects of oxygen deprivation, or *hypoxia*, they won't be able to help their children."

"What the devil are you saying, spiker?"

"Your family didn't put on their masks first. They didn't shield themselves from attack because they believed themselves too powerful."

"They were *unstoppable.*"

"Until I stopped them."

My knees still felt weak, my head light, as I stood there among the grasping, fragrant plants, the slumped-over dead witches, and between the two most powerful alpha leaders I'd ever met. Malcolm was fully engaged, intensely focused on me, and it was terrifying.

Even so, I didn't back down. As much as I'd hated Saul Roso, the alpha had changed something in my psychological makeup when he'd tried to murder me. He'd thrust my threshold for handling fear of death into a whole new realm.

Malcolm was facing me now. I couldn't decide if he'd done it so slowly, I hadn't noticed, or so quickly I hadn't seen it.

"There are two scenarios we're working with here, spiker. Either you come to me, or you die. It's very simple, really."

We have company. Lucas spoke to me inside my head. *I'm sensing twenty to thirty wolves. All alpha, all moving in fast. Guess the bastard isn't as stupid arrogant as he used to be. I'm going to have to shift. Won't be able to talk.*

Malcolm was suddenly closer. Just on the other side of the fern that separated us. I hadn't seen him move. My heart was pounding so hard I thought my head would pop off. Sweat dripped down my temples, rolled down my spine.

"Those aren't my only choices, Malcolm." I opened myself, let the energy in the room pour into me. I went from zero to overflowing in seconds. There had to be a lot more than thirty alphas in the vicinity. I had to warn Lucas.

"Not thirty shifters," I said, "I can feel them. He's got more like sixty out there."

One side of Lucas's mouth lifted. "What makes you think they're all his?" He let go of me, shifting as he spun around to face his old alpha. This time he didn't bother with his hybrid or Bengal tiger form.

He went straight to the prehistoric age.

"Are you *shitting* me? You're a *prehistoric*?" Malcolm's mouth fell open. "A Smilodon-shifter? How in the world did you keep this from me?" His voice nosedived into alphahole mode. "*How dare you keep this from me? I am your alpha.*"

The roar that tore out of Lucas's throat shook the entire solarium. Malcolm's wolves began launching themselves at him, two and three at a time. Lucas was holding his own, but that meant his attention was diverted.

I blinked and Malcolm was in front of me in hybrid form, his hand around my throat, hot breath blowing into my mouth, furious gaze boring into mine. I'd wondered what he would look like as a wolf, and now I had a pretty good idea. His fur was brown and gray, with white around his muzzle. Long, sharp fangs protruded over satiny black lips.

"*Submit.*" He threw me into the lap of the closest dead witch, who happened to be his mother. Her body was cold and stiff, and smelled like decaying roses.

I coughed, rolled my head around. Malcolm hadn't squeezed me a fraction of how hard he could have. It was stupid to have allowed him to get that close, stupid to have not been prepared. I opened my senses more, let the life energy in the solarium pour into me. The ferns to my left wilted, the star jasmine shriveled, the philodendron to my right flopped over.

"Your eyes. They glow with your wolf." Malcolm sniffed the air. "You are exquisite. I smell your power, taste it on my tongue." His gaze darted from wilted plant to wilted plant, then landed on me. He held up the necklace. "Stop drawing power. You can't spike me. You'll die."

The plants around the three witches shriveled and browned.

"Stop this, Neely. There's no need for you to hurt yourself." He licked his lips, sneered. "Submit to me and this will all be over."

"I. Don't. Submit."

"You will." Twin veins protruded from Malcolm's temples and ran all the way down to his cheekbones, disappeared, then popped out on the sides of his neck. Probably weren't the same veins, but they were oddly aligned and appeared as if they were. The veins in his head throbbed and his breathing escalated, his chest expanding and contracting, a rapidly rising crescendo of breath and heartbeat.

My breath caught as more power flowed into me. Every plant I could see was either dead or dying. I took a moment to feel bad about that, but I didn't dwell on it.

"I was going to tell you to back off, give you a warning, but that's not going to work, is it?" My voice was low but strong, and threaded with crackling electricity. I hardly recognized it as my own.

His hands thickened, scalpel-like claws extended. "This isn't necessary. Your death isn't necessary."

"Do you know what your two biggest mistakes were?" My voice dragged lower. "First of all, you shouldn't have come after Lucas. When you look back and wonder where it all went wrong, know that it was when you tried to murder Lucas Blacke."

"Is that so?" His upper lip curled, revealing those deadly sharp

327

teeth. "I've been trying to kill him for years. What's so different about now?"

"Me."

With a howl, he kicked a dead fern into a cement bench wedged against the window by his dead uncle. The pot fractured, the bench cracked, and the window behind it shattered. And then he was *there*, the way he hadn't been a breath before, his hand around my throat and squeezing all the oxygen out of me. I went down hard.

"You didn't answer my question," I wheezed.

"What question, *spiker*?"

Somewhere in the background, I heard flesh ripping, screams, growls. Lucas had his hands full. Malcolm would kill me before Lucas could get anywhere near me.

"I asked ... if you knew ... what your ... two biggest ... mistakes were. You ... only heard ... one."

"You're going to tell me the other one *now*?" He laughed in my face. Spittle clung to my lashes and dotted my cheeks. "I love the way you think you still have power in this situation." He shook the charm at me and let out another laugh. This one rode the barrier between deranged and sane. Tipping more into the former.

His claws lengthened until they were like sharpened steel blades. He raked them over my throat. One swipe and my trachea would be on the outside. My body went hot and cold at the same time, as if my nervous system couldn't make up its mind. Abject fear does weird things like that.

"What was my second mistake, *spiker*?"

I reached up with a trembling hand and tugged the hood of my sweater over my head. "You didn't offer to take my cloak."

Slam. I was locked onto his brainwaves, and had been for the last minute. With all of the energy I'd drained from his plants and anyone else in the vicinity, I drove into his head, taking the same path I had with his aunt.

Top of the head. Straight down.

"You c-can't."

The charm spell was squeezing my brain in a vise, but I wasn't dead, thanks to the protection field on Dottie's stolen warlock cloak.

It wasn't strong magic. The witches told me that it would only stave off the inevitable for a very short time, but that it might buy me some time.

I was finishing this. Now.

Malcolm was weakening, rapidly losing control over his muscles. The claw hovering over my throat dug feebly into my flesh. I prayed he hadn't sliced my carotid and kept spiking into his brain just in case he had. There was so much resistance. More than I'd ever felt from anyone.

The witch charm was strong. It shot a bolt of fire into my brain and my head went swimmy for a half-second. Just long enough for Malcolm to press his advantage. His claw sank into my neck, straight through my upper trachea. Fluid bubbled in the back of my throat and I coughed, choking on my own blood as I gasped for breath.

Not again. Not like Suyin—goddamn it, not Neely.

I heard the words inside my head, and a furious roar outside of it. A blur of tan fur blew past me, slamming into the wolf alpha. The beast's claws ripped and shredded the alpha wolf's body. Blood and viscera spattered the walls, and me. I was still inside Malcolm's head and saw everything. I tried to scream but gurgled instead.

Lucas.

I shoved everything I had into Malcolm's brain, but he was still wearing the charm and I wasn't getting enough oxygen. His energy should have tasted like spun sugar and felt like a hazy, happy dream. Spiking Malcolm was a miserable experience. Sparks went off in my head like a light show and pain blanketed my body, wrapping tight around me until all I knew was agony.

With a mental *whoosh*, Xavier Malcolm's life force exited his body. I was thrust out of his head, the recoil sending me crashing against the remains of the concrete bench. I was sure I'd broken something vital. Blood ran down my face, neck, and chest. My body was leaden with pain, dizzy with residual power.

Every plant in the solarium was a dried, brown husk. I studied Malcolm's body. Another husk in the dead room, though he wasn't dry or brown, just empty inside, body and mind. But then, he'd always been empty.

Beyond that were around twenty Blacke shifters, some in hybrid form, some in animal. I recognized Dan Winters, Amir Gamal, and even Margaret Lentz. The carcasses of thirty-odd shifted wolves were at their feet, some in pieces, some intact. Blood soaked the bodies, the floor of the solarium, and the shifters.

"*Lucas*," I whispered, my voice gone.

He shifted back to human and stumbled toward me, gripped my throat with both hands.

"It's okay, sugar cookie, I've got you. I'm here. I should have killed him the second we walked through the door. I'm so sorry."

"I don't think this cloak works too well," I whispered.

Lucas squeezed my throat harder and I cried out. It *hurt*.

"Shh. Hang in there, sweetheart. This is bad." He looked like an avenging angel kneeling beside me—magnificently naked and drenched in the blood of his enemies, his people a silent audience behind him, his countenance glowing with the aftereffects of battle.

Then he leaned down and whispered in my ear. "Just once, we should go out on a date that doesn't involve killing an alpha leader."

I tried to laugh, choked instead, and passed out.

CHAPTER THIRTY-FOUR

WHEN LUCAS DROPPED ME OFF AT THE BAKERY, IT WAS AFTER TEN P.M. I couldn't believe it was still the same day on which we'd taken down Xavier Malcolm and lived to tell the story.

I kept running my hand over my throat, expecting to feel a wound. Lucas had healed it completely. It was as if Malcolm had never touched me. He had though, and the scars I was would carry on the inside were far more extensive. Unfortunately, they were the kind Lucas couldn't heal.

He'd offered to come in with me, but I knew he had to get to his group. The man had responsibilities. I kissed him and thanked him, and told him I'd see him the next day.

I let myself in through the cafe, smiling at the light tinkling of the Costa family bell. Locking the door behind me, I wound through the chair-covered tables and tossed my purse on the counter. Grabbed a bottle of cold water from the cooler, picked up my purse again, and wandered into the kitchen.

There was a plate of fresh *pan dulce* on the worktable and a note from Diego, saying he hoped I was okay. *Empaths.* I grabbed a pink *concha* and went up to my apartment.

I finished the pastry and the water—slowly, as my throat was still sore on the inside—and draped the protection cloak over one of my kitchen chairs, after shaking the pink crumbs off it. Was it okay to wash a warlock's protective cloak on the gentle cycle or was it a dry-clean-only garment? I wasn't sure.

After that, I took a shower. It reminded me of the one I'd taken with Lucas, so I got out fast. It was ridiculous how much I missed him, and he'd only been gone twenty minutes.

When there was a knock on my back door, I didn't bother putting on normal clothes, shoes, or fixing my hair before going downstairs. My prairie girl nightgown, yellow fuzzy slippers, and wet ringlets would have to be good enough for the man.

I dashed downstairs and swung open the back door. It was Margaret Lentz.

Strangely, until that moment, I hadn't been tired. I wasn't jogging around the block, but Lucas's healing had given me a burst of energy. After seeing Margaret on my doorstep, I was so exhausted I could barely stand.

"What do you want?" I set my jaw and stared her down as I drew a little energy. I wasn't putting up with any bullshit tonight.

"Alpha Blacke asked me to bring your car back." She thrust the Mini's keys at me, one eye twitching.

"Thank you," I said, and I thought that was pretty damn nice of me.

"You're welcome. Neely?" Her voice has lost that holier-than-thou tone. It was softer than normal, and without the snooty edge.

"What is it, Margaret?"

"I did ... some bad things. To you. I want to apologize. It was not my intention to—"

"Yes, it was. It was absolutely your intention 'to.'"

"Yes." She bowed her head. "I didn't like you. You're a threat—or, at least, I believed you to be one. But, there's more." She looked at me, her eyes glazed with misery. "May I please come in?"

I read her. No hesitation, no questioning of my morality, nothing. Was I a changed person because of Xavier Malcolm? Surely. But I was also a changed person because of Chandra and the witches and Bill Bill and Amir, and because of Lucas Blacke.

From her thoughts, I could see that Margaret meant me no harm. In fact, she truly was sorry. She needed to tell me something, and it was pressing in on her hard, so I decided to let her tell me rather than glean it from her thoughts.

I might be different, might be more apt to read someone now, but I was still me.

I showed Margaret to a table in the café. Grabbed two bottles of water from the fridge, some napkins, and the plate of *pan dulce* from the kitchen—after removing the pink *conchas*, of course. My goodwill only went so far. No one was getting my pink *conchas*.

Margaret burst into tears as soon as I set the plate down. "I didn't know Lisa was Alpha Malcolm's spy."

"I know." I handed her one of the napkins, sat down across from her and opened my water bottle. I wasn't thirsty, but it gave me something to do with my hands.

"She really had me going." Margaret blew her nose into the napkin, then got up and put it in the trash. She even washed her hands in the public bathroom after. It was that, more than anything, that made me think I might get along with Margaret someday.

"No one knew. I would imagine that's the first rule of spying."

"Yes, I suppose so. Makes me feel like an old fool, though." Margaret took a shaky breath and opened her water bottle. Took a sip. "I was awfully rude to you. Lisa had filled my empty head with a lot of ridiculousness, but it was my fault for letting my head get that empty."

I set a *mantecada* on a napkin in front of me. Stared down at it. "I killed Lisa, you know."

"Yes. It's common knowledge in the group." Margaret also selected a *mantecada* and set it on a napkin. Her hand shook as she peeled the red paper away from the lower half of the muffin. "If you're feeling guilty about it, don't. She would have slit your throat without a second thought."

"Does everyone know what I did?" I didn't know how I felt about that. It wasn't a secret, but people were already afraid of me. Now they'd be chucking rocks through my window and gathering up the pitchforks.

"Word travels fast. Oh, and Alpha Blacke said to let you know that the Malcolm pack has left town—the ones capable of leaving, anyway."

She smiled. I flashed back to the blood on her muzzle in Malcolm's solarium, and shivered. "We're still holding those two Malcolm pack alphas."

I'd almost forgotten about William and Dick. Lucas was in for a long night.

Margaret took a bite of the *mantecada*. "You know, these are tasty, but there's something missing. I'd never know it if I hadn't had one of José's muffins first."

"*Mantecadas*."

"Yes, *mantecada* muffin." She ate another bite.

"It's magic, I think." I took a bite of my mantecada. "Because I found his recipe and Diego and I have followed it perfectly. We've deviated a bit to see if that was it, we've even added things to it. We can't figure it out."

Margaret nodded. "Yes. Magic. That's probably it." She cleared her throat. "Neely, I have something I need to say, and I want to tell you right from the start, I didn't know what I was getting into when Lisa approached me. She asked for some money to help run you out of town, and I thought it was a good idea. I thought you were the dangerous one, old fool that I am."

"You are neither old nor a fool," I said. "Stop putting yourself down and tell me what you came to say."

So, she told me.

"BOTH BAKERY BITCHES HIRED the hitman? I thought it was just the snake." Chandra laughed so hard I thought she would hurt herself.

"Yes. Margaret Lentz told me tonight." I glared at the phone when she laughed harder. "This would be funnier if it wasn't so scary. Also, if it wasn't *me* who was being targeted."

"Come on. Can you imagine the conversation? Margaret, with her circa-90s teenager slang, talking to some hardcore assassin?" Chandra continued, in a spot-on imitation of the older woman, "*Hey there, uh feller, we need one of you, er, gangsters to bust a cap in someone's heinie for us.*"

I waited for her to stop laughing. "You know, *busting a cap* is much older than hip-hop. It's an Old West saying."

Chandra laughed harder. "You're such a nerd."

"I like documentaries, okay? They calm me."

When Chandra finally stopped laughing, she said, "We're going to have to cut her loose—unless you want to challenge her. She's gone too far."

"No and no, you don't. It was Lisa Cesar's plan and Margaret got swept along. She thought she was running me out of town, not hiring someone to kill me."

"You sure about that?"

"I read her, so yeah."

"Good for you." She sighed, a deep one. "All right. I'll take care of Margaret and the assassin. That sounds like a good band name, doesn't it?"

"I really hope you're having a good time," I said.

"It's been a shit few weeks, but this? This is good." She went quiet for a moment. "Hey, I know why you did what you did for Alpha without telling me—the kidnapping, I mean." She cleared her throat. "I get it. We're cool."

"I had to act fast, Chandra. He was dying. I could feel him dying."

I gathered the remaining *pan dulce* and took the platter to the counter to wrap in plastic. Margaret had finished hers and I'd given her a white *concha* to take home. Sure, hire an assassin to take me out and I still send you home with pastries. Must be the baker in me.

"I couldn't. Feel him, I mean."

Carefully, I set the platter down. "You didn't feel him fading through the group bonds?"

"No. That was why Amir kept close watch over him. None of us could feel him anymore." She was quiet for a beat. "But you could."

One of the *mantecadas* rolled off the platter and onto the floor. "Because I'm a telepath, I guess."

"I don't think so. Neely, you might not want to hear this, but when do I let what you want to hear get in the way of what I need to say?"

"Pretty much never." I bent over to pick up the pastry.

335

"Right. The thing is, I believe you felt Alpha Blacke because you have a deep connection with him."

"*Deep?*" I whipped back into a standing position. Too fast. My head went swimmy and the *mantecada* went flying out of my hand. "What do you mean by that?"

"What I said. Look, I'd never betray a confidence, but Alpha didn't expressly tell me I couldn't say this, so I'm taking that as consent."

I gripped the phone tighter.

"When you were trapped in that dream spell, he was the only person who could reach you. There was a point where even the witches..." She paused as if choosing her words carefully, which made me nervous. "Look, you weren't *breathing*, Neely. Your heart wasn't beating. To the witches and to the rest of us, you were dead. But he wouldn't let you go. I thought I was going to have to knock him unconscious to pry him away from your dead body, and I'm not sure I could have."

"Lucas did that?"

"Yes, Neely. He held onto you when everyone else had already given up. He knew you were still there, when all signs pointed to you being gone. I'm far from an expert, but if that's not a powerful connection, then I don't know what is."

CHAPTER THIRTY-FIVE

THREE HOURS AFTER THE PHONE CALL WITH CHANDRA, LUCAS KNOCKED on the back door. I hadn't gotten any sleep and I was so relieved to see him, I nearly wept.

"Using the door?" I asked, by way of greeting. "This is new."

"May I come in?" His expression was serious and somewhat grim, so I didn't tease him anymore. I simply moved aside so he could enter.

We went up the stairs to my apartment, and Lucas kicked off his sneakers and dropped onto my bed. He was dressed in khaki green shorts and a faded *Space Jam* T-shirt. He smelled like sage soap and shampoo, and looked worn thin and sad.

"Did Chandra tell you that Margaret helped Lisa Cesar hire the hitman?" I sat down beside him and he pulled me half onto his chest.

"Yeah. She's going over there now to find out who they hired and put a stop to it."

"Wait. Move a little. There." I shifted into a more comfortable position in the crook of his arm. "You know Lisa Cesar was the mastermind behind the hitman. Margaret was duped."

"I heard. Chandra said you read her. Good. You should read everyone, all the time."

"Don't start."

337

"I won't. That wolf shifter is a pain in my ass—too nosy for her own good."

"Meh. I think she's bored."

"*Bored?*"

"Yeah. You know, it might be smart to put her busybody ways to good use. Think about it, if you needed a spy, no one would suspect her."

"I don't spy on people. Much." Lucas twirled a lock of my hair around his finger. "Hardly ever."

"Yeah, right. Anyway, if you gave her a job, she wouldn't have to entertain herself and get into trouble."

"She already works part-time at the grocery store. That's not enough for her?"

"Apparently not."

"All right. I'll talk to Chandra."

"Good idea."

The conversation trailed off. Lucas let my hair spin away from his finger and started plucking at the sleeve of my flannel nightgown.

"Was Lestat traumatized by his time with the witches?" I asked, to get him talking again.

"Dan brought him there, you know. For his *safety*. Ha. That cat may need therapy." He wrinkled his nose. "She put a *shirt* on him."

I pressed my lips together to keep from laughing. "Dolores put a shirt on Lestat?"

"Of course, Dolores. Who else?"

"What did the shirt look like?" I flipped onto my belly and pressed along the line of his body, half on top of him, half off.

"It's orange and has a picture of a tiger on it. She had to have conjured it out of thin air, because she only had my cat to herself for a day." He stopped plucking at my sleeve. "The worst part is, Lestat likes it and won't let me take it off."

This time I didn't even try to hold back. I laughed until tears sprang to my eyes.

"You're just as bad as they are," he grumbled.

I laughed even harder at that.

"*In other news*, the Cortez women are moving to Sundance. I offered Maria a job running the clinic. She has an interest in running the apothecary shop, too, which should work out well all around."

"That *is* good news." I swiped the tears of laughter from my eyes. "That family deserves some peace."

"Yes, they do." He smoothed my sleeve with his fingers. "We'll hear from more of Malcolm's wolves. They're floundering, now that their leader is dead."

"Like Roso's wolves did after he was gone?"

"Yeah."

I let some time pass. "Did you challenge William?"

"Yes. Dick, too. They're back home, either preparing to fight or preparing to flee. Either way works for me."

"You let them go?" I was stunned. After what William had done, I'd expected Lucas to challenge him the second he had the chance. "Why?"

"With Dick, I figured forcing him to leave the San Diego pack was punishment enough."

"And William?"

"Willa called. Begged me not to kill him." He dropped my sleeve and began stroking my back. "Also, I'm really getting tired of having to murder my old friends. It's hard on the soul."

I reached for his free hand, weaved his fingers through mine. "Will you have to fight any other wolves?"

"Yes. I foresee several challenges in my future. Malcolm's pack was full of stupid alphas."

"I don't want you to fight."

"Me, neither. It messes up my hair." He winked and kissed my forehead.

More sarcasm and affection deflection. I decided not to push him. He deserved not to have to think about what was coming.

"Hey, I'm sorry about William being an asshole."

"Yeah, me too." He let out a long sigh. "Listen, I need to talk to you. It's ... it's serious."

My eyelids drooped. "I'm on empty right now. Can it wait until the morning? Please?"

He stared at me for a beat. "I shouldn't let it, but yes, it can."

I inched back the covers and crawled beneath my cool, clean sheets. They felt so good against my skin, I almost moaned.

"Get some rest." Lucas rolled off the bed and shoved his feet into his sneakers. "I'll talk to you tomorrow."

"Wait."

He stared down at me through eyes circled with pure gold. His animal was close to the surface. The man was on the edge.

"What is it, Neely?"

I'd thought I was too tired to feel nervous, but I was wrong. My heart drummed against my ribs as I babbled my next words at him.

"I know we aren't in a relationship or anything, I mean we had sex, but that was just sex and I get that, but I'd really like it if you stayed here tonight—if you can, of course, I understand if your group needs you." I finally stopped blathering like an idiot and just blurted, "I want to sleep with you. Please stay with me for at least a little longer."

Without a word, he kicked off his shoes, stripped to his black cotton boxer briefs, and slid under the sheets with me.

I turned out the light and we lay in the dark together, he on his pillow, me on mine.

"Malcolm was my kill, you know."

"Are you waiting for an apology?" I asked. "Because you'll be waiting a long-ass time."

"You can't fight all my battles for me."

"Some of your battles are my battles, too. Maybe you need to remember that."

We let some silence pass between us.

"Thank you again for saving my life," Lucas said. "Even if you had to spike me to do it."

"I was wondering when you were going to bring the spiking part up." I reached for his hand, finding it quickly because he'd been reaching for me, too. "Not apologizing for that, either. I couldn't let you die."

"I know."

I rolled to my side, faced him. "Lucas, are we friends?"

His fingers flexed, tightening around mine. "Yes, we're friends, but we're also more. And we're going to have to decide where we want to take this soon, because I'm getting used to..." He said the rest in his head. *I'm getting used to you. In my bed, in my head, in my life.*

"Me too."

He sighed. *It's new for me. This feeling.*

I didn't tell him, but I kind of liked that it was. "Will you do something for me tonight?"

"Fine. I won't ask you to play our sex theme, but I'll probably hum it."

Dear heavens, I hoped so. "No. Something else."

"What?"

"Do you remember the promise you made to me at Malcolm's house that first night?"

"Yes."

I let go of his hand and flipped onto my side, giving him my back. "Say it to me again. Just once and just for tonight. All bets are off in the morning."

He curved his body around mine and tucked my bottom tight into the cradle of his hips. His lips gently grazed my ear, sending shivers down my spine. My eyes slid shut, his whispered words escorting me into sleep.

"I promise I won't leave you."

I AWOKE at seven a.m. in a blind panic, thinking I needed to set out the pastry dough, take the chairs down, and make the coffee.

Then I remembered I wasn't running the bakery right now.

At first there was relief, then, sadness.

Lucas was gone. He'd taken my new romantic suspense book with him, but he'd left something in its place on my nightstand. One of the witches' silver charms with a tiny heart-shaped rose quartz inside. Beside the necklace was a note.

The witches removed the spell on the quartz and put a peace blessing on it instead. Fingers crossed you don't turn into a frog when you put it on.

~L

No further explanation for the gift, of course. I was silly for expecting one. I put on the necklace and instantly felt centered. I smiled, and picked up the note to read again. Underneath the paper lay a tiny black box. When I examined it, I saw that it wasn't a box. It was a USB drive. There was no note with it, just the drive.

I got up, got dressed, and went down to the cafe to make coffee, since I didn't have a coffee maker in my apartment. The mornings were cooling down and I thought I'd take a chair to the front patio and watch the traffic go by. Might even get to see more than six cars if I timed it right.

The USB poked my hipbone as I tucked it into my pocket and settled myself on the patio of my uncle's, of *my*, bakery cafe. I knew what was on the drive. It was the footage the information trader had given Lucas. He wanted me to see it before I decided if I wanted to take what was going on between us further.

I sat there and thought about it, warm cup of coffee cradled in my hands. Blacke shifters drove by. Some waved, some pretended not to see me. A regular leaned out his car window. "*When are you reopening, Neely? I miss my daily coffee and* mantecada."

Because I didn't have an answer for him, I shrugged and smiled, and made a mental note to bake a dozen and drop them by his house.

I wasn't ready to close the bakery permanently, but I didn't want to run it alone. I wasn't ready to watch the USB, but I needed to see what was on it to make a decision about Lucas. I wasn't ready to fully embrace who I was, but I needed to for the sake of the people I loved as well as for myself.

For now, though, I was content to sit on my front patio, wave to the people who waved to me, and sip my coffee in blessed ignorance.

ALSO BY C. P. RIDER

Spiked

Thanks for reading *Summoned*!

If you liked this book, please consider leaving a review on the retailer site where you found it. I'd appreciate it very much.

For a FREE short story from Lucas Blacke's point of view, story-related downloads, and updates on new releases, sign up for my mailing list! www.cprider.com My newsletter goes out once a month and I am serious about protecting your privacy.

Chandra-serious.

Thanks again for picking up *Summoned*.

C.P.R.

ACKNOWLEDGMENTS

A big thank you and lots of grateful hugs to:

Alexandra Pitones and Coralie Tate, for being the best beta readers in the universe.

Rosalie Redd, who proofread this story for me at the last minute.

My cafe sisters. You are a constant source of positivity and support. I am grateful for each and every one of you.

ABOUT THE AUTHOR

C.P. Rider writes paranormal and urban fantasy romance. You can find her at www.cprider.com or on Facebook and Instagram.

facebook.com/urbanfantasyromance

instagram.com/c_p_rider

Made in the USA
Lexington, KY
30 November 2019